P9-CDA-739

Fathom

Tor Books by Cherie Priest

THE EDEN MOORE BOOKS
Four and Twenty Blackbirds
Wings to the Kingdom
Not Flesh Nor Feathers

Fathom

Fathom

Cherie Priest

TOR®

A Tom Doherty Associates Book

New York

FATHOM

Edited by Liz Gorinsky

Book design by Kathryn Parise

A Tor Book
Published by Tom Doherty Associates, LLC
175 Fifth Avenue
New York, NY 10010

www.tor-forge.com

Tor® is a registered trademark of Tom Doherty Associates, LLC.

Library of Congress Cataloging-in-Publication Data

Priest, Cherie.
    Fathom / Cherie Priest.—1st ed.
        p. cm.
    "A Tom Doherty Asscociates book."
    ISBN-13: 978-0-7653-1840-4
    ISBN-10: 0-7653-1840-7
    1. Monsters—Fiction. 2. Angels—Fiction. I. Title

PS3616.R537 F38 2008
813'.6—dc22

                                                    2008034251

First Edition: December 2008

Printed in the United States of America

0 9 8 7 6 5 4 3 2 1

To the Sunshine State, and my relatives who originated there.

(Yes, that's pretty much all of them.)

Acknowledgments

Thanks go first to the usual suspects: My fabulous husband, Aric, who lets me stay home and write these things while he trundles off to his office job each day; my amazing editor, Liz Gorinsky, who, bless her heart forever, was subjected to not one, not two, but *three* separate Draft One versions of this project; my superfly publicist, Dot Lin, who's always quick on the draw with the promo materials; my impossibly patient agent, Jennifer Jackson, who gets shotgunned all my ridiculous ideas and yet never uses live ammo when she shoots back; and my ever ready webmaster, Greg Wild-Smith.

Next, I'd like to cast grateful, friendly props to a few members of the Seattle-area writing crew—namely, Kat Richardson, Richelle

Mead, Caitlin Kittredge, and Mark Henry—for the lunches, the parties, and the companionable revelry that only fellow zombie aficionados can provide. They've been exceedingly kind to the new girl in town, and I love them all to pieces for it. And speaking of the locals, thanks likewise go to Duane Wilkins at the University District bookstore, because he's a signing-organizing madman and a true friend of authors everywhere.

I'd also like to send a shout-out to Chief Kenneth A. Price, Jr., over at the West Manatee Fire Rescue, for taking the time to answer pestering e-mails from a faraway author with some really odd questions. I did not honestly expect an answer to something as off the wall as, "Can you tell me about the fire department on this very small island about ninety years ago?" but he came through in style. Mind you, I only *selectively* followed his historical notes, so if anyone reads this and thinks I've gone off the deep end with my facts—please don't bother poor Chief Price about it. He knows his stuff. Anything I've botched herein is entirely my responsibility.

And as a final note—because such things are important to some people—the song that Edward sings can be roughly, approximately hummed to the tune of "King Volcano" by Bauhaus.

Fathom

Lake Wales, Florida

It's as if you've asked me to build an ark. Only this . . . this is even stranger. It's not that I don't believe you, and obviously it's not the money."

Edward shielded his eyes against the gleaming, glaring afternoon sun. Below the hill where he stood, the scorched gray-green tops of live oaks and winged elms stretched as far as he could see in every direction. Here and there, the view was pocked with low, swampy places and trailing streams of tepid water thick with algae.

"It's just this *place*. And I should tell you," he continued, "this is the highest point on the peninsula. Can you believe that? This little mound is as high as the landscape ever climbs away from the ocean."

He rubbed at the grass with the shiny black toe of his shoe, pushing past the topsoil and into the gritty red dirt just beneath it. "But you say this isn't clay? It looks like clay. Except..." He jabbed at a clod and it disintegrated like sand. "Except it's awfully dry. And that color, it's much redder than clay."

The broken clod looked like an injury, there on the ground.

"It isn't clay," his companion said. "It's iron."

Edward nodded. "Iron," he echoed. "Through and through. A small mountain made of it, and God knows why. But this is the place, you say?"

"This is the place. Build it here, as tall as the earth will stand it. Send it into the sky. Make it a sanctuary."

Edward tugged at his collar, wiping at the sweat he found underneath it. He gazed across the landscape and then back down at his feet. He did not look over his shoulder. It was one thing to hear that voice made of gravel and mulch; it was another thing to see the speaker, both oddly shaped and terribly misshapen.

Edward found it easier to listen than to look. "And you'll be here? You'll stay here, I mean?"

"I'll stay, and I'll watch. I'll wait in your sanctuary."

"I like the sound of that, yes. A sanctuary. I'll buy out the land as far as we can see from this point, and we'll reshape it. I know a man who does great work with landscaping." Edward was warming to the idea, building momentum as he pushed it around in his head. "We'll make it into a proper garden. We'll plant orchards. We'll have birds, and butterflies, and how do you feel about swans? We should have at least a pair of them. There's plenty of water to keep them happy, and we could import fish, too. Do you like fish?"

For a long moment, there was no answer. "It depends."

Edward was afraid that he'd asked an inappropriate question, but his escort did not offer a formal objection or complaint. "Well, all of that—the fish, the swans—it's all a ways off yet. This will take several years, if not longer."

"A man with your resources should be able to speed things up considerably."

"Money can accomplish only so much. You're talking about tons upon tons of stone and metal. I'll need to hire workers, arrange for the transport of materials, and contact my friend the landscaper—and that will only be the beginning. I'll do my best, I assure you. But I'm only human," he said. "Perhaps there's something that *you* could . . ."

"I'll assist you any way I can. But my abilities are better suited to breaking things down than building them up."

"But there are others like you, aren't there? Is there someone else who can help?" Edward had always wanted to know, and here was a perfect window for asking.

His companion laughed, and it was a bitter, raspy sound. "Yes and no. There are none who would answer any call of mine, if that's what you want to know. The ones who remain despise me. I chose this exile because I was tired of their scorn. I was exhausted by their contempt, and I would rather bury myself in the Iron Mountain than endure it another day."

Edward Bok did not know how to respond. It had been several years since he'd first met his strange friend, and in that time he'd rarely heard anything so revealing or personal. He was acutely aware that he knew precious little about the creature that stood behind him.

But he was not a stupid man, and he'd inferred a thing or two. He'd gathered that the creature was alone, and that it was angry. He'd surmised that it was very old, and that it was suffering terribly as a result of some punishment. But the thing was selective about the questions it answered, and Edward had grown careful about what he asked.

"Exile," Edward repeated, wondering how best to ask more.

"They won't come after me here, if that's what's bothering you."

Edward shook his head. "No, I'm not worried. I trust you."

"Why is that?"

"I beg your pardon?" Edward wanted to turn around, but only shifted his head to peer over his shoulder.

"Why would you trust me?"

"Do I have a choice?"

"Everyone has a choice. You have more at your fingertips than most people do."

"Because of the money?" Edward frowned. "I do my best to share the wealth. I build libraries and fund schools. I—"

"Don't defend your expenditures to me. I'm not your god, and not your accountant. I don't care where or how you spend your funds, so long as we agree in this one great venture."

"We agree," Edward said quickly. "Of course we do. I gave you my word, didn't I? I'll build your tower, and I'll cast your bells. I'll make your sanctuary according to whatever directions you see fit to give me."

"Don't do it for me, you ridiculous man. Do it for yourself, and for your children and grandchildren. You have a grandchild now, yes?"

"I have two."

"That's twice the reason to build the tower, then. You're building it for them, and for everyone else you love. You're preparing to save the world, Bok. Don't behave as if you're doing me a favor."

Edward withdrew a handkerchief from his pocket and used it to swab his forehead. The air was dense with humidity, and the sun felt too close; it cooked the sweat on his face and seared pink burns into his skin. "I didn't intend it that way. I only wonder, sometimes, why you're going to the trouble."

From behind him, there came the muffled crackling noise of

rocks being tumbled in sand. And when he finally twisted on his heels to look, he saw no one and nothing there.

"All right," he told himself. "I'll get started."

He began by purchasing fifty acres, including the Iron Mountain itself. He declared his intention to create a wildlife preserve; he arranged for the pipe-work and water system installation, and imported nourishing topsoil by the ton. The iron-rich sand and dirt could hold only so much life, and it had to be supplemented. The landscaper, Frederick Olmsted, would not even *visit* the site until that much had been prepared.

In 1924, once the groundwork had been established, Olmsted came down from Massachusetts with an army of gardeners, stocked with native and imported flora of every stripe. He believed deeply in conservation, and he applauded Bok's plans.

Mr. Olmsted also wanted to save the world.

The landscape architect plotted the grounds, set down trails, and laid out the gardens. He arranged the oaks, pines, and geometrically styled orange groves. He planted date and sabal palms, papyrus, creeping fig, and hollies. Wafting up through the clattering ruckus of construction and digging came the sweet, light scent of jasmine and camellias.

So when the land had been cleared, and the pipes had all been laid, and the gardens were under way, Bok turned his attention to the sanctuary's centerpiece: the Singing Tower. His friend Milton Medary designed it.

Medary drew his inspiration from the best of art deco and Gothic overindulgence. He looked to the great European cathedrals and he liked what he saw there; he wondered how it might be shaped to better fit the heat, the sun, and the shifting, sandy earth of the peninsula.

He brought cream and lavender marble from Italy and pink co-quina from St. Augustine by the cartload, by the truckload, by any kind of load that would carry it deep into central Florida, through heat that could bake or kill anything that breathed.

It wasn't easy. It wasn't quick.

Foot by foot, year by year, the ornate tower stretched itself up to the clouds.

While the tower grew, and while the gardens sprawled, and while tidy rows of orchards were groomed around the Iron Mountain, sixty great bells were cast in bronze. Shaped like cups and designed to work with a special clavier, the bells ranged in size from sixteen pounds to twelve tons.

The largest bell could have hidden a horse.

On February 1, 1929, Calvin Coolidge dedicated the property as Edward Bok's "gift for the visitation of the American people." The ceremony was well attended and highly publicized, but only one spectator watched from the very top of the carillon.

It watched in silence, and in pain. The bells burned its skin, and the noise of the crowd made its head itch. But it watched, and it was pleased with the results.

Less than a year later, Edward Bok died. He was buried at the foot of the tower, directly in front of the big brass door, in accordance with his final request.

The Orchard and the Island

According to Marjorie's letter, her daughter, Bernice, was not adjusting very well to the move. Marjorie was aware that Bernice and Nia had barely seen each other in recent years, but since they were cousins—and almost the same age—they might enjoy each other's company for a few months.

And wouldn't Nia like a break from working in the orchard?

She could come out to the island, where the new house was only a few yards from the beach. She could have her own room, and swim at her leisure. She and Bernice could even catch the ferry over to Tampa and see the Gasparilla parade if they liked. The city was not so far away.

Nia's mother and grandmother balked at the idea, but Nia was tired of climbing ladders and picking oranges like a field hand. A sunny beach on a distant island sounded like a much better way to spend the summer than working for free on the family farm; and anyway, she was eighteen and she could go if she wanted to.

She didn't remember much about her cousin. When she thought on Bernice's name, all she could muster was a memory of someone small and fast with curly blond hair and a smile that could cut glass.

She knew that her cousin was beautiful, and that she'd been living in New York ever since Marjorie had remarried ten years earlier. She knew that her cousin was a little "wild," or so her grandmother said with a tight little grimace bunched at the side of her mouth.

"Marjorie lets Neecy run too fast. She doesn't keep that girl close enough," Grandmother declared during the living room gossip session that began as soon as Marjorie's letter had been read by everyone present. "She's never whooped the girl, not even once . . . and Bernice has deserved it plenty more than once. Lord help me, but it's true. If she came up here instead of tempting Nia down south, I'd do it myself. Better late than never."

"She's too big for that now, Momma," Nia's mother said. She twisted her lips around the sewing pins she held there while she worked. "She's a couple years older than Nia, even."

"She isn't too big to beat. She's just too far away."

Nia held the envelope hard in her fist. "I want to go," she said. "Aunt Marjorie invited me, and I want to do it. It sounds like a nice house they're building, right on the beach."

Grandmother grunted and said, "I'm sure it's real nice. Marjorie's married money both times."

Nia's mother pulled a pin out of her mouth and folded it into the skirt she was rehemming. She mumbled around the remaining pins, "Nothing wrong with falling in love with a rich man."

"No, but she could've picked one who wasn't a crook."

"What's that mean?" Nia asked. She squinted down at the letter, which she was fairly certain contained no mention of her uncle Antonio being a crook.

"He's a Yankee—and an Italian, to boot," her mother said with teasing cheer. "Your grandmother thinks they're all a bunch of crooks."

"No," she argued. "Not all of them. But this one in particular, yes. He's a crook, and a carpetbagger, too."

Nia's hands were going sweaty around the bunched letter in its crushed envelope. "I don't care if he's so crooked, he's got to screw his socks on every morning. I want to go. And I'm going to."

Grandmother spoke around Nia, as if she weren't there. "Marjorie's let that girl go native, too. She's practically a Yankee herself now. She'll be a terrible influence on yours, I'm telling you. If I were you, I wouldn't let her go."

"You can't make me stay," Nia insisted.

"I *can't* really make her stay," her mother agreed, talking to Grandmother past Nia's head, "if she wants to go. We could use the help, but I think we'll be all right. It might be good for her—getting out of town, doing a little traveling. You used to like traveling, Momma."

"I'd enjoy it now, if I didn't have a grove to run. Last time I traveled anywhere was with your daddy, back when that one"—she cocked a thumb at Nia—"was just learning to read. But that's neither here nor there. I still don't like Marjorie's *tone* in that letter."

"What's wrong with her tone?" Nia demanded.

"It's bribery—that's what she's doing," Grandmother answered. "She's trying to bribe you with her money, and with the way she lives. She's tempting you with how you won't have to work, and you can swim in the ocean like a little heathen if you want, and you can stay in her nice big new house over there . . . like what you've got here at home isn't just as good."

Nia's mother shook her head. "I don't think she means any of it like that."

"Maybe she don't. But that's how it reads to me. Go on down then, if that's what you want, girl. We'll get along without you, if you want to spend the season getting picked on and run ragged by that wild girl. She's older than you, and she's been around a lot more, and she's not going to let you forget it. Bernice didn't write that note, and I promise you she didn't ask her mother to write it, either."

Grandmother's words were still humming in Nia's ears when she finally arrived on Anna Maria Island, a small strip of sand that jutted into the ocean, south of Tampa.

After a long trip by truck, by train, and by ferry, a servant escorted her to the brand-new house at the edge of the beach. After he left her, she made her way into the courtyard behind the house, where two women were shouting at each other.

Nia poked her head around the wall's edge and flinched as a plate shattered just a foot or two away from it.

"Hello?" She used the quiet word to announce her presence, and it almost didn't work; but Marjorie spied her niece and threw up her hands as if someone were pointing a gun at her.

The brunette woman in the tailored white suit smiled spontaneously, and stiffly. "There you are! Welcome, dear. I'm so glad you came. I assume Roger took your things to the cottage. . . . Did you have any trouble finding us?"

"Oh, no," she said, and she resisted the urge to add that she'd found her way by following the racket. Nia tiptoed into the yard to give her aunt a hug. "Roger's directions were good. And Bernice, it's real good to see you again, too," she said to the sharply dressed, blondly curled beauty with a fistful of expensive porcelain.

"Bernice," Marjorie said through clenched teeth. "Nia is your *guest*. Say hello."

"*My* guest? I didn't invite her."

Marjorie pried the bit of china from her daughter's hand and set it back on the long covered table before Bernice could throw it. "Yes, I know, but it's been a long time since you've seen each other. Since . . . since your grandfather's funeral, I think. Or no, we all went to Gasparilla that next year, didn't we?" The last part came out thoughtful, as she tried to count back the years.

But then she turned to Bernice and her voice dropped. She breathed the next part in an exhausted whine, and underneath it, Nia could almost hear a long-buried accent that sounded like her mother's. "Just for now, please? Let it go. Take Nia over to the cottage and help her get settled in."

Bernice liked the begging well enough to release the remaining plates, but even Nia could see that her truce was a temporary arrangement. "Fine," she said. She relaxed and folded her arms across an expensive ivory suit jacket. "And hello, Nia. So Roger took your things to the cottage already? I'm *ever* so glad we won't be forced to carry them in this *dreadful* heat."

Nia stepped aside and let Bernice take the lead. "Yes, your father's assistant took care of it. He met me at the ferry."

"My *step*father's assistant." She casually lifted another glass and smashed it into the wall as she walked past it.

"Aunt Marjorie," Nia dragged her heels and called over her shoulder, "will you be joining us?"

"No, dear. I'll stay and finish setting up for the party. Mr. Coyne doesn't think it's going to rain tonight, so we can leave everything out in the open. I want it to look nice for tomorrow. And don't go far, girls. Supper will be ready at eight."

They left her in her perfectly trimmed garden behind her new house, carefully picking up shards of glass and arranging the surviving cups and cutlery.

Nia wondered how they'd ever have enough settings left for the party; but she knew her aunt had plenty of money, so there was probably more dinnerware waiting wherever the broken plates had come from. It must not be a problem.

She let Bernice lead her out of the courtyard, and together they wandered among the jungle-thick trees back out to the dirt strip that passed for a road.

"Nee-uh," Bernice said her cousin's name with an exaggerated snap. "That's a weird name. I don't like it. I want to call you something else."

"Then I guess you don't expect me to answer."

Bernice reached into a pocket in her skirt and pulled out a silver cigarette case. "You're *my* guest. I'll call you whatever I want. Nia," she said again, not calling the name but turning it over in her mouth as if she were trying to tell how it tasted.

"It's short for Apollonia. Use that, if you'd rather," Nia suggested. Then she said, "Give me one of those, if you don't mind."

"Certainly."

Nia accepted a skinny white cigarette and let Bernice light it. They stopped together in a patch of shade and puffed together in silence until Bernice spoke again. "Now where exactly are you *from*?"

Nia checked a nearby tree for large insects and, seeing none, she leaned against it. "Tallahassee."

"Where's that?"

"Up north, on the mainland. Up in the panhandle."

"Is it like this island?"

She thought about it. "Yes and no. We're in the middle of a forest there, and we're a long way from the beach. But it's hot, and the greenery's the same."

"But it's a city, right?"

"A city? It's barely a town."

"Hmm." She acted like she was going to say something else, but instead she twitched her head and swatted madly. "Could you—something's stuck in my hair!"

Her arms flapped like a wet dog's ears while Nia held her head steady enough to detangle a buzzing beetle. When it was free, Bernice fluffed and combed her short shiny hair with her fingers.

Nia played with the bug and tried not to act jealous. She'd never had the nerve to cut her own hair short; it was kept off her neck with a limp brown braid. Her mother would have a fit if she ever cut it; and besides, she didn't have any curls to fluff anyway.

"What is that thing? Will it sting me?"

"It's just a june bug," Nia said as it launched off her hand with a hum. "They don't sting anybody. And they're not nasty like the palmetto bugs."

"What are those?"

"They're roaches bigger than your thumb. And they *fly*."

Bernice shuddered and clutched herself. "I've seen big roaches before. We have them all over the place in the city. I just didn't know they lived anywhere *outside*. Forget this. Let's go back to the cottage. The less time I spend outdoors, the better. Then again—" She scowled and changed her mind. "—Antonio's in there. That son of a bitch."

"You really don't like him much, do you?"

"I haven't got the words."

They crushed out their cigarettes in the sandy dirt and meandered along a path that alternately widened and tightened to accommodate the trees that no one had yet cut down.

"That's funny." Nia dusted her hands off on her skirt. "I thought I heard a bunch of good epithets back there at the courtyard. What was all that about, anyhow?"

She grunted something between a cough and a chuckle. "Epithet," she said, like she hadn't heard the rest. "What's that, a curse word or something?"

"Yeah. A curse word or something."

"Then just say 'curse word.' I thought you came from a farm. You don't talk like it."

Nia said, "Sorry I'm not as dumb as you expected," and she waited for Bernice to change the subject again. Their arrival at the cottage gave her plenty of opportunity.

"This is it," she announced. "This is where we've been staying while the house was getting finished. And that's Antonio. You don't have to talk to him if you don't want to."

"Hello," Nia said to the alleged crook, but she couldn't muster a smile to go with it. He was hidden in the screened area that kept him shadowed and relatively cool, and all she could see was the shape of a man in a hat, holding a drink in his hand.

Bernice reached for one of the handrails that flanked the wooden steps. "On second thought, let's not go inside. We might as well get a nice view for the smell."

Antonio nodded passing acknowledgment at Nia and disregarded Bernice with skill born of long practice. Nia mumbled that it was nice to meet him, and he responded in kind, with a similar level of enthusiasm.

He leaned forward to set down his drink, and for a moment his face slipped into a patch of sun. Nia thought he was good-looking, with deep-set eyes, dark-slicked hair, and a strong nose. Or perhaps he only looked handsome because he was well-dressed.

Bernice turned away from the porch and wobbled on tottering high heels back down into the dirt-rut road. Nia quit staring at her uncle and followed her.

"Let's go out to the dock. " She peeked down at her watch. "It's almost seven thirty, but we'll be back in time for supper. It's not very far."

Nia had never seen such an expensive watch before, and certainly not on someone her own age. She thought it was pretty, but it looked weird on a half-deserted island.

Bernice reached for her cigarette case again and offered her cousin another before she even asked.

Nia fell into step beside her. "Are you sure we'll get back in time?"

"I'm sure. You ever been out here before?"

"No."

"Well, I have, and I'm telling you it isn't very far. Welcome to the middle of nowhere." She took a particularly long drag on her cigarette, using the time to think or plot. When she finally spoke, her words were dry and a tiny bit menacing. "There's going to be a party tomorrow."

Nia tried not to wonder why the simple statement sounded like a threat. "The courtyard looks nice," she said. "Your mother did a nice job of putting it together."

Bernice nodded. "It's all real nice," she agreed with a scowl that guaranteed she didn't mean it. "It's their anniversary. Mother and Antonio have been married for ten years. Tomorrow will be their first day in their new house, and ten years together. Hoo-*ray*. At least *someone's* happy to be here." She kicked off her shoes and climbed onto a rickety gray pier, dropping her feet into the water and twirling them around. The hem of her skirt trailed in, too, but if she noticed, she didn't care.

Nia glanced up at the sky and observed, "We're on the wrong beach. If we wanted to watch the sun set, we should've gone to the other side of the island."

"It doesn't matter. We've got all summer, and then some." Bernice stirred the water with her toes while Nia settled down onto the dock beside her and let her own feet dangle. "You know what?" she said. "You smoke like you've done it before, not like you're trying to show me how smooth you are."

"I've smoked before," Nia admitted. The men who worked the farms smoked on their breaks, and if her mother wasn't watching, sometimes she'd smoke with them just to taste it. If they were going to treat her like a hired hand, she figured she'd act like one.

The girls sat and smoked while the sun sank behind them.

Nia was about to mention the time again when she saw something strange in the water. At first she dismissed it as a trick of the moonlight, but it seemed to come closer, so she nudged Bernice. "Who's that?" she asked.

"Where?" Bernice strained and stretched her neck.

"There, did you see her? Someone was . . . swimming."

Bernice frowned. "I don't hear any splashing."

"She's gone now," Nia said. "I didn't hear the splashing either, but I swear, I saw someone. It was a woman with long hair."

"You're crazy." Bernice pulled her feet out of the water and shook them dry. "There's no one out there this time of night except those big damned fish. What are they called . . . dolphins."

Nia lifted her own feet out and felt around for her shoes. "Dolphins aren't fish," she said.

Bernice was already walking away.

Nia glanced back at the water and saw the mystery woman again. This time, the woman didn't duck away, but she stayed there, her naked torso rising up out of the water. She was much closer to the pier, only a few yards out in the bay, and Nia could see her more clearly. Her skin was dark, and her hair hung so long that it floated around in the water at her waist.

Somehow, Nia suspected that Bernice would not turn around even if she called out again—so she did not tell her cousin that the woman's silvery, empty eyes followed them both until they were back in the trees.

At supper, Marjorie seated Nia between Bernice and Antonio, who scowled and spit at each other around her, or through her, if she leaned forward too far. Occasionally, Antonio made a vague stab at conversation; but Bernice would not let the smallest comment go unattacked.

"It's not so hot tonight, is it? Not as bad as it has been," Antonio tried.

Bernice laughed sharp and loud. "How would you know, you lazy bastard? You've been sitting inside all day on the porch."

Antonio squeezed his fork and lifted it to his mouth, where he unlocked his jaw long enough to snatch a mouthful of fried plantains. Marjorie stared at her plate and fiddled with her food. Under the table, her thigh lurched.

"Honestly, Mother. If you want to say something, have out with it. There's no need to get violent. Besides, that's the table leg you kicked just now, and the last two times you hit Nia in the shins—only she's too nice to say anything."

"You could take a lesson from her." Antonio swallowed his plantains and picked up another forkful.

Marjorie stumbled into the conversation. "Please don't antagonize her, dear."

"Yeah, Antonio. Don't antagonize me."

"Now *you* stop it, too," Marjorie fussed.

"This is *my* house." Antonio almost shouted. "I paid for it, and I'll antagonize anyone inside it if I damn well please."

"We're not in *your* house yet."

"Sweetheart, please don't talk that way to your—"

"Shut up, Mother."

"Don't tell your mother to shut up!"

Bernice jumped to her feet and wadded her napkin. "Nia, let's go."

Nia froze, fork poised midair. "I'm sorry? What?"

Bernice snorted. "Didn't you hear me? Or were you still daydreaming about your new friend, the mermaid?"

All was suddenly quiet.

"What? No. What mermaid?" Nia took another bite, and while she slowly chewed, she played with her fork. It made faint screeching noises as she pushed the tines around, following the pattern around the dish's rim.

Bernice stood behind her own chair, hands planted on the seat back. No one spoke, and all eyes were on the visitor, so she quit scribbling on the china and tried to explain herself. "When we were outside, I thought I saw a woman swimming by the dock. But I probably didn't. It was awful late—right before supper. What was it you wanted again, Bernice? Where did you want to go?"

"Outside. Mother, Nia and I are going for a walk."

"We are?"

"We are. *Now.*" She pushed her plate away and dropped her napkin with a flounce and a flourish.

Marjorie smiled like she was too tired to muster more of a reaction. "Go ahead. But it's dark out there, and there are hardly any people. I don't want you getting lost. You could get bitten by a snake, or worse. Take one of Mr. Coyne's lamps."

"We won't need it." Bernice leaned over and whipped Nia's napkin out of its place on her lap. She squashed the small cloth and threw it onto the table. "There's plenty of moon. Come *on*, Nia."

Nia stood and gently shoved her chair under the table. "Well . . . Aunt Marjorie, Uncle Antonio. Thanks for supper. We'll be back before long."

Bernice grabbed Nia and pulled her out the door.

Once they reached the porch, Nia reclaimed her arm with a swift yank. "For future reference," she grumbled, "don't talk *for* me, and don't tell me what *we* are going to do."

"You're full of shit," Bernice complained. "If you really had a backbone, you'd have used it in there. You're just as pathetic as they are."

She turned on her heel and strutted down the stairs, trying to let the porch's screen door clap Nia in the face. Nia caught it, and then caught Bernice by the sleeve of her jacket.

She glowered at Nia, arm flexing and curling. "Let go of me," she commanded, squaring her feet and ripping her arm away. "This jacket cost more than you'd earn all summer flinging oranges into a bag."

She tripped with the effort of escaping but recovered at the last second, just in time to skip lightly down the stairs and out into the yard, as if she'd meant to do it that way all along.

"You're an idiot for wearing it out here, then," Nia told her. "But I bet you didn't bring anything better."

"Better? I've got more expensive stuff than this by a mile."

"No, not more expensive. *Better.* Clothes you can wear outside without worrying you'll mess them up. Look around, would you? You're in a forest, practically a jungle. Hardly anybody lives here, so who are you trying to impress?"

She glared, then changed her mind and flashed a gorgeous grin. "You're right. And you'd know better than I would, wouldn't you? Maybe you can loan me something. I bet you've got *stacks* of clothes for wearing outside."

"I don't think we're the same size," Nia said. She didn't think Bernice would be caught dead in cotton, anyway. "You're a lot skinnier than me," she added.

It wasn't very true, but it had the right effect. Nia meant it as a little bit of an insult, and Bernice took it as a compliment.

"Aw, aren't you a sweetie! Look," she said, pulling out the cigarette case again. "Let's just have a smoke, huh? Let's be friends again; I like it better when we're friends. I'm sorry for being such a pain."

"I believe you. Really. And I don't want to smoke again, right now. I'm too hot. Let's just walk, okay? Isn't that what you wanted?"

Bernice shrugged. "Sure, we can walk. There's nowhere to *go,* but I couldn't stay in *there.* I can only put up with those guys for about an hour a day. I guess we could visit the new house again. The beach out at the edge of the lot is quiet—there aren't any weirdos fishing or swimming . . . or anything else. And I think it's low tide now, so we can look for sand dollars."

"We should *definitely* get a lamp."

"I told you, we don't *need* one."

Nia scrutinized Bernice's sharp, hollow face.

Her cousin was right. The moon was high and full, and she could easily make out the trail to the house. It was a straight shot across the narrow part of the island, and she could find her way back by herself if she had to . . . in case Bernice pulled something funny, which looked like a distinct possibility to Nia. No one goes beachcombing in high heels.

She relented. "Just for a little bit. I've had a long couple of days, with all that traveling, and I want to get some rest."

"Don't worry." Bernice pushed a long lock of moss out of her path. "This won't take long."

"What won't take long?"

"You know. Our walk. I want some fresh air, or the closest thing to it. This whole island feels stuffy, like it's some kind of place where they keep plants. Like one of those big glass buildings that smells wet inside."

"A greenhouse?"

"Yes. It's horrible."

"No, it isn't."

Bernice kicked at something in the dirt and stomped sourly forward. "You only think so because you're from around here. You're used to it. To everyone else, this place is hell on earth."

Nia kept her gaze locked on the back of Bernice's head as it bounced in front of her. It was awkward to talk when they were walking single file, so they didn't speak again until they passed beneath the thick, heavy willow that marked the entrance to her aunt and uncle's new property.

"We're back," Bernice declared with a dramatic, silly stretch of the vowels that proved their grandmother right. The girl *had* gone native up there in the big city. "It's just a few more yards to the beach, right over there. You can hear it, right? Go on over the dune, down to the water if you want. I'll be there in a second. I think I left something in the courtyard. If I don't see it right away, I'll worry about it later. Go on. I'll catch up in a minute."

"I don't know."

"What are you, a scaredy cat? Afraid of the dark?"

"No," Nia said. But she didn't want Bernice out of her sight, because she didn't trust her—even the slightest bit. She looked out at the dune and over at the dark house with its prettily laid-out courtyard behind it. "Don't be like that. I'll go. You promise you'll catch up in a minute?"

"Sure."

She could feel Bernice watching her as she walked toward the dune. She took a few steps into the coarse strands of sea oats and let herself disappear over the sandy hump, then peered back over the barrier that separated the front yard from the beach.

And she slipped back into the yard.

3

Why They Call It That

The rush of the waves sliding onto shore masked the swishing of Nia's feet through the grass, but she could still hear the quiet shatter of something wrapped in cloth muffling the sound of breaking glass. Already the shards of newly busted ceramic plates sparkled on the ground.

Arms folded, Nia leaned against the nearest wall and marveled at Bernice's demented efficiency. "Exactly how stupid do you think I am?" she asked. "Jesus. I may be poor, but I'm not *dumb*."

Bernice didn't pause. She picked up another glass and wrapped it in the corner of the tablecloth, and with a satisfied swing, she slammed it against the wall. She reached for another one.

"Stop it!" Nia ordered. She wanted to physically accost Bernice, but something about the girl's determined, mechanical motion made her hesitate. "What do you think you're doing?"

Smash.

"Why? Why are you doing this?"

The vandal stopped, and faced her cousin. "Now *that* is a better question."

"What?"

Bernice wrapped another plate in the cloth and wound the fabric around it. "You asked me a couple of really dumb questions; then you asked a good one."

She paused, reflecting before giving her response. And then, in a sudden and weird shriek she shouted, "It's because I hate them! And I hate this place, and I hate this house, and I hate this stupid party, and—" The plate fell loose from the tablecloth and Bernice's twisting hands, and it dropped to the grass. Her words came in a fierce panting that made her sound like a wild animal. "I hate *him,* because, because . . ."

And then a light went on behind her eyes. She calmed down to an angry grumble. "I hate him for coming into my room after Mother's asleep."

Bernice stalked slowly toward Nia. She clung to her story and the corner of the tablecloth. Everything came sliding away behind her. The remaining glasses and plates, the silver candlesticks and flatware, the large glass punch bowl and the crystal cake pedestal all went clattering to the ground.

Nia slinked away from her, reaching her hands behind her back and feeling along the courtyard wall. "You're lying," she prayed.

"Lying? Why would you accuse me of lying? No one *ever* believes me." Bernice's eyes were huge and wet, and she pouted her pixie lips. She hadn't released the tablecloth. It dragged along the sand like a tremendous red train on a crimson wedding gown.

"I wonder why. You . . . Don't. Stay away from me."

"That's what I used to tell him. I'd say, 'Antonio, get away from me or I'll yell for my mom!' But he never listened. He'd tell me to hush up, and he'd unbutton his shirt, and he'd take it off and leave it hanging on the bedpost. Then he'd slip off his shoes and undo his pants, and lift up the corners of the bedspread so he could crawl into bed beside me."

"You're lying," Nia insisted. She tripped over a patio stone and almost fell into an alcove in the wall.

Bernice's tablecloth snagged on the circular fountain and she tugged it loose. She guided her free hand down the front of her shirt, letting her white, manicured fingers hang for a moment where her breasts were pressed forward under the fabric.

One by one, she folded the round glass buttons through the slotted holes until Nia could see the top of her lean, pale stomach beneath the cotton and lace of her brassiere. Small beads of sweat gleamed on her skin and dripped down into her cleavage. Without glancing down, Bernice swept the moisture away and wiped it on her skirt.

"What are you doing half-naked out here?"

Bernice whirled around to face Antonio, who stood in the archway entrance to the yard. His brown linen suit looked black in the shadows of the banyan tree, and he wasn't wearing his hat. The ocean wind kicked up, and his hair rippled wildly.

He paced across the sand and grass and tried to grab her arm, but she turned too fast and he caught her hair instead. Accepting whatever handhold he could seize, Antonio wrenched her around so hard that she toppled over herself and sat tangled in the table-cloth.

"Your mother wanted me to come and check on you, because she's worried about you. I'll never understand why she gives a damn. Close your shirt, you stupid little slut."

He turned his back to her.

"What was she talking about?" he demanded, and even in the mostly dark, Nia could see how red his face was. "Was she making up stories about me again? I know she does that; I know what she likes to tell people. But you can see through her, can't you? You're not a dumb kid. You're a nice kid, I think. You can tell she's a liar, I know you can."

Nia thought he was going to add something else, but then Bernice reared up behind him.

There wasn't even time to call his name before Nia heard a wet blow.

He stumbled forward, slinging his arm back to push her away. A long silver knife rose out of his back, just beyond the reach of his searching fingers. He doubled his elbows up, trying to get a hold on it. He fell.

Nia wasn't sure whom to shout at, so she didn't shout at all.

She ran to Antonio and knelt beside him.

Bernice didn't try to stop her. She simply backed away from them both, unspooling herself from the cloth.

Antonio was lying on his side, trying to rub the knife on the ground to snag and remove it. Nia pulled the knife as quickly but gently as she could, and threw it away with a horrified grunt.

His blood looked black and slick as it gushed heartily over her hands, as it bubbled out of the wound with every breath he struggled to take. Bernice had stabbed him hard. By luck or design, she'd hit something important. Nia took a corner of her dress and pushed it against the gushing hole.

"Where is she?" Antonio wheezed.

Bernice darted in close to swipe the knife, then ducked away again—out of Nia's reach. She stood a few feet away and fondled the weapon, running her fingers along the wet edge.

Nia pressed her makeshift bandage against Antonio's back.

She leaned on it as hard as she dared, and kept her eyes on her cousin.

The silver cake knife made Bernice confident.

Overconfident, Nia thought, or at least she hoped.

Bernice shifted her grip on the blade and pointed it down, prepared to attack again. "I like you, Nia," she said, and her words were so cold, they left frost in the air. "So I'm going to give you one good chance to get out of the way."

Antonio had slipped from Nia's hold. He was flat on the ground and dangling near unconsciousness. He gurgled and twisted himself over with a surprising burst of effort that sent him halfway onto Nia's lap. "Get Marjorie," he said.

"I will," she promised, but his eyes were already glazed, and his chest was not inflating the right way. He was certainly dying. Nia was still pondering the costs of protecting an almost-corpse from an armed madwoman when the armed madwoman pounced.

Nia wasn't so off guard as Bernice had thought, and the ensuing attack was less than professional-grade. Bernice staggered wildly across Antonio's limp form, stabbing from above in a way that let Nia catch her forearm.

But she couldn't keep it. She fell to the side, and there was a brief moment where Bernice could have run her through without resistance . . . but she wanted Antonio more. She used Nia's weakness to finish him, burying the blade through his chest and between two ribs—using all her weight to jam it down, up to the gilded handle.

He did not gasp or groan, or even quiver. She may as well have jabbed a rotting apple for all the response she got, nothing more than a small drool of warm, sticky blood seeping an anticlimax through his shirt.

Nia rose carefully to her feet.

Though Bernice must have noticed, she didn't look. She stared down at her handiwork, absorbing every sloppy detail. Nia couldn't read her expression. Bernice might have been pleased to see him dead, or she might have been disappointed by how easy it was. It was too dark to tell.

But Nia did not believe for an instant that Bernice would let her go. In that fragile moment of silence over Antonio's body, she scrutinized her cousin and tried to think.

Bernice was taller by an inch or two and solid enough, but Nia was lean from living in the sun and working in the orchard. She was no muscle-bound farmhand, but she wasn't a pampered city girl either. She was heavier than Bernice, sure; but she didn't have an ounce of fat on her—even where she would've liked some.

It would take Bernice no more than a second to retrieve the knife from Antonio's body.

Nia was smaller than her soon-to-be opponent, and she was wearing a longer dress. This was not Nia's home territory. She didn't know her way around the island, but chances were good that Bernice didn't either, whether she claimed she did or not.

Nia glanced over her shoulder, checking to make sure all the broken glass was behind her. Then, as inconspicuously as she could, she pried off her shoes.

The careful shuffling broke Bernice's spell. She peered down at her cousin through tightly slitted eyes. "Nia." She said it calmly, like a passing introduction. "Mother will never believe you."

"Yes, she will, Bernice." She tried to give her cousin's name the same cool treatment. "But she'll spend the rest of her life denying it."

"She doesn't *have* to. Nia, think how *easy* this would be." Her tone abruptly changed, sliding from an earnest plea to something more casual and chatty. "Hey, do you know why we had to move here?" she asked with earnestness, as if she actually wanted to share the answer. She walked over to the fountain and sat on its edge. The cake knife in her hand clinked against the tile and stonework.

"No. Why?" Nia wondered how much space there was between herself and the archway exit.

"That dirty wop." She gestured down at Antonio. "He and his business partners had a falling out. He was a bookkeeper for a hooch parlor, and in that sort of business, you don't get fired for skimming—you get dead. So when word got out, he took the money and took off running."

"You're lying again."

Again, she was almost comically serious. "No, not this time. You can ask Mother. She knew about it; he had to let her in on it; otherwise, she wouldn't have believed he was in enough trouble to make a run for it. Mother's the one who suggested the island. She had some friends down here, the ones who let us stay in their cottage while this place was being built. I swear to you, Nia. This would be *so easy*."

"So he really was a crook? Grandmother said she thought he was."

"She did? That's funny. Yeah, she was right."

Nia made a small shrug with her eyebrows and added, "Grandmother thinks everyone from farther up north than Tennessee is a crook. This time, she was just a lucky guesser."

Bernice smiled, wide and friendly. She started to stand, and Nia twitched, prepared to run. She couldn't do it—she couldn't hold the cool, easy stance that her cousin adopted so easily.

Bernice sat back down.

"This is what we'll do," she said. "We'll say we found him this way, and we saw two men leaving through the woods. Everyone'll think his old partners caught up with him, and no one will be able to prove a thing."

"Those kinds of businessmen don't kill people with cake knives."

Nia's grandmother had told her about them; they were the men who ran the racetracks where the family sometimes sold produce to vendors.

"Oh, what do you know, anyway? They . . . they'd probably want to keep it quiet, right?"

"Then they could just make him disappear or something. That's how they work, isn't it? I've read stories about people like that."

"Shut up, would you?" Bernice stood up, despite Nia's cringe. "Look, I don't want to hurt you or anything. You're family. Besides, we'd make great friends and we'll have a wonderful time this summer with *him* out of the way."

"And besides," Nia added, catching Bernice's momentum and riding it, out of fear more than conversational flow. "You want someone to help your story. Your mother might swallow it, but the police never will."

Bernice approached Nia, tiptoeing over Antonio and coming to stand in front of her.

Nia hated to allow her so close, but she knew that if she wanted to make it out of the courtyard, she had to draw Bernice farther away from its exit archway, or she'd never beat her out of it. There in the courtyard, the ground was crisscrossed with paving stones and the grass was clipped close; it would be a fair race between them. And out in the open, it was only a short dash to the beach.

"Nia?" She stopped a few feet away. "Nia, you've got to help me out. Nia, what do you say?"

Nia took a deep breath and used her toe to nudge her shoes farther away from her feet. "Let me think about it."

Then, with as much commotion as she could manage, Nia dived to her left and dodged the flicking knife—which caught on and ripped her dress, cutting out the hem her mother had only recently fixed.

Bernice jumped after her, snaring her nails in Nia's hair, trying to twist her fingers into the braid there, but Nia grabbed the wall and used it to launch herself free and through the arch.

The grass was soft beneath her naked feet, and she prayed to God that there weren't any sandspurs. Down at the dune, she took a flying leap and landed on top of the small ridge, then hopped down the other side into the thick, powdery sand. It trapped her briefly, but she dug in with her toes and hurled herself forward onto the beach.

Bernice was right behind her. She hit the sand with a quick grumble and then recovered, only to sink under her next steps. Her tall shoes dug into the sand and tried to bury themselves.

Nia kept running, knowing it would take precious seconds for Bernice to figure out that she ought to take her shoes off, and then perhaps a couple more to unfasten the skinny buckles and cast the things aside.

An endless strip of beach sprawled before them, and a small beacon of light gleamed weakly at the island's tip where the lighthouse was perched. Nia thought that there must be a keeper there, and surely a backwoods yokel who worked alone all night would have a gun.

The distance between the girls widened as Bernice cursed and hobbled; but she finally forced her shoes away, and once her feet were free, the gap began to close.

Nia prayed that her head start would be enough.

Sand flew up behind her as she charged down the strip, and her legs burned with exhaustion. The light in the distance wasn't growing close as fast as she thought it should, and God, she was tired. She tried not to pant so hard; it made her side cramp and her throat catch.

But Bernice was almost on top of her again, breathless and tireless, too, so Nia jammed her feet into the sand, crunching down into shells and seaweed, crab claws and shrimp tails, in a gritty plume. A thin wave trickled over her path. Mere yards away, a larger wave rumbled and rushed after the first.

The tide was coming in. With a burst of inspiration that fueled a second wind, Nia wondered if Bernice could swim.

She turned and ran into the oncoming waves, knowing the water would slow them both. But if she could go deep enough, if she could make it into the surf where the waves were higher than both their heads, she could get out of Bernice's reach long enough to think—maybe even long enough to swim to the lighthouse. It couldn't be more than a mile, since the island wasn't much longer than that, and she could always tread water while she caught her breath.

Black and warm, the Gulf foamed around her ankles and sucked at her toes.

Bernice splashed in after her.

Nia trudged ahead, plowing through water that was up to her knees, then her thighs. Her dress soaked and sagged around her, slowing her some, but she'd expected that. She dived headfirst into the next oncoming wave and pulled herself under the water with arms that were not quite as weary as her legs.

I've made it, she thought, swimming out to sea, kicking for all she was worth. But the tide was against her, and she was only a few strokes into her flight when Bernice's hand wrapped around Nia's foot.

She panicked and floundered, sputtering as she tried to stand and breathe. Bernice's grip slipped, and she dropped the knife in order to hold her cousin with both hands, drawing the other girl toward her like a fish on a line.

Nia flipped over and kicked with her free leg, pounding Bernice in the jaw with a resounding crack and sending her sprawling. She let go of Nia's leg, leaving long red scrapes where her fingernails had clutched at her, and although the wounds must have stung in the salt water, Nia did not feel them. She threw herself back into the water and swam like mad against the incoming current, trying not to think about her bloody leg.

Something big and solid rushed by underwater, bumping against her side.

Terror shot up her spine. Besides her freshly scratched leg, her clothes reeked of Antonio's blood, and the Gulf abounded with sharks.

Oh God, she prayed. *Let it be a dolphin.*

She couldn't hear Bernice behind her anymore. Only the sound of her own feverish splashing filled her ears. She glanced over her shoulder, causing her eyes to sting with the sticky-sharp heat of the ocean. She still couldn't locate Bernice, so she quit swimming and stood up. When the waves rolled past and around her, they came to her collarbone.

Her cousin bobbed a few feet away, eyes closed and mouth shakily agape. Water lapped at her face and she winced, but her eyelids didn't flutter or open. She coughed and sucked in salt water, but did not seem to awaken. Her head slid under the next wave and bubbles popped to the surface as she started to sink.

That thick, strange form pushed past Nia again.

A moment later, Bernice's body bobbed as if it had been bumped, too. She did not respond, but drooped even farther below the surface.

"Shit," Nia swore like one of her grandmother's farmhands. "Shit!"

Making damn sure she didn't see the knife, Nia grabbed Bernice's collar. She hauled her cousin along behind her, walking backwards so she didn't have to take her eyes off the injured girl. Her face was still underwater, but Nia figured that it could stay that way until she could get them both onto the sand.

The mysterious thing collided against them again, and Nia frantically tried to believe it was a dolphin. Anything else would have attacked already, or that's what she told herself as she tried to get a better hold on Bernice.

Desperate, she grabbed Bernice's hair and lifted her head up. Her eyes were half-open, but Nia saw nothing there except for the whites, and in the darkness she was so drained of color that she seemed to glow. Water dribbled from her nose and mouth.

"Come on," Nia said through gritted teeth. Her fear of the thing in the water had tipped until it was greater than her fear of Bernice, so she shook her cousin and tried to bring her back around. Anything, anyone—she'd talk to anyone right now; she just couldn't be alone with it, out there in the water. *"Bernice?"*

Nia wrapped an arm around the other girl's chest and pulled her as far above the water as she could, but Bernice was dead-weight, and it was all she could do to merely tow her. By the time they reached a waist-deep tide, Nia was almost completely exhausted.

Bernice hacked violently. She began to breathe again with a wet gasp.

"Nia?" She choked on the name. She rotated slowly in Nia's grip and clung to her. "Nia, I think—"

With incredible force, Bernice was torn out of Nia's arms and back underwater.

It happened so quickly, Nia couldn't tell which way she'd gone, but she knew without a doubt that this was no farce. A few waves away, Bernice's hand shot up and thrashed, then disappeared.

"What's going on?" Nia yelled, and she was starting to cry because she was too afraid to do anything else. *"Where did you go?"*

Her feet tapped something cold and hard. The knife? She ducked under the waves and felt for the blade, rooting around until she touched the fine silver handle. She almost had it. She'd almost pulled it to the surface when another hand latched itself on to hers.

Out of pure shock, she blinked.

She shouldn't have seen anything at all, but she could swear there was another pair of eyes, swaying before hers in the swirling undertow. She tried to scream, but it was muffled by the water.

You can come, too, then.

She shook her head furiously and twisted her arm, but the hand that held it might have been made of steel or stone.

"No," she burbled. "No."

It was not Bernice. It couldn't be.

What felt like seaweed looped around her legs, constricting and binding her as she fought. She needed air. The hand released her and she tried to swim, knowing the surf was only a few feet deep, but not knowing which way was up. The weeds grew tighter, pulling her in all directions at once, rubbing her skin raw and squeezing all the air out of everything.

Stars fizzed across her sight and she felt so light, she was sure she must be floating. She nodded her head, trying to clear it, and opened her eyes again—not feeling the burn of the salt so much as tasting it with her whole body.

The eyes were still there, evil underwater. Her fear was the only thing keeping her conscious, but even that hold was slipping.

The eyes peered closer, zooming up to her face.

"No," she mouthed, waving the creature away. She squinted over her arm and pulled her legs up to a fetal position. "Stay away. . . ."

Never.

The world was going dark. Nia wondered where Bernice was.

Come join her. I can take you both. I will make you strong beyond belief.

She shook her head. *No.*

She tried to push the eyes away, and the feeling of lightness passed, and she was sinking.

The last she remembered, the eyes were retreating. They looked angry, and Nia wondered why. She felt so heavy. She settled to the ocean floor and thought disconnectedly about how this must be what it felt like to die.

"But who are you?" she asked the eyes before they vanished.

I'm Arahab.

Bedtime Stories of the Gods

Under the water, beneath the place where sharks circle low, their noses hovering above the sand, and below the shimmering, shifting schools of fish that move through the Gulf, there is a safe place where an old, long-abandoned being may rest and wait.

She collects other things like herself, or other things that she might fashion after herself. She holds them down and presses them against her. She makes herself mother and master, and maker, and queen.

Arahab holds the blind, water-sick young woman and coos into the still girl's hair.

"Before you, I took another," she says. "I plucked him from the water as I plucked you, pulling him down into this abyss where I hold you now. By that point, I'd been watching him for years.

"First I saw him as a child. He was still a boy when he reached into the river and drew the girl out. She was small and frightened; he hid her in his house and tried to make her family buy her back. The lawmen came, and the family cried out for justice. They were powerful people, powerful enough to pay a ransom—but they were also powerful enough to bring down vengeance. The little Spaniard was afraid. His plans had not been fully formed when he seized the child; for look at him, he was just a child himself.

"But he was learning. He was gathering ideas, and coming to understand the way the law of men shows mercy, or fails to.

"Since he was only a boy, the courts gave him a choice. He could go to prison, or he could go to sea. I held my breath, and I smiled when he chose the boats and the waves. I waited for him to learn.

"He sailed on the *Floridablanca* and learned which ropes to tug to pull the sails, how to watch the sky for a sign of the weather, and how to guide a wood-framed vessel by the stars above and by his compass.

"And he learned that a war on land will take to the waves, in time.

"His ship was overtaken. It was pounded and ruined; it was blasted with cannon and riddled with lumpy round bullets; it was overrun with uniformed men who seized whom they liked, executed whom they pleased, and took whatever moved them.

"But my little Spaniard—who was now less little, and more man—he survived the battle and fled from the government ship. He could find no honor in serving a nation whose best efforts met failure; he could not justify risking his own life to further a cause in which he did not believe. And out on the seas, between the land masses where men build their cities, there were other men like him. Other men had seen what bounty the water might bring; they, too, had learned the ways of the ropes and the sails; they, too, had buried in their hearts the ways of the stars and the horizons that stretched from world to world's end."

Arahab uses her terrible, ancient mind to share the scene with the water-sick woman in her arms. Her memory is perfect and infallible. Her recreation is flawless and fearsome.

The water-sick woman listens and watches.

She has no choice, but she has no desire to do otherwise. She learns and waits, and clutches her new mother. Mother means life, and strength, and air. Without her mother, without the primordial voice that rumbles and hums beneath the ocean floor, without her mother's arms around her body, there is no breath and no being.

"He found a crew and a ship of his own; he severed his ties to the land, to its laws, and to its lords. He called himself king of the coast, and in time he chose this coast. It was not an empty place, even then. Even then, there were men traveling between the ports, between the islands, between the nooks in the Gulf where other men had gathered to trade. But there was not so much competition on the west side of the peninsula, few others stalked the ships that sat low in the water, fat with gold and slaves.

"The Spaniard learned to kill, and he learned to sail with a flag of terror. His ship moved fast across the Gulf and around the rocky edges, rough with coral, where the land sticks its fingers out into this place of mine. He accumulated wealth, and captives, and ransoms. He earned esteem, and respect, and fear. He investigated the forgotten places where the fresh rivers flow into the salt; and in these places he found estuaries and wells and places where things can be hidden, and lost, and forgotten.

"I waited for him to learn some more.

"Out in the open water, he laced his guns together with knotted rope and slung them around his neck. He leaped from deck to deck, and he fired them quickly, one after another, one shot into one body, and the next, and the next. The wood that creaked underfoot was baptized with the entrails and vomit of men, and women, too. He learned that wealth and power cost blood, and he took the lesson to heart. He learned it well.

"I waited for him to learn the rest.

"Once, he chose a woman from his captives. He did not yet fathom the way a heart is won, or which hearts are worthy of winning. He chose poorly, and she resisted him. He should have cast her into the water, wrapped in chains, but he resisted killing her. The crew saw his hesitation as weakness, and they, in turn, resisted his rule.

"In desperation, and in anger, and in fright, he ran her through with his first mate's sword. It met her at the throat, and nearly took her head. And with that sacrifice, he learned much, much more about the company he should keep. He regained control of his ship, and of his heart. He seized the next vessel and annihilated its contents, man and beast and treasure alike.

"I only had to wait a little longer, though if I counted out the years to you, you might think it an eternity. When I wait, I am patient. I have more seasons and suns behind me and before me than you'd ever dream. I have more time than any God you've ever prayed to.

"I waited until he had finished, almost. I waited until he'd had a long life, and a long career for a man of his kind. And I knew he was mine—I knew he was meant to join me, when his greed would not let him retire to die an old man in his bed. He tried to be wise and withdraw while the odds might let him vanish; but there was one more boat, fat and low in the water with gold or slaves. And it sailed under a flag he hated, a flag from the country that first compelled him to leave his land-life and come to my domain.

"He called his crewmen off the beach where they were sorting out their spoils, and he said to them, 'Look, in the bay, you can see it there. It's a beautiful ship and it is heavy in the water. One last venture, then. One last ship and its treasure, and then we can part ways. You can go to your island, Roberto; you can return to your Sanibel in Spain, Arturo. This is the last of the wealth we've grown between us, and now it is divided according to rank and skill. But one last ship, my men. One last ship and we will call ourselves kings and retreat to distant shores, distant homes, and distant memory. It is fair and fitting that we have been so long spared the squad or the noose.'

"And the sailors on the shore agreed with him, and they rallied beside him, running to the ship and raising the anchor, unfurling the sails. They urged their ship into the bay, and out through the water, and they drew their vessel alongside the easy victim, and they raised their flag of plunder.

"But the other ship had a secret. Its flag was a false one, and its mission was one of deceit. It had set itself against the shore to serve as bait, as a tempting lure to draw the Spaniard out.

"When the attack began, the other vessel lowered its treacherous sheet and raised its true colors. It was no merchant ship but a ship of war, a ship called the *Enterprise* from the New World. The other craft returned fire and the Spaniard was furious. It was a trick that he had taught them, the lure and the attack, and now they used it against him.

"Overpowered, outmanned, and outgunned, he found himself alone on the deck as his men died or surrendered around him. He was no fool. He knew that they would not let him leave or live. Even if he raised his hands and let them take him, he'd only face execution at a later date. He would not allow such a thing; he was not made for public humiliation such as that.

"And down below I waited for him; I smiled and was pleased, for I had been waiting on him for years, and the moment was at hand.

"He rushed to the bow and he seized the anchor's chain. He slung it around his neck and wrapped it around his shoulders. He faced the New World ship and he saluted its commander. And he said to him, 'Gaspar dies by his own hand, and by no enemy.' He turned his back to the deck and he cast himself into the water."

"I caught him." Arahab breathes cool bubbles into the woman's ear. "I caught him, as I caught you." She tightens her hold and smiles when the woman returns the embrace.

It might be heartfelt, or it might be a reflex from a dying body too long left without air.

"I swam beneath the ship, and let him fall into my arms. He struggled against the chains he chose, but he did not struggle against *me*. Even as the sky left his lungs, and even as his chest convulsed, and his eyes burned from the unfamiliar salt, he understood that I was there to take him, and he did not fight *me*.

"I brought him here, held him close, and told him great stories, as I now do for you. But you, I have more to tell—because to all the great histories of the earth, I add the story of how my son came to me, as well.

"And he, my cherished son, was a bold and wonderful thing. I gave him tasks, and he performed them. But then I gave him a quest, and he hesitated.

"He made me promise him a boon, for attempting the quest I

assigned. I admit and I grant, the quest was a tremendous one. So he asked of me, before he agreed, 'I want to be a legend among men; I want you to make me a myth. Let them remember my name forever, and throw festivals in my honor. The very men who scorned me and refused me—the society that forbade me entrance, and deemed me unfit to join it—let them recall me as a hero.'

"I gave my word, and my word does not bend. He set out to do my bidding.

"I sent him to another ocean, in another vessel. I gave him a crew of creatures I'd claimed and altered to better move on board, eels and sturgeons, octopi and dolphins with intelligence and strength greater than anyone save their captain. Together they would go deeper and farther and faster than any man could dive or swim, or any whale could sink.

"I sent him to a trench, to a great crack in the earth's face, to a split that reaches past the water, past the lava, and down to the earth's very bones."

The woman without air shifts, makes a softly questioning sound.

Arahab understands the query, so she nods, and then she says, "I will tell you why. It is because of the thing that sleeps below. He sleeps much farther down than I hold you now. He sleeps at the center of the world, almost. He sleeps beyond the touch of men, or machines, or even me. Or so I've come to fear. This thing that sleeps, he coils himself tightly because he must—his size is so great, and his body so tremendous, that he scarcely fits within this world at all.

"At least, that is how I remember him. It has been so long since last I gazed upon him, I almost could not say. There is a chance that my memory fails me. A few million years here and there can cloud the details.

"But he is large, and he is sleeping, and by his very absence the rest of us are pushed aside and forgotten. We are shunted to the fringes and overrun by lesser beings. Long have I stood aside and watched, insulted. Long have I waited and been disconnected, and disgraced, and disregarded.

"While the Leviathan rests, the rest of us are wraiths—despondent and abashed. So I have made it my goal to awaken him. But he will not rise easily, or quickly. He has gone so far and sunk so deep that it is no longer easy to touch him. But there are places where the skin of the earth grows thin. There are cracks through which he can almost be seen; he rises almost to the surface, and a very small portion of his bulk can be reached with diligence. These places are scattered throughout the globe, but they are difficult to navigate.

"And that is why I took the Spaniard.

"I took him for being wise, and merciless. I took him for being strong and quick. I embraced him because he was tough and driven, and he would not be stopped.

"His errand was to reach the slumbering Leviathan. All I asked was that he touch the old god, and I believed it might be enough to rouse him. *Reaching* him would be the trouble. 'Go to the trench off the Chinese seas,' I told Gaspar. 'The crew I've created will lead the way, down through the waters and into the gap—down between the waves and into the fissure. At the bottom of the earth you will find him, quiet and unmoving. You will glimpse only very small portions of him. His size is too immense to see more. Touch him, and do it kindly. There is no need to strike or scar him, for you cannot harm him. There is no need to shout or scream, because he cannot hear you. Rouse him, and the world will shatter and realign. Rouse him, and I'll make you more than the myth you've asked.'

"The Spaniard agreed to these terms and he set sail with the strangest crew that ever did pilot a vessel. They led him into the Chinese seas and down to the trench itself. The vessel, which he called the *Arcángel*, closed in upon itself and dived down between the waves, into the sand, and down to the trench itself.

"The crew braced itself against the terrible pressure, the awesome gravity of the earth's center. They found it hard to breathe, even the creatures whom I fashioned from the ocean's deepest living things. The crushing weight of the water squeezed them tight, and I realized that the ship was too small and the task was too large. I had set it adrift, and it was barely a seed, being crushed in the fist of a god. I clung to my hope that the Spaniard would see the mission through; and I waited for him at the trench's edge, down at the bottom of the world.

"I waited for him like a father awaiting the birth of a child.

"I waited, and hours passed. Days followed. Weeks went by, and I feared that my Gaspar was lost, and the *Arcángel* with him. And finally, when I was prepared to abandon all hope, the *Arcángel* emerged from the trench—as if it had been expelled, as if it were coughed up out of the deep.

"All aboard had perished, succumbed to the burden of the water's impossible load; but my Spaniard remained. He alone had guided the vessel back to the portal, and he alone had forced the sails to press against the pressure. He alone returned with the *Arcángel* to the surface of the water, though he was weakened and exhausted by the trial.

"I was pleased to see him, even *relieved* to see him, despite the fact that he failed me."

The woman in Arahab's arms sighs, and the last small vapors from her lungs are expelled from her nose. There is nothing left in her of the air-breathing, two-footed girl who ran along the beach. There is nothing left of the human she was born as.

Her transformation is ready to begin.

"I carried him down with me again, so that he could recover and later, perhaps, try again. I would consider a new strategy; I would conceive a new plan.

"But he had failed me, and there *was* a price to pay. As he was quick to note, I had promised him a legend if he would attempt the quest, and I had not rested my oath upon his success. And my word does not bend. So I granted him the gift.

"His name has passed into legend, now. His name will go down farther into history and into myth, as I swore. But that myth was not written by his peers, or by his family. It was not created by his friends. It was made by liars and enemies, and it became a story for lighthearted bedtime sharing between children. It became a fairy tale, written by idiots and told by fiends.

"I removed from the face of the earth every trace that he'd ever lived. There remains neither note nor relic to confirm he ever breathed before I claimed him.

"So he can have his legend, and my word has not been bent. But it is not the legend he would have chosen for himself. And, I think, it gives him great grief. His enemies insult him with their fondness, and with their familiarity. But there is always a price for failure.

"This is not to say that I hate my wicked little son, far from it. I love him, as I love you—and I have loved him longer. And this, my daughter, is where you join the story."

If the woman hears her, she cannot signal it. If the woman cares, she is beyond the ability to demonstrate it. She sleeps, and listens.

"I have realized my mistake. It was not that I chose the wrong mortal, for I did not. It was not that I charted the wrong course, for the course was sound. It was not that my timing was false, for to creatures like the Leviathan and me, time as you feel it is meaningless. It was that the task I assigned was too much for one man. One man can do only so much against the forces I sent him to meet. Mere legend and mere lore cannot move him to the ends of the earth, and deeper and farther than that. Mere myth is not enough to push a man into darkness and beyond it.

"And so, I give him a new goal. I give him a new prize, and a new direction. I will send him again to that place where the bottom of the ocean is close enough to the surface that a man might touch it. But I cannot ask him to do this alone.

"And so, now I give him a *woman*. And another chance to take the *Arcángel* down to the bottom of the earth, where my father might hear my son if he carries a newer, more powerful call."

The woman in Arahab's arms does not open her eyes or signal that she's seen, or heard. She does not move, or gasp, or agree, or dissent. She does not acknowledge hearing any of this, though she'll remember all of it later.

The Cocoon

The tide receded and sunlight seared Nia's eyes. It must have been morning.

Footsteps crunched in the sand. Nia, lying on her back, tried to turn her head to see who was coming, but her neck was terribly stiff.

In the distance, the waves chased each other back and forth across the sand, and seagulls argued over edible creatures the tide had stranded on shore. Up on the dunes behind her, the grasses whispered in the Gulf breeze.

The footsteps crashed closer. People were coming.

She wasn't sure how she'd made it onto the beach.

"What's that?" someone wondered aloud.

"It looks like a girl. Maybe we found one of them?"

"No. Wait."

The two men stood over her and stared down in disbelief.

Help me, she whispered. *Something's wrong. I can't move my . . . anything.*

"Damn, Rick."

"Where'd that come from?"

"Maybe it was on a ship. Maybe we should bring the sheriff."

Nia would've jumped, if she could've moved. *Help me,* she tried again to cry.

One of the men flicked his finger against her arm. She felt the sting of the tiny blow, but his knuckle thumped solidly; it did not snap the flesh. She struggled to move, and to ask questions. The man had said, "Maybe we found one of them." Her cousin must still be missing.

"What do we do with it?"

"I don't know. Go ask Missus Marjorie. It's her property. Or it's *on* her property, anyway."

Nia listened to their retreating footsteps. She was lying on her back, staring at the clouds. *Come back,* she prayed, because she could not speak. *I think you're looking for me. I'm right here. Oh God. Oh God.* Panic surged through her limbs, but no fear, no anger, no amount of willpower could make them move.

A small crab scuttled across her toes and into a nearby tide pool. Its claws made a quick clicking noise when they moved across her. It wasn't the right and soft sound of crustacean meeting skin.

She struggled for memories, but retrieved only blurry glimpses of the night before. There were bright eyes underwater, and wet darkness. There was blood. Someone had a knife.

Help me, come back. Get the sheriff, please. I have to tell him something. Please come back, I think I'm still bleeding. Go get my aunt Marjorie. Does she know yet? I have to tell her I'm sorry.

The men returned, and with them walked an extra set of gritting footsteps.

"You found it here, like this?" Marjorie asked, peering down into Nia's line of sight.

"Is it yours?"

"Mine?" She shook her head. "No, I've never seen anything like it."

One of the men screwed up his face and applied a battered straw hat to his balding head. "It don't belong to nobody, but it's on your land, ma'am. What do you want we should do with it? We can't leave it out on the beach."

"Why not? What harm does it do?"

No one answered her, but Nia could almost hear the stares.

Marjorie sighed. "If you really want to move it, you can put it in the courtyard up behind the house."

The man in the straw hat reached his arms around Nia's waist and gave a mighty heave. His friend did likewise, grabbing hold of her thigh and calf in an ungraceful fashion. They hoisted her up and lurched unevenly across the sand, dropping her on the ground, then yanking her back into the air.

Nia hated them both—their groping hands and sweaty bodies. The grass on the dune tickled at her back as they pulled her across it and down into the yard, where they gave up on carrying her and concentrated on dragging her.

They made a final rally and jacked her into a seated position.

A pair of painted Mexican tiles cracked where they sat her down.

"Where do we put it?"

"That spot where the wall dips out. We can sit it on the shelf."

She smelled blood. Even though she wasn't breathing and could not gasp, she knew its odor, and it triggered more moments from the night she'd been there last; the fractured memories flashed through her head and burned themselves out like embers.

There was Bernice, sitting on the edge of the fountain. Her dress was sprayed with gore. There was a red tablecloth; she wore it like a gown. Silver glinted in the starlight, and there was shattered china.

It was an awkward process, but with many rough curses the men propped her into the cubbyhole. They stood back and surveyed their work. They shook hands. They smiled and joked about a job well done.

And they left.

From her new vantage point, Nia could peruse the whole scene, not that there was much of a scene left to peruse. Someone had scoured the place good; a passerby would never know that anything unusual had happened there, unless he looked very closely—as Nia had time to do.

Someone with nothing better to do would see the dark stains on the grass, stains that could easily be mistaken for shadows. Someone might notice the stray silver fork lying in a corner by the mosaic bench.

Later, someone might check his shoes and find a slim shard of glass wedged in the sole.

This happened, Nia swore to herself.

The fountain had been shut off, so no water spurted artfully over the small ceramic fish. The table where all the anniversary party goodies once were stashed had been taken away. Plywood boards were nailed across every opening in the house, even the second-story windows.

What was that name again?

She very strongly suspected that she was losing her mind.

The first few months, she talked to herself incessantly and nonsensically. About anything. About nothing. She repeated history lessons learned years before and recited snippets of poetry and songs she'd picked up here, there, anywhere. There was one phrase in particular that stuck, and repeated, and wore a groove in her memory.

One impulse from a vernal wood may teach you more of man, of moral evil, and of good than all the sages can. And oh, how she hated that damned vernal wood.

The courtyard couldn't keep it at bay. No one mowed the yard, and the grass grew tall, tangled, and nasty. Raccoons and possums prowled at night; cicadas shrieked. Once, Nia thought she saw a great cat—a huge beige panther that moved through the grass more quietly than an owl sweeping through the air.

Our Father, she tried to pray, but eventually she could not remember the rest of the words. So she told herself stories instead.

I was born in the middle of the night. A thunderstorm—or it might have been a hurricane—was tearing through the Gulf and smashing into Tallahassee, where I was busy being born.

Windows broke, wind blew through the halls, and my mother was lying in a cast-iron bathtub screaming at Aunt Marjorie, who was telling her to push.

Later that night, the clouds lifted and they wrapped me in a cotton blanket, and my aunt Marjorie, she held me close in what had once been my grandparents' living room, and they stared at the sky, watching the stars fall.

They fell by the thousands; Aunt Marjorie swears by it.

I've never seen a star fall since.

For a long time, she watched the leaves and moss and animals encroach on the courtyard with interest, since there was nothing else present to entertain her. She gave the small things names and placed them in the plots of penny dreadfuls, or concocted fantastic impossibilities of romance between the frogs and the mice.

But in time she gave up. She quit those ramblings and left herself alone in silence, unable or unwilling to keep herself company anymore. The boredom numbed her mind, and she came to something like peace with her unchanging surroundings.

The scenery didn't change much.

Winter and fall meant it was cooler sometimes, and for maybe a week or two it actually got cold. Nia would have shivered if she could, but at least it never snowed.

She'd only seen snow once before, back in Tallahassee, when it floated down in sparse waves of small flakes that died as soon as they hit the ground. It was unbelievable even that far north, but her grandmother said there'd been a terrible freeze a few years before, and all the world must be turning colder. Soon they wouldn't be able to grow oranges there at all.

Times were changing and the world was changing, and farms were dying. An orchard could die, too, just as easy.

Summer and spring meant bombastic thunderstorms every afternoon for ten minutes, a wet break that took the edge off the stifling heat.

Nia's spot was surrounded and shaded by several large trees—a banyan, a magnolia, and a mimosa. The sun never beat her directly, and the rain was deflected as well.

Eventually the island's population grew.

Two mad boys with paint sometimes assaulted the back porch, splashing obscenities in red and white. Nia hated them deeply; the sour smell of the paint overwhelmed the flowers, and she, of course, could not escape the stench.

Indeed, her senses were uncomfortably heightened despite the immobility. Strictly regimented carpenter ants tickled her ribs until she would've sold her soul to scratch them away, and she could almost count each raindrop that pelted her body during a storm. Even the slight shifting in the concrete beneath her caught her attention, the way the bricks adjusted as grass grew into the cracks and forced them apart with knotty tangles. During the spring while the vandals were away, the huge, leathery magnolia leaves held soft white flowers, so sweet and close in her nostrils that she could tell which individual trees had produced the drifting petals. Her ears became so sharp that she could hear termites across the yard, slowly turning the vineyard frame into pulp. Their grinding jaws worked day and night until the wood dropped to the grass and rotted where it lay.

In time, the porch fell in as well, and cracks formed in the boards that covered the windows. Curious island residents came in the afternoons to peek inside, marveling at the cool emptiness within.

Most of them avoided Nia, looking over their shoulders as they left, fearful that she might hop off the ledge and follow them.

6

The Exposition of Songs

E dward Bok was dead.
He had been dead for several years, but he lingered—
wandering his wonderful garden grounds, slipping past the cat-
tails in the moat, and watching the alligators in the far pond snap
lazily at waterbirds. He remembered little, and he was disinclined
to communicate, so no one noticed his presence except for the bell
player's daughter.

Her name was Ann and she was four years old, going on five.
She followed Edward from place to place, across the water and
into the trees, past the swans and down the woodchip trails between the tidily trimmed stretches of bright green grass.

She couldn't see him very well, and sometimes she couldn't see him at all; but she heard him when he sang and she found it more interesting than the bells above her. The bells rang every day twice, sometimes three times. The ghost who walked the woodchip trails sang only once a month, when there was no moon.

She gradually learned his song. She came to know it better than she knew the lever pressings that rang the big bells in the tower at the top of the Iron Mountain.

> *Underneath the flesh of the earth*
> *Below the skin of the sky*
> *Deeper than death the Leviathan sleeps*
> *All children must let the king lie*
>
> *He shifts his back and the mountains fall*
> *He shakes his head and the oceans cry*
> *Give him no dream and don't bid him wake*
> *All creatures must let the king lie*
>
> *Thousands before and thousands more*
> *The centuries pile themselves high*
> *We bury and bind him with quiet hands*
> *All gods must let their king lie*

She did not know what it meant any more than Edward did. But she repeated it for the same reason as the ghost. She liked the lifting and dipping of the minor keys and the stomping, heavy feel of the stanzas. It sounded like a very sad birthday song, or a very old carnival tune. It was the voice of a music box with bent and broken tines.

Her father wondered where she heard these things, and he told her to stop repeating them.

So she left the words aside, and contented herself to hum.

7

Of Sharks and Pirates

Four years after the murder in the courtyard, Bernice quivered
unsteadily against José's supportive arm. He led her to a low
stone wall that separated the sand from the street. She sat down
and he sat beside her.

She was wearing blue silk and a white sweater that came to her
elbows; she'd picked out the dress because she believed the shade
matched her eyes—and it did, when they peeked out from beneath
a deliberate fringe of coy yellow bangs.

Her companion was a slender man in a wheat-colored suit. He
wasn't wearing a hat, but that was not the only thing that separated him from most of the other men on the street that night. His
wavy, blue-black hair hung down past his shoulders, and it was

tied behind his neck in a ponytail like a woman might wear. Once or twice, as the evening progressed and scores of inebriated revelers walked past the low stone wall, a young partygoer began to tease the strange-looking fellow with the beautiful young blonde. But the jests rarely survived contact with José's mild, passive stare.

He made no threatening moves, and he made no countercalls to defend himself. He didn't need to. The teasing was good-natured and celebratory, inspired by a city in the midst of a festival dedicated to piracy and folktales; and besides: even the drunkest passerby could detect some intense *otherness* in the man who sat on the wall.

This otherness, which most people nervously read as simple foreignness, went deeper than his hair or the smooth, lazy way he silenced the friendly taunts from reveling passersby.

There was oldness around him, too, a strange kind of gravity that went deeper than the lines on his face—the telling tracks of age that marked him as a man perhaps in his sixties. Even sitting there almost perfectly still, next to the water, he wore a weight that was heavier than years, and he wore it as if he'd been born to it.

He sighed when a round of impotent cannon volleys finished over the ocean behind him, and he placed one long musician-slim hand at Bernice's waist. She shifted her legs and crowded closer into his loose embrace. If they hadn't placed themselves so snugly against one another, and in such a deliberate way, they might have been mistaken for father and daughter.

But if no one could guess anything else true or accurate about José Gaspar, they could guess that he was wealthy—and if wealthy, then that explained why he was able to keep company with a mate so far his junior.

Tampa was warm and the Gulf winds made the air thick with currents that smelled like salt, roasted peanuts, and the too-sweet stink of funnel cakes. That night, the world was a buccaneer's carnival of pretend-coins, cheap beads, and dressed-up boats that were painted to look like an artist's memory of a fairy-tale ship.

José took Bernice's hand and felt along her wrist, smoothing the skin he found there and pressing it gently.

"All of this—it's all for you, isn't it?" she asked him.

"Why do you do that?" he asked back. His consonants were sharpened against an accent that might have been mistaken for Cuban. He purred the rest of his words to her, because he knew how nice it sounded. "You know the answer already."

"I don't understand it, though."

"You understand enough." He did not care to explain further. It was a gentle lie, anyway. She knew some of what had happened, but there was more to know, and he kept it from her.

He resented the sting of the festival's mocking familiarity, and he disliked leaving any legend to the meddling pens of wealthy Anglos. In one hundred years, he had gone from holy terror to un-likely folk figure. Arahab had kept her promise and his legacy lived, but his history was mangled and appropriated, and he was left with a ludicrous party that remembered little, insulted every-thing, and meant nothing.

But he was forced to admit: it *was* a grand party.

"When I was a kid, my mom took me out here to Gasparilla once or twice. They have it pretty much every year."

"I know."

"It's a lot of fun," she said. "Crazy food, crazy boats, and all the pirates all over the place! I'm surprised you're not more excited about it."

"It's delightful," he answered in a tone that told her nothing.

The invading boat was preposterous and the pretense weak, but beads were flung and the alcohol flowed—and the sidewalks were packed with people shouting the corruption of his name. Night had freshly fallen and everyone was drunk, everyone was happy.

How willingly the city suspended its disbelief; how happily it put its faith in a whitewashed past and a clean-cut felon.

Let them, he decided. *Just give me another drink, and give me her body again, and they can take what they want from my corpse.*

"Happy Gasparilla!" a man shouted. He was dressed as he imagined a pirate must have dressed, and he was so deeply, thoroughly wrong that José laughed.

"That's a very nice sword." He grinned.

The drunkard beamed a blinding smile from a mouth with perfect teeth. "S'not real," he said. He jerked it out of a makeshift sheath and waggled it happily.

José nodded. "I know. But if it *were* . . ."

"But if it were!" the man thought he agreed. He staggered off toward the loudest part of the festival, back to the street with the parade—back to the automobiles that puttered along in rickety lines.

Bernice heard the subtext, even if she didn't grasp it herself. So she asked, "If it were real, then what?"

"Then he'd be dead in under an hour. The thing he carries is too heavy to swing and too broad to slice. It's a bad copy of an old design, one that went out of fashion before I was born."

"You never swung a sword?"

"Not unless I was desperate, and I was never *that* desperate. Who brings a sword to a firefight?"

"Not you." She squeezed his arm. "You were smarter than that."

"If I weren't, I would never have survived as long as I did. How are you feeling?" he asked, suddenly shifting the subject. "It's a change at first, I know. Even though you spent your whole life before on the land, it's as if you never stood before, isn't it?"

"Yes," she admitted. "I never thought feeling dry would feel so odd."

"We can sit here as long as you like."

"No, we can't. Mother said—"

"I know what she said." José stopped her. "And obviously, we'll do as she wishes—but there's time. She won't miss us for days, if she misses us at all."

"She'll miss us. We belong to her," Bernice added.

There was something chilly underlying the words. They sounded perfunctory and strange. She was not altogether insincere, but she was thinking about the things she said, and if she meant them.

"We owe her," José corrected her.

"She'll notice if we're not back—that's all I mean."

"My love, this is only a reintroduction; it isn't a mission. There's no need to rush or push. We have all the time in the world. More than that, even."

Bernice shook her head. "That's not what *she* said."

"It's what she meant."

"You talk for her now, when she's not here?"

"No." He fondled her hand some more. "I know my boundaries. I know the rules, and she wants me to teach you. And I will. But I will undertake your instruction on terms of my own. So long as I succeed, she'll hold no grudge against me."

"I'd rather have a mission. I don't want you to lead me around like a little kid, I want to get *started*."

"There's nothing to start. She's still gathering information from below; and when she knows what she needs from us, she'll send us up here to get it. This is time for *you*."

Her eyes narrowed, but she smiled. "For us?"

"If you like. The festival carries on, there is plenty to drink, and you and I will live forever if our mistress sees fit to keep us. There's plenty to celebrate."

Behind them, the tide rushed and retreated, creeping onshore and splashing brine and spray against the low stone wall where they sat. The moon was rising by slow, smooth degrees, and lights were burning brightly in the restaurants and bars along the strip.

Bernice rose to her feet, steadier. Her eyes were glittering and cruel, and it was almost more than José could bear, so much did he admire her.

"We'll need some money," she said.

"We have some money," he told her.

"I want more. And I'll take it, because that's what pirates do, isn't it?"

He grinned at her, aroused by her aggression as much as the sleek lines of her body shifting beneath the snug fabric of a dress that stopped at her knees. "And you're a pirate now, is that it?"

"Would you keep any other company?"

"I might, but not for long—and I've known the very best of the very worst. Do you think you can impress me?"

"Do you think I can't?"

He knew that he'd dared her, and he was pleased to see her take the bait. She called herself his siren, and it was truer than she knew.

Out in the water, a number of boats bobbed on the swells. Lanterns were strung Chinese-style along their prows, and between the craft hung anchors that dropped into sandbars. Seabirds prowled the sky and peered downward, hunting leftovers.

"Which one is the Mystic Krewe's ship, the main one?" she asked José.

He nodded his head at the largest and most brightly lit craft. It was painted to look old, bright, and vicious. The effect was less violent than toylike. "That's it. The *Gasparilla,* if ever a more awful name was assigned to a vessel."

"It's *your* name."

"No. You only think it sounds that way. If you knew any Spanish, you'd hear it for the insult it is."

She shrugged. "They don't mean it like that."

"It doesn't matter how they mean it."

Bernice glared out over the inky water and squinted into the whitely dotted lanterns. She wanted to surprise him, and she did—but only a little. He could have predicted that she'd jump up and run, but the leap and the splash took him off guard in a way that charmed him.

With a stumble and a hop, she lunged into the surf. She swept her arms like she was making a snow angel, and drew her body under until she was scarcely more than a fish-gray streak just below the surface.

He watched her briefly, for a flickering jerk of a second. Then he followed her over the low stone wall and into water that was as black as the sky.

On the one hand, he was disappointed. This was supposed to be walking time, feet-on-earth time. Mother wanted her new child to remember what it's like to move with the land beneath her, because enough time had passed that Bernice was close to forgetting. The mind remembers, but when the body's been cradled long enough, it loses the sensation of standing upright and lifting itself forward.

On the other hand, it was a joy to watch her swim. Neither mermaid nor dolphin, not fish or ray, she tore through the water as if she were a shark freed quickly from a net. There was terror and power there, in the tight, squeezing kicks that started at her hips and the fierce tearing of her arms, shredding the sparkling wave tops into frothy nothing.

The water was warm to him; it was bathwater and brine: tepid and tasting of sea rot.

For one shattered second, he remembered falling into it before, and feeling rust and iron, and the weight of a chain around his neck. It was almost too much, the fear and the eyes that watched him underwater, and the grasp that took him by the throat, by the waist, and by the pelvis to pull him deeper, down into the arms of a creature strange and strong beyond time, beyond belief.

He shook the reminiscence away and swam after her, the siren skimming faster than a skipped stone toward a ship with a name he would never have chosen himself.

When he got closer, he could see it more clearly, and it was brushed with carnival colors too bright to be masculine and too pretty to intimidate. This was a party craft, made to shuttle rich people from event to event, from extravaganza to private soiree.

He saw the corruption of his name painted clearly on the side in a script like a woman would write.

Bernice reached the craft's edge first. She grasped a decorative net and twisted it in her hands; she pulled herself out of the water, and the moonlight broke itself against her back.

She took his breath away, even though he could see through her glamour now, when she was wet and illuminated. Under the glorious cover of the soaked dress, her skin was translucent and tinted with the runny blue and green in which she had marinated all this time. Her limbs were too slick to be human. Her hands were too finned for gloves, and her hair tangled into seaweed locks like the island Africans used to wear.

The once-woman climbed up the ship's side and slipped onto the deck.

The once-pirate came, too, up and over. He stood up straight beside her. Some leftover habit, some fragment of a survivalist tick made him reach to his chest. But there were no guns slung there to grab, no triggers to squeeze. No one- or two-shot pistols strung together like fireworks.

His fingers grazed his shirt and found nothing. He did not notice the gesture; he could not even remember what he reached for in the first place.

But Bernice was already moving. He would watch her move, then, on planks if that was as close as he could bring her to solid ground. He was pleased to note that here, too, she crashed like a shark.

There was a woman hanging over the rail. She was throwing up, or thinking about it.

Bernice grabbed the woman's ankle and threw it into the air, and the woman went over the side with a splash that no one noticed except for a man in an expensive suit. He was stunned, and slow with liquor. Bernice seized him, and he looked confused.

She shoved him down, throat-first, across the rail the woman had unwillingly vaulted a moment before. She clutched the back of his neck and held it like a handle, using it to beat his head into the wood again, and again, and once more before he coughed blood and gave up his struggles.

The blood delighted her.

She stood back and gave the man a kick that sent him through the side rail, splintering it. A second kick finished the job, and the suited man splashed into the ocean, but did not try to swim.

He sank, and Gaspar thought bitterly that Arahab had better leave her new visitor alone.

Charged, svelte, and eager, Bernice followed a drifting tune through a set of double doors that led into the ship's interior.

Someone with terrible timing opened the left door right as Bernice reached it. Her hand was on his throat before he could remove his grip from the lever. She pulled him into the open night and opened her mouth, which stretched to reveal lines of teeth in needlepoint rows.

The man was wearing a costume; he had a black patch over one eye, so he was spared the full view of her bite when it came at his face. Regardless, he squealed and screamed when her teeth punctured his cheek.

She slashed again with her mouth. She wielded it like a scissoring set of daggers, cutting through the soft dips in his neck and scraping against the bones inside it. The connection made a dragging crunch, but it sounded to Gaspar like the clinking of wineglasses.

Inside the boat's belly, the music was still jingling forth in bells and violins.

Bernice followed the music, and José followed her.

The song pinged up out of the boat in a minor key that was made of metal and broken wires. He couldn't place the tune, but it sounded wrong for a festival like this. It was more ancient than vintage, and too old-fashioned for a rich soiree.

As he ran behind Bernice he could feel the old tug of the ocean, even though the boat was a preposterous farce, covered with fittings and fashions that didn't remotely match the era they were meant to evoke. He felt like a cat chasing a ribbon; it was mindless and happy, and purely instinctive.

He couldn't *not* run through the narrow, wood-paneled corridors.

He couldn't *not* smile at the trail of blood his mate wiped around the corners.

With no blunderbuss or pistols, without even a blade to hand, he chased her, knowing that between the two of them, they were a deadlier crew than any he'd ever commanded while he was alive.

She dashed around corners, all slick and ferocious, all beast and all woman. She ripped through the bodies she met and cast them aside, where they leaked themselves into husks.

Gaspar counted four more. He skipped over them and added them to his idle tally.

And then he rounded a corner and he saw her holding an oil lantern. She'd pried it off the wall, where it had hung on a hinge. In theory, the lamp would rock with the motion of the ship and keep a steady flame; in practice, the hinge had snapped under Bernice's fierce little fingers and she was prepared to cast the lantern to the ground—except that José grabbed her wrist and held it aloft.

She wrestled him for it out of surprise and indignation. She twisted in his grip, thrashing, while a boy on the floor cringed away from her.

The boy didn't understand what was happening, but he recognized evil when he saw it, so he retreated fast, scuttling halfway under a desk and silently cheering José. The boy had not yet gathered that the pirate had nothing like rescue in mind.

"No," Gaspar said to Bernice, lifting her up off the floor until her toes dangled and dragged. "No, not the lamp. No fires. We can't sail a ship while it burns—or rather, I do not *intend* to."

She gave one more kick, then settled down. "Can we do that? Take it out, I mean? How many people do you need to move a boat like this? Don't you need a crew or something?"

"Between us and the ocean, I think we can take it ourselves . . . if you will help me, and do as I tell you."

"You don't get to order me around. Mother said so."

"Of course I won't order you around. You will do as you wish, and I will only tell you how best to do it. Would you like to go for a sail, or not? This is a ridiculous little ship, but it's put together soundly. It would be a shame to destroy it."

"You said it was an insult."

He nodded. "It *is*. But it's an insult that's prettily made, and I can appreciate it as such. Come," he urged her. "I want to take her. I want to sail her. It's been long enough since I pulled a rope or leaned myself against a wheel; let's take her and go." The low waves of the Gulf lapped at the boat's sides, slapping it gently and rocking it so barely that Bernice didn't feel it.

"Where would we go?" she asked.

A line shaped like a smile stretched across his face. "I know somewhere," he whispered to her. "I know a spot where I left treasure, once. It's been many years, but I would be shocked if it was gone. Arahab erased me from their history, left me only in their lore. No one knows that my trail is real enough to seek."

"Treasure?" Bernice repeated.

"Gold enough to bury you. Pearls enough to anchor you. I left it on an island—" He glanced up to reference the sky, then remembered that he was below the deck and could see nothing above him except for a light and a painted ceiling. "I left it nearby. Work with me without complaining, and you can have your pick from the things I stashed away."

When she did not argue, he considered this a victory and turned to the lad on the floor.

"Who owns this boat?" he wanted to know.

The boy's eyes widened. "The Krewe, they own it."

"Is that why you're dressed so? You're a member of this crew?"

He nodded. "Ye Mystic Krewe of Gasparilla."

Gaspar shook his head. "You look absurd. I would never have taken you onto any ship of mine."

"This *is* a ship of yours," the boy said hastily. "This is yours—all of it. Take it, no one will care. We're just playing at pirates, like we do every year. But I could help you with the ship. I know how to sail her."

"Do you, now?" Gaspar was honestly amused. "You think I need your help?"

"I don't know if you need it or not. Probably not. I bet not. But I . . . I'd like to help. I'd like to really sail it, not just sit here and—"

Bernice leaned forward; her hand extended, reaching for the boy like she meant to help him up and guide him out.

But José was faster. On top of the table there was a letter opener shaped like a sword, insistently adhering to the theme. He took the opener and used it on the boy's throat before he could object or negotiate any further.

The boy toppled to the floor and started to shed a thick puddle of blood that rolled and stretched with the motion of the boat.

"Why'd you do that?" Bernice asked. "I was starting to like him."

"You've answered your own question, darling. We aren't here to make friends. And besides, there's no trusting the young— especially not when they like to bargain. If he'd had the good sense to beg, I might have heard him out. But this is no place for discussion, and the open sea is no place for parley."

"Is that where we're going? The open sea?"

"No," he said. For a moment he was almost annoyed with her, but it passed quickly. He reminded himself that she was a child of the city, and that water was a mystery to her. "We'll stick near to the coast unless the authorities compel us to do otherwise. My old island isn't far. But first, we should check the other decks, and make sure we are unaccompanied."

"You check 'em," she said, her back turned away from him. She'd found a box on a counter and she was distracted. She flipped the lid open, and it chimed that eerie tune he'd heard on the decks above. She shut the lid and it stopped.

As far as José could tell, there was nothing inside it.

"Can't you—?"

"I thought you weren't going to order me around."

"I'm not," he insisted. "But if you'd prefer to put your little play box away and trade it for something much more valuable, then you should cooperate with me."

The words were hard for him. They were strange when he lined them up and put them before her, because he was not accustomed to asking. He was the captain, and he shouldn't have to ask for any-thing. He ought to tell her what to do, and she ought to do it.

But Arahab had warned him, and he was cautious.

It was easy to believe that this was a new breed of woman, dif-ferent from the kind he'd known and commanded half a dozen lifetimes before. It was easy to believe that something fundamental had shifted; but José knew better. Women don't change. Men don't change. Only the trappings of their interactions look different.

Until he could learn the boundaries and specifics of those trap-pings, he made a point of being gentle and conciliatory. He thought it would be better to study the rules and commit them to heart be-fore making demands and giving orders. She was only a woman, after all, and he was a man and her captain. The authority was his to wield or leash.

Besides.

He found her crassness and stubbornness charming, or so he told himself. In the back of his mind, he could imagine her in the fuller, dirtier clothes she would've worn in another time. He closed his eyes and he saw her on the deck of a ship less cheerfully decorated, in a distant century. He was seized by the impulse to find her a costume, even something ridiculous, even something inappropriate and incor-rect. His mind could fill in the blanks and erase the imperfections.

When he opened his eyes again, she was still toying with the music box.

He hated the little song it burbled. He reached for it, intending to take it away from her and smash it; but he changed his mind and left her there to play.

After all, she was only a child.

José wandered back through the narrow wood corridors that shone with polish like no pirate's craft had ever seen. He passed a corpse or two but he didn't pause, since he'd already admired her handiwork. Every day he came to know her better, and every day she reminded him that she was only a girl—and she was maddening, infuriating and spoiled.

To give credit where credit was due, at least she did not expect José to do the spoiling. She was willing to take the things she wanted without his assistance, and maybe that was why he gave her such a long rope: not to make a noose, but to tether himself to her swiftly shifting form. She wanted it all, but was willing to take it for herself. He could respect that.

It was difficult, though. She was sitting on a very fine line. On one side, he wanted to hate her. He wanted to tear her apart with his bare hands. On the other side, he wanted to worship her.

He sloshed back and forth between his desire and disdain, clinging to her beauty as if it would anchor him somewhere sound.

Up the stairs, and past the one that was slick and staining dark, José watched the corners and the shadows in case they were not yet alone.

It was an idle sort of reconnaissance. No one was left, and the other partiers in their other boats had made enough noise to hide the assault.

José wondered who brought the boat to anchor in the first place. No one he had seen looked sturdy enough to work a ship. Not the lady in the beaded dress, and not the faux piratical fellows in their preposterous garb—none of them looked capable of hoisting a sail or steering a rudder.

He decided that it didn't matter.

He stepped onto the deck and stared at the stars again, and he knew exactly where he was. The world had changed, but it had not changed so much that the sky would mislead him. There was the moon, half-full and casting pale slivers of wobbly light across the Gulf. There was the great bear, and the crow. Over there, the twins. A few degrees this way, and that way, and he knew where to find his old island.

He was being watched. It occurred to him gradually, and without alarm.

He nodded his head down at the water to greet the figure there.

She rose up, all night-black skin and long hair, up to where her waist would be if she were the woman she appeared.

Where is that coming from? she asked.

"What do you mean?"

The music. Don't you hear it?

He did hear it, one stray note at a time wafting up from inside the ship like smoke. "It's a music box. Bernice found it, and she seems to like it. I suppose she'll keep it."

Arahab's eyes glinted sharply. *Is that all?*

"As far as I know. Might it be otherwise?"

It might be. I know the song, and I do not care for it.

"Then *you* take it away from her. She won't have it from me." When she didn't respond, the silence between the deck and the water was uncomfortable, so he broke it. "It's only a tune, you know. A harmless thing, if unpleasant on the ears."

Is that what you think?

"It's what I must assume. An empty box on an empty boat. I promised her that we could trade it for a bigger box, full of proper treasure. I thought she was greedy enough to put it aside, but sometimes I don't understand the way she thinks, not at all."

I know that tune, she said again. *I know who wrote the words that accompany it.*

"Does it upset you? I can force the issue if you like. I'll take it away from her if you cannot bear to hear it."

Then the woman in the water said, *It means something.*

José smiled, confused. "What does it mean?" he asked, but then she was gone.

He watched the water, knowing she wouldn't return but

wondering where she'd gone. Finally he walked to the anchor and turned the crank to lift it.

The chain withdrew with a rhythmic series of soft clanks, and the noise was loud against the distant hum of a city in the midst of a carnival. The *Gasparilla* shook and rocked. The anchor came aboard and the boat began to drift.

José reached for the ropes that would move the sails.

8

The Exposition of Evidence

The two men with clipboards entered the derelict courtyard. The NO TRESPASSING sign did not apply to business as official as theirs. And as far as Sam could see, the sign was so regularly ignored that it may as well have been an invitation. "Why do they even bother to leave that up?" he asked. "No one pays any attention to it."

Sam kicked one leg, trying to shake away the burrs and bugs that had collected in the folded cuff of his pants.

Dave shrugged his big loose shoulders. "It's private property. Or maybe it isn't. I'm not sure."

"It's going to be soon, if Langan buys it." Sam's glasses were

retreating down his nose on a slide of sweat. He used his middle finger to jam them back up his face. They slid down again almost immediately. "It's a nice house," he observed, removing his hat and
using it to fan himself.

"Nice and expensive."

The house was an architectural mix of art deco and Spanish
colonial, stuccoed from lawn to roof in a pleasing shade of light
coral. Black iron accents barred the windows and guarded the
balcony that once overlooked the Gulf, though since the house's
abandonment, the view had become blocked by tangles of weeds
and vines. The grass-covered dune that marked the end of the property and the beginning of the beach had grown up high and thick.

Sam could hear the ocean, but he couldn't see it. "How long has
it been empty?" he asked the off-duty fireman who accompanied
him.

"Three or four years. Nobody's ever lived in it. The woman
who owned it moved up to Tallahassee."

"After the murder."

"That's right," Dave agreed. "After the murder."

"You think it'll make the place less likely to sell? I'm surprised
it's got any takers as it is."

Dave waved his arm in a swipe that indicated the house, the
yard, and the fountains. "Why? It's prime property, isn't it?"

"Times are hard. Black Tuesday brought a lot of people low."

"Not everybody. Not this guy."

"Langan."

"Whatever he's named." Dave wasn't dressed like a fireman.
Nothing was burning except for the afternoon temperatures, and
this was only a bureaucratic visit.

Sam replaced his damp-rimmed hat and checked his clipboard. He brushed away a brightly colored bug and squinted

down at the text. "So the original owner—not the murdered one, I mean, or maybe him, I don't know—but whoever built the place paid up for the fire insurance. Do I understand that correctly?"

"Not this far along, no. They only paid up through the year; but the new guy—"

"Langan," Sam said.

"Yeah. He'll want to pay to have it covered, if he really buys the place."

And Dave and Sam were each pocketing fifty bucks extra for looking around. Langan had asked for someone reliable, someone who knew a little about construction or insurance. He'd asked for a report on the structure's condition, since he lived out of state and might not be able to see the property for himself before purchasing it. Sam thought it must be nice to be that kind of rich: so rich that you can buy big things without looking at them first.

The house was practically new, even if the property looked like it'd been left to run wild for a hundred years.

Florida did that to man-made places. It devoured them with jungle in a matter of weeks if no one made a stand and hacked the greenery back.

Sam made a note on the clipboard's last sheet of paper. "We'll need to mention the grounds," he said. "Langan is moving here from . . . where?"

"I don't know. Out of state."

"I thought the chief said he was coming in from New England."

"Maybe."

"Hmm." Sam folded the clipboard under his arm. "Then he might not know how fast the grounds go downhill here, when no one looks after them."

"He'll find out."

"But we shouldn't surprise him with it. The house looks great, but the rest of it is a mess."

Sam dodged a wall of swaying palmettos and glanced down at the shadows underneath it, praying that they were empty of snakes. He ducked his head sharply to avoid a low-hanging curl of moss.

A feral cat scooted across Sam's path and shot around the side of the building. The creature was fat from slow lizards and friendly island fishermen, and Sam wondered if the house's new owner would tolerate a resident feline. The cat settled down beside a rosebush and began to preen.

"Get out of here." Dave picked up a broken roof tile and chucked it in the cat's general direction. "Stupid cat. Better not get too comfortable."

The animal hoisted its tail and hopped down off the wall. It disappeared through the arch and wandered back into the main yard. "Don't do that. He'll keep the mice down."

Dave didn't argue, and he didn't throw any more tiles. But the cat didn't reappear. "Look at this damn place. This courtyard is going to need a team of gardeners to bring it back into shape."

"You said it yourself: Langan can afford it."

The winding sidewalks were choked with grass; and in the courtyard's back corner, the latticework of a small vineyard collapsed upon itself beside the blue, gold, and crimson mosaics that decorated the benches. In the center of all the confusion stood a circular stone fountain adorned with sea-blue tiles that were clotted with grass and thorns. Rainwater had pooled in the fountain's bottom, breeding mosquitoes and scum.

And there was something else.

At the far edge of his consciousness, Sam felt a distinct and unnerving prickle that made him wonder if he was being watched. He checked over his shoulder and saw Dave kicking at the edge of the back porch's foundation. He turned a full circle and met a pair of eyes that were not quite level with his.

He let out a quick gasp and squeezed at the clipboard, wrinkling his papers.

It wasn't a loud noise, but it caught Dave's attention.

Dave checked to see what had distressed Sam, and he laughed. "Oh yeah, that. Weird, ain't it?"

"No," Sam said quickly. "It's just . . . it's just a statue. I've never seen one like it before, but everyone's taste is different, right?"

Dave grinned. "Don't blame these people—the ones who built the house. They didn't buy that thing."

"Then why is it here?"

"My brother and a friend of his moved it up from the beach, a couple of mornings after the murder. They don't know if maybe it fell off a ship or what, but they handed it over to the widow. She told them to stick it over there. Then she skipped town, and as far as I know, she ain't been back."

"Hard to blame her," Sam murmured. "Her husband gets stabbed to death . . . right here." He peered down into the knotty grass and wondered where, exactly. Beside the fountain? Under the entry arch? The body must have fallen down and bled itself dry somewhere close.

"I'll tell you what strikes me funny, though." Dave abandoned the porch edge and meandered along the stone path until he stood beside Sam, in front of the strange statue set in the courtyard wall.

"What?"

"The widow's daughter went missing, too, at the same time. But she never stuck around to look for her. It's like she knew the kid was dead or gone for good."

Sam nodded a little. "I guess that's strange."

"Sure it's strange. Your kid vanishes the same night your husband dies, and you don't even hang around? What if the kid came back, or if she got hurt, or kidnapped? Nobody knew. But I think the widow knew. I think that's why she didn't stay."

"You think the widow killed them both?"

"No, no. I didn't say *that*," Dave said quickly. "I met her once, and she seemed like a real nice lady. She was real torn up about the whole thing. She looked . . . she looked *lost*. You know? But she didn't look surprised, and she didn't act like a lady who had a lot of questions. It's hard to explain."

Sam still hadn't taken his eyes off the statue. He gazed at her with fascination and suspicion, like he half expected her to blink and look away.

She crouched in a cubbyhole built into the courtyard wall, a spot that was originally meant to hold a potted plant or a garden urn. And she—because it was hard for Sam to think of the statue as an "it"—she was made from an indeterminate gray stone that was streaked with mineral deposits.

Life-sized and seated, she had one arm wrapped around her face and her legs were drawn up to her chest. The other hand she held out, fingers open as if to ward something away.

A ladybug scaled that outstretched arm. Sam followed it with his eyes.

"Who do you think she's supposed to be?" Dave asked.

"Who says she's supposed to be anybody?"

"She must be *someone*. Look at her face—what you can see of it. She looks too real, you know?" Dave didn't have the vocabulary for what he meant, but Sam understood well enough.

"Yeah. It looks like a portrait, not like a decoration."

"That's it. What you just said. But come on, let's wrap it up. It's hot out here. Let's do the survey, set the address, and get back to the station."

"It's not so bad in the shade."

Dave cleared his throat and grumbled as he walked away. "It's hot. And it's going to get worse within the hour, so hurry it up."

"I already know what the insurance charge ought to be." Sam tore himself away from the statue and let his gaze wander around the courtyard. "Whenever you're finished checking the place out, I'm ready to go."

But even as he said it, that peculiar feeling was creeping back up his neck. And there was something else, too, some undercurrent to his discomfort that he had a hard time placing. It was the sensation that he was missing something—like he was looking at something important without seeing it.

"I wish I could get inside," Dave complained. "They nailed this thing up tight, though. I'd yank the boards off, but I'm not sure if we're supposed to do that or not. I don't know if Langan wants us going inside."

"He told you to look around, didn't he?"

"He wasn't real specific. I thought he meant the outside, and I can tell by looking around out here that the place is sound. But I'd like to look around inside all the same."

Sam wrinkled his nose and stared hard at the grass, not looking up at Dave. "Why?"

"Never been inside a house this nice. Have you?"

"No," Sam lied. He had a rich aunt in Georgia, but Dave didn't like to be one-upped, and Sam didn't like talking to Dave enough to start a conversation on the subject.

"Then don't you want to go inside?"

"I don't care," he said, and that much was true. "If you want to pull off a plank and go in, I won't say anything about it, if that's what you want to know."

Dave was already working his fingers around the sheet of plywood on the back door. He reached into his back pocket and pulled out a folding knife, then worked its flat blade underneath the nails. "Good. Because I want to be thorough. If anybody asks, if Langan or anyone wants to know, that's why I'm doing this. He paid me to check the place out. Least I can do is see that the man gets his money's worth."

The wide, thin wood strip splintered and peeled back. Dave pushed his hand into the interior and levered the barrier until there was space enough for him to reach the doorknob. He tried it and it twisted easily.

"It isn't locked," he announced.

"Great," Sam said.

Sam's eyes had settled on a dark spot in the grass, and he was no longer paying attention to anything Dave said. Rationally Sam knew that there was no more blood left between the paving stones, that years had passed and there was nothing left of the crime once committed there.

But while Dave squeezed himself around the boards and into the house, Sam looked more closely at the spot in the grass. He was almost certain that it was blood, regardless of the facts.

He sank down low and his knees popped. His clipboard did a small slide between his fingers, but he caught it before it hit the ground. His glasses tried to escape again, too, but he caught them and held them firmly while he investigated the dirty patch.

Something wet had dried to a crusty, reddish brown. Sam didn't have a free hand to swipe a finger along the mess, and he wouldn't have done so anyway. But it *did* look like blood. And it couldn't have been there very long. It rained almost every day.

Dave staggered around inside the house and swore. "It's dark in here!"

"Hard to believe," Sam mumbled, "what with all the windows boarded up."

The blood—if it was, in fact, blood—could've belonged to an animal, he supposed, but where was the rest of it? Animals don't hang around and bleed, then wander off. Something must've carried it away and eaten it.

He stuffed the clipboard up under his armpit again and ran his palm lightly along the top of the grass, ruffling and spreading it. A bright, quick gleam of reflected light shone up from the ground.

Sam paused.

He let go of his glasses so he could fish around between the bristly green blades. Eventually he retrieved a sharp sliver of metal shaped like a triangle. A small round grommet dangled from its end. It looked like a hinge, but not for anything so hardy as a door.

He turned it around in his hand and wiped a smudge of dirt away. He held it up to his nose and forced his glasses closer to his eyes, which sharpened his vision by a small amount.

"Brass?" he guessed aloud. Not gold, at any rate. This was shinier and cheaper, and it wasn't tough enough to hold anything heavier than a book cover.

Sam considered this, and strained to see the object better. He'd known of big books to be bound that way, and maybe those brown fibers strung from the grommet were leather.

Dave cursed loudly and caused a crash. "I'm going upstairs so I can see!" he shouted.

"Knock yourself out." The upstairs windows were boarded, too, but Dave would figure that out soon enough, so Sam didn't holler a warning.

Over there, beside the fountain, there was a streak of something rust-colored and nasty. More blood? He climbed all the way to his feet and went to look. He couldn't be sure, but the consistency was the same.

A nub of soft material sank under his shoe. He lifted the edge of his heel and found a burned-down lump of wax. It was the last inch of a candle.

A swift gust of ocean air shook the mimosa tree, and the shadows in the courtyard shifted, waved, and broke. He returned one hand to his glasses and kept his eyes on the ground, where he found several swaths of grass that weren't shaded, but charred. Patches of earth had been scorched; and when he stood up straight, Sam thought he could detect a pattern. The burned spots had a shape like a circle.

"Dave!" he called out.

"What?"

"Down here! Take a look at this!"

Dave took a moment to reach a window, and even though it was boarded, it was easier for him to hear. "At what, the statue? I saw it already!"

"No, not that! Come back down here, would you?"

"In a minute!"

Sam began taking careful notes: how many burned spots, where they were placed, and so on. Behind him, the statue watched and withheld comment. Even so, Sam got the oddest feeling that she approved, and she encouraged him.

He wrote quickly and precisely, in slanted handwriting that other people found difficult to read. He cataloged positions, guesses, and theories. He mentioned proximity to the building, likely flammable materials, and estimated a time for the spotty, contained fires.

Dave stumbled back downstairs and squeezed himself between the door and the plywood. He popped out into the yard with a grunt. "What are you going on about?"

"Come and see." Sam waved down at the ground, using his clipboard to cover a bigger chunk of yard with the gesture. "Come on, this is strange. Really strange. Someone's been using this yard for something."

"Like what?"

"Like," Sam hesitated. "Like for cooking, maybe. Do we have any new transients on the island, do you think? Look at this; someone's made little fires all over the place. You can hardly see them because of the trees and the shade, but if you look close, there they are."

Dave dutifully scowled down at the ground, paying extra attention to the spots Sam indicated. He stood up straight and wiped a dirty streak of sweat off his forehead. "Sure. I see it. So what?"

"Is that all you have to say about it?"

"Yeah, *so what?* Langan will need to put up a gate. What's the big deal?"

Sam's ship of logic ran aground on Dave's willful ignorance, and he tried to find a way over it. "It's . . . it's a fire hazard, isn't it?"

"Oh yeah." Dave nodded slowly. "Yeah, I get it. We can charge him more for insurance. Good thinking."

"No. No, that's not what I'm thinking. I'm thinking . . ." But he couldn't finish the thought, because he wasn't sure where he was headed with it. "I was thinking it's weirder than hoboes cooking, that's all."

"Why? What else would it be?"

"I don't know. Maybe I'll ask around."

"Go nuts," Dave told him. "Write it up, submit it to the chief, and we can bill the buyer extra for the fire hazard. As long as you're the one doing the paperwork, it doesn't matter to me."

"Don't worry." Sam didn't trust Dave to write his own name correctly, much less file readable paperwork.

Some people might have been inclined to complain about the extra effort, but Sam was not that sort. He'd rather do it right himself than enlist inferior assistance. Dave was all right, but he wasn't much of a clerk. That was fine—Dave didn't make his living as a clerk. And when it came down to it, Sam wouldn't have made much of a fireman, either, so he supposed it all worked out.

Dave dusted himself off, gave the courtyard wall a final jab with his toe, and announced that he was ready to head back to the courthouse.

The courthouse was barely half a mile away, so the men had walked to the house via the beach. The island had no fire department of its own, but it had a fire wagon—left behind when the bridge had washed out during a hurricane. The truck languished in storage on city property, and the chief would've thrown a fit if they'd fired the old thing up just to ride over to the beach house.

Sam finished noting the number and positions of the small fires. He straightened his clipboard and shoved his pencil into its latch.

"Fine," he said to Dave, even though Dave was already out of earshot. "I guess we can call it a day."

9

The Exposition of Monsters

Moments after Sam left, a curling, crackling, gravely noise whispered through the shaded courtyard.

A tall, rough-edged creature assembled itself from the gritty mulch beneath the grass and disintegrating leaves. It cobbled itself into a manlike shape with sticks for bones and dew for blood; it gave itself eyes made of crumbling bark, and it fashioned a mouth from yellowed strips of dead palmetto. Everything it used smelled of some quick rot, accelerated and nourished by the wet, warm air.

It stood up straight and was taller than a man usually comes.

It paced toward the statue in the courtyard wall and when its makeshift feet thudded against the earth, they made small, rhythmic crashes like sand and shells in a leather bag.

"Hello," it said, but the voice wasn't made by any clod-filled chest. The word sighed forth and it might have come from anywhere, or everywhere. The palmetto lips shifted, shaping themselves to project and pretend. It wasn't a very good impression of speech, but it was a show for courtesy's sake and not a strict necessity.

Hello, Nia said back in her helpless way. The response echoed in her head and traveled no farther.

She was awake, inasmuch as she was ever awake anymore. It was easier to let her mind go numb, to switch off for days at a time. It was easier to insist that her eyes were closed and that her ears heard nothing. Sometimes, she even dreamed—or she thought she did.

But the two men in the courtyard had caught her attention with their chatter and she'd watched them, not closely but idly. What was the point in watching closely? What could she contribute, or warn, or assist?

"They've gotten it very, very wrong, haven't they, dear? All of them. The ones who light the fires, the ones who found the fires— none of them has it even halfway right. Probably, for now, it's just as well."

Its brown, flaking eyes twitched and cast dust.

Nia was unsure but unafraid. Nothing frightened her anymore, even the things that ought to . . . even things like the creature that assessed her so callously and fed her questions and answers in a roundabout way. She didn't know what it meant, but she didn't know if it mattered.

"You're coming along nicely, for what it's worth. It won't be much longer now." It cocked its head to the left, and a bright red centipede scurried out of the place where his ear should have been.

"I ought to say, it won't be much longer 'in the grand scheme of things,' to borrow one of Edward's worn-out phrases. I don't suppose that makes you feel any better."

She wasn't sure what the creature was talking about, but she couldn't respond, so she let it slide.

"Also, I doubt you would be cheered to learn that all of this—" It swept a fingerless hand at the wall, the ground, and the sky. It left the appendage pointed at her. "—all of it was to save you. The water witch, she would've killed you. She would have drowned you and fed you to the creeping things with shells and claws. But I thought . . . I thought I might find another use for you.

"I watched the way you fought, and the way you ran. You were afraid, but you were thinking—and it might surprise you to know how rarely I've found men who can manage both states at once. I think the water witch was right to try a woman this time. And the woman she took, that woman was kin of yours."

My cousin. So beautiful. I wanted to be like her.

"I know terribly well how complicated kinship can be. I've learned it over the lifetimes of continents, so it means much more to me than to a flesh-and-blood spark like yourself. You're born, you live, and you're gone, and it's as if just one short cycle of the tides has passed. Before I've had time to notice you, I've absorbed you.

"But if you lived a longer stretch, and if you saw the arc of time as I do—like the curve of the planet's surface, like something immense, taken for granted more than known—then you'd have time to know real betrayal and real conflict. In the end—" It paused as if to take a breath, but a thing so made does not need to breathe. Soon it recovered its intent. "—in the end, most of it comes down to kinship, of one kind or another."

My cousin, Nia thought again. A name flitted through her memory, but she couldn't catch it and didn't try very hard. *She isn't dead, is she?*

It had lost its train of thought. It picked it up again and continued. "The other girl, the one she took—that girl must have been wicked from the inside out. Did you know that, when you were with her? Did you see her for what she was all along, or did you only figure it out too late?

"The water witch must have been watching her from the moment she landed on the island. She used you, too, though you couldn't have known it. Convinced you to lure your cousin into the ocean. She won't come far onshore, herself. The earth slows her. It weighs her down and costs her too much to cross. So yes, you were used that night. First you were used by the water witch, and then I used you myself.

"At least, I set you up to be used. But I think that once you understand, you will not hold it much against me. Once the cost becomes clear, you'll come to agree that what I did, I did for the purpose of good."

Nia watched the creature shift and settle in its improvised bones. It moved a shoulder in a guilty shrug and she wondered idly where it had ever learned to lie.

I can't trust you, can I? Not even a little bit.

The thing met Nia's eyes with a perfect, dedicated stare. "No, you cannot. But there's no one else to tell you anything, except for the water witch herself—and you already know what she's made of." It shuffled itself loosely, and its grassy lips simulated a scowl. "Eventually, the imbeciles who frequent the ground at your feet will succeed, and then the water witch will learn of you. If you've ever been given to prayer, I might suggest that you do so now— petition whatever gods might hear you. Ask them for time. Beg them for the incompetence of men. Because if those ridiculous people setting small and futile fires ever achieve their goals, they'll summon up their water witch and then, my darling, she'll destroy you before you have time to be born.

"So wait, girl. Pray, and watch. Even from incorrect procedures you might learn something. You sleep through their rituals now, but you'd be well served to observe them. Watch them confound themselves. It'll tell you plenty."

From the feet up, the creature began to dissolve itself, not so much collapsing as letting the ground absorb it. But before the last of the shoulders, neck, and head disappeared, it offered one final thought.

"You can help a thing who loves the world destroy it; or you can help a thing who hates it save it."

And the creature was gone.

Nia was shocked, but what could she do? She couldn't speak, couldn't act. Couldn't warn or advise. She could only wait and reflect.

Something had spoken to her, and something had heard her respond. The creature had even taken credit for her condition. Could it be believed, even if it could not be trusted? If nothing else, Nia came away from the encounter with a fresh feeling she'd all but forgotten.

This really happened. Something caused it. Something knows about it.

And it logically followed that there might be an end in sight after all.

Now, finally—after several years of immobility and a desperate kind of resignation—Nia had something to be afraid of.

It was hard, dragging her consciousness up from the basement where she'd stored it. It was hard, forcing herself to awaken all the way and watch, and listen.

It was terrible, when she was paying attention.

All the awful sensations came back; all the distracting, distressing touches of wind, water, and insects assaulting her stony skin.

The sun was blinding and hot, and the shadows were soft and tickling when they brushed back and forth, creeping here and there along her body as the treetops swayed.

She had to strike a balance if she wanted to keep what was left of her sanity. If she withdrew too far, then she slept too much. If she strained too hard to stay alert, then the frustration made her want to scream, all the time, every second.

She tried to train her mind. Sleep some, wake some. Find a cycle.

At first she couldn't find a good pattern; she missed the things she meant to catch. As she dragged herself up from the comfortable depths of sleep, she'd detect a whiff of smoke, or smell a hint of charred fur or flesh. Down below on the yard before her, there would be fresh spots of burned grass; among the walkway's paving stones there would be pieces of wax, broken matches, or half a bloody footprint.

When she wasn't watching, people came and went; small animals were killed and chants were called.

Until finally, she caught them.

It might only have been that their routine changed, and not that she had become more vigilant.

Night had dropped itself onto the island, smothering the sand like a blanket putting out a fire.

A man in black clothes touched Nia's shoulders. One of his lean hands pressed against her arm while the other hand arranged something light and scratchy on her head.

If she'd been able to jump, she would've lurched when she realized how close his eyes were to hers. They stunned her with their immediacy, six inches from her own and staring hard, staring like he believed there was someone inside. And although it had surprised and unnerved her when the crudely shaped beast had spoken, this was somehow worse. It was one thing for a monster to know her nature; it was another thing for that thin-faced man to gaze at her as if he gathered the worst.

Another flicker of awareness flashed across his face and was gone, and he was gone, too—retreated back into the yard to join six other people who were similarly dressed.

Maybe she'd been wrong. Maybe he didn't know after all.

But she'd seen it, for a second. Not perfect knowledge, but an inkling of the truth. She couldn't decide whether she should cling to it and hope for more, or recoil, because around the edges of the black-clad man's concentration there was mania, too.

He lifted a hood off his back and draped it over his head. His companions did the same, and together they stood in a half circle, candles in their hands. The tiny orange lights painted their faces with wobbling warmth.

Nia looked closely. She stared as hard as she could, but she could scarcely tell them apart. The first man was quite tall; two others were fairly short and might have been women. The other three were of average and comparable builds. She was desperate to see their faces, but the hoods hung low and cast impenetrable shadows from their hair to their chins.

The air reeked with the pungent metal stink of blood. One of Nia's feet felt damp; she was glad she couldn't see it. But she could see what was left of something cat-sized and torn apart. In the center of the semicircle, a stripped rib cage reared up sharply out of the lawn. A long strand of vertebrae coiled at the edge of the fountain.

A tail, she thought. *Skinned and cast aside. Who* are *these people?*

The group fell into expectant silence.

One of the smaller figures broke it. "How much longer?" It was a woman's voice, low with age and a bit of fatigue.

The man who had touched Nia responded. "Quiet. Not much longer. Every night we get closer."

"So you *say*," said a third person, a man with a voice a little higher than the woman's. "How are we supposed to know? How do we tell?"

"We're summoning a goddess, not looking for a letter in the post. She's all-powerful. She'll let us know. Anyway, it's obvious the stone woman was a sign that we were on the right path."

The older woman wasn't convinced. "The stone woman arrived four years ago, and nothing new has happened since she got here."

"That's *our* fault," he insisted.

"*Your* fault," she argued.

"Fine, then. *My* fault. All the signs indicated that a harbinger had come, but it took me time to find her. I kept my eyes trained on the water and the beach; how was I to know she'd be brought here? How were any of us to know?"

"Just one more mystery," the woman grumbled. "One more secret, added to the stack."

"This isn't your mother's faith. There's none of that 'many are called, and few are chosen' nonsense. Few are called, and no one fails to answer. She picks us and we obey."

"Then she could leave us better instructions."

The leader's hood hid his annoyed expression, but she could hear the glare in his voice. "This isn't the sort of knowledge you let just *anyone* get their hands on. A little secrecy is a little security."

One of the shorter characters spoke up and turned out to be a man after all. "But it's been so *long*."

"For who? For us? For her? How long do you think four years is to a goddess? It's probably not even a blink. Not even a breath."

"But we're no gods," the woman said.

"Not *yet*."

"If she waits much longer, we'll never survive to accept her promise—and yes, I know that her idea of a long time and ours don't perfectly match. But how can we claim her reward when she won't acknowledge us?"

"She *has* acknowledged us." The leader thrust a waving hand toward Nia. "*This* was her promise, don't you get it? This was her sign that she remembers us, and she wants us to be faithful."

"According to *you*," a younger male complained. "I don't guess the stone lady came with a note attached?"

"No. She didn't come with a . . . note attached." He was forcing himself to stay composed.

For the moment, Nia was terrifically glad that she could not move and could not speak, because that meant she could not laugh. Laughing would probably make the situation worse. Everyone in the circle knew that much, too, so no one made a peep.

"But it's as clear as the Scriptures. Look at her. Born from the ocean like Venus, twisted in awe and terror. Transformed by the other side, as some punishment, no doubt." An idea came to him. He leveled his voice and added as much menace to the rest as he dared. "She probably doubted. It's the only crime to their kind— disbelief is disrespect, and disrespect earns death." He glanced again at Nia's eyes and again she felt that awful tingle of understanding and connection. "Or *worse*."

New sounds could suddenly be heard over the courtyard walls. Words spoken casually, with no intent of hiding them, slipped across the lawn.

The leader swore, and the others looked back and forth at one another as if searching for directions.

"Put out the lights," the leader hissed. "Put them out now."

Flames were hastily extinguished and smoldering candles were whisked under robes.

But the conversation still came closer. It was idle and argumentative, and Nia thought she recognized one speaker as Sam, the clerk with the clipboard who had visited a few days previously.

A fragment floated close enough for all the quiet, hooded people to hear.

"I'm telling you, the place is deserted and no one has been bothering it!"

"You're wrong!"

"I'm wrong?"

"Yes. And you don't even seem to care."

"Out!" the leader mouthed, and he put just enough air behind it to give the word some audible weight. "Out the back, through the arch. *Now.*"

Hoods came down and robes were wadded up, but without the candles, and since they were shaded from the moon by the towering trees, Nia couldn't see any faces. She watched them gather themselves together and flee. One of them grabbed the rib cage with its dangling shreds of meat, and one kicked madly at a patch of earth that had caught a spark and tried to flare.

And last of all, the grim-faced leader dashed up to Nia.

He tore a brittle crown off her head, cast it into the pulpy remains of the vineyard, and fled.

A round bob of yellow light slid into the yard, followed by Sam, who was holding the lantern that cast it.

"Do you smell that?" he demanded, lifting the lantern and illuminating his own face and the face of the fireman who'd joined him once before.

"Smell what?"

Sam frowned and made an exasperated, exaggerated sigh. "Fire? You don't smell it? Don't you fight them for a living?"

"Shut up," Dave said. "I smell it. Not like a bonfire or anything. Just a little bit of smoke."

"With wax," Sam added. "Candles. Someone blew out some candles over here, and they didn't do it very long ago."

He swung the lantern to brighten the corner where Nia sat, and he gave her a good, long look.

Dave rolled his eyes. "If you dragged me all the way out here just to get another look at the naked statue, I swear to God—"

It was Sam's turn to snap. "Stop it. Look, there's something on her."

"Where?"

Sam stepped closer. "On her feet," he said, as his own feet landed on something crunchy and slightly damp. He dropped the lantern to his knees. "Dave. Dave. Dave. Look at this. *Dave.*"

"I'm looking, I'm looking," Dave said, starting to sound nervous rather than annoyed.

The men stood there, lantern lifted and eyes cast down to the grass. They'd found the tail. Someone must have kicked it away from the fountain in all the commotion of escaping, and it had turned up underneath Sam's shoe.

"What's that?" Sam asked.

"It's disgusting."

"I can see that. What is it?"

"It looks like . . ." Dave wasn't about to admit that he didn't know, so he reached for logical answers. "It's part of an animal, don't you see?"

Sam was sweating more than the balmy night called for. He shoved at his glasses again and tugged at his shirt collar. "I see, I see. What kind of animal? And what part of it?"

Dave crouched down and beckoned for Sam to lower the light. He found a stick and used it to poke the strip of bone and muscle. "I can't tell. Maybe it's a snake," he guessed. "It looks like it could be a snake, one with all the skin peeled off it."

He stood up straight and took a deep breath. He brushed his hands against his knees, rubbing away some dirt and grass. Having come to a reasonable conclusion, he felt much better.

"A snake?" Sam was less certain, but he was also willing to leap at any plausible solution. "Do you think? I've never seen the inside of one. Those don't look like ribs, though. They look like backbones."

"Snakes have got backbones, don't they?"

"I thought they were more, I don't know, *ribby* in the middle."

"Have you ever seen the inside of a snake?" Dave asked.

"No."

Dave's grin radiated smugness. "Well, then. What would you know, anyway? We catch them and kill them sometimes around the house, little black snakes and garter snakes. Once in a blue moon, something meaner. On the inside they just look like, I don't know. Like that, more or less."

"Sure," Sam agreed, but he still backed away. "But look at all this blood. So you think something caught it and meant to eat it?"

"Probably an owl. Maybe a cat."

The corner of Sam's eye snagged on Nia again, her sharply outlined form crouching at the edge of the lantern's glow. Happy to have an excuse to leave the nasty thing on the ground, he approached her, wiping his shoes on the grass as he went.

"Where you going? Come back here with the light."

"You should've brought your own," Sam said. He held the lantern aloft and let the watery rays pour down over Nia's form. "Hey, if an animal killed that thing, then it probably wouldn't take a moment to rub the bloody corpse all over this statue, would it?"

"Why?" Dave asked, tempering the question with reluctant caution.

"No reason." Sam stood up straight and turned his back to Nia. He sniffed again at the last withering curls of candle smoke and shook his head. "Let's go. I'll write another report and see if anything comes of it."

"I don't know why you bother."

Sam didn't answer right away, and when he did, his reply was irritated, but not resigned. "I'm not sure either, sometimes. But we told this guy we'd check his house—"

"Not his house, yet."

"You know what I mean. And I'm not going to tell him that the coast is clear and he ought to buy the place, not until . . ."

Dave followed him out of the yard. "Until when?"

"Until I know what's going on," he finished weakly. "Or until it stops going on, whichever comes first. None of it sits right."

"You worry too much. We get paid either way."

"I know. But that only means we've got no reason to lie. He buys the place, he doesn't buy the place. We still get paid."

"In my book," Dave griped, "that means we should leave it the hell alone."

"You and me, we're working off two different books, then."

10

Captiva Island

Bernice made an impatient little noise and braced her hands on the rail of the *Gasparilla*. "Where are we going?" she asked.

"I told you," José said. "My old island. It's not very far from here."

She cocked her head to the right and frowned, but it wasn't an unhappy frown. "It's been a long time since you've been there, right?"

"True. But I imagine it's right where I left it."

"The treasure?"

"The island." He smiled at her over his shoulder. He leaned against the wheel, and the small ship's path curved out of the bay, slipping past the last of the party boats. "The treasure I cannot vouch for. It's probably there, but there's always the chance that someone has stumbled across it. Still. It would very much surprise me if it's gone."

On Bernice's shoulder there was a wide smear of blood. It reached into her hair, where it plastered one shiny blond curl against her ear. "And you said there's gold there?"

"Necklaces, rings, earrings. Not to mention the diamonds."

"Why is all of it jewelry? Most of the bootleggers I've met preferred cold, hard cash."

"Bootleggers?"

"Kind of like a pirate. Like a land pirate. My stepfather was one—or anyway, he worked with some of them."

"Ah."

Open ocean sprawled before them, and the full expanse of a perfectly cloudless sky stretched above. He would hang close to the coast, but he loved the possibility of it all—the vast and black spread of water tipped with white where the moon grazed the waves.

He said, "Then times have changed. In my day, precious metal was heavy, and it was heavily taxed. The travelers we met were wearing their fortunes, because it cost them less to transport it that way."

He was happier than he could ever remember being.

For the first time since he'd thrown his body overboard, tangled in chains and determined to die, he was truly delighted to find himself alive.

It almost made him change his mind. Seeing the Gulf, wild and whole—and glancing again at Bernice, beautiful and awful—for one rebellious moment he thought it might be worth making a break for it.

He could take to the open sea; he could dash for . . . for what?

Again he looked at Bernice, standing at the edge of the deck.

She leaned over the side and gazed down into the water, and it looked like her eyes were on fire. Even in the dark they glittered.

He could take her with him . . . but to where?

There was no good reason to even finish the thought. When he was alive, he'd taken to the water as soon as he'd been able. For all his life he'd known the feel of a rolling deck under his feet, and for most of his afterlife, too, riding the water or waiting beneath it. If he cut himself, he wondered, would he bleed anything but brine?

His smile, nearly fixed from cheek to cheek, spread another fraction. A good breeze lifted and pushed at the sails, and again, he thought his chest might implode with pleasure.

In the back of his mind, though, behind all sense and beneath his happiness, the half-formed plot unfolded unencouraged.

I could race with her to the other shore. We could run inland, as far as the earth would hold us. No one could touch us there, not even Mother. No more errands, no more . . .

No more ocean.

Not worth considering. The prospect fled even the furthest corners of possibility. Why nurture it? There was no indignity or price worth that one last loss. He was immortal, so far as he knew, and his Mother was the queen of her kind, mistress of the tides. He might escape her if he wished hard enough, but it would cost too much.

But deep down, still underneath and mostly unheard, a small part of him mustered a faint objection. *It was not so long ago that I settled for no master. Even the seas, I commanded.*

The *Gasparilla* strained against him, only a little—only a nudge as the wind hauled it across the calm Gulf surface. He adjusted to account for the extra air and looked up at the stars so quickly that Bernice didn't see him do it, even though she was suddenly standing beside him.

She put an arm around his waist and asked, "What's it called? The island?"

"Captiva. You'll like it there," he murmured, unwilling for the moment to be drawn into old stories of prisoners and plunder. "It is beautiful. You might say that it's captivating."

She hopped down off the stand where the pilot's wheel was mounted and went back to the rail. "I never liked living on an island *last time*."

He'd forgotten about that. "But you won't be *living* there now. We'll only visit, and we'll leave richer than we came. Surely you find that acceptable?"

Bernice thought it over and then shrugged, tossing her sticky curls. "I guess. Is it hot there?"

"Is it hot *here*? How far do you think we're going?"

"It's kind of hot. It's not that bad, though," she corrected herself quickly. "It's nice with the breeze, here on the water."

José tried to relax; he tried to shake off the irritation. "Yes, the water is fine. And I think you can suffer a few minutes of excessive warmth on shore—it won't be the end of you. I wonder if . . . I can't remember. There was a crown, a woman's crown—a tiara, I think they call them. It was white gold with a blue-green diamond set in the forehead. I'm almost certain I left it with the chest at Captiva."

"And if it's there, I can have it?"

"I can think of no fairer home for it than upon your brow. I was saving it for someone who was worthy of it," he said, more because it sounded nice than because it was true. He'd held on to the crown for the same reason he ever held on to anything—it was valuable, and eventually he could have sold it.

"Aren't you sweet," she said, batting her eyelashes and being deliberately, overtly coy. Between her fingers she was holding something small and shining. She twisted and tweaked it. She held it up to the sky and let it catch moonlight.

"Not in the least," José cheerfully assured her. "I only believe that you'd slit my throat and take it if I tried to keep it from you."

She laughed then, merry and fierce. The object in her hand bounced into the air and she caught it in her palm; she tossed it again, and caught it again.

"And you can't even contradict me! What's that you're playing with?"

Bernice lifted it to show him, though it was too small to see from where he stood at the wheel. "It's a mermaid, I think. A weird-looking mermaid."

"Where did you get it?"

"In that music box. You know how they sometimes have little dancers or ballerinas in them?"

"Yes," he said. He didn't know, but he could guess what she meant.

She grinned and held the trinket up to her eye, examining it more closely as she spoke. "I used to have one like that. My mother got it for me from this little shop in the city. In New York City, I mean. We went to this little import store when I was just a kid. I heard this music box playing and when I pulled it down to look at it, there was a little shepherd girl, like Little Bo Peep. And when you opened the lid, she popped up—she was on a spring, or something—and she would twirl around, holding her bow, or her staff, or her . . . whatever it was, anyway, she stood still and spun around in a circle while the music played. I think it was from France."

"That sounds right," he said. "They make things like that there. I think perhaps they always have."

"I wonder if this thing came from France." She waved the small figure, pinching it between her thumb and finger. "It's ugly. It's a little monster mermaid. It almost makes me think of Mother."

José heard the emphasis, and he knew which Mother she meant

this time. Arahab was monstrous, yes. But not ugly, or at least he didn't think so. She was exceedingly different from anything that ever walked the earth, but she was never meant to walk. Mother was made . . . not *for* the water, but maybe *of* it.

He hadn't thought about it before. It hadn't occurred to him that Arahab was ugly. Years before, he'd seen great whales and sharks that lumbered near the surface, graceless and heavy; but below they were swift angels, perfect and fast, and awful in the oldest sense of the word.

She was like that, too, their Mother was.

Behind his ribs and in the back of his skull, José objected to the idea of someone calling her ugly—even if that someone was Bernice. It wasn't strict love that he felt for Arahab. It wasn't strict respect, either. It was something else altogether, hovering between the two and incorporating a touch of fear.

"It sort of looks like her, doesn't it?" Bernice asked, wagging the ugly mermaid. "Not its split tail, like legs that end in fins. That's not what I mean. I mean its face, maybe. The way it's all blank and cold."

"I wish you wouldn't," José said, not looking to see how she waved the broken piece of the music box.

"Wouldn't what?"

"Never mind, love. Get rid of it, already. Throw it overboard, if that's what you intend to do."

"You haven't even looked at it yet."

"Who cares? If it looks like Mother and it makes you think of her, give it to her. Be gracious. Turn your insult into a gift."

Sullen, Bernice hoarded the mermaid in the cup of her hand. "I wasn't trying to insult her."

"Prove it," he said with a sharpness that signaled a command. He was tired of the subject; he only wanted to sail, find his island.

If she'd leave him alone and let him concentrate, he could have them there in an hour. It would take another hour more to find his old spot and retrieve the promised treasure, and then they would need to take to the water again—without the *Gasparilla*.

The ship was too conspicuous. It was only a matter of time before someone noticed it was gone. The odds were good that the boat would be missed before the people who'd been drunkenly sleeping or playing upon it. Those men and women, and that boy—they'd been wealthy, José had to assume. The *Gasparilla* was a gauche, unholy tragedy of faux cheer and incorrect nostalgia, but it had probably cost a fortune.

Someone would miss the people, too, if only to note their absence and then mount a great cacophony of outrage and vengefulness.

But if José knew anything about humanity, they'd miss the boat first.

Bernice made another grumpy whimper and then reached her arm back. She launched the metal mermaid into the *Gasparilla*'s wake, where it sank.

"There. I made a wish, and it's gone. Are you happy now?"

"Perfectly, yes."

"You're a grouchy old bastard."

"You're not the first to suggest it," he said. He pressed his torso against the wheel and enjoyed the spokes, enjoyed the wood spreading out like a hand to grasp him. "Tonight, though. Tonight there's no reason to be anything but fine."

Bernice snorted. "Fine? Aim low, why don't you."

"Fine, yes. It's much more manageable than joy or bliss. The weather is fine, the water is fine, the wind is fine, and we have this fine ship. You have no reason to feel otherwise."

"All right, *Captain*," she said.

He didn't mind that she added a note of mockery to the word.

She didn't understand, so he couldn't hold it against her, even when she continued to tease him.

She left the craft's edge and came back to José at the wheel. Folding her legs beneath herself, she sat at his feet. "How much longer until we get there?"

"Not long. Be patient."

"I'm not very good at patient," she confessed.

"I know. Do it for me, or, if nothing else will hold your attention, do it for the tiara with the diamond. You can control yourself for another hour, can't you?"

"Sure. But just an hour. How long have we been out here, anyway?"

"About half that long."

She sprawled out prettily on the deck. "And you used to do this all the time?"

He nodded and did not look at her. "All the time."

"All day?"

"All day, for weeks. For months."

"Jesus," she groaned. "I don't know how you stood it."

José shrugged. "You lived in the city, didn't you? Surrounded by people, and smoke, and trash, and noise. All day, every day, for months at a time? Well. I don't know how you could stand *that.*"

"But the city was great."

"And so was the ocean."

Bernice scooted herself over until she found José's foot, which she used for a pillow.

"Is that comfortable?" he asked.

"Terribly," she confirmed. "I might even take a nap."

"By all means," he told her.

She closed her eyes and pretended to sleep, tilting her sharp-cheeked, bloodstained face up to the stars. She folded her arms across her chest. She took a deep breath and was quiet enough for José to ignore her.

The rest of the way, he did his best not to move his foot.

After less time than he'd estimated, the sky said he was close. He watched for the shoreline. The moon could show only so much, and small lights burned here and there—but only here and there. Not many people lived on the island, or few were home. Why would they be? The big festival was under way a few miles in the distance, and it would continue to run for days.

A small pier, much too small to dock a craft like the *Gasparilla,* played host to a string of fishing boats and dinghies with oars crossed inside.

José skirted the shore's edge, staying far enough out to escape the notice of any late-night beachcombers. He withdrew his foot from underneath Bernice's head, and when she grunted at him, one eye open and accusing, he said, "I need to pull some sails. Would you care to assist?"

"Not really."

He said, "You'll be sailing with me on the *Arcángel,* you know— and it will be as first mate, not as passenger. It would be worth your time to learn a few things now."

"I'll learn them later. You said so yourself, this night is for fun, not for a mission."

"I'm the captain, aren't I? I suppose I could order you to take up a rope."

"I suppose you could *try.*"

A spike of something hot and almost angry shot through his chest. He forced it down and pushed it aside, more because it did him no good than because he was afraid of it. *She doesn't understand,* he told himself. *It's not something I can hold against her. She is only a woman, and a young one, at that. She is only beautiful.*

She was still sitting beside the wheel, now leaning back on her

elbows and saying without a word that she had no intention whatsoever of rising. Her breasts were pushed forward under the light,
gore-speckled blouse, and her hair was drying into a mess of sea
air and tangles.

"What an unrepentant little wench you are," he said. He tried
to make it sound teasing and friendly.

"And you love it," she accused. "You know you do."

"Of course I do. I'd never tolerate it otherwise."

She laughed, again because she didn't understand. The cheerfully wicked sound tinkled through the night. "You *tolerate* me. Is
that how it works?"

"I tolerate you, with love. What's so bad about that?"

She stopped laughing. A smile lingered, indicating that perhaps she was more aware than he'd thought. "It's a fine balance."

"Yes," he agreed. "Be quiet now. We're close, and it's been so
long since I've visited. I'm not sure what sort of reception we might
expect, if any. And I can't recall the closest way to the *zanja*."

"The what?" Bernice scanned the shoreline, a motionless black
line on shifting blue-black water. It told her almost nothing, so she
asked him again. "What did you call it?"

He hunted in his memory for an English equivalent. "The
hole. There's a place on the island, not so far from the shore—it's a
place where the ground sank and left the greatest pit you ever saw.
If it were a little bit larger, and if it had an outlet to the water . . .
then it would make a perfect harbor, hidden and overgrown."

"I don't get it."

"When water moves underground," he tried. "Like a river
flowing through a cave, do you understand?"

"Yeah, I get it." Though he could tell that she didn't.

As he reached for the ropes and the nets and tugged the sails
into position or out of the way, he tried to explain. "The water
carves as it moves, and sometimes, after a long time, it carves away

so much that the earth collapses. Think of it as a cave without a ceiling, and that should give you some idea. There's water in the bottom—not always, but sometimes—and in my *zanja,* the pool is deep enough to float a large boat."

"And you want to sail this thing into it?"

"No, no. We couldn't if we tried, not unless Mother saw fit to lend a hand. The pit is too far from the shore, and surrounded by earth or rock on all sides. The spring that feeds it empties to the ocean, but it gets there underground, and not by any river or stream. I only imagined that it would be a wonderful harbor. I used to dream of sailing my own ship into it, and dropping anchor, and fearing nothing."

He returned to the wheel and took its spokes in hand.

"I had even thought that one day, when I was finished with my work, I might live there. I could almost afford to buy the entire island outright, back then. At least I could have owned much of it, and owned it fairly, and legally. By then, Spain was ready to sell the whole peninsula to the old English colonies, and there was a chance I might be left alone. It was easier then, to change a name, shave a beard, and hide."

"You used to have a beard?"

"I told you, we spent months onboard the ship."

"Ugh," Bernice said. She propped her elbows up on the rail and put her chin in her hands.

"And now that I know how strongly you disapprove, I will never grow it again, my princess. But"—he maneuvered the ship around a sandbar he suspected more than remembered, and began to push toward shore—"I thought that I might become a respectable landowner, on an island like this—or maybe Sanibel, or some other. I could live on what we'd plundered for another hundred lifetimes, were I so blessed to live them. You must understand, I was a very old man for my profession."

Bernice made a short, idle hum that falsely indicated that she was paying attention.

José's arms did the work of two men, and sometimes three. He pulled the masts and mainyards into alignment. He tied everything down to hold it, and he returned to the wheel to guide the craft forward.

"I knew that I didn't have too many years left ahead of me. I would've been a fool to think otherwise. And so yes, there is this island—and there is a place here that I love, and I thought it would be fine to retire from the ocean and live here, surrounded by the water and safe from those searching it for me."

"But you got greedy. That's what Mother said."

That was true, and fair. And it did not offend him. "I should not have chased the last ship," he admitted.

She lifted her face from its nest in her hands. "So why did you? If you already had more money than a king, why chase one more score?"

He tilted his head and lifted a hand in a gesture that said nothing. "To have *more.* And since it's no more complicated than that, I don't imagine I would have made a very good retired buccaneer, so it's just as well I never had the chance to be one."

"What about now?"

"What?" he asked, not understanding.

"What about now? Can't this ship be the last one? Nothing's keeping you anymore, except—"

He cut her off. "Except for you. And Mother, who does as she likes. And things are different since we met her, aren't they? Let them catch us if they can, for all we care. Their laws have no authority over us."

Bernice stood up straighter and turned her back to the rail to lean against it. "You're not worried about anybody catching us?"

"I wasn't when I was alive. Why should I be now?"

She smiled, a malicious little streak that tugged at the blood painted on her face. "I knew I liked you for some reason."

He pretended not to hear her. "We're here," he said.

"What, now?" She turned around again and looked off into the water. "All the way out here?"

"Any closer and we'll scrape bottom. This island has no harbor for us, darling. From here on out, we swim or row—the choice is yours."

Before he could even glance over to the lifeboat strung from the other hull, Bernice was in the water again. He heard her enter hands-first in a perfect dive, with a splash so small, she could've been a fish.

Although he was only just beginning to dry off, José followed her.

Holes and Hideaways

He hit the surface with a similar splash, quiet enough to be mistaken for an oar, or a bird. The black bath engulfed him, and he swam blindly through it in the direction of his island. He had left the *Gasparilla*'s anchor raised so the boat was free to drift behind him.

They wouldn't need the *Gasparilla* to escape. They hadn't needed it to reach the island, either, but as a matter of form and familiarity, it had been an entertaining exercise. He hadn't been in a boat since his failed errand a lifetime before. It wasn't strictly forbidden, but in some way he felt certain that his estrangement from the surface was part of his punishment.

Go dash yourself, you silly craft. José pushed on toward the shallower swells of the water that foamed and crested close to the beach.

The nearer he came to a sandy place where he could stand, the more he rethought his impulse. When he finally found footing and hauled himself to a standing position, chest-deep against the waves, he looked back at the boat and saw that it was already turning and listing with no one at the helm.

A quick pang stabbed at his heart, and it embarrassed him.

It was only a boat, and an insulting one at that. But at a distance, in the dark—with its remaining lanterns burning themselves down to tiny points of light—the *Gasparilla* was a pretty thing after all. He wanted to curse her into kindling, but he found himself wishing her well, and offering a silent, thankful prayer to Mother for letting him have another night with a deck that moved under his feet and sails that flapped over his head.

His hair clung close to his face and his clothes sucked wetly at his skin. The salt didn't bother his eyes anymore; it hadn't for decades. But he felt it all the same, gritty and pungent. A breeze off the coast pressed against him, coaxing the water into rivulets that dried to taste like crushed shells and decay.

José pushed himself at the shore. The water rushed past him, underneath him, and against him as it rolled back and forth, shattering itself on the coast. His feet took a step onto sand that didn't melt beneath him, and he was back on Captiva—one of the last spots he'd ever stood on as a mortal.

Bernice had beaten him by a full minute.

She shook herself. She'd lost or dropped the sweater she'd been wearing. Light and wet, her dress revealed every curve underneath. She snapped it away from her stomach with her fingers.

The swim had washed the last of the blood out of her hair and off her face, but somehow she looked even less civilized and more dangerous—there on the sand, barefoot and as pale as the translucent things that crawl on the ocean floor.

Shark woman, José thought. The words crowded together in his mouth, and they were perfect so long as they were not spoken.

"What?" she asked, and the word clicked like a bite.

"Nothing," he told her, and the moment was broken.

She ran her hands up her forehead, pushing her wet hair back away from her eyes. "All right. We're here. Now where are we going?"

José pulled at his shirt. He tugged it away from his body and let the breeze blow through it while he looked back and forth, up and down the dark strip of shore. He shook his legs to kick away the worst of the wet. His boots held on to most of it, but he was accustomed to the sensation.

"This way," he said. "Follow me; I can find it."

Bernice made a slight grimace. José saw it just before he turned away to lead, and he stopped. "Is something wrong?"

She shook her head, but didn't shake the frown loose. "It looks like Anna Maria, that's all. I *hated* that place. Let's get this over with and get out of here. I want to get back in the water."

"This won't take long." He was careful how he said it. He nearly wanted to hit her, but he refused the impulse in favor of coddling her, because it was easier. He could force her to come if he liked. The situation was his to control, if he chose, but things moved more quickly when he led her gently than if he pushed.

She tromped through the sand beside him, following his lead between two trees with trunks that stretched and sprawled as if they were melting. "I should've kept my shoes," she said.

He agreed, pettily pleased that she was uncomfortable. "Undoubtedly. Where did you leave them?"

"I don't remember."

She probably didn't. It didn't matter, either, that she'd spent her whole life walking around; a few years on the floor of the ocean could make you forget even the most basic necessities.

When he'd first emerged, it had been hard for him, too. But he'd been alone, and for him, that was easier.

He didn't know what Bernice would have preferred. Maybe she would've liked to burst into the air like Venus, launched from her shell unattended. She was still young, though—so young that if they'd gone down together on the same day, in the same year, he could have been her grandfather.

She moved beside him, following awkwardly through the sand. It was easier to walk down by the water where the turf was smooth, if wet; up in the woods it was like stepping through flour. "How far is it to your spot, the hole or the pit or whatever you called it?"

"Not far." He doubted himself even as he said it. How long had it been since he'd seen it? And in truth, his idea of "far" was probably quite different from Bernice's. "Close enough that I halfway imagined digging that channel to the ocean. It would've made a marvelous private cove, but it was . . . impractical."

"Impractical," she repeated. "Maybe you should ask Mother about it now. Maybe when all this is settled, and she's gotten what she wants from us, and we're done, maybe you can retire like you didn't before."

The thought had occurred to him, yes. Arahab would find it a small task to carve a path between the hole and the ocean.

But he'd never asked.

"One day," he answered vaguely. "I'll bring it up, and see what she says. But before any rewards, there's work to be done, and at the moment, my standing in her eyes is only somewhat better than bad."

"I don't get it."

"I know you don't. It's because you haven't failed her yet."

"I won't fail her," Bernice said, and something about the way the words came out sounded strange to José. She presented the sentiment with confidence, yes—and something else, too.

"If she thought you would, she would never have chosen you. Though you'd best remember, she chose me once as well—and the task was more than I could complete."

They walked together in something close to silence, navigating the close-set trees and the darkness of the rain forest undergrowth with eyes that were accustomed to a much stranger, deeper darkness.

"You and me are different."

"Indeed, my love. We *are*."

12

Where Water Meets Stone

Down in the enclosed cove, the sunken hole with no outlet to the sea, a low grumbling of rocks and mulch twisted a soft sound. A rough-edged creature assembled itself, rising up from the earth. It tested its makeshift limbs. It shook one arm, and then the other, and it stepped from clod-foot to clod-foot.

If it stepped too hard or too fast, clumps and crumbs of dirt and leaves shook loose. In order to hold itself together better, it moved more carefully.

It could hear them coming.

The man and the woman—or the two things that once were man and woman—were making their way back to the secluded spot and sometimes talking, sometimes keeping quiet. Although it was quite dark beneath the forest canopy in the middle of the night, the creature knew that they could see well enough. Arahab would have seen to that when she changed them.

It wondered what other changes she might have made. Those fragile things, all meat and fluids bound in a sack of skin, how would she have altered them to keep them close?

Their skin must have toughened to the point where mere soaking would not swell or split it. Their eyes must have been taught to gather even the smallest slivers of light, and they must have transformed the way they took air; they must have learned to take what they needed from the water, yet retained the capacity for breathing above the waves.

The thing considered its own first capture and wondered at her state.

It had left her behind that house on the other island, safe except for the miserable wretches who tried to worship her. To date, they hadn't bothered her, save to smear her with blood or offerings. The damn fools wanted to summon the water witch, and they thought the stone girl was a sign. The situation couldn't have been more ridiculous.

The girl couldn't help them, and if the water witch even knew about her, that would be the end of it. The water witch would destroy the girl without a second thought, and very likely she would treat the idiot worshippers the same.

What did they hope to accomplish? Arahab wished to destroy everything they knew and loved. What did they think she would give them?

As the footsteps approached, the creature stood very still against the tall, fingerlike roots of a large banyan. It did not feel the need to hide. It did not expect to be seen, but it was interested in observing. It wanted to know what the water witch's consorts could do, and what they looked like. It wanted to see for itself how a human might transcend the flesh while keeping it.

It might give the creature some idea of what to expect from its stone girl when the time came for her to emerge. She might not be enough. She might not have been the right choice. She might not even survive the cocoon.

But it had seemed like a good idea at the time.

The creature that had made itself from the dying leftovers on the forest floor did not breathe, because it did not need to. It simply held still and watched while the man and woman walked past, moving just inches away and noticing nothing.

"How much *farther*?"

"We're here. Now," the man said.

They stood at the lip of the sinkhole. If she'd taken another step, or two at most, she would have gone over the edge.

The creature moved behind them, silently for all its bulk. It watched over their shoulders as they held hands and half climbed, half slid down the edge of the hole into the bottom. And once they were away from the edge, scooting foot by foot toward the water, the creature sat itself down at the cusp of the precipice and pretended to be invisible . . . which only meant that it did not move, and that no one saw it.

Down below, the man and woman tripped down the steep slope.

The spot was peaceful and pretty, even to the creature—who had little use for pools of water or places where things may float.

In a few thousand years, the place might yet become a proper cove. The incoming tides might beat a path inland, eroding the sand and scooping out the trees; or the sudden rush of a storm could do it more quickly.

Sunken and overgrown, the sinkhole's sides were thick with

palmettos and small trees that clung tight using roots that wiggled deep into the sandy dirt. The creature could feel them, tangled and stringy, burrowing among the bigger roots of taller trees and holding the hillside together in their own way. To the man-shaped thing sitting atop them, they felt like strings and ropes pulled taut and tied together.

Moonlight streamed in full, high enough to illuminate the hole's interior and the pond that filled the bottom. Without any tide to pull it, and away from the swift ocean air, the surface was as still as glass and as blackly speckled as the sky it mirrored.

"It's beautiful, don't you think?"

"Yeah," the woman said, and she followed it with a grunt as she skidded farther than she meant to. "It's great."

The man didn't push the issue. He reached back and took her hand, steadying her descent and completing his own. He landed at the bottom with a small jump and a triumphant smile.

"It was, for years and years, a most excellent refuge. We would leave the ships anchored by the shore and camp. The water was fresh, if not perfectly clean, and there was plenty of fruit and game on the island. A man so inclined might live here happily and unassisted for . . . for a lifetime."

"Maybe a man so inclined," she mimicked his speaking rhythm. "No woman in her right mind would put up with it for a second."

"Then it's a good thing no woman ever needed to make such an adjustment."

"Where's this treasure chest you left down here? Let's get it and go. I deserve a reward for hiking through all this mess—and barefoot, too."

"You should have kept your shoes on."

"I couldn't swim in those heels. I can hardly walk in them."

He conceded the point with a shrug. "We won't be long," he said. "Here. Why don't you swim, if you like that better than hiking." With one long, slim hand he held hers and lifted it as if he were inviting her to dance. He guided her into the shimmering pool until she was knee-deep, and smiling.

"There's not anything awful in here, is there?" she asked.

"There's less in this pool than the ocean currents we crossed to come here."

"So nothing that bites?"

"Nothing that bites harder than you, I promise."

She laughed at that, and zipped backwards with a slippery splash, all fish-quick and flexible. Out in water that was surely no deeper than her waist she lounged on her back, the tips of her hands and feet peeking past the surface.

He walked away from her, staying close in the shallows but moving to the far side of the pit.

But the woman wanted to play, so she called out, "Is there anything with *stingers* in here that would stab me?"

The man answered over his shoulder, without turning his head. "None so sharp as yours, my darling."

"Is there anything *vicious* in here?"

"Nothing half so terrible as *you,* my love."

She cackled with glee, splashed and drifted.

He worked through the thick, wet mold and grasses down by the pool's edge to the far side—where a remnant of the cave wall was strung with vines as thick as arms. He pushed his hands between the long, living curtains and withdrew them again, empty. Down beside his feet he found a stick, or a dried-out root. He pried it loose and wiped away some of the mud that covered it.

"What are you doing?" The woman called from the water.

"Looking for your treasure." With long, solid stabs, he rammed the stick through the vines. The baton slipped easily among them, meeting resistance shortly behind the vegetation where the rock stretched up out of the ground.

"Is it back there someplace?"

He rammed the instrument forward again.

"Is it back—?"

"Yes, darling. It's back here someplace. But it's been a long time since I left it, and things have grown quite a lot. Give me a moment and I'll find it." And soon, he did.

The stick passed through the growing drapes, and nothing stopped it. The man let go and let the thing drop; it landed with a wet clatter somewhere beyond where anyone could see it. He wormed his arm amid the vines and wriggled it back and forth. Plants tore and leaves tumbled; the living curtain gave way and a hole opened.

In the water, the woman stopped splashing. "Is that a *cave?* You're not going to drag me into a cave, are you?" She rotated herself in the water and began a slow swim in the direction of her partner. "I'm not following you into any damn cave."

"No," he replied as he pushed his arms, head, and part of his torso into the darkness on the other side. "It isn't a cave. It's only a ledge."

A scraping, splintering grind echoed around behind the hanging vines. The man emerged slowly, his shoulders and hands inching backwards at last as he drew the chest from its hiding place and into the open night.

Behind him, the woman quickly appeared from the water—standing close and curious. "Let me see."

"One moment." He levered his fingers beneath the hinges and gave them a pull. He was rewarded with the squeak of stretching leather and the uneven ripping of old metal.

"How long has this been here?"

He forced his full hand between the lock and the soggy front panel. It cracked and split with a damp pop. "Perhaps a century or so. Since . . . I can't recall the year. It would have been 18 . . . 1815?

1820? It was before I went into the water, but not terribly long before."

The box was more of a trunk, covered in mold and difficult to
hold or wrangle. The man adjusted it on the ground, backing it up
against a rock and using that spot of solidness to secure it while he
pried and twisted at the fastenings.

After another round of jabbing and rending, the lock finally
snapped and the clasp fell away.

"Here we go," the man said. The lid was falling apart in his
hands as he lifted it away. It crumbled into sodden pulp once its
hinges were gone, and the heavy loot within settled and scattered.

"Wow."

"Yes." He dug his fingers into the coins and baubles. He
combed through them and separated the treasure from the green-
black cake of mildew that coated it. Beneath the glaze of mire, the
trunk's contents sparkled with vivid brown light.

The creature at the edge of the pit blinked slowly.

Out in the water, over the sandy breech, the ocean was singing
a peculiar song. The creature felt a tightening in its coiled, cobbled insides. The sound rushed; it was air over waves, and a ferocious sweep under the surface.

Water witch, the creature thought. It knew that the witch had a
name, but it would only use that name if forced. She might not
notice him. She might have only come for her underlings, whose
eyes were round and crinkled with joy at their fresh discovery. But
the odds were against it.

The creature almost wished it hadn't left the trinket in the music box. It had seemed logical at the time. The ruse was a means of
making sure, of knowing with absolute confidence that the witch
was still there, watching and lingering, and that she was as close as
it feared she might be.

Besides, the creature wanted to see her interacting with her pets. It needed to see how she worked with them, and how she treated them. How resilient were they, really? How helpful were they, really?

It owed its own static and frightened recruit some knowledge of what she'd be up against.

And the time was at hand. The monstrous water witch arrived at the island's edge and was furious to see no passage to the cove; but then she sank herself deep and felt around for an outlet that ran beneath the shore. She found it shortly.

The creature sensed her furious push from the ocean, against a current that struggled through sand and stone. She did not need much water to work, only *some*—only enough to dissolve and draw herself along like a salmon swimming upstream.

In the center of the pool she emerged with a geyser and a shout.

Her children jumped and turned their backs to the moldering chest, slapping their hands down and drawing quick breaths. They were caught off guard, and they were so frightened that they froze. Transformed or not, changed or not, beloved of the water witch or not—they were still seized with the very mortal fear of being eaten.

"Mother?" the man gasped. The woman straightened herself beside him.

In one of the witch's enormous hands, black and rough like sharkskin, she held out the mermaid trinket from the *Gasparilla*'s music box. *What is this, and why?* she demanded.

The man said. "I don't understand."

Did you cast this? Did you throw it down into the water? Her voice was too low to be shrill, but too severe to be merely a shout. *One of you did, I know.*

"I did it," the woman spoke up fast. "I found it on the boat—"

Out there, the decorated thing that's about to break itself in the tide?

"Yes," she said.

You found it there?

"She did," the man interjected. "It was in a box, down below. A music box; I told you about it when you asked about the song. Please, before you get any angrier with us, won't you explain? It is only a toy. She meant no harm with it. What is it, and why have you chased us into this confrontation?"

The water witch settled in the water, melting herself until she was shaped like a woman only from the belly up. The rest remained in the pool; she hid her lower half in the dark water, as if to cover it with a tremendous skirt. She crushed the mermaid in her palm, concealing and destroying it. *You cannot lie to me*, she said more calmly. *I made you what you are, and I can see inside you, the way you work and the way you plot.*

"Then you know that we hide nothing. Please, Mother," he begged. "Explain to us our transgression."

Her yellow pupilless eyes smoldered. You *hide nothing,* she agreed with him. She turned her attention to the woman. *You found it in a music box. Do you recall the tune that it played?*

"I don't," she said.

And you played with this, before you cast it over the side?

"I did."

But you do not know why I've come?

"I don't."

While the water witch fumed and tried to read the hearts of her offspring, the creature on the hill nodded to itself, pleased at the mermaid's successful summoning, even if the very nearness of the witch made its twig-filled face twist with disgust.

The song was not so hard to reproduce. The witch was not so difficult to beckon or banish after all. One needed only to know the correct arrangement of the right old tunes.

She glowered down at the stiff-limbed, stubborn woman, and

she opened her hand. The mermaid was unrecognizable, so badly had she bent it. *This was a signal,* she said with care. *It was an urgent request, charmed and loud. It was a cry for assistance and aid.*

Having found the track of her subtle lie, the witch followed it. *I was afraid for you both. I could smell your hands and I thought that something tragic had occurred. It was as if you screamed my name and it was a scream of terror, and I wished to answer but I feared for the circumstances. I did not mean to treat you so crossly, children of mine. But you worried me with your*— She tossed the metal lump to the woman, who caught it and held it tightly. —*little toy. I can only wonder where it came from. I would ask that you be more careful with the things you throw away.*

She gave the woman another long look that was neither kind nor unkind. It was not a threat, but it carried with it elements of a warning.

And be careful also of the wishes you make, and cast. Baubles such as those may carry them far, and betray them as likely as grant them.

With that, she sank with a leisurely motion until the top of her head disappeared beneath the glassy surface and was gone, leaving only a circular ripple to mark her passage.

The creature also let itself sink, back down into the soil and through the tangled-tight roots of the slope. It emerged down at the water's edge, where it hid in the shadows of the overhanging vines—though it was careful not to dip even one corner of its lumpy feet into the pool.

It hung back and waited while the man and woman caught their breath.

The night was still again, and the pool was as perfect as a mirror, except by the very outside edge . . . where a long black hand reached out slowly, crawling spiderlike from the lip of the water toward the blocky brown foot of the creature.

It spied the hand too late. Before it realized the witch was still there, her hand had seized its foot, and the creature roared—sending the small, frightened people scattering back behind the trunk and into the vine curtain, where they sought shelter.

Arahab snatched the foot and dragged the creature into the wet; it struggled and swore, and it clutched at the earth. It reached with its center, grasping hard for the roots in the sinkhole bank and trying to anchor and draw itself forward and away, doing its best to keep from being picked up.

But the water witch wormed her fingertips through the creature's loose, leafy skin and she held it firm.

As it grew wet, it began to disassemble; and as it fought, it came apart all the faster. It changed tactics. It lunged against her, thinking it would be simpler to be torn apart and regroup later, but she halted the plan before it got under way.

She rose up again out of the water, huge and enraged. She held the creature by its neck and squeezed it with both hands.

You? You were the one who made the call and bade me come?

"No," it insisted.

Don't lie to me, Thing. Neither of those two— She gestured at the place where they hid. *Neither of them knows enough to make such a device. They would not know whom to ask, or what questions to bring. They lack the power to summon my sort.*

When she said *my sort,* the words were laced with razors to cut the insult deeper. She shook the creature, tormenting it even as she held it together. She had swollen herself until she was large enough to lift the creature aloft. The pool in which she stood was nearly empty, as she had used almost the entire contents to build her imposing, powerful shape. Her bottom half was a tentacled, finned anomaly that was forced to spread in order to support her.

"*Our* sort," the creature threw the sentiment back at her. Its voice did not choke despite her grip, because the sound did not emanate from within its throat.

Furious, she hoisted the creature high and slammed it down into the mud where the emptied pool had left the ground wet. Its body split and would have shattered with the impact, except that she held it together in its beaten-sack shape with the force of her will.

You and I share no sort, no kind, and no kinship. We are in no way the same, and you have no power here. To emphasize her point, she beat the creature again, over and over until it was pulped and crushed like the mermaid that had drawn her out in the first place.

She hit the thing in time with her words, because she knew they would hurt it more than the blows alone.

Exile. Fiend. Traitor. She ground the creature down with her palm, burying it in the mud and leaving it all but immobile, so damaged was its form. *Outcast.*

It lay there and jerked, broken to the point that it could not move the crude body it wore.

I ask you again, did you create that call?

"No," it said.

She beat it again, although it was scarcely more than pulp.

Why did you make it? she demanded.

"I did not make it. I did not call you. I would not dare it."

She threw her wet fist down again, determined to erase him, to rub him into nothingness. *You would not dare it? But you would dare to watch, and dare to follow. You traced them here, because you knew what they carried.*

"Yes," it confessed.

Its answer caught her by surprise. *You'll admit that much?*

"Yes."

She stood up straight and stared down into the crusty puddle where its body had been before. *But you were not summoned?*

"No. I only heard the song, and wanted to know who had brought it and why. My crime is only curiosity," it told her. "I heard it and I followed it. But you know as well as anyone of *your* kind . . ." It was being careful now. It had pushed the ruse too far, almost, and it needed to retreat. "I do not have the power to fashion such an enchantment. Who am I to summon you? If I were to make my very best effort, I could not summon the queen of the waters. If I were to work with the finest tools, and act upon the finest advice, the greatest result I could manage would not be enough to tug upon your smallest pet."

She turned her head and eyed the place where her children had vanished.

"Not the tiniest fish," it clarified, lest she infer its true intent. "Not the smallest water horse with a curled and coiled tail. Not the littlest crab with the most insignificant claws. I have not the will, nor the skill, and certainly not the desire to attract your wrath."

She considered this.

The creature on the ground rested and struggled to pull itself back into a shape that would let it crawl away from her. It prayed to the universe or to the unseen that the water witch might swallow the lies and think no harder on the matter. It prayed that the long years between its exile and her outburst had dulled her memories. Let her contempt protect him. Let her disdain provide false proof.

It watched her eyes flicker with uncertainty. It had successfully worried her, but it had not completely thrown her off its treachery. Quickly, before she had time to give it any more credit, it added, "What reason could I possibly have to draw a goddess to me, when destruction is the finest treatment I deserve?"

She nodded, because it sounded like a fair plea—and it was presented in the obsequious manner she most preferred. As a matter of form, she pretended to object. *Be careful with the titles you assign, you low and ridiculous insect.* The pool at the sinkhole's floor began to fill itself again as the water witch descended and returned the liquid to its proper location. *Your praise is ill-considered,* she accused. *I do not trust you, and I do not believe you. Your treachery has passed into myth, and your deceptive spirit serves as a warning to all of us who remain. But no pathetic orphan could have crafted a signal so effective.*

"I am a wretched ghost," it affirmed, though it lent the admission more heartfelt misery than it would have liked. With exhaustive effort and a trembling twitch, it mustered enough stability to extend a penitent hand. "Pity your tragic servant, Mistress. I have meant you neither harm nor offense, and I only beg an undeserved pardon."

That much is true; you deserve no pardon from me. You deserve no quarter, and no mercy. Arahab turned away from the slimy patch of earth and drew herself down into the frothed and muddied pool. *We should have destroyed you long ago. We should have taken your last breath as well as your domain, and cast you into the formless void.*

And the pool went still, its surface barely bubbling from the disturbance that the water witch left in its wake.

What was left of the creature's battered shape cracked itself into a vicious smile. "Hag," it spit. "You *tried.*"

Being Ware of Wishes

Insurance was not Sam's passion. As far as he knew, it wasn't anybody's passion, but someone had to calculate and process it, and so far as the Bradenton Fire Company was concerned, that someone was Sam.

He sat sweating at his temporary desk in the purgatory warmth of the attic of the Anna Maria courthouse, and he scowled.

Upon the desk lay a letter from the county's chief, its envelope cut and its contents spilled. Several phrases leaped up from the hastily handwritten note. One said, "No action necessary or practical at this time." Another mentioned a conversation with the mayor. Yet a third indicated that perhaps Sam could find something better to do with his free time than trespass repeatedly and to no real purpose on private property.

"It isn't private property, exactly," he complained to the empty room. "Not if no one owns it. It's city property. Langan has to buy it from the city."

The papers rustled in response, stirred by the chain-driven fan above and a quick, light breeze through the window behind him.

Besides, wasn't he working? For Langan, if not for the fire department precisely, he was 100 percent on task—investigating a potential property for an out-of-town investor. Just because he wasn't working for Chief Porter, that didn't mean he wasn't working.

The final line of the letter proposed that Sam locate Dave more or less immediately, and return with him to the mainland.

Sam had an assortment of arguments stacked up against it.

For one thing, he could barely stand the sight of Dave for more than an hour at a time, and he wasn't looking forward to the journey home. For another, his bureaucratic little soul had hit its threshold for refusal.

He'd filed no less than a dozen letters with various island city officials, and down to the last scrap they'd been ignored. So he'd filed a second set of meticulous documentation about the goings-on at the beach house, and that second set had been likewise disregarded.

In person, then, he had addressed every correct and proper agency. They all rebuffed him, sometimes gently, sometimes condescendingly, and sometimes with outright anger.

He simply couldn't understand why no one thought it was even *interesting*—much less important—that criminal activity was taking place in this closed, quiet community right beside the ocean.

Granted, he didn't have a great stash of evidence to show.

For that matter, he remembered grimly, he had no evidence at all. His carefully collected specimens from the courtyard had vanished from storage at the courthouse where he'd made his temporary headquarters; and no amount of outraged inquiry could retrieve the items or solve the mystery of their disappearance.

The secretary had stared at him as if he'd pulled a cat out of his pants when he suggested that she ought to look into this travesty, and possibly seek police intervention. She told him to notify the police if he liked. The policeman's name was Bud, and he lived down by the lighthouse between the pier and the main road; but he'd gone down to Longboat Key for a fishing vacation, and he wouldn't be back for a week.

Sam seethed at the unfair, incorrect, and inexcusable disorganization of it all.

Even when he took into consideration that this was a small city, accessible only by ferry, there was no good reason whatsoever for civic untidiness. If anything, he would think that a smaller population would make it easier to keep everything in order.

But no.

As long as things were quiet, no one cared what went on in the dark.

Well, Sam cared. Or at the very least, Sam was intensely interested—and he'd met with so much resistance that he couldn't let it go.

Sometimes he wished he could be more like his traveling companion. Dave had long since let it go, or hell—maybe he never had it in the first place. If Sam knew Dave at all, Dave was down at the Sandbar trying to talk the man behind the counter into bringing out some of the bathtub liquor that everyone knew was made in the back.

Another insulting word blared up from the letter. "Impractical."

If Chief Porter wanted to get technical about it, selling fire insurance on an island with no ready access to a fire company was completely, ludicrously impractical—but people wanted it. The chief insisted that they could drive their American LaFrance pumper out from Bradenton in no time flat if the ferry was waiting right, and anyway, there was always the old engine stuck in storage.

Sam rose from the desk and pushed his shirtsleeves as far up his arms as the fabric would permit. The lone window behind him didn't let in half so much breeze as heat, and he was warm enough from being angry.

Downstairs, the phone rang and the secretary answered it. Outside, a rickety truck rattled along the sandy street like a big mechanical insect.

"Also impractical?" Sam said aloud. "The steadfast refusal of proper pavement." Even if the fire engine could arrive at the island in time to fight a blaze, the truck would never make it down the streets. It would be too heavy, with all the water and equipment. The machine would bog down before rolling more than a few feet off the pier.

He reached down and grabbed the letter, wadded it up, and threw it into the metal trash can.

His time and money were almost up. One way or another, he'd have to return to Bradenton within a couple of days, with or without any proof of the strangeness down at the house on the shore.

But with every hour that passed, he was more convinced that something weird was going on. It wasn't just the traces of little fires; it wasn't just the bones and the blood that he found smeared and scattered around the property. It was the way people looked at him when he tried to call attention to the issue. It was the sudden darting of their eyes, or hasty laughter.

And now he was being sent away. Urged home. Kicked out.

The secretary's voice was low and measured. She was taking a personal call on the company phone. Otherwise, he'd be able to hear every word from his borrowed space, like usual.

Sam sighed. He was tempted to storm downstairs, burst past the secretary, charge onto the mainland, and return with the state police, or the FBI, or whoever else he could scare up with his reports of . . .

But if he were forced to admit it, he didn't have much to report.

The animal parts could be attributed to a predator of some kind—an island dog, or even a panther, someone had suggested. Sam didn't know if there were any enormous Florida cats on the island, but he was willing to bet there weren't; and even if there were, they wouldn't use knives. Some of the scraps of fur and flesh he'd found showed distinct signs of having been cut with something sharp.

And all the candle nubs, left scattered in the grass—they weren't regular candles. They had a greasy texture and a black coating. Who used black candles? No one up to any good, that's who.

He stopped his pacing and crossed his arms.

Actually, the candles gave him an idea.

Maybe the police were the wrong call; maybe he ought to look in a different direction. Candles were used in ceremonies and services, weren't they? And who would know more about ceremony than the church?

He grabbed his satchel of books, notebooks, and pens and dashed downstairs, taking them two at a time.

When he reached the secretary, he was panting, but determined. "Ma'am," he said to Francis, "What kind of churches do you have here on the island?"

"I beg your pardon?"

"Churches. For worship. Where people go on Sundays and the

like—a chapel, or a . . . I don't know. What's the population like here?"

"Ours is a fine and spiritual population, Samuel, but there aren't that many of us and there are only two churches between here and the mainland."

"Excellent. What kind are they?"

She shrugged and twirled a pencil in an idle manner. "They're just normal churches. You know."

"Normal? You mean Christian?"

"Sure, I guess."

"So you don't attend services yourself?" Sam asked, realizing that the question was a touch personal and possibly inappropriate.

But if the implication offended Francis, she didn't show it. She twirled the pencil again and stuffed it behind her ear. "I go sometimes. But I don't go all the time."

The phone made a tinny ring.

The secretary pointed at it, letting her hand hover for a few seconds while she answered the question she knew he'd ask next. "Go out to the main drag and take a left. It's half a mile or so down, on the right." Then she lifted the receiver and turned away to speak into it.

Sam backed out, then twisted his feet around to carry himself forward.

The courthouse was a small building, barely any bigger than a house, and it was made from a combination of stucco and coquina with long, tall windows, ostensibly to keep it cool. Sam didn't think the construction worked until he stepped outside and found it even hotter in the sun than it had been in the attic.

He checked his watch and noted with some relief that the sun would be down in an hour. Night wouldn't bring anything close to a chill, but at least the blazing light would be aimed elsewhere and the ocean air could blow the muggy afternoon away.

Sam thought of the courtyard, and of the infuriating fact that every time he visited, there was something new and disgusting left behind to greet him. He thought of Dave, who was happy to see nothing, hear nothing, and know nothing so long as he got paid and got to take a nap in the afternoon.

And he thought of the insulting letters and the ticking clock, and he knew he was running out of options. He would try this church, and he would try the courtyard one more time—that night, which might be the last opportunity before he was forced to go home to Bradenton.

First, the church. Then, the courtyard. He could hide himself behind the banyan tree at the courtyard's edge, and from there, he could watch through the archway and see for himself if anything sinister was at work.

Left, Francis had said.

Left into the packed-dirt street he went, and up onto the curb to avoid what small amount of traffic traveled it. Along the main drag there were a handful of stores and a market, where seagulls argued amongst themselves in the yards, bickering over scraps of trash and food. They fussed and flapped, but they hopped out of the way on their pale, webbed feet when Sam went striding past.

All the stores looked more or less the same. They were cracker shacks painted with light colors to deflect the sun, and some had porches wrapped with wire mosquito mesh.

At the market, a sign advertised Coca-Cola and pointed at a chest that overflowed with ice and sawdust. A puddle pooled beneath it, and sparrows took the opportunity to bathe themselves there, flipping their wings and splashing happily. A tin tub filled with water held stalks of sugarcane, submerged by a screen to keep the flies off them. Two little boys poked at the screen.

Three big carts of oranges were displayed in the shade of a striped cloth overhang. On either end were other bins. One held light green limes the size of plums, and the other was stacked with mangoes and grapefruit.

But Sam didn't see any sign of a church. He reached the end of the strip and looked left and right, finally spying a white board building offset behind the stores, toward the beach. If it weren't for the steeple, Sam would've assumed that it was just another house.

His initial impression changed only slightly as he approached. A narrow path went from the dirt avenue to the church's door, which was positioned up a few stairs onto a narrow porch.

A plain brown sign with white letters identified the spot as OUR LADY OF THE WATER and suggested that services were held on Sunday mornings and evenings, with a midweek Wednesday vespers for those who were interested.

If Sam squinted, he could make out a shape up at the top of the steeple; but it was difficult to identify. He was just concluding that it was the strangest rendering of the Virgin Mary he'd ever seen when the front door creaked open and a tall, gray-haired man emerged.

He was lean, with hands and feet that were too large for his frame. His face disagreed with his hair; he looked too young for it to have gone so thoroughly salt and peppered. He wore a short-sleeved black shirt that could've belonged to any priest or reverend, and light linen pants that fluttered around his ankles.

He stopped, doorknob in hand, and lifted an eyebrow as he studied Sam.

"Hi," Sam said. "I was— I don't mean to bother you or anything, and obviously you weren't expecting me, but Francis down at the courthouse told me about your church, and I was wondering if I could talk to you for a minute. If this is your church, I mean. I'm not trying to imply that it isn't, or that you don't belong here," he added quickly, unsure of what was making him so uneasy. "It's just . . . I'm sorry. It's been a weird few days, that's all."

"I see," the minister said. He lowered the eyebrow and closed the door behind himself without bothering to lock it. "And you are . . . ?"

"I'm sorry. I'm Samuel Lee. I'm an insurance adjuster from, well, I work with the fire company over in Bradenton. I'm here in town with Dave Brendt."

The minister nodded. "Welcome to the island, Samuel. I'm Henry, and this is our little sanctuary. I'm afraid I can offer you only a few minutes of my time at the moment, as I'm on my way to visit a parishioner, but if you'd like to walk with me, perhaps? I might be able to assist you."

Sam worked up a smile and some thanks, even though he was almost disappointed. He didn't want to talk to Henry anymore. He rather wanted to run away from Henry, but that was an irrational way to feel and he knew it, so he forced it back and waited at the bottom of the steps.

Henry joined him shortly, stepping down toe-first into the sandy yard.

"And what can I do for you this afternoon, Samuel from the fire company?" He had a way of speaking quickly while still pronouncing every letter in every word, as if he were reading aloud from an unseen page.

"Ah. Well." He fell into step beside the minister, whose long strides covered a lot of ground with effortless swiftness. "I suppose you know about the house on the west side of the island? The empty one, where—"

"The Murder House," Henry supplied.

"The Murder House? Yes, I guess that's what they'd call it. But I try to avoid that designation. I was asked to come here and examine it for Salvador Langan, a gentleman from Pennsylvania who is interested in purchasing it."

Together they reached the main road again and turned right,

away from the courthouse and away from the murder house, too. If they stuck to the edge of the unpaved strip, enough trees overhung the shoulder to keep them shaded.

"I can hardly blame you for your discretion. But I must assume that Mr. Langan is aware of the house's history, is he not?"

"Oh, he heard about the murder, sure. I don't know how many details he ever found out, and I don't think he much cares. Mostly he wanted someone to take a look and tell him if the structure is sound and the grounds are intact."

"And you were the lucky man to land the task?"

"Mr. Langan is a friendly acquaintance of the fire chief in Bradenton, and I wasn't important enough to keep close to the station. I don't fight fires or anything. I'm a pencil pusher, that's all."

"Don't sell yourself short," Henry said. "If you weren't up to the task, I doubt Langan's friend would've chosen to rely on you. Now, you said you were accompanied by someone else as well?"

"Dave. He *is* a fireman, but as far as I can tell, he's just along for the ride. I think he sees the whole trip as an excuse to go drinking on the beach—begging your pardon there, sir. Or is it reverend? I don't mean to be rude, I'm just unclear on what kind of church this is, or how I ought to address you."

"'Henry' is fine. Now, the murder house," Henry said again. "You wanted to ask me something about it."

"I did, in a roundabout way. Or maybe it's not so roundabout, I'm not sure."

"Then I'd ask that you do your best to be direct, and brief. I don't mean to cut you short, but we're nearing my destination and I'm afraid that it's a private kind of call, you understand."

"Oh yes, yes. I understand. It's just that the more directly I phrase it, the stranger it sounds. But here's the long and short of it: I think something strange is happening in the courtyard behind the house, and I think it might involve some kind of religious ceremony."

Henry didn't miss or skip a step. "Do you, now?"

"I do, yes. I know it sounds bizarre, but when I went there with Dave and we were looking around the place—"

"I thought you were only there to check for structural issues."

"Structural issues, sure. But we noticed something while we were there. And Mr. Langan *did* ask specifically about the grounds. And frankly, Mr. . . . I'm sorry, Henry. Frankly, Henry, I'm a very thorough man. Even when I'm not being somewhat preposterously overpaid for a small errand, I try to be meticulous in my assignments, so I truly feel compelled to treat this as methodically as possible."

"Admirable of you," the minister said. "And I mean that. It's good of you to go to so much trouble on your client's behalf. Though I can't help but wonder if theological investigations fall under your assignment's specifications."

"Ordinarily I'd say that they absolutely don't. But there's nothing ordinary about the murder house, almost by definition, wouldn't you say? Something terrible happened there, and now something unusual is happening in the same place. The distant buyer has a right to know what goes on at the property, if he's going to be persuaded to invest a sizable amount of money in it. Don't you think?"

"I do think, yes."

Instinctively, Sam reached for his satchel and began to fiddle with the buckle, but he stopped himself. "It's just that there are candles, fires, and . . . and blood."

"Blood? There was blood on the scene? Perhaps you don't need a minister after all; it sounds like you should contact the police."

"I tried that," he mumbled. "But they don't care, and I think there's something going on—and I think it has something to do with the statue."

"The statue?"

Sam got the distinct feeling that Henry was directing the flow of conversation while trying very, very hard not to appear interested in it. "Yes, the statue," Sam said again. "In a corner of the courtyard there's a statue of a woman. I've never seen anything like it. I think it's the centerpiece, or the altar, if you will."

And then, because the right ideas collided in his head at precisely that moment, he added, "I think they're worshipping her. It. I think they're worshipping it."

The minister dragged his expansive gait to a halt. "My goodness. That's quite an accusation there, Samuel."

"It's not an accusation, really—"

"Well, it's quite an assumption, or speculation. I'm sure things are different on the mainland, but this is a close-knit community. We all know each other, and we're all friends."

"And I'm not trying to suggest—"

"Regardless of what you're trying to do, please, for your own sake, don't wander the island asking about such things. Though your intentions are honorable, they're guaranteed to be misinterpreted. People will think you're accusing them of witchcraft, or worse, and it won't make you any friends."

"I'm not trying to make friends, exactly. I'm only trying to do my job."

Henry shook his head. "It sounds to me like your job has been done, and done well. And I'm afraid that I must leave this conversation now, for I've reached my destination." He indicated a bright white home with black shutters and an American flag hanging from the porch pole. "Mrs. Engle is a shut-in, and I'm running late for our weekly supper and—" He lowered his voice and winked. "—card game."

"Thank you," Sam told him. "And I want you to know, I appreciate your time. You're right, I mean, you're perfectly right. But if—well, could I ask you a favor?"

"Quickly, Samuel. Mrs. Engle doesn't like to be kept waiting."

"Yes, I'm sorry. Could you—if you think of anything—could you drop me a note in the post? Just so I can demonstrate that I tried every outlet, you understand."

Henry smiled and took Sam's hand to shake it. "Absolutely. If you could leave a forwarding address with Francis at the court-house, or drop it off at the church—I'd be happy to do that for you."

"Thank you," Sam said, still shaking the minister's hand. He released it and waved as the lanky man went up the walk to the bright white house, and once Henry had disappeared inside, Sam slumped again.

He stuffed his hands into his pockets and walked back in the direction of the courthouse, strolling slowly and with a sulk.

Henry hadn't seemed half so surprised as a clergyman ought to be when confronted with the prospect of dark rituals among members of his flock. Especially for a flock that was, as he'd been fast to point out, close-knit.

And isolated, Sam added as an afterthought. The ferry ride wasn't too prohibitive, but it was inconvenient enough to prevent people from taking it any more often than was strictly necessary. So there was no fast way onto the island.

And no fast way off it, either.

14

May the Circle Be Unbroken

S am was on his way back to the courthouse when he passed the turn-off that would take him back to the church. In the middle of the road he stopped. He hesitated. Could the church be considered public property? Henry had said it was an institution that took all comers. That was practically like declaring it a public place.

Wasn't it?

He could take a quick look around outside, and satisfy some of his curiosity. That much was definitely fair game—and required the breaking of no rules or laws. At worst, it could be described as a friendly case of trespassing.

Before he had time to change his mind, Sam glanced both ways to see if he was being watched, and determined that he wasn't. He turned on his heel and changed direction, away from the court-house and toward the church.

He crept, nearly tiptoeing through the sandy dirt even though he'd convinced himself he was doing nothing wrong. When he realized he was sneaking, he stood up straighter and walked with less care. It even occurred to him that he might *want* to make some noise, in case someone was inside. Inquiring at a church was one thing; slinking up to one was something else altogether.

He climbed the steps and reached for the latch.

What would he say if he found other people inside? Oh yes. He'd promised to leave a forwarding address so Henry could contact him later. It was perfectly true, after all.

He wrapped his hand around the latch and squeezed it, and the door swung inward.

It was not bright inside. It took Sam's eyes several seconds to adjust, and when they did, he was not at first sure what he was seeing.

Everything looked normal enough at a glance. The sanctuary held two rows of wood pews. Up front there was an altar, and a podium. The tall windows were narrowly designed and didn't let much light pass through, and the dimming effect was enhanced by the painted or stained touches on the glass. Between the darkly decorative vegetation and the watery blue light filtering past the windows, the room looked and felt like the bottom of a tide pool.

"Hello?" Sam called, not very loud and not very insistently. "Is there anyone here?"

No one answered, so he pushed himself all the way inside and shut the door. Once he was cut off in the semidarkness, he found the place truly oppressive. The heat was so thick and dense that it was as if he were trying to breathe through a barber's towel; and without the crack of daylight from the open door, the interior was so bleak that Sam could barely see to walk around.

He went down the aisle between the pews, checking the windows and noting that the colored glass laid out scenes of some kind. But the scenes were too abstract to make much sense. He thought he saw seashells and fish, and maybe a spindly-legged shrimp.

"What kind of church *is* this?" he asked himself, since there was no reticent minister handy to dodge the question.

The altar was a wide slab made of dark wood that had been polished until it gleamed. An inscription was carved on one side. At first glance Sam assumed it was a note from Christian communion: *Do this in remembrance of me.*

He looked closer, and saw that he was wrong. Instead of Jesus' request, the letters spelled out, REMEMBER US, AS WE REMEMBER YOU. Sam's voice was loud and scratchy in the dim, closed-up chapel. "Hello?" he tried again, but again he received no response.

Still, he did not feel alone.

A prickly, chilly sensation tickled the back of his neck. He wiped at it with the back of his hand.

On top of the altar were several bunches of decorative plants, but they were brittle and flaked into dust when Sam touched them. They were not flowers at all, but dried ocean weeds and scraps.

He picked gently at the arrangements and found mummified kelp and kale twisted with wires to keep their shape, and fitted with urchins, seahorses, and even the needle-thin bones of a small fish.

His eyes landed on an ivory-white coil strung like a necklace around the front of the podium. At first he thought it was another gruesome backbone, but when he touched the thing it was dry and clean, not made of bones at all. He peered at it hard, and used a trembling finger to lift one end to the shimmering light from the nearest window.

He'd seen such leavings before, on the beaches here and there.

If he remembered correctly, they were the remains of the creatures that live inside conch shells. Usually, they were sandy and clotted with sea detritus from having washed up onshore. This one had been bleached and stretched until the coiled shape had loosened, and then it had been given a clasp—in case anyone wanted to wear it, Sam supposed . . . though he couldn't imagine why anyone, anywhere, would ever want to do so.

He let it go, and it flopped back around the podium corner with a crackling whisper.

The sensation of being watched was almost more than Sam could stand. He breathed harder, even though the air was too hot to swallow; and he looked around for another exit. There was another door behind the baptismal font. It might lead outside.

He tripped over to it and gave the latch a tug. The door swung open and out, but not into daylight.

Sam had found an office. Rows of shelves lined the walls, each one so stacked with books that it drooped in the middle, and an expensive-looking mahogany desk was pushed up against a wall. The whole place smelled like old paper and seaweed, but at least it was brighter than the chapel. A window with ordinary glass overlooked the desk and illuminated the area, but it was closed tight and there was no ventilation.

The books were all written in other languages and Sam didn't see a single one that looked like a Bible. By that point, he wasn't surprised.

The only thing that did surprise him was how badly he wanted *out*. There was more to his desperation than the terrible overwhelming heat, and there was more to the urgency than the way the ambient dust tortured his nose. He sneezed once, twice, and almost a third time before he could stop.

Through watering eyes he pushed himself over to a second

door. A small cutout window in the door told him that yes, this was the way out; but as he got a handle on the latch, a loud noise from the chapel made him freeze with fright.

Someone had entered the chapel through the front door.

Paralyzed with indecision, Sam left his hand on the latch and fought with himself over whether to flee immediately, announce himself, or hide. His first impulse was to dash, but the door wouldn't move. He bucked himself against it, but it refused to budge.

Two voices rumbled from within the chapel, coming closer to the pulpit, to the font, and to the office door.

At a loss and running out of time, Sam hopped back behind the first door so that when it opened, he would be hidden behind it. But the door didn't open. It stayed blessedly shut while the two people on the other side carried on a conversation that drifted a few words at a time into the office.

One of the voices belonged to Henry; Sam could tell that much immediately. The other belonged to a woman. Sam might have guessed that it was Mrs. Engle, except that she didn't sound elderly or infirm. She sounded youngish and irritable, and Henry sounded annoyed and impatient as well. They weren't arguing, exactly, but they weren't agreeing very well, either.

". . . he'll be leaving soon."

"How soon?"

"Tomorrow, I think. We have to . . ."

Sam tried not to assume that they were talking about him. It didn't work. He was almost *certain* they were talking about him. He wished he could hear the conversation better, but he didn't dare press himself any closer to the door.

Then Henry's companion said, closer now—close enough that Sam could hear the word clearly. "How?" They were definitely closer. They must have walked up by the pulpit.

The woman made an exasperated sigh. "What, do you want to just beat her with a hammer?"

"I don't know; I don't know if it even matters."

"I think it probably matters. There ought to be—"

"What?" he interrupted. "We know we haven't got much time. If that paper-pushing fool gets anyone to listen to him—"

"So why not eliminate *him* from the equation?"

Sam's heart seized.

"Because for all we know, he might be missed. No one but us will notice if the girl is gone. And how long are we to wait? You've complained about how long it's taking more than once, so let's follow the situation where it takes us. Let the meddling outsider force the moment."

"But it *has* to be tonight?"

"I think it does," he said.

"All right," she finally said. "What time should I tell people?"

"Tell them eight o'clock."

"Eight? It'll barely be dark!"

"*Eight.* I'm going to need to collect a few things. Don't worry about what," he said, preemptively cutting short some implied objection. "Just get everyone there. I'll take care of the rest."

"But I *am* worried about what. Maybe I can help."

"I don't need any help. Do your job and let me do mine."

Henry said it with a finality that made Sam's ears pop, but the office door didn't open even though the chat ended. By the sounds of things, the woman went back out the front and Henry was milling around in the stifling little sanctuary, but there was no telling how long that would hold true.

Sam tiptoed back to the other door, sweating as much from the stress as from the heat. He gave it another cautious, firm squeeze . . . and it opened with a squeak that felt as loud as a gunshot.

He pulled the door open and wondered why it had stuck before, but he didn't wonder about it long. Wasting no time, he took a fast step into the afternoon sun and sprawled onto the ground. Even though the building was propped on blocks to protect against flooding, there was no back stair leading away from the office. It wasn't a long hop, but it was a surprising one if it wasn't expected, and Sam had not anticipated it.

He almost ripped the latch free as he fell. He let go just in time to keep from pulling the door down from its hinges with his body weight, and as he hit the ground with a thud, the door swung shut behind him.

Sam pulled himself together long enough to scramble up and around the corner.

When Henry opened the door, wondering what had made the noise in his office, he saw nothing outside. He closed the door again.

Too afraid to move and too astonished by his own behavior to do much more than quietly panic, Sam huddled against the building's blocked-up supports and hugged himself. He was crouched on the shady side of the church, and a pleasant breeze curled around its corners; or perhaps he was just so overheated from hiding inside the church that any motion in the air felt like heaven.

While he lurked there, trembling and gasping, he twisted his neck back and forth to watch both directions—in case someone came to investigate from around the front, or from that back door with the missing stairs.

He didn't hear anything. Not inside, and not outside.

But he did *see* something.

In the blank backyard made of patchy scrub and sandy gray dirt, patches of brown leaves and darker mulch pocked the landscape. The more Sam stared, the more it looked like they made a track from the edge of the woods to the door of the chapel . . . and then back out again.

He didn't want to call them footprints. The stride was too long to be a man's, and they didn't take the shape a boot or a shoe might leave. They were puddles of dried mud and crushed leaves. And if they made a path, or a track, or a trail, then it must be Sam's own imagination.

He brushed away the clinging dirt and picked sandspurs out of his pants, and then, while he still had the nervous energy to do so, he started to run.

15

The Promise of Peril

He could've run down to the Sandbar and grabbed Dave. He could've gone back to the island's lone hotel, packed his things, and announced that he was taking the next ferry east, back to the mainland, and away from that damned island. But in the end, Sam decided that he didn't want to talk to Dave. And he didn't want to go straight back to the hotel, because Dave was as likely to be there as anywhere else; so he'd returned to the courthouse, to his awful temporary office up in the attic.

Over and over again, he replayed the conversations in his head—analyzing and sorting, pretending that the words had all been committed to paper. It was easier to understand that way. And Henry had been right: Paper-pushing was what Sam did. It wasn't his passion, but it was his forte.

If his hands hadn't been shaking so badly, he might have written down what he remembered; but his hands were quivering and that was fine, because he remembered plenty enough to be scared, and curious, and confused.

The thing that bothered him most was not the oblique suggestion that he, personally, ought to be removed from the picture. Henry had shot that down, which was good of him, Sam thought. What bothered him now—barring immediate threat to his own well-being—was the "her" they meant to destroy.

It had to be the statue at the house—the house that Sam was supposed to watch, examine, and report upon. Of course, if Sam was right and Henry meant to go destroy objects on Salvador Langan's potential future property, then Sam had an obligation to prevent it.

He wanted to go back.

He wanted to go see it. Her.

At the bottom of the courthouse stairs there was a clock on the wall. Sam left his desk area long enough to tap down to the end of the stairs and see that it was not yet six o'clock. Henry wouldn't be back there until eight. Sam had two whole hours to figure out what to do.

He ran down the stairs just in time to pass Francis, who was going home for the afternoon. She said hello, and he said hello back, but he barely looked at her as he dashed for the door. He wasn't worried about being locked out. They'd given him a key, and besides, no one ever locked anything here—including the civic buildings. It drove Sam crazy, though on this particular occasion it would come in handy.

Out on the street the stores were closing up and people were walking home. The shadows were stretching out long, but it was still intensely hot, and everyone who had a reason to be indoors was sticking to it. Dogs skulked from shady patch to shady patch, children idly splashed themselves in the one working street pump, and even the squirrels looked wilted and slow.

Sam was the only person in sight who was in a hurry.

It was only half a mile to the deserted beach house, but by the time Sam reached it, he was panting and wishing for one of those iced Cokes he'd seen back at the market. He put his hands down on his knees and wheezed, while sweat streamed down his neck from his hair. Damp spots spread under his arms and slicked the creases of his thighs. He lifted one hand up and leaned against the courtyard wall, poking his head around the side. The square inside the rough peach wall was deserted except for some tiny green lizards and a seagull, all of which scattered when they saw Sam.

And *she* was there, too.

He crossed the courtyard, still breathing hard as he stepped between the overgrown paving stones and the broken tiles. The grass was knee-high between the fountain and the wall, and it buzzed with insects when he pushed through it.

Panting and shooing at gnats, Sam came to stand in front of the statue. He smeared his slick wet hair away from his forehead and pulled at the shirt to peel it away from his skin.

Why would anyone want to break her?

She was perfect, if perfectly strange. Curled and crouched, nearly fetal, except for that one outstretched hand, warding away . . . what? She looked so afraid.

"This is nuts," he said to himself. "I'm nuts," he clarified.

He lifted one of his legs and extended it as far as he could, drawing himself across a tangled patch of thorns and settling down as close to her as he could get.

From this nearer vantage point, he examined her: the way she was sitting, and the way she was posed. He'd been afraid that she might have been built into the wall, but this was not the case; she was a separate piece sitting on a ledge. He could move her without a chisel and hammer.

If he could lift her.

Sam wriggled one arm behind her, wedging it between her body and the wall. He wormed the other arm underneath her legs and gave a tentative shove. Then he leaned harder and gave a hearty heave. It was only after his firmest, sternest effort that she shifted a fraction of an inch.

She must've weighed hundreds of pounds.

He had no idea how he could transport her without a truck.

But there *was* a truck on the island. There was a wagon, anyway, the old fire wagon that had been stranded by the storm when the ferry wasn't sturdy enough to return it to the mainland.

He could get the wagon. He'd need help, but he could get Dave, if he had to.

Again he pulled at the stone girl and tried to calculate how much strength he'd need to transport her. "I can't do this," he concluded. "Not by myself."

He retrieved his arms from beneath and behind the statue. He hopped down off the wall and dusted his hands against his pants, then started for the archway that would lead him out into the open lot.

"Where are you going?"

Sam froze. He whirled around and looked back into the courtyard, but it was empty except for the statue. The open lot around the house was cluttered with trees—big magnolias and a pair of enormous banyans with roots that interlinked like long-fingered hands.

"Who said that?" he demanded.

"You can't leave her there."

"Who said that?" Sam was almost shrill, almost hysterical.

"If I show you, it will only upset you more."

Sam wheezed rhythmically and adjusted his glasses, trying hard to trace the voice. It must be coming from one of the trees. It originated over at the biggest banyan, a monster of a tree the size of a small house. The tall, stiltlike roots were dense and stringy. Someone could reasonably be hiding within them.

"Who are you?"

"You can't leave her there," the voice repeated. "The minister and his horrible underlings will destroy her."

Sam's eyes narrowed. He faced the speaking tree. "You know about that?"

"Of course I do. And I'm the reason you know about it, too. I wanted you to know. She needs your help."

"Why do you keep calling it 'she' like it's a person?"

A rustling noise behind the tree shifted, and settled, and crackled. "For the same reason you do in your own mind, and when no one is watching. You know as well as I do that she's inside there, fetal and fragile."

Sam was on the verge of losing his breath again, even though he was standing still.

"What . . . what *is* she?" he finally asked.

The speaker did not answer immediately. Another round of rustles and leafy twitches indicated that someone was stirring, and maybe considering what to say. "She is," the voice said slowly, "a work in progress."

"I don't get it," Sam complained.

"I am not surprised."

"Look." Sam threw his hands up. "Would you just come out here? I feel stupid talking to this goddamned tree. If you want me to do something—if you want me to move her, or help her, or save her, then you're going to have to help me out."

After a beat of silence, something brown and only barely more than shapeless stepped sideways, away from the shelter of the banyan's cluttered roots. It limped and shrugged as it walked, huge and hindered by some crippling hurt.

It was bigger than a man and rougher around the edges, flaking and shedding its borrowed skin and crunching bones. Sam's brain fought to describe it and process it.

It's not a person. It's not an animal. It's . . . something else, as if a child were asked to mold an ape out of things it found on the ground.

He tried very hard to muster some rational response to it.

So he fainted.

When he opened his eyes a few seconds later, he was face-to-face with the thing—for it was holding him up to its own eye level.

Strings of ants trooped in a spiral column down its neck, and the chewed-looking pulp of leaves, twigs, and dirt were arranged unartfully to approximate facial features. Gravel cheekbones flaked as the big thing spoke, a hole opening and closing where the mouth ought to be.

"No," it said. It shook him, and it set him back down.

Sam's knees buckled and he sat down hard on the sandy dirt.

"No?" he echoed.

"No. Pull yourself together, fool. She hasn't got much time."

It swung a small kick at Sam's leg. Sam didn't think to dodge, so it clipped him. The creature's foot crumbled, almost came apart, and then mostly held itself together.

Sam curled into a defensive position and tried to roll away.

"I tried to tell you," the creature complained. "But you insisted on seeing me, so now you've gotten your wish, you wretched little beast. I need your assistance. *She* needs your assistance. You can lie there and whimper like a dog, or you can behave like a civilized man, for whatever value such a performance might have."

Sam stopped retreating, but did not uncurl. "What are you?" he asked, the words not nearly so steady as he wanted them to be. He peeked up from over his arm, not even realizing he was roughly imitating the stone girl's pose.

The creature shrugged. "Get up," it said. "You have to help me move her. I cannot do it myself, and they'll destroy her at dusk."

Sam scrunched his eyes and shook his head. "No, we have until eight."

"I know what you heard," it argued. "But I also know what they're doing. They're running early, and so must we if we're to save her."

"What do you care if she's saved or destroyed?" Sam asked. "What is she to you?" The more he talked, the calmer he became. In an hour more, he might be merely frantic.

The creature crouched beside him, leaning down and looming over him. "Because I made her. And soon, she'll be properly born. But for the moment she's helpless, and I am not at my strongest. I cannot protect her here."

Sam sat up. He did a slow scramble backwards, trying not to appear like he was fleeing. "Wait a minute. Wait a minute. You know what I heard? How do you know what I heard?" he asked, but even as the question escaped him, he was looking at the thing's brown, rotting feet and thinking of the almost-footprints he'd seen outside the church. "You were there. You heard it, too. You locked me in there! You pushed against the door so it wouldn't open!"

"You needed to know, and he wasn't going to tell you. Now listen, time is short. We'll need a vehicle of some kind. Something mechanical and strong, to carry her away."

"You want a car?"

"I want anything that will move her."

"I don't . . . I don't have anything like that."

The creature frowned very well despite its lack of eyebrows. "You can get something like that, can't you?"

"N-no. I don't think so. And even if I *could*"—he was sitting upright and no longer retreating—"we couldn't very well get it off the island. There's a fire truck here in town, in storage behind the courthouse, but I couldn't get it any closer than the road over there. I could never drive it through this dirt. It'd bog down."

The creature's frown loosened. "So you *could* get such a vehicle. And you *could* bring it close enough for us to bring her to it."

"What? No. I mean, it's theoretically *possible,* that's all. It's not something that I can make happen just now, on a whim. And even if we got her into the truck, we couldn't get it off the island. It's too heavy for the ferry."

"Then how did it get here in the first place?"

"There used to be a bridge," Sam said, but he wasn't thinking about the bridge. In the pause that followed, he was considering how difficult it might be to actually take the truck and bring it to the edge of the house's lot. He wondered if it had gas in it, and if he could figure out how to drive it, and if he could—

"Do it, then."

"I beg your pardon?"

"Get up," the creature commanded. When Sam didn't react quickly enough, the thing reached down and lifted him, hoisting him by his underarm until he was back on his feet. "Now go get it. I'll worry about the rest."

"I just told you, I *can't.*"

"And I just told you, you *will.*"

The creature moved fast—faster than Sam would've thought something that size could move—and it seized him again by an arm and pulled him close.

Sam struggled and kicked, knocking bark, sticks, and leaves loose but doing no real damage. It was only when he was so near that he couldn't help but look that he noticed the creature wasn't breathing, and that its eyes could not possibly see. They were fashioned from the sheddings of a magnolia pod, with the bright red seeds for pupils.

The concrete knowledge of this did not prevent Sam from knowing, in the bottom of his stomach, that the thing *did* see. And it disapproved.

And despite the creature's claims that it could not move the statue by itself, Sam had his doubts. The creature was powerful enough to lift a man by one arm with no visible effort; it was strong enough to shake him back and forth like a dog worrying a stick.

"There is much at stake here," the creature said. And although its mouth twisted and moved, and pretended to have lips, the sound came from somewhere else—not within its body. "That girl, in that cocoon, I am giving her the tools to save your entire world—everything you know, and everything you love. Everywhere you've ever been, and every place you might one day go."

"I didn't realize any of that was threatened," Sam said. He tried to make it sound flippant, but failed.

"All of it, and then some. Now go get the vehicle and bring it back here. I can carry her myself, but I can't carry her far."

It dropped Sam and turned its back, and stomped back into the courtyard—leaving Sam stunned, confused, frightened, and thoroughly motivated.

He scuttled to his feet and glanced wildly around the lot. The creature was gone, but Sam could hear it. There were crunchings, scrapings, and draggings, and none of it sounded easy. Powerful though the big monster was, it wasn't moving her quickly or without effort.

One after the other, Sam straightened his legs and forced his knees to lock him into a standing position.

Could he do it? Really?

He knew where the old engine was, closed up in the storage garage behind the courthouse. He'd seen it through the window, covered with junk and dust. But it might be empty, and it might be broken. There was no way to know if it would run—or if he could successfully drive it if it *did*.

From over the courtyard wall, the creature bellowed. "Don't stand there trying to talk yourself out of it!"

But Sam was afraid of stepping so far outside the rules. He was afraid that he'd lose his job, or cause trouble, or contribute to the chaos he saw in the world around him. He was a man who'd made a mission of order and routine, and now he was being asked to break and enter, abscond with city property, and then steal something from a private citizen for whom he was supposed to be working.

"Go!" the creature bellowed.

Then again, there was a monster on the other side of the wall.

He picked himself up and broke into a run without dusting himself off. Fueled by terror, and something lighter, something stranger, Sam tore across the lot and slowed down only when his shoes sank into the sandy ruts that passed for a road at the edge of the property.

Ten minutes later he arrived at the deserted courthouse, exhausted and sweat-soaked and gasping for breath even as he felt around the side of the building to the storage garage.

The garage was unlocked.

16

Found Objects and Stolen Machines

The courthouse's garage annex was more like a big shack than a proper building, and it housed city gear like lawn shears, police tools, and—as Sam noted with only a passing glint of amusement—homemade alcohol-distilling equipment, which had no doubt been seized at Prohibition and not returned, though the law had been repealed.

Most of the room's contents were covered with a fine layer of dust, but there were indications that the place was sometimes visited. A pair of large saws had been wiped clean and had fresh flecks of wood stuck in the teeth; one of the big dust cloths that covered the truck had been recently pulled back, perhaps to retrieve the gardening supplies that were occupying the passenger's seat.

He climbed up the side and into the driver's seat, smearing himself with dust and shoving the spades, gloves, and buckets out of the passenger's side as he fumbled for the keys.

It had been an easy guess. They were right where he expected to find them: in the ignition, where they, too, were collecting dust. When they swayed under Sam's hand, they kicked up a small cloud. He wrinkled his nose and fought a sneeze. He felt around the dashboard and looked for the choke, located the gearshift, and positioned his feet on the appropriate pedals.

The big machine gagged and objected, with a gurgling metal grumble like a train being strangled. And then, once Sam stumbled upon the correct sequence of commands, kicks, lever pulls, and key turns, the great engine turned over and the slow, heavy pistons began to fire.

That's when Sam realized he had forgotten to open the double doors that secured the garage.

They swung out on giant wooden arms, but if Sam got out of the seat and tried to open them now, he was sure that the truck would die and never restart. Besides, what did it matter if he damaged a little civic property in the midst of stealing some?

He eased the clutch, jammed the gas, almost stalled the truck, and then lurched forward into the doors, which buckled outward and flopped down to the ground.

The truck rolled out over them, jumping the edges and snapping the boards with its terrible weight. It crawled into the yard, over a small tree, and around the corner of the courthouse.

Once he made it into the street, Sam began to feel pretty good about the whole thing. The road was mostly empty, and he was going at a pretty good, pretty loud clip—or so it felt. In reality, he figured that anyone capable of sustaining a steady jog could have caught up and climbed aboard, but who would bother? The truck shambled and jangled along with a momentum that felt unbeatable and a noise level that would surely prove off-putting to all but the most dedicated pursuer.

And who was there to give chase?

Even if anyone realized that Sam was stealing the truck, there was no good way to get it off the island, so where would he take it?

He took it back to the courtyard, or as close to the courtyard as he could get. The machine bounced and rolled, bumbled and re-coiled at top volume over the half-paved road. It hung up in the sandier places and resisted the thicker gravel patches, but since it wasn't carrying a load of water, it wasn't so heavy as it could be, and its own inertia pushed it forward.

The seat squeaked and strained beneath Sam with every bump.

He coaxed the truck as close to the edge of the private drive as he dared, knowing that the sand would bog it down. He let the engine idle in its low, coughing rhythm and scanned the trees for the massive creature whose commands he followed because he did not know what else to do.

"Here," the thing called, and the voice sounded terrifically close, though the monster itself was yards away—three-quarters of the way between the courtyard wall and the unpaved drive. It was car-rying the statue, but carrying it slowly, with intense strain.

"Come and help me," it suggested.

Sam wasn't sure. If he let go of the clutch, or if he released any one of the precariously balanced pedals and the truck's engine were to stop . . . could he fire it up again?

"Come *here*," the thing commanded.

"But I'm not—"

"You're better than nothing."

Sam leaped down from the truck's seat and the engine sput-tered to a halt. He was certain that he should've left it in park, or left something braked or braced, but he didn't know enough about the way the truck moved to get very technical with his operation.

He ran across the yard and met the beast in the middle, where it was half-carrying, half-dragging the unwieldy girl in her frozen pose.

"Take her leg, take her thigh. Hold her from that end."

Sam did as he was told and shuddered beneath the sudden, sharp weight of her body. His feet sank and his hands slipped, but he squeezed and clutched, and he held up his section as best he could.

"Now, *walk*."

"I'm trying," he insisted.

"Try faster. In a matter of seconds, we will no longer be alone."

"I don't understand," Sam tried to say, but the girl's weight smothered his protests.

"Later," the creature answered. "Once we're on our way."

The creature was wilting beneath the load; it was coming apart in small pieces—fragmenting and snapping with a sound like a tree limb being twisted from a trunk. Whatever the monster had used to make itself, the materials weren't strong enough to transport stone . . . at least, they weren't strong enough to move it very far.

When they reached the truck, Sam and the monster were forced to set the girl down in order to unlatch the truck's back gate. It unfastened with a clang and dropped hard on its hinges.

"Up," the creature said, grasping the girl's torso and hoisting one arm underneath her chin.

"Up," Sam agreed. He reached for her foot and seized it. With one hand under her knee and one wrapped around her ankle, he helped maneuver her onto the truck's back bed between the metal tanks and rubber-coated canvas hoses.

There wasn't much room, but there was enough to hold her and to hold the creature, too. It jammed itself into a cubby beside her and hunkered down low while Sam climbed back into the driver's seat.

"Hurry," it said again.

"I'm *working* on it."

His knees twitched as he wrestled with the keys and the levers, the knobs and the pedals. The engine resisted restarting, but Sam was determined, and he yanked the clutch in and out, forward and back.

It retched to life with a curdled hiccup and jumped forward, only to retreat. Sam punched his foot against the gas, and the truck surged again, then settled back onto its wheels.

"Shit!"

"What? What have you done?" the creature asked. It sat up and peered nervously over the tanks, at the edge of the courtyard perhaps five hundred feet away. "You *must* make this machine move."

"We're stuck," Sam explained with a whine. "The truck's too heavy, with you and the . . . and her, and the tanks. It's stuck in the sand."

"They're *coming*."

"Then get out and *push,*" Sam snapped back. "I can't help, I've got to drive. If you want this thing to move, get out and give it a shove!"

It understood enough to agree, so it abandoned the stone girl and slipped down off the back of the truck. It pushed the tailgate closed and began to thrust with its weight in fast pulses.

The truck began to rock, and Sam tried to match the monster's stride with extra gas on the upswing.

The noise was enough to wake the dead or draw a crowd, and the engine's stink as it billowed smoke and fuel made Sam's eyes water. He was glad he wasn't the one pushing, back there by the exhaust, but he hoped that the creature would really put its goddamned back into the effort, please, because over the engine's ear-popping, pounding song, even Sam could hear people coming.

The vehicle rocked back and forth on its wheels and the monster rocked back and forth on its knees, and finally, just as a black-robed man came to stand in the archway, the truck sprang up out of its rut and pitched forward.

The engine's strain lightened as the truck started to move, and the monster continued to push behind it until they reached the firmer, packed street at the edge of the block. And Sam was glad for the extra assistance, because the man in the archway had started to run—and he was not alone.

The minister had thrown back his hood and was closing in at top speed, followed by half a dozen others in various stages of covering themselves with the long, dark garments.

"Idiots," the creature complained as he gave the truck one more encouraging heave and leaped into the back.

Sam gave the truck as much gas as it could stand, and it began to pick up speed.

"What did you say?" he yelled over his shoulder.

"Faster!" it ordered, failing to answer the question, while offering a suggestion that Sam would've been thrilled to act upon.

"It won't *go* any faster!" he swore. "We're too heavy!"

The furious passenger almost took a swat at Sam's head from pure malice, but the man's objection had given it an idea. "All right," it said. "I think I can help."

Between furtive glances over his shoulder and back at the road, Sam watched the creature as it yanked at the water tanks. "Oh no *way*. You couldn't carry her by yourself, but you can throw those things around?"

"I can't . . . throw them . . . around." It shook the tank until the brass-fitted hinges that held it to the truck's bed stretched and snapped. The hinges peeled away, and the monster used all its bulk to tip the tank forward.

The tank teetered and fell, smashing down onto the tailgate

and shattering it. The gate popped off and slammed into the street, tripping the nearest pursuer—a man whose long legs gave him enough advantage to send him ahead, but no extra reflexes to dodge an incoming gate.

It cracked him across the chest and knocked him to the ground.

The creature sat down behind the tank, which rolled from left to right between the edge of the truck's bed and the supine statue, which was faceup and contorted. Every time the tank revolved toward the girl, the creature would jam its own body between them to absorb the worst of the impact. Every time the tank collided with the thing's makeshift body, it made a sound like a lead pipe hitting a dead oak.

The truck dropped heavily into a pothole and then yanked itself up and over, which rattled the tank enough that the creature could wedge one arm and leg behind it. Then the creature steadily levered the metal cylinder forward, and out the back of the truck—which had no more barrier to hold its cargo in place.

Leaving long drag-marks in the painted metal of the truck bed, the tank went over the side and into the face of an angry woman.

Sam swallowed hard and kept driving.

When the first shot rang out, he almost fell out of the truck.

"Ignore it!" the creature ordered, but Sam wasn't concerned about the creature getting shot—he was worried about getting himself shot, which was another thing entirely.

He held his head down, hunkered it tight over the big round steering wheel, and did his best to guide the truck down the half-paved, half-packed road.

"Someone is shooting at me . . . ," he whimpered quietly, but the creature heard him anyway.

"*Keep going.*"

"I *am,*" he said. And then he added to himself, *Because once the shooting starts, there's no good reason to slow down and let them catch up, now, is there?* The stakes had gone from arrest and disgrace to death, and Sam wasn't entirely sure how he'd traveled that spectrum in the span of an hour, but he didn't like it very much. And the creature could quit telling him to keep going any day now, because there was no chance in hell that Sam was going to do anything else.

All of this only raised the question of where exactly he thought he was going with this old truck and its cargo.

Behind him, Sam heard the tearing, rending squeal of metal being yanked and stripped. Encouraged by a fearsome shove from the enormous and increasingly battered-looking creature, the tank crashed to the truck's bed and rolled swiftly out the back, where it collided with another running, robed pursuer.

Sam ground the full weight of his leg down onto the gas pedal and ducked his head between his shoulders as he drove, and the truck gave a happy leap forward.

Pleased by this—since it was the first truly good sign he'd seen all afternoon—Sam lifted his head a fraction and glanced over his shoulder again.

The creature stood behind him, at almost its full height.

It leaned down and over so that its head was next to Sam's. "How far is it to the ferry?"

"The ferry," Sam repeated, feeling silly because of *course* that's where they were going. "It's—"

But before he could finish, another loud report sounded, and the creature's left eye was blown out of its head.

The thing's neck bobbed, and it lifted one hand to feel the hole the bullet had left.

"Too bad we're out of those tanks," it griped.

"Are you . . ."

While Sam tried to divide his attention fairly between the road and the huge, misshapen face that loomed a few inches to his right, he saw (more closely than he would've liked) how the creature's moldering skin rearranged itself.

It was restoring the spot, filling the gaping, bloodless wound with maggots and mulch. Within seconds, a new pupil was fashioned from the hull of an acorn, and the terrible face was no more terrible than it had been to begin with—though the eyes no longer matched.

"That's . . . that's . . ." Sam wanted to say "disgusting," but he restrained himself and returned his attention to the road. He glanced down at the mirror on the truck's side. In it, he could see that the minister was shrinking in the distance. He wasn't even bothering to shoot anymore.

"How much farther to the ferry? How long until we can get her off this island?"

"Not very far, I don't think. It's hard to tell. It's getting dark," he pointed out.

The creature looked up at the sky, a reflex or a habit left over from some unknown tic. "Yes," it agreed.

"Is that good or bad?" Sam asked.

The creature shrugged, and winked its new eye to adjust it. "Neither. It is only dark. But," it added, "I imagine that it will be good for *me*. It's better if no one sees me."

Shutters and shades were snapping up inside every home and store they passed. The rambling, rattling fire truck and its fugitive passengers were attracting attention, but that was mostly because they were peeling along the main drag at twenty-five or thirty miles an hour. In a town that still relied mostly on horses or feet for transportation, a speeding truck was a sight to behold.

It occurred to Sam that this was why the minister had put his gun away. He had followed them almost into town. Even though it was late in the day, there were still people present . . . and even though the minister was obviously not alone in his wicked plans, the entire population was not allied beside him.

Sam thanked heaven for the small blessings and kept his head low. He didn't know what else to do, other than drive.

Over the Waves

L ying on her back in the fire truck, staring up at the blacken-ing sky, Nia was deeply conflicted.

When the afternoon began, she had no idea that she was in any danger, though she'd gathered from the monster and the squirrelly little man that there was real peril, and she was being rescued. And it was easy to figure that she was being rescued from the robed people with the candles and the dead animals.

It was the most excitement she'd seen in years.

How many years? She wasn't sure. Several, at least. She could distinctly, and sometimes indistinctly, recall snaps of cold between stretches of hot—and though she no longer counted sunsets or sunrises, she would have estimated that a thousand or more had passed since . . .

. . . since that night at the Murder House.

Since she'd seen those awful eyes underwater and wondered what they meant, as she sank down to die. Since she'd frozen, and sunk, and stopped doing anything except watching and wondering and waiting to die again, in slow motion.

She couldn't see either of her rescuers. One was in the driver's seat, crouching there as if he was praying that no one would see him. The other was kneeling beside her, off to her left and out of her immediate view.

Between them, she was more likely to trust the squirrelly little man.

He was small and frenetic, with round wire glasses and a head of hair that wouldn't lie down smoothly, but he seemed like an organized and generally helpful fellow. Unfortunately, it was perfectly plain that he was even more in the dark about what was going on than *she* was.

This left the monster.

She strained inside her prison, trying to inch her vision far enough to get another look at the leafy, dirty, powerful thing with the improvised body and the voice that came from nowhere and everywhere all at once.

She couldn't see it, except for the rough curve of its upper thigh and a glimpse of its crooked elbow.

The ride was rough, but she knew it wasn't far. The ferry was less than a mile from the house, or it had been when she'd been alive— although that was a strange way of thinking about it. She tried to think back, tried to remember walking from the ferry to the cottage. There was a footman, or an employee, or something. Somebody. Someone Antonio had employed. He'd carried her things, she thought.

It hadn't been far.

Her back bounced against the metal floor. She tilted and tipped, knocking her arm against the bed's wall and clacking her knee against the creature.

The creature turned and looked down at her.

There, she could see it better. Its filthy face—not merely dirty, but made of decomposing filth—gazed down and its leafy lips cracked into a mirthless smile. It wasn't a grin of greeting or a signal of joy; it was just a U-shaped crease in an inhuman face.

Behind it, stars were blinking one by one against the sky.

Where are you taking me? she asked, knowing that it had heard her and answered before.

It answered this time, too. "Away," it told her.

Away from what?

"From the water."

"Who are you talking to?" the man asked.

The creature smiled again, and the smile looked more honest, if somewhat more sinister than its previous attempt. "Her."

The man tried to crane his neck far enough around so that he could see her, but he couldn't do that and drive at the same time. "She can talk?"

"No, but I can hear her."

"She's alive in there?" He sounded almost frantic, almost awed, horrified and hopeful at once.

"Yes. But not for long."

The man's foot slipped away from the gas pedal, and the truck seized. He put his foot back into place and pushed some more, and the truck kept going forward at its astonishing clip.

"What do you mean by 'not for long'? She's going to die in there?"

"That's not what I mean at all," the creature assured them both. "I mean, she's going to come out here. Very soon. Though we'll all be well served if she can wait until we're past the water. We need to reach the mainland, and carry her as far from the water as we can."

"But this truck is too heavy to ride the ferry. That's why it's been here all this time—the bridge washed out, and now there's nothing to take cars back and forth. Even without the tanks, I don't think it can—"

"It doesn't matter. We'll carry her. And when she emerges . . ."

Sam leaned his head toward the creature, waiting for the rest. When nothing further came, he prompted, "Yes? When she emerges?"

It lifted one hand in a funny shrug. "Then we'll see."

"You don't *know*?"

"I'm not *sure*. That's not the same thing. What's that, over there? Is that the dock?"

"That's, yeah. That's the ferry. And look, see—there's no way the truck will—"

"I told you." The creature sank down, hiding close beside Nia. "We won't take the truck, just the cargo."

"And how are you going to—?" The man didn't finish, because there wasn't time. They'd arrived, and the ferry was waiting.

Sam cut the engine and climbed down out of the seat; Nia felt the wagon sway when he left it. She felt it bob on its springy wheels as he stepped away, up to the man who moved the ferry from shore to shore.

The creature turned to her and stretched itself out so its body was flush with hers. It whispered to her, and its voice was lower than a parent's, less loving than a lover's . . . but it conveyed qualities of each.

"You've been so patient," it said. "And I've been patient, too, also without recourse. I've been alone much longer than you have. This either makes me more accustomed to the silence, or far more desperate to end it. I know not which."

What's that supposed to mean?

"Later," it said. It touched her face with one lumpy, fingerless hand and ran that same misshapen stump along her arm, down to her breasts and ribs. "Let him make the arrangements. We'll put you on the boat and hold our breaths until we reach the other side, and then, you'll have all the explanations you can stand. I'll give them to you—and to him, because we're going to need him for a little while longer."

Who is he?

"His name is Sam. Other than that, I couldn't say. He's predictable and easy to bully. He's also competent when it comes to following instructions, and he understands the ways of this world far better than do I." It patted her arm. "Once you're awake, you'll need no rescuers—no guardians, no guides."

Nia thought to herself, careful not to project, *So it knows how to lie. And I know it is lying now, because it already admitted that it does not know what will become of me when I am born.*

It did not seem to hear her, or if it did, it had no response.

Sam was returning, outpacing another man and trying to move fast enough to earn a few seconds alone at the fire truck.

He reached the truck and whispered down to the monster and its child.

"I've made up a story. I'm transporting the statue to Bradenton, like Langan wants. The ferryman's name is Mel. He'll help me load her. But you—" He hastily indicated the creature. "—I don't know what to do about you."

Rather than answer, the creature began to dissolve. In less than the length of time it takes to draw a breath, it had collapsed into a pile of dirt, twigs, and leaves. It left no shape, and no trace that it had ever moved or spoken.

Nia felt a strange pair of hands grab at her lower legs. "This thing, now. I've seen it before."

Mel was an older man, by the sounds of it. He might have been the same man who piloted the ferry the first time Nia had crossed the water, for all she knew. She tried hard to remember that trip; it felt like it'd taken place a thousand years before.

A thousand years, a thousand days. She couldn't tell the difference.

There had been a man, though. He'd been lanky and knobby, all elbows and knees, and he had a curly white puff of hair that blended seamlessly into the curly white puff of beard that covered half his face. He hadn't talked much. And maybe that was Mel.

Her suspicions were confirmed when he approached her side and leaned down over her. It was almost dark, but she could see all that white, halo and disguise rolled into one.

Sam helped to scoot her back, dragging her across the metal truck bed and catching her when she slipped over the edge. "It's from the courtyard of the . . . well, you know. The Murder House, everybody calls it. I work for the man who just bought it," he said, and Nia knew that was a lie, but it was a quick and easy lie, and she was glad that he'd thought of something so plausible.

Mel caught the parts of her that Sam failed to catch. "I heard someone was interested in it." His hands were huge, and shockingly strong for a man whose hair had gone so snowy. "What's all this trash back here, beside her?"

"It's not trash," Sam said quickly. "It's . . . soil. For a garden, I think. All these gardening supplies were in there already. I only borrowed the truck, you know how it is. Someone else will come and pick it up after we leave."

"Did you leave the keys?"

"They're in the ignition."

Mel's tight leather arms strung themselves underneath Nia like a sling. "And someone will come and get it? It can't stay here at the dock."

"Probably the reverend."

"You think?"

Sam nodded and strained to carry his portion of the stone girl. "He'll probably be waiting when you get back from dropping us off on the mainland."

Shuffling sideways step by step, the two men lugged Nia onto the ferry. She felt their feet shift when they met the small barge; she felt the water beneath her dip the flat-bottomed craft left to right. It threw off their balance, and they struggled harder to keep her from falling over the side, into the ocean again.

She couldn't decide whether to be frightened or hopeful at the thought. How much worse could it be, back in the water, under the sand? Now that she no longer needed to breathe, how much more pleasant might it be to end up buried that way?

But then she remembered the eyes, gleaming and glittering and dead—flickering under the waves like fresh bait.

And then she prayed that they would hold her steadily and true.

"You should've boxed this thing up first," Mel said.

"I thought about it, but I couldn't find a crate that would hold it. And then, when I asked Mr. Langan, he said that I should just move her loose like this."

"Her?"

"It. You know. I'm real sorry about the trouble," Sam said.

"It's no trouble."

Mel and Sam worked Nia into a semi-upright position against the hull. She looked out at them, over her hands—the one outstretched, and the one that covered her mouth. And she looked beyond them, too, because she could only see straight ahead.

Behind them, a nebulous shape with the color and scent of soil was creeping across the pier, over the gray-brown boards, and onto the ferry.

She could smell it, even though she wasn't breathing. She could hear it, even though her ears were closed. And she could see it, through eyes that shouldn't have seen a thing.

It moved, undulating snakelike and curling like smoke as it shifted its bulk to join them . . . to join her. And she heard it whisper, "Cover her. Hide her from the water's eyes."

Although Mel didn't seem to catch the instructions, Sam did— and he jumped nervously. "I should cover her up," he announced. "Let me go get a drop cloth from the truck. I'll go get that and we'll tie her down, cover her up. You can get ready to leave, and I'll get the cloth."

Nia thought that, yes, just as the frantic undercurrent in Sam's words suggested, they needed to hurry.

The creature was on board and it had oozed out of sight, but Nia could still smell the faint corpse odor that it wore, and she knew that it lingered somewhere close. And at the edge of her senses, just beyond the part of her that knew quite clearly what it was hearing, there were angry voices and there was the burning fuel stink of torches.

They're coming, she tried to say.

"I know," the creature replied, from some hidden nook that was closer than she'd suspected. "But we'll be gone in time."

Are you sure?

It didn't answer.

But she could hear Mel over at the pilothouse pushing buttons or pulling cranks, and she could hear Sam flapping a big burlap cloth away from the back of the truck, and then Sam was running back to the ferry.

"Lift the line there, fellow," Mel ordered, and Nia saw him pointing at the rope that hitched the ferry loosely to the pier.

Sam grabbed it as he hopped on board, pulling it up behind himself and pushing at the pier, as though his own slight weight could push the boat away faster.

He dropped the loop of rope down onto the deck and took his twisted bundle of tarp over to Nia. With a loud snap, he flipped the fabric open and brought it down over her, and then she could see nothing else except for the dark underside of the scratchy shroud.

Getaway and Gone

Behind her, there came a tickling, sliding press that stank of old plants rotting and becoming rich. The creature sidled up to the crook of her back and beneath her, almost cradling her.

"I can hear you," it said, shaping itself to match and hold her. "Not only when you speak, that isn't what I mean. I can hear what's inside, the way your body is changing and moving, transforming like a larva into something great and beautiful and strong.

"But," it added, "I do not love you, except in the way that a craftsman might love his tools. I do not care for you except in the way that a scientist might ponder a particularly vexing problem, and think to himself, 'I believe I've constructed an answer.' I did not create you, my small-boned thing of fauna and flesh. But I have preserved you in my own way; though not in any image of mine, and not as a companion, but as a tool. Even if I could create a new thing of my own power, I would not. I was never any god, nor parent."

What were you, then?

It leaned itself back against the side of the boat, which bobbed and skimmed slowly across the water's surface. Back on the sand, beside the pier, Nia heard footsteps pounding and the staccato press of horse's hooves, too, riding up to the water and begging for the boat's return.

But Mel could not hear them half so well, and he only waved a long, sweeping hand at them. He shouted, "I'll be back again in an hour. Wait there. I'll come back."

The creature had not answered her question. When the shouting up on the deck had finished, the earthen thing spoke again. "I was a shepherd."

Then where is your flock?

Sam came scrambling down to the canvas covering and he lifted a corner so he could see underneath. "Are you—?" he began, but when he saw the creature, he emitted a yelp.

"Hush," the creature said. "I'm here, yes. You didn't think you'd left me behind, did you?"

Sam stammered through the rest. "No, of course not. I hoped not. I mean, I don't know what to do with her, obviously." He raised the flap higher to let himself underneath with the stone girl and the monster, even though it would look strange to Mel if Mel were to see it. "But how did you get on board?"

"I have my ways," it said.

I saw you.

"She saw me." It produced that facsimile of a grassy grin again, and this time it was tinged with pride. "Soon, she'll be able to see much, much more. Like I was telling her, I can hear it—the way the time is drawing nigh." It pressed its head against her shoulder as if it were listening hard.

"You can . . . you can hear what's going on in there?"

"Yes," it said. "But I'm not listening for what she's saying; I'm listening for what she might be feeling. It's something like . . ." It searched for an example that it could borrow from the human behavior it had witnessed over the years. "It's somewhere between waiting for an egg to hatch and thumping a gourd to see if it's ripe. There's motion within her now, finally. She's almost ready."

"Well. Okay, I guess." Sam huddled down beside her, but as far away from the creature as he could get while remaining beneath the shelter of the cover. "So what does that mean—she's going to hatch?"

"It means she's quickening." Sam's face was blank, so the creature answered with easier words. "Yes, it means she's going to hatch."

Sam stared hard at the stone girl, whose features he could barely see for the shadow of the drape. "And . . . and then what?"

The creature did not lift its head from her shoulder, from the curve of her neck. For something that insisted it needed no companion, Nia thought it was an awfully clingy sort of creator.

"You don't have any idea what's going to happen, do you?"

It shook its head, rolling it in the corner where Nia's neck met her arm. "You must leave, go back out there to that man who moves this boat. It will not do for him to see you here, or to wonder where you've gone. We are pursued, remember that. When we reach the end of the water, we must move quickly."

"Right," Sam said, and he started to untangle himself from the canvas.

The creature seized one of Sam's hands, and it was an awful feeling, but Sam did not jerk away. "And there's this, too. Keep us covered. The night has eyes, and the water does, too. We must not be seen until there's shore beneath us."

Sam nodded vigorously, and, as he climbed out from under their private tent, he tucked the ends of the canvas around their edges and lashed them there with a bit of the boat's rope. He didn't tie them tightly enough to bind them, but it was enough to keep the ocean breeze from pulling too hard at the sheet.

The nearly cool air inhaled itself from around the creature and the stone girl, collapsing the thin shelter until it lay across them both so snugly that their outlines could be seen beneath it.

What kind of shepherd were you?

"What?"

You said you were a shepherd, and I don't think you were talking about sheep.

It changed the subject. "How are you feeling?"

Same as always, she replied, which was not strictly truthful.

All the while that the creature had been discussing her interior workings, Nia had wanted to argue with him. She hadn't felt any transformation within; she hadn't been aware of any shifting in her personal chemistry, for all her guide insisted upon it.

But while it was quieter, and while she was lying there sheltered by the rough sheet and held in awkward repose by a monster she could barely describe, she was forced to admit that something was . . . off.

A stray current or a hard nudge of wind shook the ferry in an idle way, and with the sudden motion she felt it—a tiny slosh. Inside.

The creature lifted its head.

"I heard that one. Oh yes. It won't be much longer now."

And then she felt another liquid twitch inside her chest. And a third, lower—down in her bowels, like the onset of some dreadful gastric distress.

There was a burning, too. It began warm and gentle, but it sharpened itself until it moved between her ribs like pinpricks of fire, one after another, and then scores of them at once. Hotter it became, until something was boiling and she couldn't get away from it; and then it was no longer boiling, it was melting—it was flowing and searing, lava and steam.

Nia tried to scream, but the creature did not budge or offer any comfort, except to say, "Let it come. Don't fight it."

But how could she not? She was being cooked, from her heart out to her fingernails—from her intestines to her eyelids.

"Stop struggling. You'll only make it harder."

How do you know? she demanded. *You keep saying that you aren't sure, and you—*

She couldn't go on. She couldn't rail at him and survive the misery both. The pain was too strong, and entirely too much.

For the first time in years, she tried to breathe. She did her best to thrash and fight, to draw in air through a mouth that did not open and through nostrils that had been closed for too long.

She wanted to stretch and shift; but she believed with all her bubbling, stewing soul that if the shell of her skin were to crack, that she would not emerge in butterfly fashion—she would spill and light the decks, spreading flame like petrol that's been sparked and splattered.

Let her die, or let her drip and trickle and leave behind the prison shell, setting the ferry on fire with the acid that was coursing—yes, she could feel it coursing now—through her veins.

Did she even have veins anymore?

She wasn't sure. But she could definitely feel a pulse and a pounding. She could certainly detect motion within, where before there had been nothing but well-shaped stone.

She strained and stretched.

And something broke.

It cracked with a small burst, and even through all the amazing, blinding pain, Nia was taken aback. Once again, she tried to breathe. She went through the mental motions of taking a big, deep, full breath . . . and there was another crack, and something split—just a fraction of an inch.

"Yes," the creature assured her. "Yes, now. Go on, but don't fight so hard. Don't tear yourself, and don't thrash too much. You must be born quietly, and—" It closed its mismatched eyes as if it were looking at something, somewhere else. "—and quickly, too. There's not half an hour before we reach the end of the water."

Help me.

"I can't."

Help me, please.

"I can't."

Help . . . "m—"

Her jaw popped, from reflex or from memory, as she tried to gasp out words.

The creature laid a flat palm across her mouth, not to smother but to hush. "Quietly," it said.

"I . . ." Her skin was stretching, swelling, and coming apart. Seams were forming and widening, tearing, and revealing something softer underneath. Where the new skin hit the air, it felt like fire, and where it touched the burlap cloth, the fabric scratched like sand in an open wound.

She tried to writhe, but the creature held her tightly. Its outer covering of leaves and mold and shredded flecks of curly moss was abrasive to Nia's fresh hide; its skin chafed against her and its strength was terrifying. Even as the creature restrained her, even as it was professedly weakened, its grip was like being pinned down by a tree.

Nia's teeth bit through their gritty covering, filling her mouth with gravel. She pushed it out with her tongue, into the creature's hand.

It took the gravel and dropped it away, then returned to covering her face. And even though it had told her it could not help, it used gentle, sharp-tipped twigs like fingernails to peel away the stone covering from her eyes, where the muscles were not strong enough to shatter the rock on their own.

She tried not to cry as the stone came away like the rind from an orange, even though it hurt worse than any scab being picked away from a scuffed knee.

She whimpered and wheezed. She tried to kick, and her left leg straightened an encouraging bit, but the right one wouldn't budge. Her right arm cracked at the elbow, then at the armpit, and for the first time in a long time, she could lower it.

Shaky and horrified, she beat her right hand up and down against the side of the boat until her fingers felt broken—but they were only free. Fragments of the shell hung between the webs and powdered themselves into dust when she squeezed them; larger strips collapsed along the veins on the back of her hand, and when she made a fist, the last of the crust on her wrist fell away.

With one hand fully clear, she was able to more easily escape the rest.

She reached for her other, frozen hand and pushed it hard, and when it broke it felt like all her bones were on the outside, breaking. It hurt like nothing she'd ever even heard of before, but any pain was worth it.

Her left thigh flexed and more stone split, revealing gray-white skin beneath. She braced her back against the creature, and against the side of the boat, and she straightened herself until she was no longer crouched and bent.

Left, then right, her ankle turned and cast away dust as it worked itself loose. Her knee made a bursting noise when the joint bowed and snapped closed, then open again.

And side by side her legs were straight, and her back was straight. Her left arm was proving difficult, but she grasped it with her right hand and wedged it against her thigh, and finally that one, too, gave way.

Her neck was still coated with a thin scab of smooth rock, and her torso was held immobile by a vest of the formidable stuff, but she took more breaths. As deep as she could inhale, as hard as she could exhale—and fine fissures compromised the remainder of the sheath.

She coughed and sprayed more flakes; pebble-like fragments fell from her nose.

The creature wiped them away, and left his hand off her mouth.

After all, she wasn't screaming. She was panting, pulling every possible bit of air into her chest and forcing it out, and then beginning the process anew—relearning how to breathe, sorting out something that once was unconscious.

"Good girl," the thing told her. It took its hand and put it on her head, where it began to pick at her hair.

All this time it had been growing there, beneath the stone helmet that coated her head and dragged down the tendrils into tentacles harder than granite. And then, because no strength of hers would move it, the creature held her close and groomed her, pulling its fingers along and around and through the compressed locks. It scraped at the seam where the shell met her forehead, and it tugged the covering back to show the tresses underneath.

They were thick with dust, and matted beyond brushing. But when the creature extracted a strand with its mold-covered palms, her compacted mane was several feet longer than last she saw it.

The creature hoisted a small corner of the tarp, and let the moonlight beam down long enough to see the way it glimmered, red-brown with flecks of gold, like a starfish.

It lowered the sheet again, and balled the excess fabric in its hand, pulling the sheet around her as it held her there in the dark, waiting for her to quit gasping.

Sam came sneaking back to the tarp. He picked up a corner and whispered out the side of his mouth, "We're almost there. But I've got to ask you, what do we do when we get there? How are we going to move her, and . . ."

And his eyes gathered enough light to show him what the tarp concealed.

Nia blinked out at him, her eyes big and bright although her face was dusted with the crumbs of her shell. She was still having trouble breathing, but she was learning fast, sucking at the air like a newborn baby snuffling after a nipple.

"As you can see," the creature said. "We won't have to move her anymore."

"C-cl-clothes," Nia said, her eyes never leaving Sam's face. And even though her voice was thin and cracking, she managed to put an order into the broken word. "Clothes," she said again, more clearly.

She folded her arms across her breasts and drew her legs together, folding them beneath herself.

"Okay." Sam nodded. "Okay," he said. He released the edge of the fabric, then picked it up again for one more look before dropping it and running.

Nia and the creature heard Sam's pattering footsteps hunting around on the deck, stumbling from edge to edge in search of a suitable garment—or any garment. As long as he had a task, he was all right. The man needed nothing except instructions.

"Y-you . . . never . . ."

"I never what?" the creature asked.

Nia fought with her own throat, and wrestled with her own lips. "Whuh-what kind . . . of shepherd."

It shook its head. "That's not important."

"It must be," she said, and it was her first full sentence. "Or el-else . . . you would've told . . . me . . . by now."

"But it's *not* important; it's only interesting, and that's not the same thing. Right now, we must confine ourselves to that which is relevant to our circumstances—which is to say, things that will continue to keep you alive."

"What . . . about . . . you?"

"Me?" it said with a touch of surprise. "I'm not altogether certain that I'm capable of dying. Or, if I am," it added, "then there's precious little that you or I could do against such a force that could harm me."

"What . . . about . . . *him*?" she asked, nodding her head toward the deck.

"Him? Don't let yourself become too fond of him. He's been useful thus far and we'll keep him around as long as we can. But let me be direct: He is not a priority."

Nia didn't like the sound of that. She also didn't like the sound of Sam's slapping feet, searching prow to stern across the ferry for something that would cover her. And perhaps it had been a strange thing to ask of him, but even given the change, and the time, and the astounding set of events that had led her to the rickety wooden craft, she couldn't pretend that it didn't matter.

Likewise, she couldn't pretend that she was clean yet.

The shell's residue was worst around her body's natural creases, under her arms, behind her knees, and between her legs.

She wanted nothing more than an hour of privacy with a bathtub, but she imagined that no such luxury would be forthcoming.

Sam skidded to a stop beside the tarp tent and shoved a wad of clothes underneath. He didn't pick up the fabric to see how his offering had been received; instead, he offered his apologies through the barrier.

"That's all I could find. I'm really sorry, it's not much and it's old and it's dirty."

"Better than nothing," she replied. And then, because she hadn't meant to sound short or ungrateful, she said, "Thank you."

"Better," the creature told her.

"What?"

"You're speaking better already. I think you're going to be all right."

Nia unrolled the clothes and found a man's linen shirt with long sleeves, a pair of pants that were almost as long as she was tall, and a scarf for her hair. The shirt had once been white, but even in the dark Nia could see that it was browned around the seams. It smelled old, and dusty, but clean.

She pulled it on over her head because it was big enough that she didn't need to unbutton it. The pants she kicked aside, for they were more trouble than they'd be worth. The shirt hung almost to her knees, anyway.

Taking the sleeves one at a time, she rolled them up above her elbows.

A few minutes of fumbling and a triumphant grunt later, and Nia was as dressed as she was going to get. She wished for shoes, but, as her mother used to say, "If wishes were horses, then beggars would ride."

Nia would walk, and she'd do it barefoot if she had to.

When she was finished, she pulled her body away from the creature's—and, since it did not appear to take offense, she brushed bits of its composting flesh off the shirt.

They were still sitting together, under the covering of the canvas sheet, and there wasn't much room to maneuver. Sam was perched on the rail beside them, or so Nia thought from the tell-tale whisks of his shoes against the boards.

The timbre of the waves was changing, becoming shallower or faster, indicating in some understated way that the water was less deep and that the end of the trip was near.

"What are we going to do?" Nia asked slowly, but loudly enough for both Sam and the creature to hear her.

Sam made a little noise like he wasn't sure, or maybe he was shrugging. "I've already paid for the trip, so hypothetically, we can make a run for it as soon as the ferry is tied up. I mean, I don't even know how—" He searched for a pronoun to indicate the creature and decided on the masculine. "I don't know how *he* got on board in the first place."

"I'll find my own way," it promised. "You two, get to shore any way you like. She's strong enough to run, or jump. If you're fast enough to keep up with her, then I suggest you do so."

"How fast can she go?"

"Much faster than you, but she doesn't know that yet. I'll have much to teach and tell once we're away from the water."

Nia pushed out one of her feet, not kicking exactly, but getting the creature's attention. "You keep saying that. Away from the water."

"Of course I keep saying that. Don't you remember what you met the last time you went into the waves?"

"I remember," she said, which was more true than not. But she didn't remember perfectly, and much of what she did recall, she couldn't understand.

"The sun had set and the water was black, like it is now. I do not think that the water witch knows your whereabouts, but my suspicion is no guarantee. And back there, on the other shore"—it waved its enormous hand—"an ignorant flock of sheep stands upon the pier, crying out to her."

Sam wrinkled his face into a frown. "To the—what did you call it?"

"The water witch. She has a name, but I won't be accused of calling her, not when there's an excellent chance she might hear me. And if those fools back there think that she'll grant any peace or prayer they offer, they have much to learn about the way the universe works."

"Or the way you work?" Nia asked.

"Hush, now. I'm leaving."

Sam heard that part and it frightened him. "What?"

"We've arrived, and I cannot risk a leap across the water. If even a speck of mildew should fall, then she will know I've passed this way. The less she knows of our escape, the better."

"Someone knows we're escaping?" Sam risked lifting the tarp, and seeing that Nia was clothed, he didn't put it back down. "Someone other than those guys?" He jerked his head toward the distant shore.

The creature thought about it for a moment. "If she doesn't know yet, she'll learn soon enough. Those damn fools have accidentally called her correctly this time."

"What?" Nia pushed the canvas up over her head, giving herself more room to breathe.

The creature made an impatient little sound and then reached for Sam's shirt. It pulled Sam under the fabric and held the man's face close to its own so it could speak quietly. "They've been trying to summon the water witch, because they are damnably stupid, and they do not know what she'll do to them when she answers."

"Trying?" Sam stammered.

"Trial and error, thus far entirely error—which is why they survive to chase us now. But they've done something right this time, and the call has sounded. It's a pitiful squeak of a summons, barely more than a cough, but she is bound to answer it. She'll go to them, and they know about us, so we need to be as far away from them as possible. Do I make myself understood?"

Sam nodded. "Understood," he repeated.

It released him and tossed him backwards, out of the sheltering tent and into the open air.

The ferry bumped itself gently against the dock, and somewhere up above, Mel was slinging a rope to secure it.

The creature stood to its full height, and the tarp ballooned around it until the covering flew free and fell away.

Nia rose to her feet. She was not shaky anymore, and she could breathe without struggling. Her hair hung in heavy, brittle tentacles that swung down to her thighs. She was covered in dust, black flecks of earth, and peeling strips of the lingering stone shell. But she was standing.

She stretched and flexed, rocking on the balls of her feet to test her legs.

"Now," the creature whispered fiercely. *"Go."*

It crumpled to the deck, dissolving into a pile of mulch and broken twigs.

Nia grabbed Sam by the hand, and with a leap that surprised no one more than herself—she bounded off the ferry and crashed down onto the dock.

19

What You Pray For

And all the while, for all its stuttering incompleteness, the call was sounding.

And all the while, in the distance below the black waters, something was struggling against the summons. Something huge and angry was preparing to respond even as she was pulled up to the pier where the little ferry docked itself day in and day out.

She was coming because she was furious and possibly frightened, because she had been brought to the surface twice in as many nights. Prior to those events, no one had been ignorant enough or stupid enough to attempt a call in a thousand years, and now she was at the beck and call of the tiny and corrupt.

It did not matter that the success was all but accidental. It did not matter that the call was only partial and imperfect.

It mattered that there was a call. It mattered that someone or something believed it ought to have control over her. Arahab did not agree.

So despite the fragile and fractured nature of the song, the old thing with a thousand names gathered her strength—and there was much of it to gather—and she pulled herself into the Gulf of Mexico again, and across it. She followed the melody's little lasso and let it lead her, for it was too feeble to force her.

Her fear was this: that someone was experimenting, and learning.

A fragment of a song that had first been sung when the sky was divided from the water was not enough to compel her. But the whole song, and assisted by a focusing object, and cast into the brine with *intent* . . . that was something else altogether.

If someone knew a part, then the whole could yet be gleaned. If someone knew even the basest germ of the facts, then the rest could be grown as if from a seed.

Unless she put a stop to it.

It was much better to cut it off now, while the will of the practitioners was weak and imprecise.

As she closed in upon them, she used the eyes she could gather— a snoozing pelican that awoke with a start, a jumping fish that slapped itself against the surface. She borrowed the sharp face of the nearest dolphin and bade it rise enough to spy.

Two people. No, three. One was a woman.

And the alpha of them, a man with a candle that burned a flame as short as a fingernail, knelt on the wooden slats in his semicircle of borrowed power and chanted wordlessly. He murmured the shape of the notes and they fluttered around him.

"Something's happening," Mrs. Engle said, more to herself than to either of her companions. "I don't like this," she added, even though there was something inside her that very much *did* like it— all of it, the uncertainty and the power both.

The water was shimmering, quicksilver on ink; and the warm air around them was buzzing with a sound more frightful than mosquitoes. Out in the Gulf, a big bird flapped itself skyward as if it had suddenly awakened, and a dolphin jerked its slick body nose-down into the surf.

"What's that?" Roy asked, and he might have been referring to any of it.

"We're being watched," Mrs. Engle said.

Henry ignored her, concentrating hard on the small sliver of power he'd found. He handled the short stanzas with caution, with care, and with increasing confidence. All the power was congealing around him, ramping up a notch with every repetition of the odd, old tune.

Mrs. Engle watched as the Gulf began to swirl. "Henry? Henry, I think you should stop."

Henry took a split second from his humming to blurt, "Shut up," and then continued. With every note the vortex spun harder, bigger, and faster.

The pier's pilings began to creak under the strain; the worst they usually faced was the steady pull of the daily tides and a very occasional storm, but the force of the sucking eddy made them bow and buck.

The candle fell over. Henry had already figured out that he didn't need it, so he let it go over the side and didn't even watch it fall. His voice was doing all the work by then. His pursed lips vibrated with the song that moved the waters and called up the old mistress.

He remembered the distorted trinket with a shape like a

dancer. He held it aloft, and behind him he heard Mrs. Engle say-ing, "No, don't. I don't think—" But when the spiral had hit what felt like a peak, and the air had become so windy that he could scarcely keep his eyes open against it . . . he threw the warped lump of metal as hard as he could.

It hit the water with an inaudible plop, the sound of its sinking lost in the miniature maelstrom.

And as soon as it passed the surface, dipping beneath the water and dropping in a back-and-forth, leaflike fall, the hastily con-jured storm stopped.

Altogether.

The sky went still, and the water was smoother than glass.

Nothing moved, and no one spoke. No fish slapped the water and no night birds called; no frogs croaked, and no sand-stranded crustaceans clicked themselves together.

Arahab rose up from the water with her hand held aloft and her fist clenched around the metal glob.

She did it so slowly and with such great control that the air didn't stir, and not even the water from which she spawned herself rippled. Although she could have made herself huge, she chose not to; she made her body the size of an ordinary woman's—about the size of her young pet-daughter, Bernice.

Out in the water she lingered, close but not too close.

Henry's mouth was moving manically, humming the song as though he were afraid to let the tune end, because then the woman in the water might leave.

"I am here," she said. "I have answered your call, and if you like, you can speak."

She said it soft and low, but Mrs. Engle heard power and ten-sion flowing underneath the words. Henry and his assistant, Roy, stood transfixed. But Mrs. Engle shifted her feet nervously. She, too, was awed and amazed, but she was also more aware.

Maybe it was only that she stood farther away from the song and from the specter in the water, or maybe there was more to it—or less. But the water woman's shape, with her seaweed hair and her blue-black skin shining under the stars . . . it unnerved her more completely than it overwhelmed her.

Mrs. Engle had seen things herself, before. In another place, and under different circumstances, with different spiritual leaders, she had been witness to ghosts and even a demon once.

But this was different. This was something at once purely alien and purely familiar. And, almost certainly, more purely dangerous.

Mrs. Engle raised one foot and moved it over half a step. When no one took notice of her, she took a whole step off to the side. Her shoulders clung to the tree and the shadows behind her because every primitive synapse in her body was telling her to *hide*.

If Henry and Roy had similar instincts, they did not act upon them.

"Children," Arahab addressed the men. She did not look at Mrs. Engle, who was busily hoping that she had gone unnoticed.

"Mm-mistress," Henry responded. He wasn't sure what title she would prefer, and he didn't want to say the wrong thing, but he couldn't stop himself from speaking once the humming had ended and she'd commanded his mouth to engage.

"Mistress?" she tossed the word back to him with a question lifting the final consonants.

"Queen." Henry grabbed Roy by the back of his knee and pulled the younger man down to a kneeling position. Roy toppled, but caught himself on his hands—a position that was prostrate enough to count as penitent, even if it had been coerced.

Henry bowed his head and tried to look at her, peering up through his hair and into the water. "What would you have us call you? We are your servants, and we wish only to worship and serve."

"What would you call me?" The woman in the water blinked

her pupil-less silver-green eyes and cocked her head in a thoughtful gesture as she considered which appellation she preferred.

"Anything," Roy added. "Your Highness."

Henry growled a hush. It rumbled out the side of his mouth
and Roy heard it, and obeyed.

"My names are as numerous as the waves. From whence do you
hail?"

Henry wasn't sure what she meant, and he wanted to ask her to
be more specific, but he could barely breathe, much less form an
intelligent question. "From . . . from whence . . . ?"

"In colder seas I am called Merrow, or Manta, Ben-Varrey or
Dinny-Mara, or Imap Umassoursa. In warmer places, and in the
waters along the center of the world, I have other names. I am
Ccoa, the cat spirit of the storms, Igpupiara, Yagim, and Huito—
Mistress of All the Waters. Would you choose a name, or offer me
one of your own?"

"Have you a preference?" Henry asked, tipping his eyes to
meet her empty ones and shuddering, but holding the gaze.

"These years, I am sometimes called Mother."

"Mother." Roy nodded, as if it were perfect.

"Mother," Henry agreed, because it was a fond word that easily
moved the tongue.

"But I am not often called," she said once their reverence was
assured and confirmed.

Again Mrs. Engle felt that shock of panic zipping along her
spine and up her neck. This was no phantom or farce. This was
no impossible complaint from a vengeful demon. This was a
goddess, and she wanted something very specific that she'd not
yet revealed.

And this was what alarmed her. "Mother" was fishing for something, and she was doing it the way a wife does when she interro-
gates a husband, knowing that she's going to learn something she

doesn't like. It was a startlingly human approach to interacting with humans.

"I want to ask you a question," Mother said. She was being careful to enunciate every letter in every word, and even the spaces between them.

"Anything," Henry assured her. "Anything at all. How can we be of service to you?"

She held out her hand, and held up the lump of misshapen metal. "This trinket you found—it is something I cast aside not so very long ago. Its usefulness has expired, though it retains the scent of power. Why would you cast it back again?"

"I—," Roy began, but Henry kicked him.

"Shut up, you don't even know what it is," he mumbled. And then, to Arahab he said, "I used it, that is, I cast it only because I thought it might work. Together with the song."

"There was a song?" she asked, with a tone that aimed for idle curiosity.

"Yes, yes. There was a song, just a little bit of one that I heard somewhere. I thought that it might please you. I thought that you might indulge us with an audience, if I were to sing it precisely right."

"There are many old songs I know, but I heard nothing of yours," she said.

"Oh," Henry said. He believed her, because he wanted to.

"It's this toy that interests me more," she said. "Where did you get it? And why would you think it might work?"

"Well, why wouldn't it?" He dodged the question. "I mean, it *did* work, didn't it?"

"On the contrary." Arahab swam without appearing to move a muscle. She glided and the water parted around her, and then she was mere feet in front of Henry and Roy. She stared up at them, not bothering to enlarge herself or intimidate them with her size.

"The . . . the contrary?"

"It did not work. I came not because I was compelled, but because it was my decision to investigate. I came because I wished to know what mortals believed that could wield such authority over me, to attempt a binding such as this."

Henry sat up from his knees and leaned back until he was sitting, his legs in front of himself as if he were prepared to scurry backwards . . . though such a course would only have sent him back off the pier and into the water.

"A binding?" he squeaked. "No, no, Mother. We only meant a summons—or, that is, a request. A polite and most decidedly servile request, I swear to you on the lives of all I hold dear. Please, I would ask that you not misunderstand our intent. We only meant an invitation; we would never be so arrogant as to attempt to bring you here by force. Is that . . . is that what . . ." He pointed at her hand, which still held the lump.

She looked down at it and closed her fingers around it. "It once was, yes. It was fashioned by a man, across an ocean, and it signified nothing in his hands alone. But something somewhere infused it with more power than either of you have ever possessed. More power than either of you have ever even heard of—it would take much, *much* more to bring me here against my will. And once it's spent—" She shrugged her arms in another peculiarly human gesture. "—it is spent. It is worthless."

"But . . . you *came*," Henry insisted. "You remembered us, as we prayed."

"Yes, I came. And yes, I remembered you, as you prayed. But I do not want you, and now that I know you are here, I cannot stand it."

"What?" Roy said it first.

"What?" Henry echoed, half a beat behind him.

Arahab let herself stretch, finally. She grew in size until she blocked out the moon and covered the pier with her terrible shadow, twice as dark as the night around them.

"Tell me how you came by the toy. I threw it down not a day ago, and now you throw it back at me again. Where did it come from, and why did you know what to do with it?"

"I found it," he said, but no one within hearing distance believed him.

"You found it, and you found the song, and you combined these things in a feeble attempt to bind me, and this came together by accident? By no design at all?"

"None, Mother. None."

"You don't even know how you did it, do you?"

"No," Henry swore.

"No," Roy added, even though it was clear that he was not being addressed.

"I just." Henry shook his head, trying to clear it or reset something that had gone completely off course. "I don't understand. We only wish to serve you."

"That has never been the case," she said, and by then she was looking down at the pier from a preposterous height. "No mortal has ever offered service without petitioning prayers and repeated requests. What would be the point, since you are all bound to die, regardless?"

"But—"

"I choose my disciples; they do not choose me. All this time and all these years you have prayed to be remembered—but if you'd had any wits about you, you'd have long ago hidden yourselves; and if you knew of me at all, you would pray that I never heard any cries of yours."

When she spoke, the night shook and the water seized itself, clutching at her unseen bottom half. There was only darkness below her, for her body cast such a thick shadow that nothing escaped. Only her pale uniform eyes—unbroken by irises, untainted by any shade—glared down from the sky.

"All these years," Henry said. He could barely utter the rest. "You knew . . . we were here?"

She leaned down low, until her face hovered hugely above and close to him.

"I knew, but I had forgotten. You are insignificant in the greater plan, and too powerless and proud to earn anything apart from my wrath."

"But—"

Henry had never imagined that his last word would be a mere three letters long. Before he could utter anything further, Arahab raised a hand so fast that no one saw it, least of all Henry. The world was dark, anyway. The night had no stars and no moon, only two gleaming eyes set against the heavens.

Her hand came down and it was only water, but it was all water: thousands of gallons, brought down faster than gravity and with the force of a hundred hurricanes. The hand slapped itself through Henry and through the planks of the pier, where it dissolved and reformed beneath.

It had been fast. It had been less than a flick of her wrist.

And there was no trace that Henry had ever existed, except for a few mangled bits of bone and gristle wedged between the boards, which had not even been fractured by the assault. There was no reason they would be damaged. Arahab had no quarrel with the quiet little dock, only the man who'd knelt upon it.

Roy she'd killed by accident. It was not a perfect accident, because she'd wished him gone; but his demise had required no additional effort on her part, and he was forgotten as soon as he was missing.

Mrs. Engle had backed herself well into the trees, and her hand was covering her mouth. Through the trunks and above them, at times, she could see the immense shape of the water woman; she could hear the anger in the goddess's voice, and she noted how little trouble it was for Mother to erase Henry and Roy.

It had been like watching a horse's tail flip at a fly.

It had been perfect, and deliberate, and facile.

The shape in the water shrank again, sinking back to a more manageable size, then disappearing completely into the water.

So Henry and Roy were dead. What good would it do to confirm it, or to search for evidence of what had taken place? Why would she creep so close to the edge of disaster?

Her curiosity was not so demanding as that. It might kill cats by the score, but it would not kill a woman who knew better than to climb down within the reach of an aggravated elemental. It would be safer by far to run in the other direction and hope for the best.

As she ran back toward town, dodging trees and ducking away from the low-hanging locks of moss, Mrs. Engle wondered what the desert was like.

She'd never seen a proper one, baked brown and dry. There were places she knew where the sky almost never opened, where the ground was so parched that it held nothing green or alive, and certainly nothing that could swim.

She was focused on her flight even as her mind wandered to thoughts of a more permanent escape. Night still hung heavy over the woods, but once she made it to the road, it was easy to see the white gravel and dirt that passed for paving.

She saw, but she did not have time to register, the shark-gray skin and slime-shined teeth of a creature that was woman-shaped, but no woman at all. She noticed the clawed hands and the stretch-mouthed monster with the wet blond curls, but there was no time to react or resist.

Bernice seized Mrs. Engle and with a lightning twist and a tearing bite, she broke the fugitive's neck and tore out the best-bleeding veins.

Mrs. Engle was dead before her eyes had finished blinking. She was gone before her fists had time to uncurl.

Bernice dropped her body and left it where it fell, between the road and the trees. She didn't care if it was found. She didn't care if it was investigated. The fleeing woman was just a loose end in a bigger story, one that needed to be closed for form's sake and for Bernice's own safety.

There had been a moment of nervousness. There had been a minute of fright when the wretched minister had gazed into Mother's face and tried to lie.

Bernice had done her best to coach him and teach him what little she'd learned, but she should've known that the man's mind couldn't withstand the very meeting that he'd sought to bring about.

Still, it had worked out well.

The minister had lied. Mother had lied. Everyone was lying, and Bernice was gleaning information even from all the half-told truths and full-blown falsehoods.

Arahab had been right: Everyone wants something, and it's always more than it first appears.

20

Beginner's Luck

Nia hit the ground running, and dragging Sam—who wasn't nearly so fast or coordinated as she was.

She had no idea how strong she was until she realized that Sam was yelping with every step; and then she saw that the wrist she was holding belonged to a man who had long since lost control of his feet.

But since she was nearly to the tree line, and since she could hear something awful happening in the water behind her, she did not stop to let him pull himself together. It might have been more graceful to carry him, but picking him up would have required her to pause.

And the more Nia heard behind her, back across the water and over at the other shore, the less she wanted to stop. It buzzed in the back of her head, radio static transmitting bits and pieces of a calamity she'd narrowly escaped.

She didn't know where the leaf creature was, exactly, but she had a pretty good idea. Alongside the radio static and stuffed into some back-brain compartment, she could hear it, or feel it, or sense it with some other sensory word that she'd never needed before.

Once, when she was a child, she'd had an uncle explain to her the way homing pigeons worked. He said it was like they had a little string in their heads, and the string was planted in the ground at their home roost—and no matter how far they flew, no matter where they went or what happened to them, the string always tugged them back home.

She imagined that the bird's string felt something like her vague but definite connection to the creature. It hadn't been there before, had it? Before she could move? Or was it only that she couldn't remember it?

Sam jangled and banged along behind her, his wrist bruising and his knees breaking themselves against the ground.

"Wait!" he gasped, but Nia wasn't interested in waiting.

She wasn't sure where she was going, but "away from the water" had sounded like a very good instruction and she intended to follow it.

She couldn't help it. She was driven by blind panic and pure exhilaration. And yes, there in the background—almost overwhelming her awareness of the creature—there was that incessant, atrocious humming.

Back by the shore, something big was swooping under the water and through it—faster than anything finned or feathered. Whatever it was, it was alive and it was impossibly large.

"Run," she said to Sam.

"I'm trying," he said, but he could barely get his feet up under himself in time to trip over them again. "Let go, and I'll follow you."

"No." They were almost to the trees, and the thing at the edge of the other shore was gathering itself.

As Sam bounced along behind her, he tried to object, but he couldn't find the words; so he argued instead. "But why would we be safer in the woods?"

"Don't know," she said. "Faster," she said, and it wasn't a command so much as it was warning that she intended to speed up and she was taking him with her.

"But we'll lose . . . that . . . that guy. That thing."

"That thing knows what's it's doing."

She didn't know how far she needed to go, but she wasn't taking any chances. She didn't know where she was precisely, but she could guess that this was the mainland and that she could head quite a ways east without hitting another ocean, so east was where she went.

Between the trees she dived and weaved, no longer hearing the confused cries of the ferryman behind her and no longer striving to listen to whatever chaos was unleashing itself across the water, back on the island. It didn't matter. Nothing could make her move faster with Sam in tow, and nothing could persuade her to release him. He was the first person she'd met in her present condition, and she would bring him with her wherever she went. To whatever end. However far.

A particularly loud yelp from Sam made her look back long enough to see that he was battered and now bleeding.

She slowed her frantic run to a nervous jog, and then to a stop. When she released his hand, there were bruises where her fingers had pulled him. There were holes in the knees of his pants, and scrapes around his elbows and knuckles. His glasses were hanging by one ear-hook, their lenses dangling under his chin.

He picked them up and plucked them off his ear; wiped them on a corner of his shirt and put them back on.

"I'm sorry," she told him. And she looked him up and down, wondering what he was made of.

"It's . . ." He wanted to say that he understood, and that he didn't take it personally, the way she'd hauled him through the forest without concern for his well-being or comfort. He *did* understand. But he was too wobbly and beaten from their flight to communicate more than a nod. "It's . . ."

"Who are you?"

He panted and leaned forward, hands on his dirty, scuffed knees. "Sam," he rasped.

"Sam. I'm Nia."

"Mia?" he peeped.

"Nia. It's short for something longer. You're bleeding."

He nodded. "Bleeding."

"Did you break anything?" she asked, though the question should have been, *Did I break anything of yours?*

"Don't think so."

"Good. I don't know if we're far enough inland or not, but my money's on not. Whatever that was, it was—"

"What? Whatever what was?" His breath was catching up, but every word sounded thirsty.

"There was something else, after we left. The creature tried to tell us before we got off the ferry. It was talking about a 'she,' and I think I saw her. I heard her," she said, even though that wasn't the right word either for the pressing feeling in the back of her brain.

And then they heard a remarkable crash, an infinite weight of water being smashed down against something soft.

Both of them froze.

Nia could hear the final trickling splashes as the last of the liquid drained, spilling between the boards of the pier and washing away all evidence of something brutal. She doubted that Sam could hear it.

Sam was anxious—even more anxious than Nia was. "Maybe we should wait for it. For him. For . . . for whatever, you know. That guy."

"I don't think we need to."

"Why?"

"I think he's anywhere he wants to be."

"Then where should we go? We did what he said, right?" Sam looked around, but it was dark and there wasn't much to see. He'd been hauled unceremoniously thus far and he hadn't had a chance to scope the scenery. "We got away from the water."

"Not far enough," Nia said. She turned away on her bare heels and started to walk farther into the darkness. "Even if we don't run, we should keep going. I'll go slow if you need to rest."

"But I don't think you need me, exactly. Why do I have to stay with you? Maybe you should just, um, drop me off at the . . . at the nearest . . . at wherever there are people," he finished weakly. "That guy, that thing—he only wanted me to help him move you. And now you don't . . . you don't need any help." He rubbed at the darkening skin on his wrist.

"Why do you think that?" she asked without turning around to see that he was coming.

He was coming. "Because, I think, he told me. Or if he didn't, he certainly gave me that impression. Look, ma'am—"

"Nia. I told you."

"Nia. Look, Nia. I don't know what's going on here—"

"Neither do I."

"And I don't know what you are or anything—"

"Again, that makes the pair of us."

He faltered, and rallied. "But I'm pretty sure that it's very different from, uh, my areas of expertise. That thing, he just needed someone who could drive a truck. I don't think—" He tripped over a long-reaching root and scampered to walk closer behind Nia, who could see better in the dark than he could. "I don't think I need to be *involved*."

"You're already involved. But for all I know, you're right, and I can drop you off at the nearest town. We can't be far from St. Petersburg, can we?" She hesitated and spun in a circle, trying to get her bearings.

"Uh, no. Not far, I don't think. We're closer to Bradenton, though. I think. Then again, you know what? I've never tried to walk it in the dark before. You've got me completely turned around." And then a miserable thought popped out of his mouth. "You didn't get us lost, did you? Oh God. We're lost."

"We're not lost," she murmured.

Her uncle's homing pigeons were crawling to the front of her mind again. She closed her eyes and concentrated, trying to navigate the unfamiliar fields, threads, and currents running around behind her forehead. She could feel a tug inside the earth; it was deep and integral, and flowing in lines, or waves. If Sam had asked, she couldn't have described the sensation, but she didn't have to describe it to grasp what it was. She was feeling the poles, and the earth's magnets that ran between them.

North gently yanked, and South tugged more gently still.

"Then where are we?"

"We're in the woods," she answered. "And we're east of the Gulf. We're going to go farther east, because that will take us farther from the water, just like he told us we ought to be."

"You're just going to obey? Just like that?" asked Sam, who was tagging along behind Nia like a puppy off its leash.

"Do you have any better ideas?"

He was quiet for a few steps as he picked along. "Don't you think, well . . . I guess you couldn't. Or anyway, you *wouldn't*."

"Wouldn't what?"

"Wouldn't go to the authorities. Find the police. Report what's happened here. Those people back there, they were going to kill us. They had a gun, or one of them did. And I know, I know, there's a lot we'd need to leave out, but I'm all right with that. I don't mind passing along a bare-bones version of events. I can leave out the big dirt-monster and the . . . and the . . . and you. Ma'am, there are people chasing us, and there are things chasing us, too—and if we can get even just the people off our case, I'd feel like that'd be great."

She didn't answer immediately. She was remembering what the creature had said about foolish people who get what they ask for. "The people have been the least of our problems."

"Oh. Oh really? Then, then why—" He stumbled over a rough tangle of palmetto roots and a small stump. "Then why was it so amazingly important that those guys back there didn't break you up with a hammer?"

"I don't know. There's a lot I don't know. Maybe it was just important that they didn't try it. We can ask our guide when he finds us again."

"What if he doesn't? And where are we going?"

"He won't leave us for long." She put her hand on the side of a tree and used it to push herself forward.

Sam tried to copy her, and succeeded only in scraping his hand. "Why not?"

"Because he's gone to a lot of trouble. He won't abandon us now." Or he wouldn't abandon *her*, at any rate. She felt uncommonly confident on this point—that even despite its repeated statements to the contrary, it had preserved her in part to keep from being alone.

"So where is it? He, I mean. Where is he?"

She twisted her shoulders in a shrug. "If I were him, I'd want to see what's going on back there. He probably stayed to watch and make sure."

"Make sure of what?"

"That we got away clean. He said that something was coming. He wanted to see that it didn't come after *us*."

"Selfless," Sam muttered.

"I don't think so," she answered, even though it hadn't been a question and Sam had said it only to himself. "Wait. I smell something."

"You . . . you *smell* something?"

"A campsite or something. Don't you smell it?"

"No."

"Well, *I* do. Stay close and follow me," she said.

They crept up through the trees and found a semicircle of cabins. Nia sat Sam down at the foot of a wide palmetto patch and told him to stay there while she looked around. She didn't hear anything, and she didn't see any signs of recent habitation, but the smell of the campfires felt fresh in her nose. Then again, everything felt fresh in her nose. The wet green scent of the pines, the crisp nutty smell of oaks, and the crunchy, fuzzy tang of the dangling moss tickled her nostrils and teased the back of her tongue.

So maybe it was only the newness. Perhaps she was unaccustomed to the richness of it all, and none of the signals were more recent than a week or two.

"What time of year is this?" she asked Sam, who had not stayed where she'd left him, but walked along behind her, trailing in her wake and believing that he'd been sneaky about it.

It startled him that she'd spoken so softly, that she'd known how close he was following. "It's, um, it's March. End of March."

"Not exactly high tourist season, then."

"What?"

"These cabins, it's part of a campground or a park. I don't

think there's anyone in any of them. It doesn't smell like it, anyway, and I don't hear anything." She went up to the nearest window and held her face against it, buffered by her hands. "This one looks empty."

"You said they all looked empty."

"No, I said they smelled and sounded empty. This one looks empty, too." Around the front of the cabin was a thin door made of something light and fragile like balsa wood. A secondary screen door overlaid it. Nia pulled it open; then she fiddled with the knob.

"Is it locked?" Sam asked.

She began to say yes, but when she gave it a firm twist, it came loose from the wood and splintered the area around itself. "No."

"You broke it!"

"I didn't mean to." Using her elbow and part of her shoulder, she pushed the door inward. "It's old. And look: the wood is, there were termites." There weren't any termites, but it was dark and Sam wouldn't know the difference.

She'd startled herself with the knob. She hadn't given it any effort, but it had broken without any resistance. The knowledge of her new strength made her nervous; it made her want to tiptoe and not touch anything.

"Termites, yeah," Sam said. If he disbelieved her, he was disinclined to argue with her now, so he followed her inside.

The cabin was only one room, with no privy and no sink, and it was dusty from disuse or neglect. Thin gauze curtains hung on either side of both windows. They weren't closed, though, so for what little protection they might provide, Nia shut them. The material was scratchy and fine; she thought it might be mosquito netting.

"I need . . ." She scanned the room, and her eyes settled on Sam. "I need to find a pump. I need to wash off; I can't stand this."

"But we're supposed to stay away from the water."

"We're supposed to stay away from *bodies of water,*" she clarified, having absolutely no idea if she was telling the truth.

"Are you sure?"

"Yes." When she moved, the edges of the remaining flakes dug into her skin and scraped it, scratched it, and attempted to pierce it. "There'll be an outhouse somewhere around here, and there ought to be a pump, too. They have to get fresh water to the campgrounds somehow."

Sam was on the verge of offering to help her look, but she headed him off at the pass.

"Stay here. It's dark, and you don't see as well as I do. Stay here so I'll know where to find you when the . . . when, you know. When he catches up to us."

"I can take care of myself."

"But as you've already said, you don't know where we are and you don't know what's going on. You don't even know if you're necessary, so if I were you, I'd hold my horses and clam up. If you really want to help"—and she knew that he *did*—"you can look around and see if you can find me some shoes. Or even some pants."

"Shoes?"

"And pants. Or just pants. I don't know what the odds are that you'll turn anything up, but I'd appreciate it if you'd see what you can find."

"I'll look around. And you're not going very far?" It came out sounding afraid, which Sam didn't like very much. He hated feeling like a small child whose mother was threatening to leave.

"Not far, no. It can't be far." She held her nose up and sniffed, first left, then right. "The outhouse is back that way, I think. No one's used it for a while, but it's back over there. The pump will probably be near it."

"If you're such a bloodhound, keep your nose open for the sulfur."

"I beg your pardon?"

Sam pushed his glasses back up his nose and sat down on the edge of a squeaky cot. "Your nose is pretty good, and the fresh water here smells like rotten eggs. The water pump will reek of it."

Nia went back out the front door and drew it shut behind her, even though it didn't lock and it provided only the barest, most limited protection from any element, real or imagined. She pushed the screen door shut as well. It squealed on a rusty metal hinge and slapped against the frame.

She held still and listened hard, but heard no response from the night.

21

Wet Away from the Water

Crickets sang and small nocturnal things scampered to and fro beneath the canopy. A light breeze puffed intermittently from the ocean, bringing air that was sharp with salt and a few degrees cooler than the warm, heavy layer of atmosphere that clung close to the ground.

And yes, there was a faint yellow pall around the edge of the air currents.

Nia smelled the brown, bitter taste of eggs and fire, and she knew that the water pump was nearby. She found the pump with her nose, and then her hands. She felt her way down the corroded metal lever and, remembering not to move with too much force, she pried it up and pushed it back down.

A whooshing gasp of damp, smelly air squeezed out.

Again, she cranked the handle, and a third and fourth time before anything but old gases flowed.

The water first slipped out in a trickle, then a stream. And then, if she kept one arm moving, it came out in a steadier gush. The contents of the well pooled around her ankles, soaking and sinking them. There wasn't any soap, but Nia was willing to take what she could get—and if that meant she had nothing to wash with, then she'd make do. Now that she knew the well wasn't dry, she could afford to get muddy.

She pulled off the too-big man's shirt and sat down, in the dark and on the ground, in the pond of stinking water.

It didn't fill up too swiftly, because the ground was more sand than dirt and it drained liquid away almost as soon as it could collect; but the longer Nia pumped, the more the water gathered and the deeper her improvised tub became—until there were inches enough to soak all the hair between her legs and all the stretches of untouched, shell-covered skin along her thighs. The added damp didn't dissolve the remaining debris, but it helped to loosen it. When she picked at it, she noticed that some of her fingernails were impossibly long; they had grown until they were almost as long as her fingers, but they'd curled inside the stone cocoon and molded themselves to the curve of her hands.

She bit them at the corners until they broke, and while she pumped with one hand, she filed the other's claws against the rust-speckled pump until the edges were no longer so sharp that they could gut a fish. She alternated hands, continued to pump, and the puddle held steady enough to dip her. The rhythmic splash of the sputtering crank added its melody to the insects, the frogs, and the night birds.

Her hair was beyond hope. She'd never had the nerve to cut it off before, but now the time might be nigh. Was such a style still popular? Did women still crop their hair tightly against their heads and wear it like men sometimes?

As she slipped the scarf off her head and held the rocky, tangled locks under the stream, the bits and pieces of binding gunk washed free. Much like her nails, her hair had been growing all the while. And with nowhere to go, it had folded back upon itself.

It was thick between her fingers, and knotty. She couldn't comb her way through it with her hands, because it had become too dense. Even while wet, its texture made her think of the black men who came from the islands. Sometimes her grandmother had hired them to work the orchards, and she'd seen them there—climbing up ladders in their thin cotton pants, their exposed skin dark and shiny with sweat. Some of them shaved their heads until nothing remained but a shadow; and some let it grow long and kinked, rolled into natty tendrils that looked like the roots of a tree, or like cords of braided rope.

That's what it felt like, when she crushed a fistful of hair in her palm. It felt springy and strong, and the color was strange too—redder, golder, and even whiter, in strips and streaks, than it had been before.

She rinsed all the hair she could, and when the worst of the dust had been cleaned away, she did her best to braid her mane back out of her face. The braid sat heavy and too thick down her back. Its ends dangled in the water around her hips.

A bright spark of white and warmth flicked to life at the edge of her vision. She turned to see what it was and saw that Sam had found a lantern. The small room with the squeaky cot and the dingy curtains leaked light from its windows, but it was a pleasant, unobtrusive light.

She heard the cot springs groan again, and she listened to the scraping patter of Sam's feet as he moved about the cabin, opening drawers and pushing boxes.

She leaned forward, pressing into the arm that was still mechanically moving up and down, her elbow mimicking the joint of the pump. With her free hand, she began to pick and pull stray pieces of shell and strips of rock out of the curled bush of hair that sagged heavily against her inner, upper thigh.

It hurt, but not so badly that she stopped. She only wished for a pair of scissors or a razor to make the cleanup faster. It would have been wonderful to shave the last of the peeling mineral veneer off her skin, out of her hair. She would have done almost anything for a bar of soap or a rag, but all she had was an unreliable, ill-smelling stream of forcibly pumped groundwater.

At last she felt like she'd done everything she could possibly do. She gave the lever another series of insistent jerks and built up enough water pressure to rinse herself off, then stood up. Her toes wormed into the milk-white puddle bottom, and she thought that maybe she didn't need shoes so badly after all.

The longer her skin was exposed, the firmer it grew and the less easily marred it became. When she noticed this, she felt a pang of fear that maybe she was returning to her statue-stiff state. But the skin still flexed when she commanded it. Her arms and legs and neck and waist twisted and bent smoothly without resistance or discomfort.

She undid the loose braid that restrained her hair and let it fall in a wild spray, springy and ropy and wet. She shook her head and splattered the area around herself with drizzle, then stood up and retrieved her shirt. Rinsing and wringing, she squeezed out the worst of the damp and dusty dirt.

With a flip of her arms, she billowed the shirt open and crawled back into it, even though it was wet enough to cling immodestly. It would dry. And there wasn't anything else to wear, anyway.

It was hard to decide that she didn't care, because from leftover mortal habit she certainly *did* care. But caring and feeling the need to act were not the same thing.

An idle, amused thought slipped quickly through her head. *My mother would be embarrassed to death if she saw me like this.* And then she went on to involuntarily wonder about her mother. She also thought about Aunt Marjorie, who had supposedly gone to live there with her mother, at the edge of the old grove outside Tallahassee.

How long had it been since she'd seen them?

Had they given her up for dead?

Perhaps not. Perhaps up north in the shade and scent of the pretty white blossoms that sprouted on the knobby-limbed trees, her mother and aunt had held out hope on her grandmother's farm. They might have been waiting all this time.

Or they might not have.

People who live their lives near water are often forced to come to terms with it—that sad fact that there aren't always bodies to bury, and there aren't always traces left to commemorate. Even if they never knew that Nia had rushed out into the tide . . .

And she could feel it again, in terrible memory, the bath-warm water of the Gulf foaming up around her ankles as she ran headlong into the surf, into the water where Bernice didn't know how to move herself.

If they'd searched the island and turned up nothing from sandy shore to shore, they *must* have concluded that the ocean had taken her. And it is rare that the ocean returns its prizes.

But sometimes things too firm to decay and too tough to be nibbled by fish will sink, and sometimes the tides will push them back out, regurgitating them the same way that an owl or a snake will reject the bones, shells, and spurs of the things it swallows.

"So that's me, then," she said to herself. "Rejected, and unable to decay."

Her own voice stopped her. "Decay," she said again, and there was meaning in the word that she couldn't put her finger on. It was packed with significance—though she couldn't tell precisely how.

"Yes?"

She jumped, creating a little splash in the puddle—which was almost gone. The soil that was more sand than dirt drank it up fast, and sucked it down in a filtering spiral, down to the rock below.

"What? Oh, it's you."

"It's me." The creature was standing beside the pump. It was damp in a comfortable way, like it enjoyed being wet for all it hated the water and the things that lived within it.

"Are we—" She fumbled for the sentiment. "—safe?"

"Safe?" It laughed, and chunks of debris fluttered down into the disappearing water. "Never. Not under any circumstances, ever again—if ever we were before. But for now, I think, we're all right enough. The water witch has other problems to pursue. She is not looking our way, which is the best we can hope for. How are you doing?"

"I'm fine."

"Fine? Is that all?" It fashioned its leafy lips into something close to a leer. "I would hope that you're significantly better than fine. You left Samuel in a cabin?"

Nia was getting used to the creature's random and obstinate shifts in conversation, so she ran with the flow of it and said, "Yes, where the light is. I don't know if that's safe or not, but as you just said yourself, we're all right enough. And, bless his heart, the man can't see in the dark."

"But you can?"

"Better than he does. You really don't know, do you?"

"Know what?" it asked.

"What I can do. You made me, and you have no idea."

It began to walk toward the cabin, and Nia joined its long-legged stride. "I didn't make you. I modified you. I cannot create. I can only transform."

"I don't understand."

"You're back," Sam observed almost happily. "Hey, Nia, I found some shoes." Indeed, he lifted up a pair of work boots that were brown and rough, but sound. "They're a man's pair, but they aren't very big. They were under the cot here, and . . ." And he faltered, trying not to notice that she was naked underneath her wet white shirt.

"Thank you," she said. She took the shoes and upended them, shaking them to see if anything would scatter out. She pulled back their tongues, loosening their laces, and wormed her feet down inside—where she found a warm flannel lining that was not too badly weathered or worn. The warmth of them she could have lived without, but the softness was pleasant, and it made her feel more civilized, somehow, to cover her bare feet.

While Nia pushed her toes into position and tied the laces, Sam was sitting on the far end of the cot and trying not to look at the way she was shaped beneath the clingy wet fabric. It was already beginning to dry, but it was not so dried yet that the darker tips, angles, curves, and crevices were not readily apparent.

To distract himself, Sam turned to the creature and asked it a question. "So tell me, um, Mister. What do we call you?"

It turned the idea over in its head, considering a response but seemingly incapable of deciding on one.

"Don't you have a name?" Sam pressed. "Anything we could

attach to you for simple communication purposes? She's Nia, short for something longer; and I'm Sam, short for Samuel. But who are you?"

"You bandy those names about too casually, Samuel. But it's natural for you. A title does not bind you the way it binds some others. Other kinds," it clarified. "I did have a name once, but I wore it as a title . . . and that name was stripped from me. By the time the first men first set ink to paper with their very first quills and sticks, I had already been exiled and unnamed.

"So I began again. I scavenged, combing the vacant and unwanted areas between the points of power. I sought a new purpose and a new authority; I assumed a role that no one else wanted. Even if any of them had been aware that such a role existed, no one would have seen the value in it."

It was talking to itself more than to them. It scarcely seemed aware that they were still there, still listening, still waiting for an answer.

"But there is power in the leavings of life, in the castoff of cells and the discarded refuse of growth. Something must feed it. And when it dies, something must break it down, something must cycle it again." It met Nia's eyes. "Or preserve it against that cycle."

"Decay," she said. It was the same word that had earlier stuck in her mouth. "That's what you're talking about."

"Decay. The breaking down of things that once grew up. What could rise anew if the corpses of the old things did not nourish them? So, yes, you could call me Decay and you'd be correct. I break down, or I can prevent the breaking down. This is where I've found my niche, and recovered my strength."

It settled down lower, spreading its legs against the stones of the tiny hearth. It shrugged its massive shoulders and set its hands on either side of itself, leaning forward in a pose that was meant to convince and assure.

"There is no more Death," it declared. "Death as a task and title was undone, and its mechanisms were given to the elements. It was spread across the fire, the water, the force of the earth's pull, and the passing of time. It was given away to the dominion of others, and its own dominion was disbanded. But this left . . . gaps. It left possibilities, even as I felt that all possibilities had been removed."

Nia thought she understood, but the enormity of it choked her throat. This creature that called itself Decay had been demoted . . . from Death? She wasn't sure where to begin her frantic wondering, so she listened instead, and hoped to hear something less heavy and hard to fathom.

"But," Sam pushed, "what are we supposed to call you? Have you no name? Nothing at all that we could use to mention you, or simply discuss you?"

It nodded slowly and spoke without any hurry.

"If I must give you a name . . . if only to close the question . . ." It was hunting for something, left or lost deep in its memory. "A long time ago, in this very place, there were primitives of your breed. They glimpsed me, and they invented stories to account for me. They called me—" And it emitted a string of sounds that were beyond Nia's or Sam's capacity to pronounce. "I believe it meant, He Who Feasts upon the Moss Graves."

At the end of this proclamation, silence filled the dimly lit cabin while Nia and Sam each tried to find a way to condense the small sentence into something that would fit in their mouths.

"Moss . . ." Nia said. "Moss-feaster?"

The creature visibly brightened, insomuch as a thing made from the rotting forest floor can do so. "Mossfeaster. Yes. You have your name now. Call me that word as you like, and I will answer to it."

Sam made a dubious face. "Is that a promise?"

"It's more like a prediction. Now," it said, climbing to its feet and stretching to a height that almost hit the crossbeams of the ceiling. "Is there anything else we can take from this place? Anything else you might require?"

"I'm thirsty," Sam said.

"There's a pump out back," Nia told him. "But otherwise, I think we're finished here . . . if *you're* finished here."

"Oh yes," it said, stomping toward the door. "I needed nothing in the first place. The rest was for you, and for him. But now we need to move. We need to push ourselves farther, away from water."

"You keep *saying* that—," Sam said, rising from the cot to follow.

"And I keep *meaning* it. We still have several hours before the sun rises, and I think we should take advantage of them. Darkness won't hide us from the water witch any more than daylight will, but we should move while our flight is fresh. We should cover all the distance we can."

"Where are we going? How far from the water can we go—do we need to go all the way to Georgia?"

"Not so far as that," it said. "Inland, and north. There is a town there, near a larger city. The city is called Ybor, and the water witch has business there."

They went down the creaking stairs and into the woods. Sam was carrying the lantern and bringing up the rear. "Wait, but. But you just said that we wanted to get away from her, away from the water."

"For now, yes. But soon we'll need to confront her. We must

engage the minions she's contrived, and destroy the device that she's creating. It won't be easy, and I can't set you upon this mission cold, and newborn, and uninformed. So first, you will walk with me."

"I'm hungry, too," Sam added to his earlier complaint of thirst.

Mossfeaster said, "We'll improve upon your condition, Samuel, provided that you continue to aid us. And I think that once you understand what's at stake, you'll realize that, really, you have no choice but to lend us your assistance."

"What kind of assistance do you expect from *me*? I mean, you've got"—he cocked his head at Nia—"*her*—and you're tougher than me by a mile. What on earth can I possibly do? What use do you expect me to be?"

"Someone must go into Ybor, and someone must help our little stone angel here to fit in with the rest of your kind so that they do not hunt or fear her. She is preserved well enough; water may tear down stone, but much more slowly and not without terrible effort. But she is different from them now, and not only because she is improperly covered."

"This is crazy," Sam mumbled. "All of it, it's crazy. I'm just an insurance man. I'm not really in the business of helping . . . do . . . whatever it is I'm helping you do."

"Insurance?" Mossfeaster repeated the word slowly, as if by digesting it the creature might determine its meaning. "What is that? Explain it to me."

Sam fumbled for words. "It's a preventive thing. It protects your property by promising that if it's destroyed, you'll be compensated."

Mossfeaster considered this, walking in silence ahead of them. Its colossal, semi-humped back moved up and down with each step, and the light of Sam's lantern cast jagged, sharp shadows in every direction. The trees split the light into bars and beams, chasing the night out of their path.

It stopped and turned around so that the flickering glow of the portable flame illuminated its face. It smiled.

"Yes," it said. "I approve. I will take it as a sign that this is correct and right. I've inadvertently selected a guardian for my guardian."

"Wait. No, I mean—"

"No, I *understand*. You protect property, and people. You guard them, even if it's only with money. I know enough of how your society works to understand. I think it's a sign."

"You believe in signs?" Nia asked.

It turned around and resumed walking, and it was walking straighter, with more optimistic bounce. "I *do*," it assured her. "There is more to the heavens and more to the stars than us small things that crawl and swim, and live and die, and bleed and watch and struggle against one another."

"You're not making any sense," Sam fussed.

"Leave him alone," Nia said.

"He doesn't have to leave me alone if he doesn't want to," Moss-feaster said, and through the words he still was smiling; Nia could hear it as she followed along behind. "I don't mind. But Nia, I approve of your disapproval. I am glad to see that you already wish to protect me. I protected you, and you will do likewise in return. You were the right choice, and while I had some reservations about *that* one"—it waved a big hand in Sam's general direction—"I am now reassured. We will make this happen yet. We will stop the water witch from calling Leviathan, and we will undo the thing that she has set into motion."

Sam stumbled and caught himself. The lantern shot crazy, wobbling beams in every direction, but steadied itself as Sam found his footing. "And what kind of thing might that be?"

Mossfeaster said without looking back, "She intends to destroy this world, and every one of you who crouches upon it."

"Every one of you?"

"Every one"—it nodded—"of *us*."

The forest east of the ocean was thick and dense and hard to walk, and it was rough for Mossfeaster to lead. Although the creature could twist and distort itself around the trees, Nia and Sam could only walk behind their towering leader and try to match the monster's unrelenting pace.

The Whistle at the End
of the Earth

José loved Ybor City almost as much as he loved Bernice, who strolled half a step ahead of him. He let her take a slim lead because he liked to watch her walk; he loved the sway of her body, moving shiplike through the small industrial city, dodging the streetcars and tripping lightly even in the tall, thick shoes that she wore to prop herself up. It was easy to love Bernice. Beautiful and bold, wicked and wild, capable of being sublimely civilized and charming . . . she was a fantasy plucked from the water and given to him to hold and to keep.

It might have been less easy to understand why any man would love Ybor, but José had his reasons.

It did not remind him of Spain, though that was Bernice's

assumption. She heard the nattering, clipped Spanish conversations at every street corner and inside every bar, restaurant, and hotel, and she watched José smile to overhear it.

But she seemed not to know or care that many lands speak Spanish and the accents were different from place to place. Just as Bernice could easily have told the difference between voices from England and New England, so too José could tell without trying that the men who surrounded him were born on islands.

The factory workers came and went along the walks, reeking of sweat, tobacco, and the glue that holds cigar bands together. They discussed food and women and rum, and they argued over games of *bolita* that were rigged: no, they were not—well, you know Charlie Wall is a cheater, and everyone says so.

And every block sounded for all the world like the deck of a boat a hundred years before. So they gambled with lottery balls instead of cards; and so they smelled like *cigarros* and cane alcohol instead of sunburn and salt water . . . they were the same kind of men.

Mostly the speech he overheard was made by working-class Cubans, but he heard Puerto Ricans, too, and Dominicans. The patterns of their banter were familiar and friendly, and they echoed in José's ears as the smoke and stink of the cigar factories wafted through his sinuses.

"What are they saying?" Bernice asked.

José had not been listening, either to her or to the couple she indicated. "What? I'm sorry, dear. I didn't hear it."

"I think they were talking about us."

"And what if they were?"

She made a cranky little pout. "If they were, then I want to know what they were saying."

"I'm sure it wasn't important. Or else, it was about you—I'm sure they were only admiring you," he told her, and he watched

from the corner of his eye as the couple in question disappeared
into a market. "You're beautiful and strange, here. Most of the
women in this city are dark, and they work alongside the men
making the cigars. They don't often see women like you."

"So they *were* talking about me?"

Sometimes it was easier to lie and put it to rest. "Yes, I caught
the last of it before they went inside. They wondered what a
woman of your class and stature was doing in the workers' district. That's all. They thought you were too pretty to belong here,
and they wondered if I was your father or lover—that is why they
whispered."

"Oh." Her mind wandered again, and she tumbled into silence.

She'd been doing this more and more lately, and José was beginning to wonder what was going on behind those brutal blue
eyes. It used to be that she told him everything, asked him everything, wanted his company for everything. But in the last week
she'd taken to abandoning him and Mother both for her own
agenda.

If she told them anything at all, she would make mention of
seeking out resources or hunting down old grudges. But usually,
she said nothing. She simply left and returned at her leisure, feeling no compunction to explain or account for herself.

He tried to engage her again. "We're nearly there."

"At the jewelry place?"

"It's not a jewelry place, exactly."

"It's got a funny name," she recalled.

"Poppo Efodiazo," he repeated. "And I'm sure it's not funny if
you speak Greek. It's a shop for all kinds of things, not merely
jewelry."

"But he makes jewelry, right? I thought you said that's what he
did."

"Sometimes. More often, I think, he alters and melts jewelry to be sold again. He's been known to buy stolen goods and transform them. Then he sells them or ships them elsewhere."

"So why are we using *him*? I don't like it here," she said, blanketing her discomfort with a general expression of unhappiness.

"Why not? It's a beautiful day, the factories are churning, and we have all afternoon to run a simple errand. After we're done, we can go find a shady spot to have a drink."

"Because I don't like it when I don't know what people are talking about. And I don't want to sit around and have a drink after this. After this, I want to go back to the water. It's hot and smelly here, and I don't like it."

José opened his mouth to argue, and then changed his mind. He didn't know what was going on, and he didn't want to fight with her until he knew exactly what the fight would be about. "Are you upset about something?" he asked instead.

"Like what?" she said with a snap.

"I don't know; I was hoping you could tell me."

A wash of crafty interest spread itself across her face, and it startled José. He was pleased to have garnered a reaction from her, but it unsettled him all the same.

She seemed on the verge of saying or asking something, but when she spoke up she didn't say or ask anything important. All she said was, "I told you, I don't like it here. That's all. It's hot and it stinks. We're almost there, aren't we?"

"Yes, yes. I imagine you also want to go back to Mother."

"I didn't say *that*." And something about the way she made her denial made him worry again about the things that moved her.

Most of time when he looked at her, he was, in a quiet and deliberate sense, looking down on her. After all, she was beautiful—

but not the most brilliant woman he'd ever known. She was spoiled and easily vexed, prone to fits of childish rage and irrational flights of fancy. Bernice was smaller than José, and younger than him, and in her own way, weaker. She didn't know what to do with her powers. She didn't know how to read very well and she didn't speak anything other than her Yankee English with its jagged edges and tortured vowels.

But she had her gifts. People gave her things, and told her things. People offered themselves to her, heart in hand.

With a sharper mind, she could have taken over the world by now, he thought. *Thank heaven or hell that the gods thought to hobble her, or we would all be lost in her wake.*

At the next corner they turned right and took a sharp twist into a street so narrow it might as well have been an alley. But the buildings had signs, hanging from squeaking chains and painted to advertise services that could be obtained through the recessed doorways that were shuttered against the afternoon heat. One sign had a picture of a bell painted upon it in a golden shade of brown, and the letters beneath spelled out, POPPO EFODIAZO.

"That's it?" Bernice asked.

"That's it. This is the place."

He took her hand and led her to the low stone steps. He opened the door for her and held it aside while she clomped up the uneven stairs in her expensive heeled shoes.

She hesitated. "What's a Greek guy doing here, anyway? I thought this was the Spanish part of town. Why's he so far from home?"

"This is a . . . commercial part of town," he told her, resisting the impulse to correct her summing up of the blocks. "This is a business district, and the Greek is a businessman. He has come here because his services are useful in some fashion. And it's not so strange, really." José took her hand and joined her on the threshold, then urged her inside.

The store was cluttered with a rich and diverse array of products. Metal pots and glass vases were hung and displayed side by side with odd pieces of wood furniture and tiny fountains with figures of naked children. Under the main counter's glass there were more valuable items, gold chains and pendants, earrings that glittered with gems that could have been real, or might have been paste. Along the walls, from floor to ceiling, there were frames upon frames—some holding pictures, some holding mirrors—in all shapes, all sizes, and all patinas. The room smelled like old paper and chemicals.

"Farther up the coast, there are many Greek families that live along the shore," he mentioned.

"There are?" she asked.

A new voice joined the conversation. "There are," it said. "They came to dive for sponges."

Small and swarthy, a bent little man with a shock of black hair came shuffling forward, through a parted curtain that separated the front of the shop from the back. He was wearing a filthy, thick apron made of leather or treated wool—it was too dirty to tell which one at a glance. A pair of wire-rimmed spectacles hung from ear to ear, settling heavily on his nose. Where the metal reached the skin, a sunken groove had formed from holding the weight of the thick glass lenses in place.

"Mr. Poppo," José said.

"His name is Poppo?" Bernice gaped.

"Agatone Pappanophilus," the storekeeper clarified. "But it's easier to shorten it, make it simpler for foreign tongues." He waved down José's polite apologies and said, "No, it's all right. I've come to understand that it's silly in English. Most of my customers are Latin, though."

"Latin? Where's Latin—"

José interrupted her. "Is the shell finished? You said to check back today, so here we are."

"Oh, it is finished, yes. It has been finished for days, but it needed to set, or I would've tried to send for you." When he talked, the English was muted and forced; he wrapped the words around his native pronunciations and compelled the letters to line up correctly.

Mr. Poppo took a cane from off the table and planted it down firmly on the cold slate floor. "I think the results will please you. It's a small piece, but pretty. It's a tiny conch, isn't it?"

"Yes." José nodded, following behind the man, who moved through the room with amazing slowness. "Smaller than you usually find them. But the casting went well, and the piece is sound?"

"Perfectly sound. It's a gift, didn't you say?"

"For our Mother," Bernice piped up, bringing up the rear.

Mr. Poppo stopped and turned around. "The two of you, you're brother and sister?"

"Oh no, we're not. The gift is for her mother, my mother-in-law. But the woman has been quite kind to me, and I call her Mother also," José lied without trying. "It's an anniversary present."

"Then I'm surprised you didn't want it in gold."

Bernice was going to say something else, but José squeezed her hand. "The gift is one that is meaningful, if not very valuable. She will understand the sentiment behind it, and appreciate it accordingly."

"Ah," Mr. Poppo said.

"It's—," Bernice was saying again, but José squeezed her hand harder.

He couldn't explain to her there, on the spot, that Mr. Poppo did not care and did not want to know. The storekeeper dealt with burglars and thieves for a living, and he neither wanted nor required any explanations.

They ducked around the navy blue curtain and it jingled on its rings.

"Back here." Mr. Poppo gestured with one hand. "This is where I work. This is where I set it, and after it cooled, I trimmed it and polished it. The end result is quite nice, quite nice indeed."

He limped forward into a work area that was littered with casts, molds, paints, chisels, and stray bits of leftover material.

The workshop could have worked anything, almost—or so José surmised from his sweeping inspection of the place. There were pigments set up in tightly closed pots with clumpy brushes, just the right colors for falsifying antiques. Here and there, he could see parchments and papers being soaked in a brown solution that smelled faintly of tea and tobacco. Some of the successfully aged documents had been lifted out of their baths and were hanging by the rafters, clipped to a string to dry and wrinkle.

"Back now. Farther. Not this room, but the next." Mr. Poppo saw José examining the space as he passed through it, and the shop-keeper said, "I do not care if you know how this works. For the price you have paid, you can see all you like. Your 'Mother' may be any queen or crone, but if your requests were honorable . . . or legal . . . you would have gone into Tampa and had this done there, through a metalworks, or through a jeweler. So look all you like."

He reached for the curtain that covered the next doorway and drew it back. A blast of scalding air puffed out.

Mr. Poppo nudged along, scooting with the cane and dragging a twisted foot.

"I know it's warm," he said. "But to work with metal, you

must make it very hot. And to make it hot enough to melt, my friends, you must invite yourself into hell."

José took the curtain and it felt brittle in his hand; it was purple with threads of gold snaking through it. He lifted it aside and fought against his instinct to retreat. The furnace within was shocking in its intensity, and the sheer force of the skin-withering heat was enough to push even the bravest back.

Still holding Bernice's hand, José blinked his eyes hard and tried to enter, but she held him back. She pulled her fingers away from his and shook her head.

"I can't," she swore. "God, that's awful. Forget it. I'll wait here. You go get it."

It was hard to blame her, and since there was no reason for them both to suffer, José entered the backmost chamber without her.

Through watering eyes and a stinging nose, he could tell at a glance why the place was so unbearable. Two tall chimneys released smoke out through the flat roof, but there were otherwise no outlets, no windows. There were no lights except for the fires that simmered here and there, under crucibles and inside ovens.

"Most days," Mr. Poppo said, "my son and another boy assist me here. We are quite accustomed to the heat, I promise you; but even so, we cannot work here for long. During the winter it is not so bad, but in spring and come summer, there's nothing to be done about it—except to pretend that we're devils."

"I can imagine," José replied, although he didn't have to imagine. The heat was sucking him dry, working its blistering waves into every wrinkle of his skin and clothes.

"I doubt you could!" the Greek argued. "No, today the fires are left low because the projects that await them are few, and I am alone. You should imagine it when the furnaces are all alight and metal pours from mold to mold. It is blinding and terrible, and I call myself Hephaestus, and I command the fire. I make armor for the gods, isn't that how it goes?"

"I'm not sure," José said, tired of the talk and faint from the temperature. "Please, sir. I'd ask you to hurry. *You* may be fond of the climate, but I am finding it difficult."

Mr. Poppo shuffled to a shelf that was lined with small objects in various stages of finish and finery. "Hurry, yes. Hurry, hurry. It is difficult for you to handle the heated air, and it is difficult for me to hurry." He indicated the cane and the irregularly shaped foot. "But I am part of a very fine tradition. Hephaestus, and his Roman brother, Vulcan—both of them were lame like me. There's a long and illustrious history to it. Men who work the fires, gods who work the fires . . . the skill of the deities comes at a price."

He used his cane to draw a stool up beneath him.

José watched the man's leisurely pace with impatience, wishing to help or speed the occasion but not knowing how to do so. His head was spinning from the crushing weight of the ambient fires, and he didn't know how long or how well he could stand there beside the purple curtain with its sparkling threads.

"And this." Mr. Poppo used his cane to push a dull brown shell the size of a man's fist. He inched it toward his hand and caught it when the cane's edge pushed it off the shelf. "This is why."

"Gifts for mothers-in-law?"

The Greek smiled. "Bronze, my friend. This kind of bronze, in fact. The things I melted down to make it were selected in accordance with your request. Not with tin was this made—not with the cheap shine of the lighter metal. This was made with arsenic, as you asked and as you like. Copper and arsenic, they contaminate one another, you see. They work together, firming one another and adding strength to flexibility. And if you add enough of the heavy poison, there are other benefits, too. At the right percentage, you lower the melting point and the metal is easier to pour."

José shook his head, and sweat spilled down into his eyes. He wiped it away. "I don't understand," he breathed, wishing for the water or the sky like never before in his life. "What does that have to do with anything? Here, please. Let me see it. Let me have it."

Mr. Poppo held the shell in one hand. "After a time, the arsenic finds a way inside the man who works the metal. He breathes it in and coughs it up; it settles on his skin and seeps into his blood. The toxin weakens the body and dulls the reflexes. It cripples the man as it strengthens the metal. And *that,* my friend, is why the fire gods were lame."

"Ah," José gasped. "Ah. And you? Have you worked too long with poisons?"

"Me? No." Suddenly the man was standing directly before José, holding out the shell and beaming a brilliant grin. "I broke it badly thirty years ago. It never healed right. There's no mystical, chemical weakening to it. I was clumsy, and now I'm broken. These things happen. But look at you, you're nearly overcome with the heat. We should give you some air."

And although there was a firm mask of concern on the Greek's damp, creased face, José couldn't shake the impression that Poppo was pleased to see his visitor fade under the dark glare of the furnace room.

It made José irrationally angry, and he almost lashed out, almost reached for the cutlass and the blunderbuss. *(No—he'd come unarmed and no, there wouldn't be a blunderbuss, not on land, not these days.)* He almost wanted to murder the little fellow where he stood . . . but the man was still holding the shell, detailed and perfect and waiting to be collected.

José swiped the shell and turned on his heel. He tried to make it look deliberate and hasty, but it was more of a teetering fall than a triumphant retreat. He collapsed through the purple curtain and Bernice was there on the other side, her arms folded across her chest. Impatience was written on every inch of her, but when she saw the shell, she smiled as big as the Greek.

"Let me see it," she said, meeting him in the middle of the room and holding out her hands. "Is that it? It's not very big," she observed, fondling it and holding it up to the light of the window.

"You know better than anyone," José panted, taking her arm and drawing her back into the front room of the shop. "How small things that shine may be . . . may be worth more than . . . I'm sorry." He wiped at his face and dragged his sleeve around his neck, and down his throat. "I'm sorry, it was awful in there. Let's go, now. I need to go outside."

"Sure, baby," she said, and mild alarm met with curiosity in her frown. "Are you all right?"

"Yes," he told her. "I'm fine. But that was . . . that was . . ."

"The fee has been paid, sir," Mr. Poppo said from the doorway where the purple curtain hung. "You are free to leave and I thank you for your patronage." Then he turned, scraping the tip of his cane along the floor, and went back inside to the furnace room.

José shuddered.

"What is it?" Bernice asked as they pushed the door open and toppled back out into the afternoon brightness.

"How miserable," he tried to say. He found it hard to articulate. "How odd and strange, and what a horrible job—to work a smelting furnace in a tropical land. There's something cruel about it, or at least, I think there *would* be something cruel, except for how the man seems to almost enjoy it."

"He *likes* it in there?"

"He seems to. He takes it as a point of pride, but it's unnatural,

I swear—the way he lounges in that room, barely the faintest sheen of sweat on his face. There's something . . . not right about it. It bothers me."

"Well, hell, it bothers me, too, and I didn't even go in there. Forget about it, okay? Forget about it, baby, and we'll go have that drink if you want. We can go find a bar, like you said. I don't mind. It's hot out here, but . . ." She looked over her shoulder at the door, checking to make sure it'd closed behind them and kept the Greek inside. "But it's not a big thing. We can get a drink. I have something I want to . . ." She stopped.

"Yes?"

She seemed to find it hard to begin again. "There's something maybe I ought to talk to you about, anyway. We can talk about it over drinks if you want. That would be fine, wouldn't it? You'd like that, right?"

"I'd like that, yes. It would be fine. And I'd very much like to talk to you."

"Good. Okay. Good. Pick a place, then, if you want. I don't know what's good, or where the drinks are cold. Just pick something," she repeated, and José watched her confidence falter. He wondered what was wrong, but then he felt a surge of excitement at the thought of finding out at last.

Being outside was helping José's clarity immensely, despite the fact that it was late afternoon and the day was as warm as it was likely to get. He didn't mind it in the least. It felt like an icebox after being in Poppo's lair, and it cheered him even more than Bernice's sudden attempts at openness.

She was carrying the shell, examining it as they walked, and he let her. He was leading her to a nicer corner of the town, where the bars might interest her better than the ones frequented by the workingmen as they finished their shifts. He watched her turn the peculiar little thing over in her hands; she was examining it from every angle, running her fingertips along its ridges and gaps as if she were looking to unlock some clue or compartment.

"It's pretty," she finally declared.

It *was* pretty, in an unassuming way. The detail was exceptional, with every fold and flutter seamless and smooth; and the finish had been brushed and polished down to a dull glow that shone without glittering. It looked warm without looking bright.

"I agree," he said. "It's lovely, and it's going to make her very happy."

Of Plots and Promises

After passing through a few blocks of low-set shops in front of towering tobacco factories, the cityscape smoothed itself into a cleaner strip. Away from the big brick warehouses there were restaurants with white patios and outdoor seating; there were open-air bars that served iced drinks from glasses that leaked frozen condensation onto the counters.

He selected one almost at random, a sleepy establishment with a waiting staff that wore crisp white and spoke English when asked.

The couple was seated promptly and offered handwritten menus with glasses of water. And while they settled into a cooler, more comfortable setting, the tension of the afternoon began to peel away.

Sangria arrived and the ocean breeze fanned them into early evening.

The bronze object sat on the table between them. They admired and discussed it, idly making chitchat while Bernice worked up to the things she really wanted to say. José knew better than to rush her. If he pressured her at all, she would retreat and tell him nothing. If he was patient, he could wait out her discomfort.

"So we have the shell for Mother," she broached.

"She'll expect it within the next hour or two. We should finish here and pay our bill."

Bernice was stalling, working up courage or deciding the right approach. José thought it must be quite a topic, if she was dancing around it with such outrageous caution.

"Is something bothering you?" he asked. It was a gentle nudge in the right direction, but he'd have to use it sparingly.

"Sort of," she admitted. "It's hard to explain."

"I'm listening."

"Well . . . you know what she wants to do with it. We both know. Are you okay with that? Does it make sense to you, or . . . I don't know. I'm starting to have—" She dropped her voice to a whisper. "—not second thoughts, exactly. But I'm starting to wonder if it's the best thing to do."

His heart did a little twitch in his chest, but whether it was from relief, shock, or excitement he couldn't say. "Second thoughts," he said, and slowly. "I *do* understand such things, my dear. I understand why you would have reservations. It's a gargantuan task we're helping to undertake. To remake the world, or to unmake it—this is an enormity not to be underestimated. But you do know, don't you, that we live and breathe, we walk and swim by Mother's grace and favor. Without it, and without her, we drown and fall like—" He flipped his hand toward the sidewalk a few feet away, meaning the people passing by. "—like them. Like any of them. She has given us a second chance."

"But that's part of what I want to know," she insisted. "There's this second chance, sure. But was there anyone before us? Anyone *besides* us? Haven't you wondered?"

"Yes. But if it were important, she would have told us."

Bernice scowled, and for a moment, José thought he'd lost her. "You trust her too much. You rely on her too much—you act like she really is your mother, for God's sake."

He shrugged. "But she is. For the purposes of this life, and even the one I had before it. I worshipped the water in my own way. It is the nature of sailors everywhere, and always. Even now."

"Don't do that. Don't *be* like that," she added. "Did you ever answer to anyone back when you sailed? I know you didn't. She told me about you; she told me how you were the meanest son of a bitch on the water, and how you answered to no one. But you answer to her?"

"Bernice," he said, letting the *r* roll. "We will live forever, do as we wish, and fear nothing. It's an enormous gift, and for that, I am willing to pay. The cost is not much, love."

"But—"

"But what? Has this been so odious today? Has this been such a dreadful task, that you would argue with a goddess, quibbling over details?"

"No!" she said. "That's not what I'm talking about. She wants to use this thing"—she waved at the shell—"to wake up a monster and destroy the world. And maybe I don't want the world to end yet, *that's* what I'm saying."

Ah, there was the bluntness. He wondered why she'd held it back so long. This must not be the crux of the matter, then. This must be only the preamble to what she wanted.

"There's a chance you're thinking about it the wrong way. It will be the end of one world, yes. But it will mean the beginning of another. And who's to say that whatever replaces this will not be superior? You call Leviathan a monster, but he is no such thing; he is a god."

She put away the scowl and replaced it with a frown. "I don't want another god. I'm fine with the devil I know."

"Everything changes, dear. Everything, all the time. Even this—" He fluttered his hand at the sidewalk again. "—this place, these people. All of it changes. I visited this city before, did I ever tell you that? Back when I was alive the first time, I came to this place once or twice."

"It's not a city," she grumbled. "It's barely a town."

He sighed. "I was *here,* in this very same place perhaps a hundred years ago—or more than that. But it was very different, much wilder and less civilized—for all that you think it's a jungle frontier now. Yes, I can see it on your face. I know how you think. If it isn't New York, then—"

"Oh, *stop* it."

"I'll stop when you stop. Dear, the world is going to change anyway; and so much the better if it changes in accordance with Mother's wishes. She wants little enough from us now. Once the change is complete, I imagine we'll be as free as birds."

"Has she told you that?" Bernice asked, sharply and suddenly interested.

"No, but she's never misled me yet. She promised us peace and protection when the new order comes. Why isn't that enough for you?"

"Why *is* it enough for you?" Bernice was getting flustered again, creeping up against the edge of what she meant and finding the precipice distressing. "Actually, I know why. It's because you've been out for a hundred years."

Bernice leaned forward, pushing the fabric napkin aside and accidentally putting her elbow on the handle of her spoon. "José, you got to *live*. Look, how old were you when they took your ship?"

"I'm not sure exactly," he said.

"Oh, come on. How do you not know how old you were? I know it was a long time ago, but really. You can do better than that. Give me a guess."

"You want a guess?"

"Yes, please."

A number popped into the edge of his memory. He didn't know if it was right or not, but it was probably close. "I was . . . I was in my sixties."

"See? That's what I mean. You were *old*. You had a regular human lifetime behind you, and *then*—and then you got another hundred years on top of *that*. It's easy for you to want the world to end; you've had plenty of time to see it."

Her eyes welled up and José was stricken, having no idea at all whether to believe her. She'd never cried before, not that he'd seen, so he didn't know if she could fake tears or if she would bother doing so. After all, the poor girl did have a point.

"I was nineteen. That's all the years I got before this happened to me. Now it's been another three or four, but still. That's not as many as sixty." She picked up the red napkin and dabbed at her eyes, then ran it along the underside of her nose.

"That's . . ." He searched for an appropriate response but couldn't find one that matched what he meant, so he said, "I never thought about it that way. I can see why it upsets you."

The upward curl of her lip met a downward-dripping tear. "We *can't* just let her turn everything upside down. Not now. Not when I've just gotten started."

Again lacking a good response, José's mind raced through options, alternatives, and distractions. She watched him think, with her wet blue eyes oozing sweetly and blinking themselves soggy.

Still on his guard, and still being careful, he said, "But what would you propose? We can't—and I absolutely *won't*—make any threatening move against her. Because she gave me this lifetime, she is within her rights to take it away."

Bernice's lips parted and closed, then parted again. "I'm not suggesting that we try to get rid of her or anything. I don't know how we could, even if we wanted to. And I don't want to. You've got to believe that, if you love me at all."

"I do love you at all. I love you altogether," he said, but he did not say that he believed her. "And I'm glad to hear you say that. Even if you believed that we would survive without her, and even if you did wish to be rid of her, I don't know that there's anything on earth that could accomplish the task. She is immortal, Bernice. We may be long-lived, but I'm reasonably sure that without her protection, we would die."

The change in her face was meant to be subtle, but she was too eager. The smile blossomed before she could prevent it. It was a brilliant smile, and beautiful. It smoothed the tiny ripples on the surface of her lips and made their pretty shape all the more pronounced.

"She's going to dump an awful lot of power into this thing," Bernice tapped one flawlessly filed nail against the shell. "She said it would exhaust her, and that if it fails or breaks, it would take her another hundred years to gather the strength to try again. But she's immortal. She has all the time in the world to sound this call, or whatever it is. Let the Leviathan sleep a little longer. Mother's been around since time began, and we've barely lived. Is it so wrong and so crazy to want just a few years more?"

"What are you asking?" He leaned back in his chair, throwing up defenses that he knew she could tear down with a flick of her hand. "What, should we petition Mother for more time?"

"That would never work. She's gone to all this trouble already."

"My thoughts exactly." He wanted to feel relieved. Bernice understood that there could be no negotiation and no assault. This was good; this was right. With those two options removed, there could be no—

"All we can do is trick her."

Profound and pure silence dropped between them.

"You want . . . to . . . *trick* her?"

She nodded hard. "Not in a *bad* way, not in any way that'll do her harm—I just want to inconvenience her a little. A thousand years, a hundred years, it's nothing to her. She says so all the time. But it'd mean a lot to *me*."

Dumbfounded, it was all José could do not to laugh in her face. "And how precisely do you propose we go about tricking an ancient creature who commands the power of the ocean?"

Bernice answered him with another question. "How much do you think she loves us?"

"Not enough to postpone the apocalypse on your whim."

"What if it wasn't a whim? What if you or I got hurt, badly, and she could either let us die or use some of her energy to heal us? What if it cost her just enough power that she'd have to wait a little while before bringing about the end of the world? That wouldn't be such a bad thing, would it? Even if it only bought us another hundred years, I'd be happy with that. Wouldn't you like another hundred years to wander around the world like this, with me? Think of the places we could go, and the things we could do."

"But think of the things we'll do when the new world is formed!" He forced himself to fight her on it, despite the way her plan was so fiendishly logical.

"I can't fathom them, and neither can you. And I don't want to spend the rest of eternity being a tourist in heaven when I haven't had a chance to go poking around in hell."

"You're perfectly mad. I wouldn't even know how to go about . . .

what, injuring you? Injuring myself? What kind of wound or ill-ness could require such a drain from Mother to repair it?"

The old shrewdness was creeping up Bernice's face, settling in her eyes and tightening the line of her jaw. "So you *do* think, if it came down to it, that Mother would risk a delay to save one of us."

And then he said something awful, something that tipped the balance and sealed her victory; and he knew it before he'd finished speaking it aloud. He knew, as soon as the sentiment was spoken, that his lover had won the debate and that he would give her what she wanted.

"For love or ambition, it would not matter if she *wanted* to in-tervene for our welfare, she'd be compelled to repair *my* strength regardless—unless she wants to comb the seas for another like me. By her own design, the *Arcángel* will permit no other captain."

Chance Encounters

Mossfeaster left Nia and Sam at the outskirts of Ybor City. The creature dissolved itself into the ground and was gone in that fast, frightening way that always startled the two, no matter how many times they saw it happen. Nia had insisted on finding civilization and Sam needed to rest. He'd been awake and on the run for nearly twenty-four hours, and he was wilting.

"What are we *doing?*" he asked in a childish cry, dragging his feet and slapping his hands against his legs. "You're already *wearing* clothes. Why are we looking for *more?*"

"I'm wearing a shirt, and if Mossfeaster wants us to move around town, I'm going to need to look more normal. I wish we had some proper money."

"I have some proper money."

"Not very much. You already counted it out. If we can find a spot, we can get you some breakfast, though. And once we find this Greek fellow, we'll cash in these things." She fondled the dirty string of pearls that wrapped around her left wrist. It was a very long necklace, not a bracelet; but when she looped it half a dozen times, it stayed in place like an exquisite cuff that nearly reached her elbow. On her other wrist, she wore a stack of silver bangles inlaid with mother-of-pearl and sapphires.

The opalescent beads and the metallic bands clicked together, tapping time as her arms swung back and forth. The creature had sworn that they were real, and that they came from one of *Gasparilla*'s chests out on Captiva. Even the cheapest dealer in stolen goods should offer hundreds of dollars for the collection.

Nia wasn't sure what they'd need so much money for, but Mossfeaster had insisted upon it, and he'd insisted that they go to a Greek in Ybor City to get it.

"I already counted my money?"

"Yes," she told him. "You did."

He yawned. "I'm tired."

"I know. We'll find a place for you to take a nap, I swear, and we'll find some clothes for me, and then we'll go find this fence in town."

"What?"

"Mossfeaster said we'd find him just off Seventh Avenue, in the Latin Quarter past the cigar factories. He gave me good directions," she oversimplified. It would have taken too much effort to explain the way he'd planted them in her head, and the way they pulled at her so she felt like a homing pigeon again. "Hey, look." She pointed at the end of the road. "Houses."

"Heaven help us if anybody's home," he mumbled. "What do

you want to do, just go up and say, Hey, can we have some money and some clothes?"

"No, we're going to steal some when we find some. But not here. Not from these places." As they drew closer, Nia could see that the houses were low to the ground and unkempt; they were rough around the edges, tattered at the porches, and unpainted.

"Why not?"

"Because they won't have anything worth taking," she said, but what she meant was, *Because they can't afford to lose what they have.*

The squat cracker-box houses reminded her too much of her grandmother's farm and orchards. They looked like the places where the migrant hands would stay, at the fringe of the property or on the cusp of the town's boundaries. Her grandmother had barely gotten by, so she could guess how little her employees got paid. There just wasn't much money to go around.

When they walked, they stuck to the edge of the road, close to the trees.

Past the shacks and closer to town, the street names were better marked and the houses were larger. "We need to find one where nobody's home," Nia said to Sam, then realized that he'd fallen behind her. She stopped and waited for him to catch up, and she took his arm. "We'll find a place for you to rest soon, I promise. But for now, please keep up with me."

"I'm trying. I'm tired, and I'm hungry."

Nia wasn't tired. She wasn't hungry.

"All right, fine. You see where I'm pointing?"

"Yes."

"Through those trees, at the end of this next block. I'm going to go ahead and scout. You stay out of the yards and stick to the trees."

"Fine."

As she ran, the too-big boots flopped around her ankles. She stopped long enough to remove them and return to being barefoot. The scarf that held her hair back slipped down around her neck and her tangled, dreadlocked hair burst free and trailed behind her.

Her hair beat against her back and shoulders, terrible cables that glimmered as if there were strands of metal woven into their kinks and coils. Her naked feet slapped against the earth, pounding it and crushing anything that she stepped on; nothing scraped the soles and nothing cut her in the softer spots between her toes. She was remade, or unmade. She was something new and something stronger, something heavier.

It almost made her hysterical when she thought about it. This wasn't how it worked, or it wasn't how she'd always heard tell of it. When you die, you don't freeze and stay; you become an angel or a ghost. You become light and beautiful. You don't get heavier and more solid. You don't get stronger and more ugly.

Ugly.

She didn't like the word, and something inside her argued with it. Nia didn't know what she looked like, not really. She hadn't seen a mirror yet, so that became one more goal—find a mirror and see how bad the damage truly was.

The first house smelled like tea, fire, and cooking eggs. People were home, and making a late breakfast. Nia bypassed it and moved on to the next, but through the windows she could see someone dusting, so she skipped that house as well. Three or four homes down, she came to one that was conveniently offset and shuttered up. It was a large house, but not so large that it could be called a mansion, and it smelled like no one had been there for weeks. Nia pulled one of the shutters open and peered through the window, then pressed her ear against it. She heard nothing—not the sound of late sleepers breathing, and not the bustle of a house-hold in motion.

She continued to listen and sniff from the back of the house to the sides, though she stayed away from the front door.

But there was a rear entrance, out of sight of prying eyes. It was locked, but that meant nothing to Nia. She pulled at the lever until it snapped and burst free. She pushed her hand through the hole, popping the hardware, and she shoved on the door until the latch split and fell.

She held still. No response came from inside. No one raised an alarm or asked about the commotion.

She swung her head from side to side and noted that she was in a kitchen, and that the kitchen had been very thoroughly cleaned before being abandoned. There was no whiff of smoke and no hint of anything cooked, and the air indoors was uncomfortably warm and stale. No windows had been opened in days, and the light that squeaked in through the shutter slats was dusty and thick.

Nia shut the door behind herself and made a quick, quiet investigation. Downstairs past the kitchen and dining areas there was a small parlor and a living room. Upstairs there were three bedrooms—a master and two others. All were tidy and mostly empty of personal effects. The washroom cabinets held little of interest, and the wardrobes showed signs of having been sorted for packing.

The owners were out of town, and had been gone for no less than a week. It was perfect.

She tiptoed back down the stairs and retreated from the kitchen door, which she drew shut even though it was broken.

Ten minutes later she returned with a bleary-eyed Sam, who was intensely uncomfortable about the prospect of breaking and entering, but too exhausted to do anything but lodge a feeble and formal complaint. Nia convinced him to take the smallest bedroom, because it backed up to the woods and no one would see if the window were opened for air; and the chain-drawn ceiling fan didn't squeak so loudly that it would attract any unwanted attention.

He dropped himself onto the small bed and was asleep before Nia had time to suggest that he brush himself off. But if the worst that the family had to suffer for the illicit stay was a little bit of dirt in the child's room and a broken back door, then the intrusion would have been a gentle one.

Nia left Sam and wandered back to the master bedroom, where a few clothes meant for an adult woman remained in the wardrobe.

She stripped off the baggy shirt she was wearing and let it fall to the floor. She faced the full-length mirror, closed her eyes, and then opened them again, resolved to keep looking until she got used to the idea of her new body.

Except . . . it wasn't very different from her old body, now that she had a minute to stare at it. The shape was the same, lean and not terribly tall. Her face hadn't changed much; it was still wide at the cheekbones and narrow through the chin.

But her color was off. Once she'd been brown from a life in the sun; now she was so pallid and white that she looked nearly gray— and it wasn't just from dust left over from her shell. The texture of her body had changed from ordinary skin with fine hairs and creases at the corners to something milky and matte, with veins that crept just barely beneath the surface. "Marble," she murmured, because that was what it made her think of. There was a bank in Tallahassee with floors that were creamy and gray, with streaks of blue-purple cutting through the pale like lightning.

When she squeezed herself, pinching at the skin of her upper arm, the flesh depressed and sprang back. It was not hard; it was only smooth. With long sleeves and long skirts, she could hide enough of it to pass for sickly or shade-prone. It didn't look too unnatural, she decided.

But then there was the hair.

Knotted and twisted like rope, and rough like tumbled burlap, it had lightened from its original dull brown into a vibrant mass threaded with copper and white. It was long and heavy, and she wondered if trimming some of it away would make it look more normal.

Naked, she padded into the washroom and found a small pair of scissors left beside the basin. But her hair resisted the blades, and when she tried to compel them to trim, the handles shattered between her fingers.

"Fine," she said, throwing the broken scissors onto the bureau. "I give up. It can stay—until I find some pruning shears, anyway."

One drawer at a time, she went through the clothes of the lady who lived and slept in the bedroom where Nia lurked. She felt like a petty thief, but at least she was robbing someone who could afford the loss. And besides—these were the things that the owners had left behind. Someone had gone on vacation, or had left for the hot season, and nothing that was left behind could be that important.

Nia found camisoles and stockings, socks, an old girdle, and a brassiere. She didn't want the stockings, and the brassiere was entirely too large, but the socks were soft cotton and they felt nice around her toes, so she put them on. In another drawer there were folded shirts and rolled-up nightgowns, lavender-stuffed sachets that smelled like barley husks and flowers, and dressing slippers that wouldn't have withstood a trip into the front yard.

All of it was very pretty, but none of it was very practical.

Finally, at the bottom of the last drawer, Nia found a white knit top. The shirt was too short to serve as a dress, but beside it Nia spotted a folded pair of dark brown pants. She opened them and held them up.

Nia had worn pants before, castoffs from male cousins or friends. After all, if there was real work to be done around the farm and orchard, there was no good reason to do it in a dress or in high-heeled shoes. She wondered if pants for women were coming into style, or, if not, what a rich woman was doing with them. Abandoning that line of thought, she climbed into the pants and found that they fit well enough to wear. There was a belt hanging in the closet. It didn't match, but she didn't care. It made the pants fit better. Then she found and added some lace-up shoes.

Except for the hair, she could possibly pass for an ordinary girl.

In the closet there were hats, small felt things that would have been tight even if her hair had been short and normal. As it was, she couldn't get them down to even the tops of her ears.

The scarf she'd been wearing had landed on the edge of the bed. She picked it up and used it to tie back what she could. She coiled the rest around her hand and used a pencil to jab it into a bun at the nape of her neck.

This was the best she could do. This was the most normal she was capable of looking, and it made her stomach sink. But it would have to work.

By the time she finished her transformation, Sam was stirring on the squeaky springs of the child's bed. She went to wake him up. "Come on," she told him, smoothing the sweat-plastered hair away from his forehead. "Get up. We've got work to do. I can hear the factories from here, when the wind blows right. We're not far away from town, and we need to—"

"Find the Greek with the shop in the cigar district, or find your cousin, and follow them to the water," he parroted the instructions Mossfeaster had left them. "I remember." He looked haggard and unhappy, but clearer.

Nia smiled at him.

"There's a pump out back and a basin in the other bedroom if you want to clean up. Use the back door, the one in the kitchen. We don't want any of the neighbors to know we're squatting."

They left the house an hour before sundown and set out for town while the sky was still orange and a bit pink. By then they were walking the streets and sidewalks as if they had nothing to hide, as if there was nothing unusual at all about their stroll.

The air grew darker from smoke and from the later hour, and the narrow streets were cloudy with tobacco and coal. Fragments of a conversation pricked at Nia's ears from somewhere close, around a corner or on the other side of a wall.

"Anna Maria . . . ," she heard, and she reached out an arm to slow Sam.

"Wait," she told him.

He'd learned to quit asking questions and let her lead, so he quit walking and let her nudge him off the main walkway.

She took his hand and held it with both of hers, and stood in front of him as if she were about to close in for a kiss or embrace, but she did neither of those things. She was only shielding him and trying to lean closer to the sound of the conversation. Her ears almost pivoted to better hear.

It came to her in pieces, but the gist was easy enough.

At least one murder reported. Two or three more dead on the road, from the pieces of the stolen fire engine and its heavy tanks. A church had been burned to the ground, and they were looking for . . .

"Sam," she told him, her mouth only inches from his. "Sam, we have to move fast. We have to get you out of here."

"Me?" he asked. "What for? I thought you were the one we needed to hide."

"No. Not so much. Not anymore. They're looking for you."

"Who's looking for me?"

She took his elbow and began to walk him away. "We should've changed your clothes, back at that house. We should've . . . done something about your appearance."

"What's wrong with my appearance?" he objected, but he let her lead him away and down another street where fewer people were walking. Down the road, a shift had ended at a factory and a crowd of dirty men came pouring out from the main doors. Most of them rattled back and forth to each other in Spanish. Nia couldn't understand them, but she guessed that they'd be unlikely to finger Sam as a person of interest. They had been busy all day, indoors.

She guided Sam into the crowd, and they walked in its midst down to the center of town.

"They'll have your description, and they'll be circulating it," she told him.

"Who?"

"The police. They know what happened back on the island. Or I guess they don't know, really, but they found a few dead bodies and a burned-down church and they're kicking around your name since Mel said that you were the one who drove the truck down to the ferry."

"Oh," he breathed. He might've said more to defend himself, but the bustle of the bodies pressed around him and he clutched at Nia's arm to keep her from drifting away. "Oh, that's not good. Wait." He tugged at her elbow and crushed close to whisper toward her ear, "Wait, what about the church? I didn't burn down the church. For that matter, I didn't kill anybody either. I realize that there might have been . . . interference from the water, but . . . Oh, Jesus. Mossfeaster didn't say what happened back there. Do you think he burned it down?"

"I don't even know what church they're talking about," she said. "But I didn't smell anything burning before you two made off with me, and I don't think he would've doubled back to cover our tracks. He said he couldn't touch the water, or the water witch could find him."

"So where is he now?"

"I don't know. He said he had things to take care of."

"Like burning down a church?"

Nia shook her head. "Word wouldn't have gotten here so fast. The church must have gone down when the people died. But they're saying *murder*, Sam. Those people who were following the truck, we didn't murder them. Nobody murdered them."

"Mossfeaster did, if you want to get precise about it."

"That was self-defense, and you know it. And since no one saw what happened, I don't think . . . wouldn't they talk about it like it was a weird accident? Why would they assume it was murder?" Her thoughts were racing, trying to piece together what was happening even as she tried to direct Sam along with the crowd's flow.

"People are dead, and it was strange. Murder's an easy guess. How much farther to the Greek?"

"Not much," she said, feeling the insistent pull of Mossfeaster's directions planted in her brain. "Seventh Avenue is up there."

"How do you know?"

"Because this is Fifth." She pointed at an iron sign with a white curled embellishment. The crowd was beginning to thin as the workers siphoned off down side streets and alleys. Ybor was dotted with ethnic clubs that catered to various members, and outside the core of the town there were residential neighborhoods. Few people had cars, but the streetcars chimed and cut through the streets on their cables, culling the throng even further.

They hurried past the Spanish club, Las Novedadas, and the Afro-Cuban club, and then another block down. Off to the right there was an alley, tight and dark. A sign reading POPPO EFODIAZO hung down from a pair of squeaking chains.

Down the alley they ran, but when they reached the door it was firmly latched, as if the store was shut for the afternoon. There were no hours posted, but it was early enough that someone should be manning the counters.

Nia held her face against the window and saw a wonderland of different products and items inside. But she saw no people anywhere, and she smelled metal and fire.

"Is this the place?" Sam asked.

"It should be." She knocked on the door, almost hard enough to break it.

No one answered, and no one came; but out on the main street, several passersby stopped to see what the commotion was about. Nia smiled at them, trying not to look too guilty or strange. They continued to stare until she took Sam by the arm and led him away, out the alley's other side and onto Sixth Avenue, where the few people left on the streets moved quickly toward home, out of the heat.

"Now what?" Sam inquired, and it annoyed Nia because she'd been on the verge of asking the same thing and he'd beaten her to it.

"I don't know. Mossfeaster talked like this man was a sure bet. Maybe we should let ourselves inside and help ourselves," she suggested.

But Sam's lifetime of insurance work made him cringe at the prospect. "We can't just break *in*! That'd be our second felony today."

"Sure we can."

But before she could force Sam to agree to take some action, an explosion crashed through the building behind them. Bricks split and fell as the nearest wall bulged, pressed from within by an incredible weight or force.

Nia smelled it again, the lava burn of fire filling the air in the alleys and along the streets nearby. She reached for Sam to pull

him back to a safe distance but he was already backing away—
already wondering how to flee whatever was coming.

"Go on," she told him. She didn't want to keep him there, but
she needed to see what was going on.

"But—"

"Go back down to . . . that restaurant we passed on the way,
the one with the fountain. Go wait there." She wasn't sure why it
was so important that she figure out what was going on. She didn't
know why she wanted to make Sam leave, either, but in the back
of her mind—in the homing pigeon part, the part where Mossfeaster kept one rough finger hooked inside her—she *knew* that
this was something awful, something that was part of the plan
whether anyone else was aware of it or not.

Sam hesitated until a second blast fractured the wall of the
next building over, and then he ran for it.

Hell and High Water

Nia watched Sam retreat, walking halfway backwards as he tried to figure out what was going on. When he rounded the bend and scuttled onto Palm Street, she returned her attention to the store.

A mob was gathering. The fringe of the scene was collecting people who were too curious to flee and too nervous to investigate more closely. Nia hid herself within those ranks for a minute more, then returned to the front door and leaned on it until it collapsed inward.

She toppled into a dark, furnace-hot space that was filled with smoke and stank of brimstone. Instinctively, she covered her face with her arms and hands, breathed in the saltwater shine and the mold of the old jewelry that jingled there.

But there was no way to hide from the smoke or the awful reek, and she could hear—a few rooms away—the first crackling snaps of fire catching hold of a willing fuel.

She was about to call out to ask if anyone was inside, or in danger, but stopped herself short without knowing why. Under the swirling current of blue-gray smoke that hovered at the ceiling, she detected another scent, familiar but unplaceable. It was the faint and pernicious odor of something she'd smelled long before, but possibly never identified.

Nia closed her mouth and covered her face again, but she found the pose too much of a reminder of her years in stone, so she crouched instead to avoid the worst of the tainted air.

Down on the floor the air was a little clearer, though no less hot. Nia pulled herself over it on all fours, scuffing the knees of her stolen pants against the stone floor, which felt cool by comparison to the air.

There was a counter, and she felt her way around it. There was a curtain, billowing and blue, separating the front room from the back. The pressing heat was coming from that direction—it was emanating from one of the back rooms, from somewhere deeper in the heart of the block. From the outside of the building, it didn't look like the store was very big, but she was surprised and alarmed by how far she could creep into its depths.

The second room was occupied by three startling figures. They were each individually so baffling that Nia didn't know where to look first; each one commanded her full attention, but they had triangulated themselves in such a way that her eyes could only dart back and forth between them.

She crouched in the doorway with the blue curtain draping across her shoulders.

"I am neutral, by ancient and unbreakable agreement!"

The screaming man was small and misshapen, or perhaps he

was only lame. One of his feet was curled and clubbed, and his back was bent. His hair was wild and black, and where the light of the sparkling fire caught the tousled waves, it appeared to be streaked with orange. He was wearing a tattered apron that reached to his knees and carrying a knobbed metal cane.

He waved the cane like a wand, and when he struck it against the tables and floor it sparked wildly, illuminating the room in bursts.

"I serve because I choose, and I choose to serve without allegiance or preference!" He spit the last word and slammed his cane against the counter nearest the second man, who was doubled over.

When the other man spoke, there was pain in his voice that came from deep within, as if he were mortally wounded and acutely aware of it. "We did not know," he insisted. "We had no warning that you were of our kind."

"Liars, the both of you!" The apron-clad man swung the cane again. It would have clapped against the other man's head except that it was caught by a blond woman.

She seized the cane and held it hard; the muscles in her forearm bulged and strained, and she shoved the cane away from the injured man, who moaned.

"Bernice," Nia whispered, but the syllables drowned in the chaos.

Her cousin stood between the two men, defending one and looking like she wished to kill the other. Nia knew that look. She'd seen it before; it had been one of the very last things she saw in her last life, and she remembered it well.

Nia wasn't sure if it was exquisite or terrible the way Bernice looked exactly the same, but perfectly different. Her hair was damp with sweat, and her face was streaked with soot and rage, but, as always, she was impeccably attired in a long, light-colored dress and yet another pair of impractical heels.

She never learns, Nia thought. But as she watched Bernice move and parry, twist and growl, she realized that perhaps she was wrong. Dressed like a lady or no, Bernice had gathered a thing or two about the way a body moves. While the man in the apron mounted his assault, Bernice cast herself into the fray and held her own, though her adversary was clearly not the mortal sort.

The Greek used his cane to push them back; he stabbed with it and swung it, and everywhere the metal tip made contact, fire struck and sparkled. It was catching here and there, along the drying strings of paper that hung along the wall. It was digging in, charring and climbing up the curtains.

And it seemed to Nia, who watched in stunned uncertainty from the doorway floor, that everywhere the fire caught and burned, it seared away something false.

A mask was being stripped one licking flame at a time, and underneath the mask there was only more fire. In a matter of minutes, the entire room would be consumed from wall to wall, and there would be no escape for anyone. The mask would be removed, and whatever rank little hell the Greek's store concealed would be visible to all. It would keep and broil them all, and only the Greek seemed not to care.

He had been pushed beyond a boundary that Nia couldn't see, and that Bernice was swearing she hadn't known about.

"We told you!" she hurled the cane aside, and away from the man she was protecting. "We didn't *know*!"

"Arahab knows, and you came on her behalf!" He beat the cane again and again, punctuating his words with brilliant fireworks of violence. "Do you think I did not know why you wanted the call? Did you assume that I know nothing of her ambitions and plots?"

"Then why would you give it to us in the first place?" Bernice demanded, shrill and angry. She was holding her companion up with one arm and using the other to shield them both from the Greek's frenzied blows.

"It was my *oath*," he said, and beat the cane again very close to her face. "Serve all, and none will quarrel!"

The man under Bernice's arm groaned and vomited, and the contents of his stomach were bloody and white. "José," she whimpered, not daring to take her eyes off the Greek. "José, stand *up*."

"Can't," he said through strings of spittle.

"You did this to him!" she screamed at the Greek, and her accusation only enraged him more.

"I did this? Is that what the story will be? You would frame me for such an act, when I did nothing but complete the task I was assigned?" And then, despite his bubbling wrath, he stopped as if a new thought had occurred to him; and he knew that for its sake, he must restrain it. "Get out," he commanded, and the words were fat and festering with anger.

Bernice didn't trust the order. She glanced with darting, feral eyes from corner to corner, seeking escape.

And that's when she saw Nia, still huddled and defensive in the gateway between the storefront and the back room.

Bernice's gaze snagged on her cousin, but true recognition did not come immediately. Then her mouth dropped open and she let out a little gasp of astonishment.

The Greek picked up a heavy clay crucible and hurled it behind Bernice. The makeshift discus shot through the smoke-clouded room, collapsed itself into a flaming curtain, and shattered the window high up behind her. "Take him and get out. And gods help you both if I see either of you again."

Nia watched Bernice decide whether or not to take the offer. She watched her cousin conclude that escape was more valuable than assuaging her curiosity. She watched the well-heeled girl in

the dress that was beginning to smolder take the man by the arms
and haul him bodily out the tall window and into the street outside.

Satisfied that they were gone, the Greek turned his attention
to Nia.

"Come in," he told her. The fury had not drained from his
voice yet, but even in the crackling commotion of the burning
room she could tell that it was not directed at her.

"I can't." She shook her head.

"You can," he assured her. "And you *must*."

A blast of heat behind her pushed Nia forward. She toppled
down in front of the Greek and continued to shake her head. "No,
no. I can't breathe."

He bent his good knee and tucked the bad leg underneath himself, until he was low enough to look her in the eyes. He gave her
a frank and openly interested perusal, and then offered her his
hand as if to help her up. "You don't understand," he said. "You
don't *need* to breathe. You must be fresh, otherwise you'd have realized by now that you're only doing it out of habit."

But whether she needed to breathe it or not, the air choked her
throat and the smoke stung her eyes. She refused the man's hand,
but looked over her shoulder to see that the front room was also in
flames on the other side of the blue curtain. She looked up at the
window where Bernice had escaped, dragging the man with her. It
was not so far away that she couldn't reach it in a couple of fast
jumps.

The Greek stood up straight and stretched out his arms, opening
them wide and holding the cane aloft. As he raised them, the individual tongues of fire swelled and soared together until they ate
away all four walls, and behind the walls the world was white with
heat.

Nia began to panic. The door was gone, the windows were

gone, and the room was nearly gone, too, having been eaten away
or simply undone by the spreading, sprawling flames.

"I have to go after them," she insisted through a welling stream
of tears that streaked her sooty skin with wet lines.

"No, you don't, and you *shouldn't*. Please stand up. Let me explain."

"Who *are* you? *What* are you?"

"I'm no one who means you any harm, young kindred. I know
your kind. Like them in some way, chosen by the elements and offered strength." His voice took on a pinging echo that gave each
vowel a small, definite hum. "Stand up, little troll. This fire holds
no harm for a child of stone."

The searing, pulsing waves of heat pressed against her, holding
her down even as she fought against them, trying to force her back
to rise and her shoulders to follow.

Finally and slowly she stood, but her clothes were turning
black and her nose was filled with the sickening stench of burning
hair. She cowered even as she rose, her head held low between her
shoulders and her arms clutching each other.

"There you go," the Greek said almost kindly. "That's all I
wanted to see, and all you needed to know. It isn't comfortable,
but it is survivable, isn't it?" He lowered his hands and tapped the
end of his cane upon the floor. An invisible gust blasted forth in
shock wave rings and pushed the worst of the fire back to the
walls, where it climbed and smoldered and flared from corner to
corner.

The room was still blistering, but he was right: Nia could stand
it. A stray ember alighted on her leg, scorching a round hole and
eating the fabric until she patted it away into nothing. It stung
where the spark had touched her, but when she looked down,
there was no mark.

Outside, she heard a clucking chorus of voices shouting for the fire department or the police. One voice rose above the rest, high for a man's, and desperate. Sam was calling her name, repeatedly, insistently.

He could've been a thousand miles away.

The Greek continued. "I think that you'll find a great number of things merely unpleasant but survivable once you've gotten older and lost more of your mortal habits."

Nia couldn't stand up straight, because the heat was too oppressive, but she knew that he must be right. Surely she couldn't have withstood the room of fire back in her other life. She would've expired by now, overcome by the suffocating stench and the withering heat.

"They were . . . ," she tried to say through chapped, cracking lips.

"They were not with you, I know. They serve a water goddess, and you are no such creature. You're no creation of hers, I can see that. You are preserved in a different way, and stone is a challenge to a smith like me. Paper I can reduce to ash, and even metal can return to a pliable liquid with heat enough. But stone? *That* is another fire entirely. To melt such a substance requires pressure, and the coughing force of the earth's interior. Steel may rust, wood may burn, and earth may wash away. But you, dear thing, were made by someone who means for you to *last*. Someone means to keep you close for many years."

"I'm not made of stone."

"No, but you're made *from* it. And in this case, there is no distinction. Tell me, who is your master? Who made you in this fashion, crafted you to stand against the elements?"

"I don't know if he has a name," she waffled. "He said we could call him Mossfeaster."

"Mossfeaster." The Greek turned the sound over in his mouth, tasting it and trying to tell how well it fit. He brightened, and the room brightened, too, until it was perfectly blinding. "I see, yes. I *do* see. This is the time for those of us between the cracks, is it not? Creatures like you, and like me. And like them." He sneered at the place in the curtain of flame where the window used to be.

"Them," Nia interrupted, desperate to finish the conversation and be away. "Who were they?"

"Why do you ask me? You knew them. I saw it; the woman recognized you."

"I knew her, yes. Years ago. But why was she here, and who was the man?"

He scowled, and with his anger, the walls burned blue. "Troublemakers. Emissaries from a despised party. But I am compelled to serve them, one and all. It is an understanding I have with the elders, and it is how my peace is kept. I show no preference, and I refuse no requests. My fair and impartial work is established and respected, and those . . . those pathetic *guppies* would try and rob me of this?"

"I'll go after them. I'll bring them back to you, and you can do whatever you want with them."

"Oh no, I don't want them back here. And you don't want to chase them yet, either. Give them time. Let the wretched little fiend execute her plan, for all the good it will do her."

"Why? What plan?" She asked it fast, because, survivable or not, the heat was appalling. It singed her hair and clothes even as the Greek held it at bay.

"They mean to frame me. They mean to make it appear as if I have broken a truce that is older than their greatest great-grandparents! Whether or not I loathe their precious *Mother,* I respect the peace. I would never—"

Nia peeled one of her arms up and held it out. "Yes, so you said. But I'm . . . please, I can't stay like this. Someone is waiting for me outside."

"Let them wait. No one will enter or interrupt until I drop the blaze and let them approach. And you should be patient. As I said, let the woman do her treachery. It will teach Arahab a thing or two about whom she should choose when she recruits her minions. That idiot girl—"

"Bernice. Her name's Bernice," Nia said.

"She means to betray her mistress. She has poisoned her companion, and tried to pin the deed on me."

"Why would she poison him? It looked like she was trying to protect him."

"It is a ruse, designed to distract Arahab. It will drain the Old Lady to heal him, if she elects to do so. It will cost her a great deal of power to revive him, because he's been tainted with the very metals from which she made her Armageddon call. The arsenic is mixed with the bronze to make it harder, but when mixed with water, it becomes an acid, much like its chemical kin, phosphorus. It will corrode the man from the inside out, and it will be difficult for even Arahab to wash it away. The acid is mild enough for ordinary men and women, but it's much worse for her. For us," he added. "It is hard for our kind to bear."

He shrugged his shoulders and waved the cane in a gesture of apathy. "So let her try it. It will make her ill and angry, and she deserves the misery if anyone ever did. Fire and water are not meant to mix in such a fashion, with metal corroding between them."

Nia felt like she was melting, cooking in her clothes. Regardless of what the Greek said about being able to withstand the heat, she was going crazy standing there in the midst of the inferno. But his information was too helpful, and she was too confused and conflicted to fight him for an exit.

So she asked "Why?" instead of begging to leave, even though she thought she could feel her skin sloughing off and sliding, dripping down to the floor. "Why would Bernice do that? Why would she poison anybody?"

"How should I know? I care nothing for the politicking of the elders, the elementals, or their kith."

"Well . . ." She began to cough, and then tried to choke it away lest she never be able to stop. "Can you at least tell me where they went?"

"Why would I know *that*?"

Flustered and frantic, Nia's eyes were streaming and her throat was closing up with ash. "Then can you tell me—" She gagged on the air and forced herself to finish. "—where the nearest water is?"

"Open ocean?" He used the handle of his cane to scratch the side of his head. "The fort at De Soto, I suppose. It's a few miles to the south, if that far. But I'm telling you, *don't give chase.* Just wait, and the situation will resolve itself. The man will die, the goddess will be aggravated, and the woman will be punished."

"Thank you," Nia gasped. "Thank you, I appreciate your help. Can you please let me go now? Please, I'm so . . . I can't stand it."

He looked as if he were a little disappointed in her, but he pointed his cane at the window that he'd broken to send Bernice away.

Nia didn't think twice or ask any questions. She leaped in a diving arc up to the window and through it, hands first and eyes closed. She exploded out into the street and hit the ground rolling, twisting, and gathering her body into a less crumpled shape.

Sam was there before she could finish wiping her eyes; she opened them just wide enough to see through a watery veil of stinging tears that half the block was collapsing.

"Oh my God," Sam said, because he was watching the fire envelop the buildings more than he was watching Nia recover herself. "Was anybody in there?"

"No one who'll care," she said, and as she spoke she could feel her lungs clearing and the lining of her throat growing smoother.

"Somebody's dead inside? Oh God."

"No. I mean some*thing* is inside, but he's all right with the temperature. Let's go. Come on, we have to move." She crawled and staggered to her feet, even though a well-meaning man in a nice suit was trying to tell her to lie still and wait for a doctor.

The clanging bells of a fire engine sounded a few streets away. A truck was fighting through the crowds and struggling with the narrow streets, trying to come and save the day; but the day was already lost. The Greek's store was all but gone, and the store next door—whatever it once was—would be a pile of smoldering ash within another minute.

"I wonder if they were covered," Sam mused quietly, taking Nia's arm. "No, don't. She's fine. She's with me," he told the gentleman in the suit. "I'll take her to a doctor right now."

"I don't need a doctor," Nia swore before she realized she should let Sam do the talking.

"That's all right, dear, we're going to go find one anyway." Then, quieter and into her ear. "A dozen people saw you crash through that window with a fireball behind you, so let them be concerned. Better they're worried than curious, right?"

"You're right." She shifted her shoulder and used it to rub at her face, still half-convinced that her skin was melting and dripping down onto her clothes. "Here, help me up."

"You're heavy," he observed. "I don't mean you *look* heavy—"

"I know what you mean," she said. She hadn't meant to lean on him so hard. "I don't care, it's fine. Let's go. Which way is south from here?"

"This way, but let's just get away from these people first."

The truck was coming closer, moving slowly but with great determination. The crowd was organizing itself in a loose and semi-helpful way; nearby store owners and factory people were pumping water and bringing buckets, barrels, anything they could throw at the blaze. They formed lines in advance of the truck and swung pots, casks, and kegs as fast as they could be filled—anything at all to keep the fire from spreading to the rest of the district.

Nia was still confused and simmering in her skin, still flailing her arms and resisting the urge to scratch violently at her itching flesh. Sam took her hand and took the lead, ducking through the press of people and urging her to follow.

Clear of the worst of the crowd, Sam and Nia dashed out of the fire truck's way as it careened around a corner and clipped the curb. They ducked into the next open street. People were still running to see the commotion, and business owners and residents were still screaming for water, but the pack was thinner the farther they removed themselves from the source.

"South?" Sam panted.

"What?"

"You said we were going south. How far south, and where exactly? Slow down. We can't keep running away from the fire," he told her, softer than a whisper against the side of her face. "We'll get stopped by the police just for acting guilty."

"Why?"

"Innocent people run towards a fire, because they want to know what's happening. Guilty people already know, so they go the other way."

She nodded, and her head knocked gently against his.

"And you need to cool off anyway. What happened in there?"

She wasn't sure how best to sum it up, so she told him, "I met the Greek. He's not human. I don't know what he is, exactly, but he's definitely not human. He's the one who made the fire, and he's the one controlling it. It won't go out until he makes it go out."

Sam relaxed his grip on her waist. "I hope he lets it die down soon."

She continued. "The Greek talked like he hates the water

witch—he called her Arahab, and that's what she called herself
the first time I saw her—but he said she was a goddess." She held
up her hands, counting on them as she thought out loud. "So
there's a water goddess, and a fire monster who talks like he serves
a fire god; do you think there's somebody in command of the air,
and another someone in charge of the earth?"

"Probably," Sam agreed. He didn't sound very happy about it.

After a minute of silence Nia said, "You know, the best we can
hope for is that no one will ever know that anything happened. The
world won't end, the apocalypse won't come, and Leviathan won't
awaken."

Sam didn't respond for a few seconds, and they walked together as if life were proceeding in a perfectly normal way—
except that behind them, plumes of black smoke gushed skyward.

"Where are we going again?" he asked.

"De Soto," she said. "There's more waiting for us there than just
Mossfeaster's water witch." Then another thought dawned on her,
so she changed the subject. "Listen, did you see anyone escape the
shop before I did? There was a woman in there, and a man who
looked like he was dying. There was something wrong with him;
they couldn't have gotten away very fast. They would've come out
the same window I did."

"Yeah, I saw them. They were dressed up, and they left in an
ambulance right before you came out."

"They what?"

"There was an ambulance—I think someone called the hospital when the first explosion blew out part of the building. They
must have, because they got there quick. The woman was crying
and upset, and the man was throwing up everywhere. I thought it
was from the smoke."

"So they have an ambulance, and we're on foot. We need to either find a vehicle or run like hell."

"I can't run like hell," Sam puffed, and Nia knew he was right. He was already panting, and there was no time to wait for him to catch his breath.

She stopped. "You're right, I know you are. How do I get to De Soto, then?"

"It's just . . . It's maybe a mile and a half from here, straight that way." He pointed. "It isn't far. But the ambulance took those people to the hospital. Shouldn't you start looking for them there?"

"They'll never make it to the hospital." Nia suspected, but did not tell Sam, that Bernice had already killed whoever drove it and was probably speeding merrily toward the water even as they spoke. "She's going to hijack it to get back to the water. So here's what we're going to do: You're going to go find a car, or something. Find anything that's drivable, and borrow it or steal it, it doesn't matter. Meet me at De Soto as soon as you can."

"Wait!" he clutched her arm and there was real, deep panic in his eyes.

"I can't," she told him. She pulled her arm out of his grasp, and began to run.

To the Water's Edge

José could feel his insides weakening, bubbling, and dissolving wherever the arsenic mixture spilled, poured, and oozed. His eyes were watering with runny rust and stinking phosphorus. His sphincter failed, and fiery yellow excrement spilled into the back of the ambulance.

Ceaselessly he manufactured orange bile that smelled like eggs and lava, and he cast it out from both ends. Everything the mixture touched began to sizzle and simmer, as if it were pure acid leaking from his body.

"What have you done?" he asked between heaving gags.

"You'll be all right," Bernice told him. Her calm was infuriating. She had killed the two men in the ambulance and kicked them out into the ditch, and then she took the wheel and directed the boxy vehicle along the roads. She left the siren on because she liked it, with its screeching red light and tinny wail.

José hadn't known Bernice could drive such a thing, but she had assumed the wheel and taken the controls with assurance that was—if not masterly—perfectly instinctive.

He watched her wrestle the pedals and jerk on the gears, and the ambulance stalled only once. But as the seconds swept by and the poison coursed through his system, he was losing the ability to notice much of anything except for his own grueling struggle to keep himself from falling apart. How many internal organs could he lose to the gnawing combustion of the poison? How much of his stomach could he live without . . . and how much of his intestines? For over a hundred years, he'd barely thought of himself as a man at all; he was Mother's child and construct.

But there on the floor of the ambulance, writhing and retching, he remembered that once upon a time he'd been a man with a torso that ticked with life. He recalled the need for food, the constant desire for alcohol or water or nourishment. There was forever some gastronomic distress or fluctuation brought on by the staleness of the ship's cupboards or strange molds that worked into the breads, onto the meats.

Deep in the back of his memory he recalled a night on an island where the locals had given him cooked fish and a broth that they drank like coffee, though it was thicker and had more texture. He remembered the subsequent pain in his bowels, so intense that it brought on hallucinations and bloody diarrhea. It had been some treachery, then. It had been an attempt at mutiny that had failed and failed catastrophically.

"The captain was supposed to die," he gurgled around the mouthful of saliva and vomit.

"What, baby?" Bernice called from the cab.

"They mean to kill me," he recalled, and tried to say it out loud, but the words came out scrambled and damp. The acid from his stomach, from his throat, from his intestines . . . it was eating his teeth. They were crumbling in his mouth when he clacked them together.

His lover caught the general idea, and she responded with that same maddening calm. "You'll be fine. I'll get you right to Mother. We're almost there. She'll fix you. She *has* to fix you."

"Mother," he mumbled, his head lolling back and forth, coating his face and hair with his own bile.

He couldn't remember, he couldn't recall, he couldn't focus. What was that noise? That awful, jangling, rattling mechanical sound, coupled with the piercing whine that spun around in circles over his head—where was it coming from, and what did it mean? He couldn't concentrate.

There was an island, and his first mate had wanted his ship and his crew, so he'd paid the natives to . . . And there was a meal on the beach, while drums were . . .

No. There was a small, dark shop, and it was empty when he and Bernice had let themselves inside. He'd watched her from the second room as she entered the third chamber and through the curtain that wafted and waved, parting around her and behind her; he'd watched her rifle through the jars and canisters. She'd grabbed what she wanted, then returned to him in the middle room.

She'd mixed the powders and shavings in a crucible, because there was no jar that would hold it. She'd held up the grayish reddish powder and had poured something on top of it. When the two combined, the concoction had begun to sizzle and spit.

"Where did you learn it?" he'd asked her then, and he tried to ask her now from pure delirium.

"In church," she'd told him then, but she did not answer him now because she could not understand him anymore. His tongue was coming apart, dropping into strips of saggy flesh that flopped around in his mouth or fell out in chunks.

"In church?"

"There was a church, back on the island. I did some digging around in there. I told you, I haven't liked this idea for a while. I don't want the world to end, not yet. I've been trying to think of ways to put it off, and I thought . . ." She hadn't bothered to finish her sentence, instead handing him the crucible with the foaming, disgusting mixture.

He took it, held it under his face so he could better see and sniff it.

"It'll only hurt for a little bit, and it won't be that bad," she'd promised. "I read all about it. Mother can fix you up, but it'll cost her plenty of energy to do it. Drink it, and you'll get a little sick. But you'll make me so happy. And you want to make me happy, don't you? I thought you did. Maybe I'm just stupid."

"You aren't stupid," he'd said, even though he'd long and privately assumed as much. It was only polite to argue.

Lying on his side in the back of the van, lying with a mouth filled with pieces of his own tongue swimming in acidic pus, José felt something cold against his cheek and he realized with only the dullest jab of horror that it was the van's floor against his gums. The acid had burned through his face, and now it dripped down onto the floor. Where it touched the painted metal, the finish peeled and ran.

"Hang in there, baby," Bernice said from the front seat. "I'm sorry it's taking so long, but it's not far now. I can feel it, you know? The way the water pulls at me, I know it's right over there—but I can't find a road. If I don't find something soon—" She cut herself off. "There's a road!"

She made a hard left and the ambulance teetered briefly on two wheels.

José gagged on the motion, and on the corrosive vomit. The vehicle bounced and bobbed on a barely paved strip. He could feel it, even through all the misery and disorientation and pain. He could also feel the water somewhere close, beckoning. He reached out with what was left of his determination, and he begged for Mother to hear him. Out in the distance, from the depths of the water, she heard him, and said she was coming to meet them.

What has happened? she asked, but José was too far gone to answer. He'd spent all his energy to summon her attention, and it was merely a weak cry—a hand waving in the darkness. But she heard him and she was coming. That was all he needed to know or believe.

So he tumbled into unconsciousness, convinced at last that it was safe to do so. Mother would be there when he awakened.

Dimly, as if it were happening centuries or miles away, in the darkness of his blessedly quiet mind he felt the jostlings of the rushing, crashing ambulance as it moved him closer to the shore—and yes, he felt the shore, even asleep and lost—he could feel the water up against his awareness, washing up and down like the comforting lull of a tide.

Crash, jerk, jolt, and shudder. The ambulance had stopped.

The back doors yanked open and a blaze of light penetrated his mental fog. "Bernice." He said her name in his sleep, or he thought he did. He hadn't spoken a clear word since leaving Ybor. She was looking at him, trying to decide how to remove him. She was strong, though. He trusted that she could carry him.

Bernice pulled him out by his chest, hoisted him by the crooks of his arms, and dragged him to the water's edge. Her hands squeezed and stretched the skin there, and it pinched—but the pinch was such a tiny discomfort compared with all the rest. It was a wonder that he felt it so sharply.

And then there was grass. It tickled the underside of his legs. It brushed with an itching determination along his feet and against his legs, and he understood that his clothes were gone in giant patches where the acid vomit had eroded them into nothing. It left his burning skin open to the air, and he wanted to scream about it. But he was beyond screaming. He had no tongue, no cheeks. His jaw was hanging agape, and the walls of his stomach were collapsing upon themselves. The poison was eating him from the inside out, turning his blood into jelly and his bones into fragile things, leeched of all their strength.

When Bernice dragged him over a driftwood log, he heard his hip snap, and it sounded like a slice of apple being broken between a child's fingers.

He didn't feel it at all. He could barely feel anything, even pain.

He could hear Mother's voice, though, and it was outraged and—if he dared to flatter himself—afraid. He tried to cry out for her, but the motion was gruesome; there was not enough muscle left to hold his face in its correct shape, and his effort merely shifted the festering gore.

She picked him up, pulled him into the water. He would have smiled if he'd had enough mouth left. The coolness of it soothed him, where there were nerves left to be soothed. The salt of it was tart against his body, but it was a familiar tartness that felt correct and friendly despite his open wounds.

She cradled him in her arms, not caring how little was left or how terrible it looked. Arahab hummed to him and held him. She drew his quivering, oozing form inside herself, shutting him away from the air, from the sky, and from the pain.

Even the pain.

Even . . . yes. It was gone, there in the swirling, beautiful blueness of her body—created with the ocean, reflecting the heavens. There was pleasant chill, and there was a pretty gleam of white that covered everything, blanketing the universe with calm. He heard a song humming from the water around him, and he realized that his Mother was singing to him, something old and quiet, something soothing and loving. She was singing him a lullaby.

Blanketing him with . . .

Covering him with . . .

And all of it was.

White.

Arahab held José's mangled body, even though it leaked poisonous fluids from every orifice, pore, and wound. She washed him with her hands and then she absorbed him, pulling him deeply into her own torso and closing her blank-white eyes.

"Mother?" Bernice asked. She was holding the small bronze shell between her hands. She fondled it nervously. "Mother?"

The elemental had not chosen a towering shape for this encounter, at the water's edge where the sand clumped itself around sea oats and water weeds. The lumpy dunes hid them from view, or at least gave them a touch of shelter and the illusion of privacy. Beyond the dunes, beyond the farthest reaches of high tide, a ring of trees grew in a crescent. They clung to the mainland, fearing to reach too far onto the sand. The whole earth cowered away from Arahab.

She was only a little larger than a regular human, and only a little stranger in shape. With José inside her, the image was doubled and dreadful.

Arahab, an outline—a woman-shaped sack of water with hands held apart and outstretched. José, a shamble—a man-shaped tangle of gristle, meat, and bones that floated within the translucent skin of his Mother. She was holding him more snugly and warmly than a womb.

And she was concentrating, training her pupil-free eyes inward so she could examine her patient with all his torturous injuries. Whatever he'd consumed was consuming him in turn, and it sickened her, too.

She writhed, just a bit. She buckled a bit under the atrocious weight of his suffering, then stood straight again, with only her pelvis and legs concealed by the surf.

What happened to him? she asked. The question was addressed to Bernice, who was still running her fingers around the ridges and ruffles of the shell.

"Poisoned," she said. "The Greek, at the shop where we went for the call. He did it. He poisoned José; he tricked him. He almost tricked me, too, but José got sick real fast."

Why? she asked, not bothering to pursue the how. She knew how. She could *feel* how. It was something more than a spell and more than simple chemistry. There are powders and fumes that react poorly with water, even striking smoke and sparking peculiar flames. But there was magic here, a bad old kind that was meant to eat gods.

"He said . . . he said he had to make you the call, because he was keeping the peace or something. But he wouldn't let you rouse Leviathan," she said. The word "rouse" felt funny between her teeth. It wasn't one she'd ever used. She wondered where she'd heard it, and why it sprang so easily into the story. "He said he'd kill us both to stop you."

Did he?

José was squirming. No, he was twitching. He was dying there, held suspended and falling apart. The water around him was turning a cloudy yellow, a venomous placenta too sick to nourish anything.

Bernice nodded hard, trying to answer without speaking. She didn't trust the sound of her own voice. She didn't trust the grasping flicks of her fingertips as they held and hid the bronze shell. For the first time in her life, she didn't trust her own ability to talk her way through a falsehood.

It was Mother. It was the way she glared with her unseeing eyes, closed and turned to regard José—who wasn't twitching anymore. Something taut and quietly seething pinched her face, even though it had no muscles to pinch or make it look cross.

Arahab made a small gasp, a burp of pain. She coughed and José's body flopped and wriggled inside her; she hacked again and the simmering blond liquid spilled out of her mouth. She was forcing something, harder and with more power. It buzzed in the air around her, and it hovered over the beach like a cloud of mosquitoes. Arahab called it; she dragged it. She commanded every bit of it, and it came to her—and she funneled every spark of force, or grace, or energy into her own body.

She sent it into *his* body.

No, she said, but Bernice wasn't sure what she meant.

"Mother, are you all right?"

Yes. Arahab's eyes flew open, and they were no longer blank. They were red as if shot with blood. *I'm all right. But he . . .* And then she expelled him through her chest, not in a violent burst of gore, but in a tender little birth that was slow with regret and disappointment.

"But he?" Bernice was transfixed, but not by the sight of the pulpy, repugnant mass that Arahab had deposited onto the edge of the beach. She was watching Arahab, watching and waiting. She had been expecting something, and it hadn't happened. She had been keyed up with anticipation, but this was not the outcome she had planned.

There's nothing more I can do for him.

"Wait." Bernice shook her head. "Wait, I don't . . . No. Look at him. You're just going to let him *die*?"

Arahab's slim, crimson eyes narrowed brightly and smoldered with something riotous and unreadable. *Look at him yourself, girl. He's dead. And that's all. He's dead, and you've killed him.*

"I? No, I didn't. I told you, it was the Greek, in his awful little shop. He's the one who did it. I tried to stop him—he was going to kill me, too. I was trying to help you, Mother."

Were you? She feigned a wide-eyed face. It was a mirror of Bernice's, when Bernice wasn't telling the truth; that was where she'd seen it before. "Were you so devoted that you followed my directions to the letter?"

"Yes—" She had to say it fast, because Arahab was firing questions one after another, harder and quicker. And she was rising up with each question, taking in more water and taking on a bigger form.

She swiped at Bernice and pulled the shell from her hand with a ferocious splash that almost knocked the girl off her feet.

Were you such a devoted daughter that you'd wish for my success, that you'd wish to awaken my father, my Leviathan? This time she wasn't in a cay puddle, surrounded by a rock wall. This time she was wallowing in the Gulf of Mexico, and there were tons upon tons of water at her disposal.

"Yes!"

And were you so single-minded in your pursuit of my ambitions that you strayed not at all and dabbled in no preposterous dark arts— as they are weakly known and dimly understood by the mankind that spawned you first?

"Yes, Mother—"

I made you to help him! To help me! And you would go with him into the fire priest's den, and you would conspire with him to—

"Mother, fix him! Fix him, you have to try harder!" Bernice was shrieking, hysterical. She couldn't help it. Mother was twice her size, and then three times and four times it. She was the size of a house, and growing larger by the sweeping second.

He's dead, and there is no fixing him! I could not do it. I don't hold that kind of power! No one does, any longer. The one who was once called Death is an outcast shadow, weak and shunned. Even if that creature had the means to assist me, I do not think that it would do so.

"You brought *me* back to life," Bernice insisted. She was crying now, and no matter how hard she tried to sell them as tears of pain and loss, they were tears of fear.

No, I prevented you from dying—as I did him, a hundred years before you were born.

"Then why not now? Why did you let him die now? I don't understand! Why didn't you fix him; I swear to God, I thought you could fix him!" And then she realized she'd said too much. This confession would not have been on the script if she were as innocent as she swore.

But Arahab already knew—if not everything, then enough. *You gave him too much of that elixir, and you waited too long to bring him, and now you are afraid, as you should be. Look at what you have done!*

Bernice didn't know what she was looking for, but through terrified streams of tears she did her best to see. "I don't understand," she sobbed, folding her legs beneath herself and crawling slowly back away from the water. "What happened to him? What happened, and why didn't you fix him? I *know* you could have fixed him."

You know? Arahab twisted her neck and crushed her eyes closed with pain, or with restraint, or with some other unidentifiable pressure that pushed up on her from within. *You know nothing—or worse, you know small pieces of things. You've picked up fragments here and there; you've gathered tiny bits of secondhand chatter and you think that you know all the answers!*

"No, I don't. But you saved us before, and I thought if you tried *harder—*"

If I tried harder, then what? That I would bring the poison into myself? That I would sicken myself and become vulnerable? Do you think I did not know what you were planning?

Bernice's face went gray, and her knees folded. She scrambled backwards crablike, realizing that she should not stay so close to the infuriated monster. Arahab was gathering malicious, outraged mass. She was swelling and growing, but she was aching somehow. Something about her rise was pained and forced. There was power there in the water, and there was energy untapped still waiting her command, but it was hard for her.

You know so little, she continued, *that you did not even understand the workings of the call you sent to me, from the wretched little boat that my son wished to sail. You did not know or did not believe that the intent is carried with the casting. But I heard you, my precious liar. I heard you hold the trinket to your breast and make your wish as if it were a coin, and as if the Gulf were a well. I heard your query to the gods.*

Flustered and now beyond panic, Bernice tried hard to remember what she'd wished. She remembered the act of it—the closing of the eyes, the childish toss over the side of the boat, and how it had felt like throwing a coin in a well, yes. It had felt like saying a prayer, so she assumed that no one was listening.

But she couldn't recall the plea she'd made.

Arahab answered for her, filling in the missing piece. *My lamb, you wished to be rid of me. My child, you wished to replace me. And because you are so very knowledgeable—* She opened her massive hands and spoke with sarcasm, another thing she'd learned from Bernice. *And because you are so very wise, and so cunning . . . you did not realize that you were making that wish to me.*

"If . . . if . . . if that's what you think—" She was blubbering, and she hated herself for it, but she couldn't stop. "—then why didn't you do something? Why didn't . . . Why didn't you . . . You could've kept me here. You could've killed me or changed me, or whatever it is you do!"

The creature in the water had grown to the size of a city block, and even though the beach was deserted, people far away could see her. Somewhere far away, someone began to scream. Arahab began to roar.

Because I did not know that you would harm him!

The tides that swirled inside her were sloshing back and forth, and the things she'd caught up—the fish, the weeds, the shells, and the rays—were thrown from side to side. She was a maelstrom contained. She was a vortex above the surface.

"But you could've saved him!" Bernice shouted back.

So the fault is mine, then? So I was the one who killed my son, not you? I made him to ease my loneliness as much as to aid my plans, and he was good to me, and devoted.

I did the best I could, my darling love. I gave him all the energy I could spare, and it was not enough. It has drained me, yes, and the metal venom with its water poison tastes like death in my mouth. But it cannot injure me. It can only disgust me, and a simple aversion is not deadly.

It cannot kill me . . . and I believe you did not know that.

Arahab gazed down at José's body, which was half-floating in the shallow water where the tide was leaving it, tugging it, and breaking it up on the sand where it lay. She regarded him with her empty face, gazing down as if she did not know what to do.

I wanted to fix him, she said, her voice dropping from an ear-shattering explosion down to a mournful howl. *I would have fixed him, even if doing so sickened or wounded me. I would have fixed him regardless, for I loved him longer than I ever loved you.*

Bernice was nearly at the water's edge, almost free of the sopping, slapping mess that sucked at her shoes and held her in the damp. There was no point to her retreat, and she knew it. She could never run far enough or fast enough.

She struggled to her feet, and she stood there all soaking wet and vomited upon. She held herself upright in the sandy mud and in her towering shoes, and as she stared Arahab in the face, she began to pry the shoes off her feet—using her toes to pick and pull at them, one after the other.

Arahab met Bernice's gaze, though she met it from a height of several stories. The Gulf had shrunk around her, but the tide was seeping in to replace what she had taken. The water seeks its level, as it seeks its mistress.

The mistress of the ocean brought herself down swiftly and firmly, planting one hand on either side of Bernice, and planting those hands down so hard that the wet earth shattered and shook. *I knew when I took you that you were evil. That's why I pulled you under the waves and held you against myself. That's why I saved you, because you were formless and void, and I thought I could bend you to join and assist me. I brought you in as a daughter, and as a companion to my son. I received and restored you knowing that you were made of bile and nails, so I suppose the fault is mine after all. I did not frighten you enough while I had the opportunity. I tried to rule you with love, but fear is all that will move you.*

One shoe was completely undone and kicked aside. The second shoe was nearly gone.

If Arahab had noticed, she did not comment. She only raised her head again, pushing up on her hands and baring her beautiful wet throat to Bernice, who had no weapon to push against it. And perhaps there was sorrow after all. She knew how to make the mortal sound of it, if not the shape.

I want to know this, child. If you tell me this, and if you speak the answer truly, then I may yet find some mercy in my heart. I may yet conclude that there is use for you, and hope for you. I would prefer to believe as much, because I have loved you, too, and wished for your companionship.

"What?" Bernice asked in a voice that was midway between a gasp and a whimper. Her other shoe was off, and her bare feet squished the exposed ocean floor between her toes.

Did he plan this with you, too? Was he willing to see me dead, and replaced, or did you tell him some sweet lie to deceive him? From you, I will accept and believe treachery, and it is a nuisance to me, but little more. From him, it would break my heart.

Bernice shook her head slowly, back and forth to mask the motion of her feet stepping away from the shoes. The tears swung away, dripping down her cheekbones and joining the rest of the salt water that pooled and puddled in the space around her.

"Is that all it comes down to? I can't kill you or become you, so there's no place for me in your heart or in your plans except as pet or princess?"

Arahab used her starfish eyes to glare down hard. *Did you do this alone, or did he conspire with you?* She asked it carefully, slowly. A letter at a time.

Bernice couldn't look Mother in the eye. She tried, but her neck wouldn't crane back that far and her eyes were snagged by the sight of the small bronze shell, swirling and dipping in the place where Arahab's heart should be. She reached out her hand and could almost touch it, where an enormous breast came down, almost to the waterline. She reached for the shell like a baby stretches out its fingers for a rattle.

Arahab misunderstood, and softened her crouching, looming stance above the woman at the edge of the shore; and as she dropped her tremendous body down low, Bernice's hand pressed against the false flesh. Her fingertips pushed past the surface tension that passed for skin, and she grasped the frilled end of the call.

With a swift jerk, she pulled it free.

Arahab felt the little theft. She swiveled her head, and when she shifted her position, sliding and rotating in the water, Bernice was able to meet her eyes after all.

"He did it with me," she said without blinking. "It was *his* idea."

And then she turned, one heel slurping at the sodden sand, and she ran.

Her feet pounded fast even where the water curled, bubbled, and slapped around them. Arahab had made her daughter strong and swift. A torrent of fast, irrational options sloshed through Bernice's mind as she pumped her feet one after the other, driving them down into the wet earth and knowing that every drop of water meant that the danger was still close behind.

The world has many deserts; there are huge continents with land for miles and miles, and no water anywhere to be found. I am not like José. I don't need the water to live. I never even liked it very much. I can run farther than she can chase me. . . .

But first she'd have to get away, and—

Arahab's longest tendril-like finger looped itself around Bernice's ankle and pulled her down hard. Facedown she dragged the woman back into the surf, and then she lifted her up out of the water, higher and farther than Bernice had ever been in her life.

This is what balloons see.

And then Arahab hurled her back down into the water. The blow was not a splash but a slap that would have flattened an elephant.

Bernice did not see stars.

The force of the blow from sky to sea had blinded her; her face was seared by the salt and smashed by the pressure. She couldn't see anything. She couldn't even tell if her eyes were open or closed. Her hand was closed, around the shell. It bit into her skin and carved the muscles with its ridges.

Arahab lifted her again, and there it was once more—the sky, and she was in it. Blue and white and so thin, so high that it was hard to breathe. The seconds stretched into hours. They sprawled out in front of her, and when her vision cleared enough that she could peer down onto the shore and into the trees and over them, people were running and pointing. None of them were any bigger than baby mice, pink and scattering.

Down.

The second blow was harder because it was brought down from higher, and Arahab had worked up enough steam to be angrier still. Bernice gasped, and was astonished that she could do so. She sucked in air and was shocked that she still had lungs to hold it. She couldn't feel them, after all.

Up.

Her eyes were open, because she could not close them. She couldn't remember how to do it. But when she could see anything at all, it was shot through with lightning and fire. Everything was backlit as if the sun were shining behind it, so the details were foggy.

Over there, cars were straggling slowly along roads that looked like strips of sugar scraped into the ground with a spoon. Over there, the tops of the trees were green and furry; and in the other direction she saw a strange, lumbering beast that moved fast for its size and shape.

Down.

Smashed, and crushed. Her bones had turned to powder in her skin, or so it felt. All vision in her right eye went dark as the side of her face caved against the surface, and she didn't even feel it.

She didn't feel the shell anymore, either—even though it had crushed itself through the bones in her hand. It did not matter how tightly she'd been holding it before. Now she couldn't let go of it if she tried.

She felt her body rise again. There was a shift in height and temperature, but she was so far beyond pain that it didn't matter what came next.

Through her remaining eye, and through the bloodshot and lightning haze of its faulty signals, she saw the lumbering monster running. It was trying to catch up with something smaller and swifter, with smooth gray-white skin and hair that spun and swung like a cloud of angry snakes. The running was familiar. The gait struck some chord of memory in Bernice's scrambled and ruined head.

It's Nia, she thought in an addled, half-amused burp of lucidity. *Coming to—*

Drawbacks of Rescue

Nia didn't slow down to gape at the gigantic human-shaped monster with tentacle hands. It would have been easy to stare, because it loomed high above the trees, flinging its appendage and snapping it skyward like a whip—pulling something up and slapping it down again into the water with a crash she could hear even half a mile away.

But she glanced up every now and again. She couldn't help it. The thing in the water was so big that it ate up a corner of the sky; it covered the horizon line, and yet she was charging toward it.

So she kept her head down as much as she could, and she ran through the trees, one arm held out to smack away branches and both legs pumping and pounding.

She had no idea how fast she was going. The trees slapped and scraped past her with a stinging force.

Never before had she been able to move so quickly. She'd been quick once, but now she was strong and quick, and the difference moved her through the woods with the speed of a javelin.

Behind her, something heavier came after her.

It had to be Mossfeaster.

It was calling her, urging her to wait, to listen, but she was moving too fast with too much determination. She knew where the call had gone. She knew who was wielding it, and who wanted it, and what she wanted it for, and Nia did not slow down partly because she wasn't sure she knew how. The inertia of her movement thrust her legs without any thinking behind it, and the sheer force of the speed was carrying her forward more than any real intention.

She burst free from the tree line and pitched herself onto the beach.

The sudden shift from turf to partially powdered sand slowed her with suddenness and pain. She tumbled forward, thrown from her rhythm and confounded by the new terrain.

It was strangely dark, there on the beach in the middle of the afternoon. The shadow Arahab cast pitched the strip of sand into dusk. But the shadow undulated as she moved, and speedy, broken rays of light cut through her gestures and scattered on the water.

Now Nia could stare. How could she not?

The goddess was taller than any building she'd ever seen, and wider than any whale or elephant she'd ever heard of. She was made of water as if it were poured into her skin, which was loosely held in the shape of an angry woman the size of a storm cloud. Where eyes should be, there were bright gold slits with streaks of red; where her fingers should be, there were boneless, twisting tentacles with spurs and suckers as big as tree stumps.

And in one hand there was something small and limp. When Arahab held it up to smash it down again, something caught a passing sliver of sunlight and glinted a warning flash of light.

Arahab held it aloft and smashed it down onto the water's surface with a furious, flailing motion. She beat the thing the way a child knocks a toy against the ground if it breaks, or commits some imagined transgression. She crushed it against the water from the full height of her extraordinary reach, and Nia found herself hoping for decency's sake that whatever it was, it wasn't alive.

Mossfeaster stopped behind her. Flecks of dried leaves scattered where he stood, and clods of earth dripped away to the lighter-colored sand. He wasn't panting, because he didn't need to breathe, but the rattled flaking of his decaying form created the same effect.

"It's there, in her hand."

"That thing she's beating?"

"That thing she's beating is your cousin. She is holding something very important in her hand, the little thief. She's cunning and arrogant, but ignorant, too. Forget her. Arahab will have killed her momentarily; we need only the trinket the girl clasps—and I'll tell you, I'm impressed that she's held it this long."

"Bernice?" Nia almost called her name loudly, hoping to be heard. She changed her mind and said it as a question to her companion instead.

"Bernice, if that was her name. Whatever she's holding—"

"If it *was* her name?"

"Look at her," it said, and it was backing away, into the trees again. Arahab's knuckle-less fingers were nearing the ground again. "She's dead. Her corpse has such tenacity. She must have been—"

Mossfeaster might've said more if it hadn't retreated under the threat of the water witch's fist.

Nia did not. She watched the hand with its curly, slick fingers come whistling toward the water, and she again saw a spark of sun catch something bright and small. She leaped forward, onto the wet sand where the tide ought to be, and she dived headlong.

But Bernice hit the water with the smacking crack of a cannon being snapped in two; and a tidal wave coursed out in concentric rings, lunging away from the point of impact. One such traveling ring of water caught Nia square in the face and carried her back to the edge where the sand was dry. The sand stuck against her skin, powdering her down like a biscuit on a baker's countertop.

Before she could fully halt, she got up again and dashed back to the water . . . where she was spotted by the hulking creature who was drawing stares, screams, and frantic summons from people near and far.

She could've been a storm, localized and shocking. She might've been a waterspout, swirling and thrashing over the water. She was losing her shape in her fury, not dissolving or falling apart but simply unwinding into a nebulous, angry form that lashed with whiplike appendages and lunged with the weight of the ocean.

Nia had no idea what to do, but she had a target—the glimmering slice of light that twitched, jerked, and intermittently disappeared as the water monster flung it to and fro.

There was a rhythm to the movement—up, back, and down in a lassoing circle.

Nia timed her jump, and then—just as she was ready to leap—the swinging rope of Arahab's boneless arm flopped to a halt. It dropped its load down onto the sand a few feet away from the crouching girl, formerly made of stone and presently scared speechless.

The gigantic lump of water held still and quivered around the edges. Although it had no physical eyes, Nia was certain that it was staring at her. She hunkered in its immense black shadow, poised to jump or to run.

Bernice was only a few feet away from her. It was once Bernice, anyway, that broken sac of skin and crumbled bones too pulverized to bleed. From the corner of her eye, Nia saw the pile of shattered parts move. It was a convulsive gesture made by a body too weak to convulse. And in its hand, pierced through it and smashed against it, was a brown-gold shell.

The mass of water was shrinking, splashing itself down to a size more conducive to communicating with a creature that was barely over five feet tall. Arahab decompressed and reformed smaller, but still larger than Nia. The water witch retreated until her torso was the size of Nia's body, and she stayed out in the surf a few yards away.

She was not afraid. But she was very, very interested.

What is this? she asked.

Nia was too frightened to rise up. She lingered on the sand, knees bent and one hand outstretched, bracing herself in case she needed to fly. "I'm . . . ," and she didn't know what else to say.

Arahab cocked her head and her eyes were back, all translucent and white. *You're not any kind of theirs.* She waved a hand at the ambulance, where Sam was climbing inside, trying to hide.

Nia could see him at the edge of her peripheral vision. She didn't dare look at him, lest she give Arahab an excuse to pay more direct attention.

"No," Nia agreed with a shuddering cringe. "I'm not any kind of theirs."

And you're not any kind of mine.

"No, I'm not any kind of yours."

Arahab turned her attention to the gurgling pulp that lay on the sand, now in the water. As the creature reduced her bulk, the water table rose back to its usual level and there was less sand and more waves. Bernice was moving, shaking herself left and right. It sounded like pebbles and pasta shifting in a wet leather bag.

"She's healing?" Nia said, because that's what it looked like to her.

She's healing, but she'll never mend. You're like her, aren't you?

"More like her than you. More like her than them." Nia indicated the shore, where the first astonished trickles of a crowd were coming together. "I guess," she added.

What are you, small thing?

She tore her eyes away from Arahab and openly stared at Bernice. It seemed like she was coming back together—re-forming in her skin.

You do not answer me? Arahab asked, but the question didn't sound altogether offended or aggressive. And when Nia continued to stare at Bernice, the water witch drew her own conclusions. *You do not answer me, because you do not know.*

Nia nodded at her. "Is she . . . can I look at her?"

Arahab made no move to stop her or intervene, so Nia half walked, half crawled over to her cousin. She put her hand under the other girl's shoulders and used her hand like a spatula turning a pancake.

Bernice rolled and flapped onto her back, there where the water was almost deep enough to let her float.

The right side of her head was caved in down to the bridge of her nose, but it was trying to puff itself back out again. Her mouth was stripped of skin and her naked teeth knocked against each other as her body swayed in the rippling small waves.

I know you, Arahab said.

"You don't," Nia argued softly, and without any bite.

She corrected herself. *I remember you. You were in the water, the night I took this one. You refused me. I told you my name, because you asked.*

Nia nodded, agreeing to that much. "She's my cousin," she said, as if it offered some explanation for everything.

But you drowned.

"No, I didn't."

But I did not preserve you. Arahab was working her way closer, not swooping exactly, and not creeping. She was gliding, cutting through the water without displacing it. She moved as smoothly as a marble on a mirror.

Nia reached down to Bernice's hand, the one that clutched the shell. The shell had been so thoroughly pounded into her flesh that there was no disentangling it now. It would have to be cut away more than pried.

Bernice's other hand came up, flapping out of the water. The bones were not yet repaired and they gave her arm a disjointed, monstrous look; but they were strong enough to grasp at Nia's shirt. "Save me," she sputtered, and it was hard to understand. Some of her letters were missing, because she didn't yet have lips again to shape them. "Trying to save the world. Take me with you."

She betrayed me, Arahab dispassionately confirmed. *But she is wicked, and she would betray you, too. Again, as she did before.*

"You wouldn't let me bring her, anyway—would you?"

No. Not now, when I want you to stay. I want to know what you are. If you don't know, or will not tell me, then I wish to learn for myself.

"No," Nia said back. "No, I can't stay here with you."

Arahab nodded, but it was not in agreement with Nia. *Yes. You can.* She slithered up closer, close enough that Nia could have sneezed on her. She took one properly hand-shaped appendage and extended it to Nia's face.

Nia tried not to flinch or back away, but it was not like letting Mossfeaster hold her on the ferry. It was not like lying in pain in a bed of grass and leaves; this was being touched by something wet and shapeless, but firm and grotesque. Arahab's fingers felt like the arms of an octopus looked, and when she ran those fingers along Nia's skin, they left a trail of saltwater slime.

You are too heavy to swim well, Arahab observed. *You are too tightly made to be washed away with kelp and crabs. You were not made for the water, but you can endure it, I believe. Whom do you call master, if anyone? Not the gods of fire; you are too cool. Not the lords of the air, for you are too dense. That leaves the kings of the earth. . . .* She hesitated. *But they are long since buried, and they care little for ways of men.*

"They may still have custodians," Nia said carefully. In the rear of her skull, in the homing pigeon part at the base of her neck, she could feel Mossfeaster creeping up along the shoreline, hanging back in the trees and watching the scene closely.

She could sense, but not quite hear, his impatience.

They might, but I do not know of them. Arahab backed up and squinted at Nia, who still crouched beside Bernice.

Bernice's good eye—the one that hadn't been smashed into the side of her head—opened, and with the first vestiges of her healing mouth she whispered. "I can tell you how to beat her." The words tripped and slid around on her gums.

"And a fat good job you've done of it," Nia breathed back.

"The shell," she burbled. It was stuck to her hand, molded to it.

"I know."

"No, you don't," Bernice said. *"Take me with you."*

Arahab retreated into deeper water, but it was not a withdrawal. She was only digging herself in, settling down in friendlier territory in case she wanted to rise up. Bernice's ruined mouth warped itself into a grin. "She's afraid of you."

"I doubt it."

"She's afraid of what you *might* be."

Whether or not the water witch could overhear their talk, Nia did not know, but Arahab moved a few yards more out to sea. *Too cool,* she said again. *Too cool to come from the fire gods, and too willing to wet your feet.*

"If she was sure of that, she would've killed you already."

"Shut *up,*" Nia said.

"If you help me"—Bernice failed to shut up—"I can run."

The fire gods didn't send you, did they? They might have made an emissary such as you—designed to resist the water, as you may well be. My . . . Arahab glared down at Bernice. *They have committed an offense against the little Vulcan, I know. I do not fear you, small stone child, be assured of this much. But I am also aware that there has been a transgression, and that it may lie on my hands, by association.*

Mossfeaster was retreating.

The creature had come to the very edge of the trees, but it could hear well enough to grasp that any interference would only tip the situation against them. Nia knew it, too, so she was glad that she was being left alone. She didn't understand what was happening— not perfectly—but she knew that Arahab's uncertainty could only help her.

Over by the edge of the sand, where the packed earth was strong enough to support the ambulance that Bernice had stolen, the engine hacked to life.

"Take me *with you,*" Bernice begged again, sounding stronger and less desperate—but looking only marginally better. "I have the call."

How far was it to the ambulance?

Sam was gunning the engine, using the roar of the big machine as a summons, trying to remind Nia that yes, he was there, and yes, he was waiting for her. But could it move fast enough?

From underneath the billowing curtain of her altered, tangled hair, Nia watched the water. She watched the ambulance. She watched Bernice, whose chest was rising and falling again—not breathing, exactly, but pumping back to life.

If it didn't work, she'd never survive to get a second chance.

Nia took a deep breath, whether she needed to or not. "You deserve to be left," she said to Bernice, who was floating now in the water as it rose. It climbed back up as Arahab retreated. "You deserve that, and worse."

"Probably," she agreed. "But I can still help."

"And you're going to. Like it or not."

Nia didn't know for certain how fast she was or how strong she might be, but she seized Bernice's hand—the one with the shell healed irretrievably into it—and she jerked with everything she had. She'd almost expected to yank the hand clean off, and although the prospect nauseated her, this was no time to get the vapors.

Bernice came flying out of the water, trailing her own arm like a kite.

Nia lunged, jumping as far as she could with the deadweight behind her, and she made it to dry sand in one long-legged leap. But that wasn't far enough, and she knew it. Her cousin thudded against the ground behind her, useless, but close to weightless. She was bulky but not very heavy, so Nia thanked heaven for the small blessings and dragged her onward, back into the trees.

The ambulance honked furiously, because she was running away from it.

She wanted to scream for Sam to follow her, to meet her on the other side of the trees, away from the water, but there wasn't any time for that. If he couldn't figure it out for himself, he'd have to stay behind.

Bernice flopped along behind her, dragged rag doll–style across the uneven terrain and toward the trees. Nia couldn't believe how light she was, and how little effort it took to move her. Deadweight or no, Bernice dangled and skipped like a toy on a string.

Nia couldn't afford to give any thought to her cousin's comfort, so she didn't. All she knew for certain was that the water's edge was getting farther and farther behind her; and she didn't give a damn if Arahab was too stunned to act or if she was afraid to act, so long as they stayed out of her immediate reach.

Sam, still honking the ambulance's horn, was finally turning the vehicle around. It was moving roughly, stopping, starting, and stalling. He'd done much better with the fire engine. But it was coming around all the same. It was crawling back up onto the road and honking past the gathering crowd. And although Nia didn't have time to look over her shoulder and double-check his progress, she could hear the rumbling motor over the sound of the frantic crowd, and just over the roaring splashes of something in the water.

There it was, yes.

There *Arahab* was, unstunned, furious, and ready to move.

Behind her, Nia felt a piercing spray of water that had been flung with the force of a hurricane. It cut against her back and bludgeoned her shoulders with driftwood and fish, and Bernice yelped at the stinging force of it.

But with one more tremendous leap, and one more hurtling throw, Nia flung herself into the trees and brought Bernice banging along in her wake.

She wanted to stop and declare victory, having escaped the edge of the water; but there was a horrified little part of herself that knew that no spot in Florida is very far from the edge of the water. And when she began to think of it that way, when she remembered back to some ancient schoolbook lesson about the world being three-quarters covered with water, it was hard not to feel a creeping, awful terror as she ran, cousin in hand, from a creature so powerful that she commanded the seas to bend to her will.

So she kept running. She didn't stop, even when she couldn't see the water through the trees anymore, and even when she began to pass houses and trip over the paved stretches where sidewalks met the streets.

Not until she heard Bernice crying did she slow down, and even then, it wasn't out of compassion; it was because she realized that there was no water in sight.

She slowed down and—since she was in the middle of a small, heavily overgrown neighborhood—picked Bernice up in her arms and carried her as easily as a puppy. Back into the woods they went, back between the trees and away from the houses, where Nia could pretend that no one was watching from above or below.

"Put me down," Bernice demanded petulantly, and Nia tried.

But Bernice couldn't stand very well, so she sagged back down against Nia's supporting shoulder. Nia stuck one arm behind Bernice's back and worked one hand under her shoulder, suspending her as if she were a dress on a hanger.

"I can walk," Bernice protested, but since this clearly was not the case, Nia didn't let go of her.

The battered shell still hung from her hand, swinging beside her hip. It anchored itself to her disjointed joints, swaying with all the grace and weight of an anchor.

"You can't walk. We'll stop for a minute," Nia said. She didn't know where she was, anyway. East, as far as she knew. She must have taken them east, because she'd been running away from the water. Yet again, that was the bulk and the whole of her cunning escape plan, and now it looked ridiculous.

Bernice thrashed herself free of Nia's support, and Nia let her go. Her knees buckled and folded. She slumped to the ground, and Nia dropped down beside her.

The forest swelled above them, treetops so dense they cast shadows like thick lace curtains. All the trunks were skinny and rough, and palmettos carpeted the ground with their spread-fingered fans of sharp, fibrous leaves. Birds twittered and squirrels chattered, and a smooth-skinned snake screwed itself into the ground to escape them.

"Let me see you," Nia said, positioning herself in front of Bernice.

"No."

"Let me see how bad it is, and if I can help."

Bernice snorted, but wouldn't lift her head. Her caramel yellow curls were sticky with a blue tarlike substance that must've been blood, or something worse. Her head was still crushed and dented on one side.

Her arms were mending, though, and her legs were coming back together, too. The things that had been pulverized were knitting into solid bones again. Nia could see them under Bernice's skin, the way the fragments sought one another and clung, and stretched, and hardened.

"That must hurt," she observed.

"Everything does." She was slurring less, and her lips were working better. In fact, it cheered Nia somewhat to notice that Bernice even had lips. Watching her talk without them had turned her stomach.

"You look . . . it looks . . ." Nia hunted for words. "Not as bad as it did." It was true, and it was encouraging. She still felt like she was damning with faint praise, as her grandmother used to say.

Bernice managed half of a laugh, which made her head bob and her chin tap against her throat. She had not yet looked up. "You look . . . different. A little weird. No offense."

Nia withdrew and leaned her back against the nearest tree, which set her a couple of feet back from her cousin. She kept a wary eye on her, but she did not doubt that the other girl was too damaged to go very far. And besides, Mossfeaster was coming. She could sense it, and almost hear it. Soon, she would have a second pair of eyes to keep watch.

And there was always the chance that Sam would catch up. *Or not,* she thought. With no direction more firm than "east" and no roads nearby that she knew of, she wondered if they hadn't lost him.

She was almost upset at the thought; but she was forced to admit that if he was altogether gone, then it would certainly be for his own good.

28

Determining Differences

What'd they do to you, anyway? You're . . . you look bigger or something. You look harder. I figured you'd lived. I never thought you'd drown or anything; you know how to swim. Don't you?"

Nia said, "That was the point." She'd led her there, into the water, trying to get away. She remembered it vividly, as if it had only just happened. As if it were still happening, somewhere in the back of her mind—in another place very close.

"The hair's kind of a mess, though."

"I know, but I don't know what to do about it."

Bernice grinned. Nia could only tell because there was a twitch at the ear, and a tightening of the sprouting skin across her jaw. "I used to know a guy in the city. He could do anything with any-body's hair."

She held up her hand, or she tried to. Her wrist hadn't healed enough to hold itself out straight, so the bronze shell still weighed it down. Her skin was coming together around it; her bones were molding themselves to its edges.

"I didn't let it go, even when she tried to make me. I didn't give it back. How am I going to get it off?" she asked. For a second, she sounded small and scared.

"I don't know. Are we safe, do you think?"

"No. There's no such thing as safe. Where do you think we'd be safe, huh?"

Nia shook her head and drew her knees up to her chest. She wrapped her arms around them and hugged herself that way. "No place, I guess."

Nia examined her cousin's hand, running her fingertips along the lumpy skin.

Bernice held still and let Nia look. "She was going to use it to wake up something called Leviathan. He's supposed to be an old god, asleep under the ocean. If he wakes up, he'll destroy the world. But I didn't let her. I saved the world, did you see?"

"I saw."

The telltale crackling of Mossfeaster's impending arrival chased away the last of the wildlife. Now the forest was silent except for the rustling assembly of the monster.

"I should warn you . . . ," Nia tried to tell Bernice.

"You don't have to warn me. I've seen it before, the thing that's coming. Mother beat the shit out of him, over on Captiva."

"No, she didn't," Nia argued out of reflex.

Mossfeaster shook its head, and a collection of leaves and dirt shook loose in a fluttering spray. "Yes, she did." He looked at Bernice then, and said, "Though it's worth your well-being to know, small traitor, that I permitted the abuse. On my own territory, I am stronger than she remembers."

"So what were you doing there, then?"

"Watching." The creature came to stand in front of Bernice, then crouched down beside her. It lifted her hand into its own giant, loosely shaped pads and examined the shape and structure of the mutilated lump, melded beneath the skin like a peculiar tumor. "Imagine, if you like, an old machine with many parts. The old machine is solid, and in good working order—like the water machine Sam stole from the island."

"The what?" Bernice asked. She didn't struggle against Mossfeaster's inspection. She let the monster turn her hand left and right without complaining, even when the bones ground against the metal.

"It was a fire truck," Nia clarified for her cousin's benefit. "It had big water tanks in the back."

"Oh."

"A fire truck, as you said. Imagine an old machine like that, and imagine that it has been left for many years. If you found it again, and you needed it to work, you might have to test it a bit first. You might press its buttons and pull its levers to make sure that everything has held together." Mossfeaster traced a line around a spot where the skin was forming a tent across the shell's opening. It was as taut as a drum, and when Mossfeaster tapped its thumb against the tightly stretched membrane, it made a hollow sound.

Nia shrugged. "Sure."

"If any given part breaks or falls into disrepair, you would not have the means to fix it, so you hope for the best. And now, you must imagine that the machine is an entire planet, and that there are mechanisms in place that regulate the way it will operate."

Bernice had her head down, and Mossfeaster looked over it at

Nia. With a twitch of its head, it indicated that it wanted Nia to come closer. She frowned, not gathering what it meant. Mossfeaster used its head to indicate Bernice, and then Nia understood.

She crawled away from her tree and sat down beside her cousin. She draped an arm around her shoulder and carefully locked her elbows to pin her without alarming her.

"Humans have laws and manners, water and wind have their currents and tides, and—I'm going to ask you to hold still, now," it said to Bernice.

"What? Why?"

Mossfeaster didn't answer, except to tell Nia, "Cover her mouth."

"Cover my—"

Nia pushed her hand across Bernice's mouth and was relieved to feel a thin cheek and not naked teeth beneath her palm. But Bernice struggled and bit on general principle. Then she began to shriek through Nia's fingers as Mossfeaster tore the shell, one strip of skin at a time, free from her mutilated hand.

As the creature worked, it continued to speak in the same casual tone. "Fire must have air and fuel, and rocks may stand or crumble depending upon their composition." It ignored the hideous ripping sound of her slick, tight skin as it dug around, fighting the tendons and stringy muscles for possession of the object. "So, too, are the laws of those you cannot see. The old gods, the old kings and their kind—they, too, have their governing principles."

Bernice wrestled against Nia, but Nia was stronger and she had Mossfeaster to help. She tried not to look at the gruesome operation, but it was hard to turn away. Even as Mossfeaster drew the shell back and held it away from Bernice's body, the meat inside her hands flailed in tentacle strips and tried to hold the thing. They stretched and begged for it, even once it was free altogether.

When the shell was extracted, there was little left of the hand that had cupped it; but one piece at a time, the torn ends found one another and settled down to join again. The dark bile that passed for Bernice's blood oozed back beneath the flesh and left long stretches of scars that looked like they'd been painted with pitch.

And when the creature had finished, and it held the bronze thing up in its hand, the shell gleamed with sticky slime. Tatters of flesh hung from its ornate frills, and Bernice could barely glance at it without making a face that said she was going to be sick.

"You didn't have to be so rough about it," she accused, massaging her damaged hand with her less-damaged hand.

"Tools are for men and monkeys," he said. "And if we did not remove it, you would have been dead or worse before much longer."

"Nuh-uh. I was *healing*. I was healing around the thing, yeah. But I was getting better."

"No," it argued. "You were closing around it. It would have destroyed you from the center out, like its composite materials destroyed your lover. Don't you know why Arahab let you pluck it from her breast? Even she can't hold it long, not inside herself like that. I do not care for the sensation of it, either."

Nia disentangled herself from Bernice, who almost objected to being left without her cousin's embrace. But Nia stood up anyway; she wiped her hands on her pants and braided back the hair that had come loose during her flight. Bernice remained seated. Her hair still covered most of her face, which was probably a good thing. The caved, collapsed portion of her skull was not filling out fast if it was rising at all.

Mossfeaster tossed the shell to Nia, who caught it and turned it over in her fingers. It felt warm and vaguely unpleasant to touch. Where it sat on her hand, it left faint pink marks that looked like the start of blisters.

"This is the call?" she said, bouncing it from hand to hand. She pulled the scarf from her hair and used it to fashion a bag. She tied the shell up in knots and held the makeshift sack by a corner. "We got it? That's it? Now she can't disturb Leviathan?"

Bernice said, "I took it away from her."

"I heard you the first time," Nia told her. "And I saw you do it, anyway. But I'm not real sure I believe you did it to be helpful. You've never done anything to be good in your whole life."

"How would you know? You didn't know me for my whole life, did you?"

"I knew you long enough."

Mossfeaster growled, and it was a low-pitched, deeply annoyed sound. "The call still exists, and it will be a constant danger until its power is dispersed. Such things are not created lightly, and they are not disposed of easily. The water witch did not have time to charge it, so it is less dangerous to us now than it might've been otherwise. But it could still lift the old god out of his slumber."

Nia held the bag up and frowned. "So what do we do, bury it?"

"No, it must be lifted up out of the water witch's reach. I know a place," Mossfeaster said. "It is miles from here, farther away from the water, and safer. The call will take years to drain, but I have devised a system to speed the process."

"How's that?" Bernice asked.

Nia found her cousin's curiosity worrisome. "Mossfeaster," she said, cutting the creature off before it could tell Bernice anything else. "I trust you. If you say you've got someplace to put it and something that'll take all the power out of it, then I believe you. Where are we going, and how are we getting there?"

Mossfeaster looked back and forth between the two women.

Bernice was on the ground, peering up with one bright eye from beneath the ruins of her sweetly curled hair. Her flattened, demolished hand was swinging from its perch on her knee, but it was reshaping itself. And even her head was inflating again, rising like a yeast-filled loaf of bread, but slower. Within another hour, perhaps, her skull would be the right shape again.

Nia stood beside her, above her. But she was glaring at Moss-feaster, trying to tell the creature everything it needed to know about why they must not tell her cousin anything at all, lest she use it against them.

Already Bernice was regaining her predatory posture, even sitting on the ground, looking as if she'd been run over by a train. Every moment that passed gave her time to heal, and Nia was suddenly wondering if she'd made the right decision after all. She might have torn off Bernice's arm to take the shell and left the girl to die. She might have done any number of things differently.

But the choice had been made, and now it petrified her with uncertainty.

"Mossfeaster," Nia begged it with the only name she had to call it by. "I don't care if she's almost saved the world. You can bet she's got a terrible reason for it."

"I don't care about that," it said.

"She killed—"

"I know she did. I'm sure she's killed more people than you could guess, and I'm sure she's done it with a smile. But she has been useful to us, even if it was against her own volition. Whatever she wanted, whatever she meant, and whatever she tried, she has nearly died to keep the call away from her Mother. She has proved that we share at least part of a goal in common. As for the rest of what she plots, I cannot say—but I will watch her."

"Watch me all you want," Bernice grumbled. "I'm just trying to help. I got your goddamned shell for you, didn't I?"

"You didn't get it for *me*. You didn't even know I was coming."

"Stop it," Mossfeaster told them both. "Stop it, and let's start moving. Sam is waiting with the ambulance. I told him to wait at the road."

"Which road?" Bernice asked.

"I'll take you there. We aren't far." It waved down at Bernice, indicating that she should rise.

She made a show of hauling herself to her feet, moving shakily and refusing assistance except from the tree she gripped. She used her good hand to draw herself up against it, and finally she stood under her own power. Weak, wobbly, and with legs still crooked in places, she was upright and defiant.

"But . . . but as long as she's with us, Arahab will follow us!"

"As long as we have the call, she'll follow us anyway." Mossfeaster was moving, wandering back the way they'd come. "It doesn't matter. The water witch cannot easily go where we are going."

"She'll slow us down!"

"*You* slowed us down when you were made of stone, little troll. As a matter of philosophical consistency, it would be illogical to leave her. Now, help her. Come."

Nia sulked over to Bernice, who was standing and shaking in place. "I don't trust you," she informed her.

"I don't trust you either. I'm the one who saved the world."

"You did not."

Nia offered her arm, and Bernice tucked it around herself, leaning into the assistance and using Nia's weight to prop herself up. Together, the two of them walked and limped unsteadily behind Mossfeaster.

Back at the main road they found the ambulance, empty and pushed to the side of the road. There was blood all over the back of it. Nia wanted to ask Bernice whose it was, but she was pretty sure she wouldn't like the answer, so she didn't let the question air.

Bernice brought the subject up herself. "Is this the one I took?"

"I think so. I saw Sam trying to drive it."

She made a small noise that said she was impressed. "The

clutch is crazy sticky. It's awful to drive, but it was all I could get my hands on in a pinch."

Mossfeaster paced around the vehicle while Nia deposited Bernice on its back bumper. "Samuel?" the creature called. "Samuel, where have you gone?" Then it turned to the girls and added, "He wasn't able to find another means of transportation. He ran behind you, Nia. You're much faster, but he wore himself out trying to follow."

"I'm over here," Sam announced, floundering through the underbrush as he stumbled up to the vehicle.

"What were you doing?" Nia asked.

"Hiding. This thing's stolen, you know? People are going to be looking for it, and I'd rather they didn't find it while I'm sitting inside it."

She nodded. And then, flipping a thumb at her cousin, she said, "This is Bernice. She's coming along. She's the one who stole this ride in the first place."

Sam looked her up and down with a frank and frightened glare of appraisal, but he knew better than to pry for details. "Fine with me. Mossfeaster says we're going east."

"Always east, until it's time to go west."

Nia helped Bernice crawl up into the back of the van, then sat down on a gurney from which she could monitor the other girl. "Now you're being cryptic. Great," she said to Mossfeaster.

"It isn't cryptic; it's precise. We're seeking the center. I told you, I've made a place for the call. We'll put it there, out of reach, and we'll drain it dry."

"And then what?" Bernice asked. She was huddled on the van's floor, and her body shuddered when Sam started the engine. "What's going to happen to us?"

"To us?" Mossfeaster climbed up into the van and shut the doors behind himself, closing them all in together. "To me, nothing. To her—" It indicated Nia. "—precious little." Then it turned its attention to Bernice. "Your Mother fears that she's offended those who favor fire, and until someone tells her otherwise, I'm content to let her believe that Nia is their emissary. If she is careful, she can expect to be left alone."

Bernice shifted and hugged her legs. "And what about *me*?"

At first no one answered, but Mossfeaster shrugged and said, "Eventually, she'll catch you and kill you. There's too much water in this world for you to hide forever. Do understand, little shark: You may travel with us if it suits you to have company while you repair yourself. But we are not your guardians, and we will not protect you. You have chosen your own path. Now she's going to chase you down it, and you will run that way alone."

East, into the Center

In the center of the peninsula, the land was not so easily cooled by the wind that blows across the ocean. The air was thicker and warmer, and in the afternoons when the thunderstorms wandered through, it was much wetter. There was no salty breeze to dry the dampness out, so it hung close to the ground and scarcely stirred.

East, and away from the water, the rain forest foliage thinned, and there were fewer trees. The landscape stretched into patchy places where the low spots became swampy, and the higher spots grew short, scraggly trees and tall, whip-sharp grasses.

Where it wasn't white and brown, the world was a blackened green.

Nia had never been so far away from the water. She'd never seen the peculiar stretches of Florida that look like picture books of Africa. It was strange to her, the way it was dry except for the oil-dark puddles that stretched for acres, but felt so heavily wet to breathe. Even with the windows down, there wasn't enough motion in the air to take away the worst of it.

The ambulance looked and felt like an oven, and every half hour Mossfeaster would swear that they had almost arrived.

When the vehicle overheated outside of Lake Wales, the passengers all unloaded themselves and set to walking.

Even Bernice, with her battered head and mutilated hand, could move again. She walked slowly and uncomfortably, but the few hours between the shore and the state's interior had given her time to rest and heal.

Nia watched her cousin struggle to put one crooked foot in front of the other. It was difficult to match the sight with what she knew of the girl a few years ago. The broken, hobbling woman who shambled as if she were a thousand years old . . . she couldn't be the swift and wicked thing who casually murdered and dressed like a photo in a catalog.

Maybe she'll always be like this, Nia thought. *Healing but never healed, that's what Arahab said. Or maybe that means something other than the obvious.*

She made a point of walking alongside Bernice, keeping the slower pace while Mossfeaster and Sam pushed on ahead. The sun didn't so much shine down as press down, shoving against them with fiery hands that made them drag—except for Mossfeaster. He seemed to enjoy the warmth even as it dried him out. With every step, he'd shed another dusty puff of dehydrated leaves and dirt.

"You don't have to keep me company," Bernice said to Nia without looking at her. "I'm slow, but you don't need me anymore, right? That's what your big freaky friend said."

"That was the gist of it. You made your own bed, and now you've got to sleep in it. That's how Grandma used to put it."

"Grandma. I guess you lived there with her? With them? Before you came down to the island, I mean."

Nia nodded.

"Have you been back there? Since . . . since everything?"

"No." Nia thought of telling her everything—how she'd been awake and alive again for only a few short days, how she'd been trapped at that house on the beach in the interim. It was that same damn house, the one she'd visited out of boredom, curiosity, and familial politeness, to which she'd been anchored by death and magic. But she stifled the impulse. She knew Bernice well enough, knew better than to tell her anything at all that she might use later.

But Bernice pressed, trying to squeeze out more. "Why not? I thought you liked them."

"And you didn't?"

"I barely knew them," she said.

Nia almost argued, but then realized that Bernice might be telling the truth, just this once. "I guess you moved to New York when you were pretty small. Do you even remember Grandma?"

"I remember that there *was* a Grandma. I have this idea of her, like she was a big woman who wore men's clothes that didn't fit her too good. I think of her wearing overalls like a farmer, and having her hair held up in a scarf like the one you were wearing."

Nia mumbled, "She *did* work on a farm. And it was her farm, too, after Grandpa died."

"So they might still be there, right? Up in Tallahassee? Isn't that where you came from? There might still be a farm there, with Grandma and your mom, and maybe my mother, too." Her voice sounded funny, or maybe it was just the condition of her mouth.

Nia didn't like where this conversation was going, so she wasn't sure how to answer. It gave her a pang that tasted like sorrow and terror when she thought about Bernice showing up at the orchard. It made her throat clench to imagine how that might go. So she lied with caution. "I heard that your mom was going back to New York. If you'd look around, you'll see—times aren't real good. I don't know if they've kept the farm or not. Lots of farms are going bust, and if Grandma couldn't keep hers, I don't know where else they'd go."

"So you didn't go looking for them?"

"No," Nia said. She did not add that she'd not had time. "Things are different now. What would I say to them, anyway? It's been years since we've been gone. They probably think we're dead, and it would only confuse them and maybe hurt their feelings if they found out different."

"Why would it hurt them? Maybe they'd be happy to hear we're all right."

"Happy? Only if you could make up some story they'd believe. And it'd have to be pretty crazy, but pretty believable—if you wanted them to think you'd been alive for years, but you never let them know you were safe. I can't tell them I'm all right, because then they'll wonder why I didn't say something sooner, and I'm not—" She glanced sideways at Bernice, who was watching her closely through that matted hair. "—I'm not as good at lying as you are."

"Thanks," she said.

"You're welcome, I guess." She wanted to stop talking, but she couldn't. She hadn't had anyone to talk to in so long, except for Mossfeaster and Sam. "So, tell me, would you? And I know there's no way I can believe you, but I want to hear you make something up anyhow. Why did you do it?"

"Why'd I do what?"

"Any of it? What's wrong with you, Neecy?"

Bernice grimaced. "Don't call me that. That's what Daddy

called me, before he died." She took her time working up an answer, but the words she picked weren't very complicated. "You ask that question like you figure there's no real answer. And maybe there isn't. What do you want me to say? You want me to make up some big defense? I don't owe you that. I don't owe you anything. I saved the goddamned world today, and I don't have to tell you a thing. I've always got my reasons, how about that? You and me are different, that's all."

"It's not just me," Nia protested. "You're different from a lot of people."

"Maybe. Maybe not. Maybe I'm just lucky or something."

"Maybe you're just crazy."

Bernice's face twisted, unable to decide on a frown or a smirk. She settled on a smirk. "Anything's possible, isn't it? I wouldn't have said that once, but now? Anything's possible. Hey, wow. Would you look at *that*?"

"What?"

"That." Bernice pointed west. And there, rising above the rest of the landscape, appeared a tall, thin streak against the sky. They must have been a few miles away yet, but there it was: a pink, fleshy colored needle standing alone on a hill.

"That," Mossfeaster said over his shoulder, "is the tower. And that is where we're going, in case anyone was concerned about getting lost. If we get separated, now you know where to meet."

Bernice stopped and cocked her head to the right. A tattered curl dipped away, and Nia could see that she had two eyes again; the one that had been crushed back into her sinuses had filled out, and although it was red and watery, it was blinking and aware. "That's it? A tower? That's how you're going to get that thing away from Arahab?"

Mossfeaster kept walking, and everyone else did, too, so Bernice resumed her shamble and caught up quickly.

Nia wasn't sure how she felt about Bernice's speedy hobble. Her performance was improving faster than her appearance, and it worried Nia. This was just one more way for Bernice to lie, if she wanted sympathy or if she wished to feign weakness.

The creature at the lead faltered, and then tipped its head toward a pair of dirt ruts that might have served as a road. "But we're going to detour, slightly. For safety's sake."

Bernice rubbed at the side of her head and asked, "For whose safety? Mine?"

"For everyone's. I don't know how fast your Mother moves through groundwater, but if she wants to lash out, she'll try it from the lake nearby. I prepared this place years ago, back before either of you became what you are now," Mossfeaster told them. "I should warn you that it's haunted, but the haunting is benign and barely even interesting. Edward loved the place so much, he chose to remain. He says he likes the bells."

"Is this even a road?" Sam kicked his soft leather shoe into the sand. "It looks more like a trail."

"Be quiet, all of you, if all you can do is argue and complain. We're nearly finished, and then you can scatter, or stay, or do anything you like."

"But this tower, you said it's safe from Arahab?" Bernice had fixated on that implication and was clinging to it.

"Yes. I chose the location because it would repel her. It is perfect in its design. It is as if the world-makers agreed, 'There ought to be a place where she cannot go.' And I found it, and I found a man who could reinforce it. And now it is a great fortress."

Mossfeaster shifted its shoulders and changed its direction. "Follow me," it said. "This other path is an old military trail, and it will take us quite close to where we wish to be. The tower is only part of the fortification."

"You're telling her too much," Nia said too loudly. "Don't you understand? You can't trust her with these things—you can't trust her with *anything*."

"What do you care?" Mossfeaster asked. It leaned its astonishing bulk forward and across a tangled stash of grass and low-growing bushes. "You're stronger than she is by far. There's no treachery she can wrangle against you, and yet you behave as if she holds you at knifepoint."

Even Sam objected to that statement. "No treachery? You obviously don't understand people very well."

"I've been watching your kind since before you could carve your names into rocks, and if there's one thing I have learned, it's this: You don't know yourselves at all. You're an oblivious bunch, deluding yourselves from insecurity, or love, or anger. Afraid of your own strength, and afraid of your own weaknesses, too. It's a wonder you've managed to survive for as long as you have."

"At least we're not obtuse," Sam grumbled.

While the rest of them bickered, Nia was observing Bernice and feeling uneasy. It wasn't her cousin, this time; it was something else—some strange quiet that filled the place. There was a sense of effort and pressure, as if they were walking uphill.

And then, there were no more birds.

Nia stopped, and Bernice went only another step or two before she followed suit. "What are you doing?" she asked, but Nia waved her quiet.

"Something's wrong," she whispered.

The thick but scraggly grass around them did not rustle at the edges of the rough road, and the ordinary sounds of rodents had vanished into a distressingly obvious silence. The air around them was heavy, but it was always heavy. And now there was nothing flying through it, nothing singing or calling from it. There was nothing but the tyrannical humidity and an overwhelming sense of foreboding.

But it wasn't until she saw the snakes and turtles charging across their path that Nia noticed the swampy patch of earth out in the middle of an otherwise bleak and featureless field. It wasn't a lake, and it could scarcely be described as a pond. It was only a spot where the ground was soggy enough to shine with a thin coating of stagnant damp.

Everything that prefers to swim but sometimes crawls was fleeing the water, running from the disturbance that bubbled at its center.

Mossfeaster froze, and then whirled around to face the rest of them. When it spoke, it was so quiet that they barely heard its words, even though they stood mere feet away.

"It isn't enough water," it assured them. "Even if she's found us, there's little she can do to us."

Bernice was rallying a good panic. "We've got to run. We've got to run!" she squeaked.

Nia grabbed her by the arm and pulled her close to keep her from bolting. "You heard the big dirt monster. We're out of reach."

But the wet patch was swelling and rising. It was bubbling as if it were oil, coming up out of the ground black and viscous. The boundaries where water and swamp grass met became more distinct as a nebulous shape struggled out from the center.

Mossfeaster shook its head and spoke directly to Nia, who was trying to hold Bernice. "If she sees me, you are lost. If she realizes you weren't made by another such as herself, she'll figure out that you're no threat to her." Then it said to the rest of them, as it sank into the ground and vanished, "Head for the tower. I'll meet you there."

Sam was transfixed by the boiling black blob in the field, surrounded by grass and black mud. He couldn't take his eyes off it until Mossfeaster was gone and Nia grabbed his shoulder. She pushed him and he stumbled, but when she pushed him again, his feet found their rhythm.

Without meaning to, she outpaced him in a matter of seconds—even lugging Bernice beside her. She stopped and looked back at Sam, who was slowing again.

"Come on!" she told him. "Come on, let's go before she gets her act together!"

"Can she just *do* that? Anywhere it's wet?"

"I don't know." Nia released Bernice and doubled back. Bernice kept running in her loping ungraceful gait, all the more awkward for its franticness. "But she's doing it *there,* and we need to move."

Sam rubbed his face with his hands, and Nia remembered how tired he must be, and how much she'd asked of him over the last few days. "I can't keep doing this," he said, and in the set of his eyes there was a looseness, like something elastic had stretched too far and snapped. "How are we supposed to run away from . . . from water? How can we keep that up?"

"We don't have to run forever," Nia promised him, although she had no authority to do so. "She won't follow you. She doesn't want anything from you. It's *us* she wants, Sam. You can walk away from this."

"How?" he asked, and there was pure confusion and resignation all over his face. "How am I going to go back to my real life after this?"

"We can talk as we go, Sam." Nia pulled at him again and he let her draw him forward. "It looks like a mess right now, but we'll sort it out." She tugged him along with every word, and he resisted, but not very hard.

He wanted to watch the lone patch of shifting swamp as it oozed and poured, as it slid from whatever banks had mostly held it. There wasn't enough water to give her a good shape; there was too much mud and muck to make a body like a woman's, if that was the one Arahab preferred. But there was water enough to move. The ground was as much sand as dirt, and it siphoned moisture away where the blob tried to crawl, so she came slowly, and with great weight.

"Jesus," Sam said. He couldn't stop looking. He couldn't tear himself away from the sight of the crawling, lurching, growing menace. First the size of a horse, then the size of a room. Now the size of a small house, and flopping itself forward, almost rolling.

"Sam, we can fix it," she said. The twisted chains that coated her forearms like a pair of gauntlets jangled. They'd been all but forgotten, but they gave her an idea. "I'll give you these things. They're worth a fortune. You can sell them, and go anywhere you want. You can start over somewhere else."

He was faltering along behind her, while Bernice had panted her way down to the bottom of the hill.

"It isn't the money," Sam said. He didn't say it with certainty, though. He said it like he felt he ought to, on principle.

"Sam, *faster.*"

And then a muddy tendril the size of a tree trunk crashed against them both.

Nia hadn't even seen it coming.

She couldn't see it when she stopped, headfirst and facedown in a patch of scrub that made for an itchy, miserable landing even for a woman with skin that was tougher than leather.

Nia scrambled to her feet. Her clothes were torn, and she'd held on to the scarf with the precious bronze shell tied up inside it, but she'd lost one of the jeweled gauntlets. Pearls and brightly speckled flecks of gold and gemstones rained from her arm and scattered in the dirt, lost in the knee-high brush.

"Sam!" she cried with all the volume she could muster. *"Sam!"*

But she could see him then, and she knew he couldn't answer.

He had landed a few yards away against a tree. Back-first and horizontal, he'd been pitched like a baseball, and the tree had stopped him—the gnarly old orange tree with a trunk like a column of twisted paper had cut short his flight.

And even though she knew, could see how his back was curled around itself, slung around the trunk of the tree where he'd fallen at the bottom . . . even though she could see it from twenty yards away, she couldn't just assume. Seeing would not be enough to justify leaving him, if he was dead, because he was the only person she knew anymore, and she would not just go without him on the mere suspicion that he could not follow.

It was preposterous, to call it a suspicion. She knew before she saw the way his bones had been shattered, and she was all too aware of it before she spied the clumpy puddle of internal tissues and blood that had been forced out his mouth when the tree trunk had stopped him.

Since she had to tell herself something, Nia started repeating the only thing of comfort that she could find.

"Quick," she babbled. "Quick, it was quick."

Maybe the strike itself had even killed him, and the rest—the hundred-foot glide through the air, the crushing crash against the tree, that final dashing set of seconds—hadn't even registered.

Like falling off a building, only sideways.

When Next Time Comes

Nia tried not to be sick, and she tried not to stand there and stare, but her legs had gone almost as uncooperative as Sam's had been, and she couldn't seem to direct them. The shell chimed beside her, dangling in its scarf. It hummed a funny, distressed call that was too high-pitched to be called a purr and too quiet to be called a message.

The shell was shaking, objecting. Hanging loose in the scarf, Nia could feel it pulling against her, wanting away from the tower and back to the shapeless, malevolent muck.

Its small resistance moved her, and made her angry.

Its protest was just one more thing acting against her, but the shell was the one thing she held in her hand, and so far as she knew, it was in no position to assault her. But it would destroy the world if she let it. So she let it complain, and it swung unhappily in its brightly colored silk sheath.

Nia was shaking, too. She was objecting, too.

And she was not prepared to take any shit from a small brown shell or a big, gelatinous puddle of muck that could scarcely lumber across the ground.

In the distance she could see Bernice's staggering shape as it cut through the trees around the great hill—the only true hill for miles.

Nia dashed across the grasslands, dodging small trees and leaping over the bushes. She grasped the shell so hard that she thought she could feel it surrendering under her grip, softening or caving to the pressure of her fingerprints. She swung her arms, and the shell in her hand pumped back and forth as she ran.

When her feet first hit the Iron Mountain, she felt it through her shoes.

It shocked her. It jabbed up through the soles of her stolen footwear and sent a current of something like revulsion, something like recognition, up through her toes and into her torso.

She tripped and caught herself, then kept running up the hill, which was something she'd never done before—because how many hills does Florida have, anyway? And what was this one doing here?

It didn't seem natural, the way it shot up sharply out of the ground—that sudden and steep plateau. Oranges grew around the base and up it. The neatly groomed trees were laid out in rows, all of them leading the way up to the top; all of the straight-line paths between them pointed up at the tower.

Nia didn't look back to see how closely she was being followed, and she didn't slow down, even when she noticed how the earth under her feet was changing. With every fiercely planted footstep, the earth under her shoes was red and fleshy.

Halfway up the hill there were more paths, though they weren't straight like the orchards. They smelled like blossoms and they were wide, scraped into the crimson soil and smoothed for foot traffic. They curled from here to there and split, and branched, and came together in artistic ways.

She skipped over them and barreled headlong through the bushes, past the trees, around small buildings and walls, and alongside fluffy, manicured forests of moss-covered trunks.

And then, directly in front of her, there was a gate. She crashed against it, stopping herself with her hands against the iron bars. The bars were twisted and black, and there were stylized animal heads—maybe dragon heads—topping every other one. She'd dented the place where she'd stopped herself; pushed the bars several inches until they'd distended out over the moat.

There was a moat, just beyond the metal fence.

It snaked around the tower in a smug, shiny band perhaps thirty feet wide. The water smelled awful, with a rusty scarlet tang that seared the back of Nia's nostrils.

And then she saw Bernice. Her cousin was huddled and cowering beside the gate, knees drawn up and elbows bent tightly around her legs, and her hands were clawing at her shoulders. She was making a noise that sounded like breathing except that it gurgled and hissed.

Nia's legs quivered as she walked to Bernice's side.

She bent down and crouched in front of her, waved her hand in front of the other girl's face. Bernice tracked the motion with her eyes, and Nia saw that the whites around the iris had gone a sickly orange. "Bernice?" she asked the name like a question.

"What did he do to the water?"

"What?"

"The *water*," Bernice insisted. "It's poisoned. All of it, over there, and around here. You can smell it. It stinks like blood."

It isn't blood, said a thin, reedy voice no louder than a whisper. *It's rust.*

Nia stood upright. "Did you hear that?"

"Hear what?"

She saw him, then—the older man with the white hair and the rounded barrel for a chest. He was wearing nice clothes, but you could see right through them. You could see through him, too, if you could see him at all.

He says it keeps them out.

"It keeps who out?" Nia instinctively knew whom "he" referred to, and wondered for a moment where Mossfeaster had gone. The creature had said to meet at the tower, but it didn't seem to be there.

Them. The nasty ones, the bad old ones. They want to end the world, but they don't like the rust. It's something about iron, or oxygen, my friend said. I never understood it very well.

"Where *is* your friend?" Nia watched the ghost and did not blink, for fear of scattering him. He was so fragile and translucent, the very first breeze or quick motion might banish him.

He was so barely there. Yet he started to sing.

> *Underneath the flesh of the earth*
> *Below the skin of the sky*
> *Deeper than death the Leviathan sleeps*
> *All children must let the king lie*

"Edward," came a louder voice. Nia was surprised when the spirit lingered despite the sound. "Who taught you that song? It wasn't *me.*"

I hear things now.

"Do you?"

Sometimes. Then he continued:

> *He shifts his back and the mountains fall*
> *He shakes his head and the oceans cry*
> *Give him no dream and don't bid him wake*
> *All creatures must let the king lie*

Nia didn't like it, the way the tune rose and fell like the lifting and dropping of the waves. Even if the words hadn't been so ominous, it would've been a rickety tune; it would've been the sound of a ship's chains swaying in the wind.

Mossfeaster was standing near the ghost, who was all but oblivious while he sang. The old man seemed to be aware that he was being watched and spoken to, but if he cared, he didn't let on.

He sang a third verse, and Nia thought it was the worst of all.

> *Thousands before and thousands more*
> *The centuries pile themselves high*
> *We bury and bind him with quiet hands*
> *All gods must let their king lie*

"Is that all of it you know?" Mossfeaster asked. It cocked its rough-edged shoulders and stared intently at the ghost. "Have you heard no other verses? There are more, if you'd like to know them."

I like the song.

"There's more of it for you to sing. Go and find the rest, Edward, or go back to sleep."

This tower. It's going to save the world, just like you said.

"Yes, and very shortly. Go on, Edward."

Edward nodded, and he dissolved into the air around them, leaving no trace that he'd ever been there.

"Where have you been?" Nia asked Mossfeaster. "What took you so long, and why did you leave me down there? Sam's dead, and—"

"I know he's dead. I saw it. And I told you why I left."

"You could've *helped*."

The creature glanced down at Bernice, still shuddering on the ground.

"You," Mossfeaster told her. "You'd feel better if you'd sit on the grass. The dirt here is what burns you, you little fool. And you," it said to Nia. "I am answering your question, too. The earth that this hill comprises, it is too dense and dead for me to navigate in my usual fashion. I move through it slowly, so it is faster for me to tread upon it like a beast. And you are better built for running than I am."

Bernice lifted her chin, and Nia was almost certain that her face was mostly the right shape now. There was still that atrocious dent in her head, but it was filling out.

"It's the dirt?" she asked.

"It's the dirt. Stand up and move, before the natural toxin weakens you further. It is as I said: This is a safe place. This soil burns the water, makes it an acid. I don't know the mechanics myself— the whys and hows of the mystery. I only know that it is so, and if you look down there, over by the swamp pit, you can see how she lingers. If she could come closer, I promise you—she *would*."

From the relatively high vantage point of the Iron Mountain, Nia could see down across the plains for what felt like miles. And down in the mucky, wet depression where there were no trees and no brush, a soggy mass was struggling against the terrain and losing.

"She can't come here?" Bernice asked again. She sounded small and cornered, and she still hadn't moved.

"No, she can't. I'm quite certain of that."

"Quite certain?"

"Get up, unless you want to hurt yourself further. I'm tired of helping you if you're just going to argue with me. Do as I say, or don't."

"I can stay here," she said. There was a faraway note to her declaration that told Nia she hadn't been listening.

"As you like," Mossfeaster replied without looking at her. "We should go. You have the call?"

Nia held up the scarf. "I've got it. Now what do we do with it?"

"We take it up there." It pointed up at the tower, to some very high point at the top of it. "You'll take the call, and affix it however you can inside the largest bell. You'll see it right away. It's big enough to hide you and me, and possibly her, too. Tie it up inside there, with the scarf or with anything else at hand. Secure it, and leave it. And do it quickly, because we'll need to be out before the bells are rung, and we must not be seen. The Singing Tower's song will undo me altogether if I listen from inside."

Nia couldn't stop staring up. "That's amazing. The whole thing is amazing. What's it made of?"

"Marble and coquina. They are elements that give me strength, even as the earth around it drains that strength away. They call it the Singing Tower, and soon you will know why." They reached the gate's entrance, and although it was unlocked, Mossfeaster urged Nia to open it. "I don't care for its texture," it told her. "You are designed to resist such things better than me, and better than your cousin, who is most vulnerable of all as a child of the water witch. I chose this place to keep her out, and to discourage her minions. I did not intend to bring one so close."

"But I *want* to come close. I *want* to come inside, if she can't get me here."

"I know," it said. "But you won't like it very much."

"Don't care," she mumbled.

Nia reached for the latch. She stood under the sharp-ended frowns of the guardian creatures that lined its spiked top, and she lifted the lever. She pushed the great gate with her shoulder and it swung inward, creaking on hinges that almost stuck.

The gate opened onto a bridge with a marbled surface and railings that had been decorated with iron swirls and flourishes. The water beneath it barely moved; it was dark green with cadaverous currents that were flushed with red. A pair of snow-white swans, each the size of a German shepherd, swam out from under the bridge and paddled away at an insolent, leisurely pace.

The nearer she drew to the tower, the bigger it looked. When the gate clacked closed behind them, she felt a peculiar sense of privacy and quiet, even though the fence was fashioned from latticed iron and anyone could peer through it. But the trees were closer together inside the confines of the moat, and the grass was taller and the flowers grew more thickly in the garden plots between the pathways. Stepping stones were laid out in paths up to the doors, and everyone in the party made a point of using them. Even Nia, who supposedly had some resistance to the rust, could feel it trying to repel her, so she lifted her feet away where she could.

"Is that—?" Nia pointed down at a flat, polished marker on the ground.

"That's where Edward is buried. He wanted to stay here, so they humored him. The *carillonneur* finds it morbid, and does his best to avoid it."

"The car . . . The what?"

"The man who plays the bells."

And as they all gazed up at the crown-shaped peak, it began to slowly wobble.

31

Subterranean Advent

Not only the tower but the hill itself was quivering, bumping softly against its foundation. The swans in the moat honked loudly and leaned themselves against the breeze, charging with their umbrella-sized wings until the sky could hold them and lift them up, away from the sliding, splashing water that bubbled around the tower's base.

"We're too late?" Nia asked, because it had to be a question. "Are we too late? But Arahab doesn't have the call!" She squeezed the shell in its scarf cocoon. "She hasn't gotten to use it!"

"She may not need it here. He is so very close." Mossfeaster's voice, always unearthly, now held a timbre of astonishment or fear that made the creature sound almost human. "I do not think she knows how very close he is."

No, Nia thought. *It's not surprised or terrified. It's in awe.*

"What do you mean *he's close?*" Bernice shrieked. "You brought us here—you brought the call here—to deliver it in person? *You're* the one who wants to destroy the world, aren't you? You're the one—"

She would've gone on, but Mossfeaster cuffed her with the back of its hand, and she tumbled against the iron fence. She huddled there, legs drawn up beneath herself and shaking, hands squeezing at her skinny arms.

"We're *not* too late for anything," Mossfeaster said, answering Nia and ignoring Bernice. "Arahab has not succeded yet, nor has she failed. The Old Father shifts in his slumber, but he may yet be soothed. Come, to the tower. Get her or leave her, I do not care— just do it quickly."

Bernice whimpered and gathered herself as if she meant to run. She was covered in the dusty cherry-colored earth, and a rash was forming where it met her skin. It bubbled and sizzled, but Bernice behaved as if she didn't notice it. She looked nothing at all like her usual self, nothing like a human being, except for the angry air of frailty that covered her like a shroud.

Nia crouched beside Bernice, balancing herself on feet that struggled to hold still even as the ground beneath them wiggled and rumbled. "We have to cross the water, but you don't have to touch it. I see a bridge."

"A bridge?"

"Come on." Nia took Bernice by the less-damaged hand and locked her fingers around Bernice's wrist.

In the distance, the tower had looked tall and thin, more like a big pole than like a structure. But up close, it was wide around the base—as big around as her grandmother's farmhouse had been. It jabbed straight up into the sky for hundreds of pink, blue, and ivory feet.

And the whole thing, every inch of it, was wavering, shimmering almost, against the clouds behind it. Flecks of stone and chips of glass drifted down and shattered on stone walkways or thudded into the glass.

Under all the rumbling chaos fuzzed a strange hum, so low that it was almost more of a growl. It made the air quiver, like heat over a dark road; and it made Nia's teeth itch.

Mossfeaster waited for her, then waited beside her at the door in the tower's base. He looked no better than she felt: awash with the deep, melodious growl from up above. The creature's skin was vibrating, shifting and shattering in clods and lumps.

"What *is* that?" she asked.

"The bells." Its voice shook even harder than its bones. "If he moves anymore, if he even blinks, they'll fall. The whole thing will fall. We have to hurry."

"He *who*? The bell player?"

"Leviathan," Mossfeaster said. "Nia, pull the ring. Open the door."

She pulled the ring. The door swung outward, and inside the world was warm, dusty, and cut with long shadows and thick beams of light. Books were piled high against corners and along shelves, and a beautiful mahogany desk was littered with papers, pens, and bottles of ink. The floor gleamed as if it were swept and polished daily, but onto it clattered the looser things from the tops of cabinets and the edges of shelves.

"Edward's study," Mossfeaster explained. "Close the door, Nia. The bell player is coming, and we have many stairs to climb."

"Stairs?" Bernice was whining, but at least it was a soft kind of whining, a token, weak objection. "This place is awful."

"Nia, go first. You have the call. As fast as you can, run. Or it will all come down, every inch of it."

The stairs were as smooth and bright as the floors, and they spiraled in an angular way out of the study and up. They shook back and forth beneath Nia's feet as she tried to scale them.

There were platforms and entrances to new levels on the second- and third-story landings, but Mossfeaster urged them past them. Nia held the rail out of habit and planted one foot in front of the other in a mind-numbing rhythm that made her teeth bang together.

"Mossfeaster?"

"Go on," it told her. "I must go another way."

"Another—*what*?"

"Keep *going*. Only two more flights to the bells. I warn you—" Mossfeaster wagged a fingerless hand at Bernice. "—you will not care for it at all. You should stay here."

"And let the place come down on top of me?"

"The farther from the bells, the better," it told Bernice. "Better beneath the rubble than in the midst of it."

Nia shook her head as she ran, and she didn't look back. "It can't fall. You said this was a safe place!" But the tower swayed like it was drunk, and she staggered along the stairs, moving up too slowly for her own satisfaction.

"There's something about the metal in the bells," Mossfeaster mumbled, as if that were a sufficient explanation. It shouldn't have been a mumble at all, but the monster's structure was shifting and bubbling, keeping time with the giant purring roar that was singing up from overhead. "This is what you were made for, Nia. You are the little stone troll who handles the metal, for I cannot do it very well. You are a new creature, and stronger than the rest." It looked

pointedly at Bernice. "Now hang the call and set it aside; its unre-
strained presence makes our predicament all the worse."

With Nia speeding ahead, the others reached the next door and
Mossfeaster pushed it open with the back of its hand. It guided
Bernice inside and to the farthest corner of the octagonal room,
where she folded up like a chair and leaned her head back against
the wall.

Nia was barely in front of them, and she hesitated when a massive wedge of rock crashed on a stair above her.

She charged back into the room with her cousin and the creature and held on to the doorframe, as if it were any steadier than
the floor.

Inside the room, there was a clavier bigger than any piano Nia
had ever seen. It was as if someone had turned a church organ inside out, displaying levers and cables, pedals and keys the size of
soda bottles. It could have been the knobby, organic offspring of a
harpsichord and trapeze.

"There's no time for this," Mossfeaster told Nia. "She may not
survive the song, but she'll stay until you return. So make your
mission fast, child."

"All right, I'm going!" Nia squinted up the spiral, which was
growing dark with debris and dust. There weren't enough windows to compensate. She bashed her leg against a freshly fallen
stone and stumbled up it, over it, back onto the stairs.

The call was hanging from the sturdy silk scarf, and it was
dangling in a swaying circle, swiveling midair like a pendulum
suspended from a gypsy's fingertips. It didn't want to be there either.

This would have to be fast.

Nia's legs weren't tired, so she wasn't certain what slowed her,
but the final flight of steps passed more onerously than the first six.
The gravity was stronger there; the higher she went, the harder it

pressed against her, and she wondered how immune to the metal she could really be if it gave her this much trouble.

But at the top of the last stair there was a wooden platform that opened into a cluttered room that was packed with the most astonishing assortment of bells she'd ever seen. She'd never even heard of such a place, or such an instrument—since that's what the bells combined to form.

From the ceiling to the floor, they were stacked and strung across beams, cords, and cables for support. The smallest bell Nia saw could have fit in her palm; the largest, at the far end, was so immense that she could have ridden a horse beneath it and it would have blotted out the sun. It was dark there, and bright, too—but only in short slivers and in cut, crossed lines where the grates around the bells were open for the sake of ventilation and acoustics.

All of them dipped and ducked in their holdings, humming and rattling as the world quaked around them.

Nia found the largest bell and stood before it for a moment, then reached up a hand to knock on it. It reverberated against her hand, vibrating so slowly that the sound it made was deep and low. She couldn't hear it so much as she could feel it, singing through every drop of blood in her veins. It tingled to the tips of her eyelashes.

She ducked her head underneath the great bell's lip, and it was black inside. It smelled like a million pennies, or like the burning room in the Greek's incinerated shop out in Ybor.

Up above her head, she felt around, and she found a loop of metal at the apex of the bell's interior. It might have been made to help them transport it, or perhaps it once might have been planned to hold a clapper. Nia didn't care. It would work.

She undid one of the knots that held the call in place in the scarf, then held the whole package up above her head while she tied it tightly up there, up beyond where she could even see it.

When she took her hands away, she waited for the swinging sway of the call to settle, but it did not. It hovered in place and hummed, fighting against the metal shell and fussing, fuming against the echo that trapped it.

When she was sure it was secure, she dodged back under the bell's enormous lip and ran back to the wooden platform, back to the sliding, shaking stairs, back down to the next floor where Bernice was sobbing.

Nia burst through the door and said, "Let's go!"

But Bernice shook her head violently and backed herself farther into the corner. "I'm not leaving. No. Forget it. I'm staying here, where she can't get me."

"Didn't you hear Mossfeaster? The bells, when they play—they'll tear you apart. I was just up there, and it was . . . it was hard even for me. Godammit, Bernice, you can't stay here! When the bells start playing, it could kill you!"

"I'll risk it," she insisted, dragging herself away from her cousin and clinging to the wall. Her fingers twined around the ornate bars over the window. "I'll stay here, up in the tower, and it won't be so bad. It'll be like a fairy tale or something. You can't make me go. You *can't*."

Nia hugged her back against the wall, even as it shifted. The mortar that held the bricks together ground together and dusted the floor with sand.

"Mossfeaster?" she called, only just then realizing that he wasn't present. "Bernice, where did Mossfeaster go?"

"I don't know." She didn't look up; she only crammed her face deeper into her arm.

Nia glanced over at the stairs. Over the commotion of the wobbling building, she heard the frantic patter of feet. "Oh no," she said. "The bell player's here. What on earth is he doing here? Doesn't he know—? He's going to get himself killed, too!"

Bernice writhed against the window, trying to anchor herself to the bars and hold herself off the floor.

The other windows were covered with shutters, and the whole place felt stifling and hot. Stacks of shelves lined the places between the windows, and collected in rows in the center of the room like the orange trees outside. The air tasted like paper and metal, and the books jerked, scooted off their shelves, and tumbled to the floor in loud, fluttering crashes.

Down the stairs and rising up them, Nia could hear the bell player coming up fast. His footsteps were steady and swift; he'd climbed these stairs dozens of times, and his legs were strong and smooth with the everyday memory of the motion. Even as the stairs rattled beneath him, he was making good progress.

Bernice had gotten quiet. Even her whimpering had gone soft and self-contained, and what remained couldn't be heard over the atmospheric wreckage of the earthquake. Nia held her breath, her foot against the door in case anyone tried to enter.

No one did. The bell player had passed them, charging up the ragged coil for some goal Nia could not comprehend. Why did he rise, when the building threatened to fall?

"Bernice." She tried again to jolt her cousin with her name, but the girl would not be budged. Nia took her by the shoulders and tried to pull her up and lift her out. "Come on, you can't stay here. I'm leaving, and you're coming with me."

"*I'm* not leaving, and I'm *not* going with you!" She kicked out and smacked Nia's hands away.

"If he starts playing, you might die! If the place comes down . . . I saw those bells, Neecy, they'll kill you!"

"But if Mother catches up with me, I'm *definitely* dead!"

"I can't just leave you here!"

She looked down at Bernice and saw a thin, angry, sick-looking beast that wasn't human and didn't wish to be. The inverted bulge on her head was still something too terrible to be covered, and her clothes were tragic. Her skin was pasty and blue, as if she were drowning on the air around her, and her eyes and lips were ringed with ghastly ripples of violet.

In the back of Nia's head, she heard Mossfeaster's voice, and she didn't know if it was because the thing was speaking to her, or if she was just imagining what it might say.

"She's objecting, she's dying, and you owe her nothing. Leave her. Stop swearing by the things you must do, and see how few are set in stone."

"No," Nia said, but she was backing away as she spoke.

"I might not die." Bernice pulled her feet up. She hugged herself hard and put her head down. Her skull bounced against the floor, which waggled back and forth so hard that Nia found it increasingly difficult to stand.

Nia went back to the door, though she couldn't take her eyes off her cousin. Inside that pitiful shell of sinew and skin, Bernice had been beautiful and wicked once, and she'd been murderous and mad. Had there ever been anything redeemable there?

But finally some other force—not herself, but not Mossfeaster or anything else she could name—hauled Nia down the stairs, because up there, in the top of the tower just beneath the bells, the clavier was being tapped and tuned. The bells would soon begin, and the tower would sing as it was meant to.

One chord, amazing in its loudness, chimed from the floors above. The big bells rang and played, plucked and pounded into a tune even as they shuddered in their moorings.

"Too late," she said, breathing hard as she set her feet down one shuddering stair at a time, then two at a time, then three.

Nia outran the tumbling stairs until she was only falling. There was nowhere to go but down and out. Nowhere to run but away. The stairs were jagged under her feet, and the descent was so much faster than the trip up.

She threw herself down the last of them. She had no other choice: the steps were slipping and rattling underneath her, breaking in places and bucking between the narrow walls of the corridor.

Nia landed hands-first against the huge doors. The weight of her body slapped them out into the garden. Outside, the world was still crumbling and quaking, but at least there was no more roof above her that threatened to fall.

The orange trees and pine trees were flinging fruit and boughs to the ground. Shrubs were leaning and tipping into ragged red cracks that opened between the footpaths. If the quake continued, the garden would sink. When Nia looked out across the plains below the Iron Mountain, she thought that maybe the whole earth would topple behind it.

As far as the eye could see, the world was moving, and up beyond sight, the bells were playing.

Above, some large piece of the Singing Tower slipped, scraped, and loosed itself into the air, whistling as it descended. Nia moved in time to dodge it. She ducked a second and third piece, too; but the fourth came terribly close. Then a fifth plummeted from someplace high, and cast a shadow as it dropped.

From the corner of her eye, Nia saw the dark patch grow larger as the slab of marble fell. Before she had time to think, her legs shoved underneath her and she escaped in the only free direction— away from the tower, across the gardens.

And into the moat.

She splashed through a film of algae and rust scum, into the filthy trough where the water burned everything it touched. There was no salt and no prickling, briny bite; there was only the taste of ashy fire and brittle chains in her mouth when she did not close it fast enough.

Nia flailed. Her entire body—her skin, and the angry muscles beneath it—objected to the water. It was thick and smelled like a volcano; it was dark, like the color of pollen in oil. There was no tide to tug it, and no current to draw it anywhere at all. It simply surrounded the tower in a flat ribbon of grease.

The water in the moat was strangely heavy and difficult to swim through. Nia kicked against it, struggling to find the surface. She'd fallen in fast, and she was heavy—hadn't Sam said so?—so much heavier than she looked. Panic clutched at her throat. What if her new form couldn't make it to the surface? Would she be forced to sink to the bottom and crawl or climb up the sticky bloodred dirt into the light?

She beat her arms and jabbed her legs scissor-style, which slowed her descent, but didn't cause her to rise much.

Her eyes fluttered open, and for an instant she could see nothing but the dark, mucky shadows. The liquid seared her eyes worse than salt ever did, but she fought it like she was fighting everything else. She fought the urge to breathe because she knew, deep down, that she didn't really need to. She fought the urge to scream because she knew it would only hurt; she fought the terrible branding smolder of the tainted water against her flesh. And she fought against the determined tug of gravity as it sucked her down deeper.

It was a test of everything, seeing how much she could stand and how far she could sink.

A pinprick of light sparkled somewhere, presumably the light of the sun glittering on the moat's surface. But when Nia tried to chase it, she found it easier than she expected, because her goal was not actually on the surface. It was a deeper thing, shining below. There was no need to swim, only to quit fighting and drop.

And she found she *could* stand it.

She could stand the ferocious burn of the scalding water between her fingers, under her eyelids. It sizzled against her softer spots like the dirt had scalded Bernice's skin, but Nia could stand it. She was made of harder stuff, made to survive, and endure.

The pinprick of white flickered and split. It twisted and fluttered in a huge, slow spasm like a dreamer shuddering against some nightmare.

When she turned her head and peered through the heavy coils of her own hair, she could see a wall, somewhere down beneath her—somewhere down along the column of rock and earth that lifted the tower up through the moat.

Only it wasn't a moat. It couldn't be. It was a lake of rancid water, hidden mostly underground—and the tower was perched atop its only island. From underneath it looked so fragile and unlikely, this arrangement of water and stone.

And whatever was beneath it . . .

As her eyes adjusted, Nia watched the writhing sparkles of light, color, or simple reflection bounce slowly in a wave; and it was only when she thought of it like a wave that she realized that what she was looking at through the water was not a wall, or a floor, or the bottommost segment of the world. She was watching something alive as it shifted slowly and with a ponderous rhythm.

She scanned the underwater lake, looking for the edges of the monstrous undulating thing, but she couldn't find them. At no point did it seem to end or fade, and at no point was there any indication of limbs or gills, or eyes, or teeth. It was smooth and vast, and if she judged its position correctly, some part of it was pressed up against the underside of the column that propped the tower up into the sky on the earth above.

It chilled her, looking at that skinny column. It didn't look any wider around than a drinking straw or a pencil, not from where Nia drifted. She knew it wasn't right, but the lake was too huge and the moat's slim margins were too deceptive. It must have been hollow, all of it: the Iron Mountain, the groves around it, the sand that stretched for miles on every side.

And what was that *thing*? Was it alive?

One sturdy flutter—a gesture that had all the gentleness of two ships colliding—flapped underneath the tower's support, and the water around Nia reverberated hard, pushing her back and tumbling her topsy-turvy away from the bottom, if there was ever a bottom that she'd been sinking toward.

She struggled to right herself, but the waves were coming faster, and she was too unbalanced to find which way was up. And besides, she wanted to see.

She could stand it.

She craned her neck and pushed the water aside, trying to shove herself closer despite the pain of the terrible water.

Beneath her, as she was pushed away and back, a fissure as long as a river split open, and something bright but black spread underneath it. The split widened, then slammed itself back into a seamless line—and the force of the motion slammed a tidal wave up, and out, and Nia could hold her place no longer. The force of the water rejected her, throwing her up and out, facefirst into the sunlight and the air. As she hung there, in the handful of seconds before she fell back down to earth and all but forgot the sinister cracking, splitting, and severing of the world underneath, she imagined an eye the size of a continent opening in the midst of an unhappy dream. And as she dropped back to earth she thought,

This is how it always goes. Easier to fall than to climb.

Isn't it?

She slammed against the ground and rolled, and the world was rolling with her; and somewhere up above, she could hear the sound of bells ringing hard—banging out a determined tune despite the quake.

The bell player had made it to his song.

He beat down the giant leverlike keys, coercing the enormous instrument into a melody that barely quivered above the violence of the background.

Down below, Nia scrambled to her feet and tried to hold that stance. She lifted her hands up to her mouth and yelled between them, *"Mossfeaster!"* But the creature didn't answer, and she couldn't see any sign of its hulking, decomposing shape.

Then, from behind her, something soft but insistent said, *"Shhh!"*

Nia froze. She stood there dripping and tender, her skin blistering but healing. She was still barefoot, and her hair was wetly fetid. She imagined she must look otherworldly, and ghastly, and she was horrified to think that someone might be watching her.

She turned slowly to look over her shoulder.

With her back braced against the wheel of a fat black sedan, a little girl held a finger up to her lips. "You have to shush," she said in half a whisper. "You have to let the dirt man sing."

"The dirt man?" Nia asked, though she didn't need to. She only needed something to say.

The child nodded, and her hair bobbed in a rabbit-brown halo. "Sit down. It'll be fine. The rocking will stop in a minute," she said. Nia could hear the worry in her words, though. The rocking didn't usually last this long, or run so rough, Nia could guess that much.

But, yes, as she listened she could hear something like words rumbling alongside the pounding cacophony of the bells. As they roared and mumbled, the swelling and cresting of the Iron Mountain began to slow, steady, and dim itself down to a gurgle of motion instead of a coughing fit.

"See?" said the girl. She pushed her shoulders against the car's wheel and used it to push herself upright. "See, lady? See? It's fine. You don't have to be scared," she said, and Nia suspected the girl was parroting some assurance she'd once been given. "The dirt man knows what to do."

"I don't understand," Nia replied, and it was the only true thing she could say.

What's to understand?

"Edward?"

He was facing away from them, the small stone woman and the little girl. He was staring up at the tower, its lavender, pink, and cream facing casting a shadow that swallowed them all. In another moment, the ground was still. But the unearthly voice continued its song for another moment more, finishing its verse and holding the last note as long as the bell above cast an echoed ring.

He said, *It's a lullaby.*

After Dreaming

Upstairs, the bell player was restoring the carillon. He tightened the cables that had stretched in the terrible quake, and he made note of which ones had snapped altogether and would need replacing. His daughter stayed out of the way for the most part; and while her father worked, she chattered at him about the big dirt man and the stone-skinned lady down by the car.

Ever since the child had first begun to mention the big dirt man, the bell player had assumed she was telling tales. The Iron Mountain was isolated, and there were few other children anywhere nearby. The girl must be lonely. She must have invented friends for herself.

But time and experience had taught him that perhaps there was more going on than he claimed. He'd seen footsteps as broad as dinner plates, nearly black with mulch and rot. He'd heard movement and rustlings, and the dim, faint echoes of something, somewhere, singing or speaking.

It worried him. But the little girl said she wasn't afraid of the big dirt man, or of the ghosts, either.

But ever since she'd mentioned the ghosts, the bell player had taken care to avoid the grave down by the front door. Just in case.

Edward noticed the bell player's caution, and he approved of it—even as he was amused by it. The spirit felt no shock or tickle from mortal feet when they tiptoed across his resting spot.

He felt no discomfort or displeasure. But he appreciated the respect.

He watched the bell player clean, straighten, and do his best to make what restorations he could. Workmen would need to be called this time. Carpenters would need to shore up the frames that held the big bells. Things had cracked. Things had rocked free, and dropped, and broken.

But it could all be fixed.

Edward drifted down and around the angular, circular stairwell.

He skimmed past the closed and debris-littered doorways of the library, the workshop, the office, and the study. He dipped down into the main atrium, and then back around to his own grave and the spot beside it that was freshly disturbed. He stopped, but only for a moment. He slipped down past the gleaming stone with a tiny hidden latch marked by a figure of the sun. He passed his own coffin on the way down, farther, lower, deeper.

The next set of stairs was the mirror of those above—angular, circular, spiraling jerkily down into the earth instead of to some high point above it.

The stairs went down through the column of stone and earth

that held the tower up on the Iron Mountain; they were not carved by human hands and they were rough, barely recognizable as stepping places. As far as the tower extended into the clouds, these reflecting notches went down into the earth.

Edward navigated the coiling passage until he reached its bottom, a place where there were no bricks and no seams—just a smooth, slick patch of blank floor surrounded by a ledge.

The ghost knew about the floor. It was damp and muddy, and if he stared at it long enough . . . if he waited and watched it for hours at a time, he could almost convince himself that some strange blood flowed beneath it, as vast and hard as a river's current.

Once every hundred years, the creature had told him, *you can hear his heart throb one great beat.*

The creature itself sat on the ledge, its broad, rough back to the dead man, its face toward the living ground at the bottom of the earth.

"You understand why I had to send Arahab away. You understand why she must not trouble you, end your dreamless sleep . . . ," it said. The words trailed off as if some other thought had interrupted them. "She'll come no closer."

It stepped down from the ledge, very gently and with all the softness it could wring from its ponderous bulk. The creature knelt, then placed its head lower, resting against the sleeping form.

"I do wonder," it whispered. "What would happen if you were to awaken, after all? Would you know me? Would you remember me? Would it matter that I've kept steward over your peace? The dreamless sleep was your own choice. This stewardship is mine."

Mossfeaster let its knees fold up and laid itself down.

"To you alone I make my confessions, and promises, and bargains. To you alone I swear. Sometimes I wish to wake you and shout, only to know that I've been heard. But . . ."

It reached out one hand-shaped palm and rubbed it gently against the floor.

"Did I tell you? I've made something new. I was not even sure it was possible, but she is smart and hard. I made her out of a mortal girl. They are stronger than they look, these spindly creatures of salt and skin."

It curled itself tighter, nearly into a ball. "But I do not think she will stay with me."

Even Edward could hear it, how the anger was only a coating for the monster's grief, smoothing and hiding it like the layers of a pearl.

"You alone abide. But if you rise, this wretched world falls, and I have nothing—not even this miserable half life farmed from the cleft between the living and the dead. And that . . . I will not let go of it. It is all that I have.

"*You* are all that I have."

Edward felt like an intruder, watching the creature whisper its secrets to a deaf and slumbering god. He knew, as surely as the creature knew, that the Leviathan must never wake to listen.

Edward closed his eyes, a leftover mortal habit that spoke of sadness, or sympathy. He returned to the rough spiral and rose up through it, back into the brighter shadows of the tower proper.

Inside, the tower was damaged but not desperately so. Books had fallen, paintings had dropped, shelves had collapsed—but the walls were built to stand, and they had held. Edward noted that the floors were ruined in parts and would need to be restored or replaced.

Several stairs were likewise broken, and he was staring down at one of the worst when he realized he was being watched. He raised his eyes and saw that the bell player's daughter had come quite close.

Usually, she kept a little distance.

Hello, he said to her.

"Hello," she said back. "Is the dirt man safe?"

He hesitated. *The dirt man is always safe.*

"Always?"

Edward did not say, "As long as we are safe, he will be safe," because she was so little. Instead he said, *Always.* And then he added, *Child, I must ask you a small favor. Will you do something for me, please?*

She nodded.

You must not enter the library on the second floor. He remembered his own grandchildren, and then he changed his approach, lest he make the library look too attractive. *Child,* he tried again, *Do you trust me to tell you the truth? Do you trust that I mean you no harm?*

She nodded again, more vigorously.

A little too trusting, Edward thought. But she was so small; it was to be expected. *I'm going to tell you a terrible truth, and it is one that your father will not believe. But it is very, very important all the same. You must not, under any circumstances, enter the second-floor library. There is a monster inside that room—an awful creature who will hurt you very badly if she catches you. She is ruined and bad, not like the dirt man.* Something else occurred to Edward, and he added it for good measure, even though the creature downstairs might have objected to it. *If you ever see the monster in the library, you should cry out for the dirt man. He might protect you.*

Or, then again, the creature might not. But the ghost believed it was worth saying, if only to give the child some comfort. He could not tell her stories of monsters without assuring her that they could be conquered.

"The monster can't hurt the dirt man?"

No, I don't think so.

"Okay," she said, as if his word was good enough for her.

Satisfied, he left her. He faded from her sight and returned to his study.

And in the second-floor library, Bernice huddled, and hated.

Twice a day, at one and three o'clock, the great bells above rang, playing their ponderous lullabies for thirty minutes even though the tower itself was in tattered shape. At first, the song was a little bit broken, missing a note from a chord here or there—because up in the tower's crown, a handful of bells had not yet been replaced. But workmen came every day, and the bells were lifted up and hung in their trapeze framework, and within a few weeks, the songs were smooth again.

For one hour every day, Bernice wished she were dead.

Hell could be no worse than the banging, beating, and clanging of the big bronze bells, casting their weird magic across the Iron Mountain. No fire could burn worse than the breeze that carried bits of iron dust through the open windows.

And . . . she was so thirsty. But there was nothing to drink except for the sulfur-and-rust water that spilled through the moat. There was nothing to swim in except for water that was wholly unswimmable.

And for all Bernice knew, Arahab lurked outside in the swampy depression.

But up in the dry, hot, miserable tower with its awful bells that rang for an hour each day, Bernice was safe from her Mother. Or, at least, Mother had not yet come for her. Perhaps Arahab was biding her time; she'd said it a thousand times before, that she was patient, and that time meant little to her.

Bernice believed that the water witch was patient; but Bernice was stubborn, too. And not the bells, not the choking ash and earth that billowed through the bars—none of it could convince her to descend the tower stairs and take her chances in the garden.

So she stayed, and she withered.

She closed the windows in the library and she barricaded the door. Workmen assumed that something had fallen during the earthquake, but no one forced the issue and the door was never broken open. She suspected that Mossfeaster might have had something to do with that.

Mossfeaster never visited her, so she had no occasion to ask about it.

She remained alone behind her barricade, inside the musty library clogged from floor to ceiling with books. Before, she'd never cared for reading. But boredom drove her to strange new behaviors, or there would be lethargy like none she'd ever known before.

Her limbs grew stiff, and her skin dried until it was crumpled and thick like old leather left too long on the floor of a closet. Her skull did not regain its original shape.

Dented, shriveled, and dry, she became a living mummy.

She hollowed out a spot beneath one far-back shelf. She pushed the books aside and entombed herself there, where she could crush her head against the thick old volumes and, every day for an hour, pretend that the bells were not ringing.

Epilogue

I.

Twice a day, at one and three o'clock, the bells chimed out across the Iron Mountain. They could be heard for miles.

Arahab heard them, from her lurking spot in the swampy depression. The bells pushed her back; their timbre and their horrid percussive echoes drove her out and away, down into the ground where the water seeped slowly through the rocks, sand, and shells.

Back out to sea she went, where she stirred up a vortex that sank three ships and killed hundreds of people. Spitefully and hopefully, she sifted through them as they drowned, but she found no one she wanted to keep.

I have time. Time is cheap to me, for there is always more.

More of this place is ocean than dirt, and through every land run the rivers and lakes I may wander. Along these currents your civilizations began, after you realized that perfection was not enough. After you wasted the gifts they took from us.

But I have time.

And in time, my waters will erode mountains and grow pink corals across your black city streets. In less time even than that, the world will forget what little it knew about me and mine. Small pieces of lore will dangle, will remain in their children, and in their grandchildren.

For I have patience, and I remain.

I remain, although my old brother is angry with me, furious because of my daughter's actions. He will not chase me here, though. I can bury myself deeper than he can. I can drench his fires, if his indignation calls for conflict. I can wait here below while my strength returns to me, absorbing the drips and steams that filter through the earth and into the great waters.

I will remain so long as the waters rise from the ground and fall with the moon's pull. This is my world, too. He cannot estrange me from it.

I am not sure I understand what weird games have been set into motion, but I do not like them. They smell to me of mortal games, of insults and punishments undeserved and unfit. I will not answer any summons unless it pleases me to do so.

The Greek and his master be damned. I owe them nothing.

II.

The woman on the ladder was wearing men's overalls just as she always did, much to the amusement of any new employees. Her long gray hair was twisted up in a tight bun with fringes that were peeling loose. One after another, oranges went into her sack and bounced against her hip as she climbed up and down, tree after tree.

Most of the employees had gone home to their families by this late in the day, but the woman was already home, so she took her time. Her two daughters were inside, cooking supper. Her trees were mostly picked clean.

Over at the market, the prices were dropping a few more pennies every week, and tomorrow on her front porch she'd find a few more men hoping for work. There were so many hopeful hands every day, these days, but she'd have to turn them away. She couldn't pay any more men. She could barely pay the ones she kept.

And she was getting old.

She didn't often miss her husband, the man who'd died and left her alone with a farm to keep. It had been a long time, and she'd beaten down her grief with backbreaking work. She'd exhausted her store of sorrow, and in its place was left a habit—worn deep—that kept her moving when younger people would've found a rocking chair and closed their eyes.

Chicken was frying up in the house. A curling current of wind brought the sizzling crackle to her nose, over the green aroma of the waving trees and their late-season fruit.

One booted foot at a time she descended the ladder, but the third step stopped her short.

Her foot settled on the rung, and she felt a jabbing pain, like a charley horse in her shoulder. It shot down her arm and up again, high on the left side of her chest. It startled her, and it stopped her.

She breathed slowly, coaxing down the sting.

With the toe of her right boot, she reached backwards for the next rung.

She leaned forward. She rested her forehead against the back of her hand. Another slicing, stabbing bolt tore through her arm; it camped in her chest. Her left lung went tight, and when she inhaled, she felt like it wasn't filling right, because there came another pain.

Her booted toe found the next rung down, but couldn't hold it.

The woman fell, and on the way down, her face clapped against the ladder, bloodying her nose. She didn't feel the landing, only that she was suddenly staring up at the sky, and the pain was gone, replaced with a light-headed, stuffy feeling that wasn't altogether unpleasant.

And then she knew. She understood when she saw that face looming over hers. One of the missing grandgirls, long-lost and transformed very slightly, but very surely, was cradling her head and speaking, saying something over and over again.

The woman couldn't hear it. And her vision was fading, one bright sparkle at a time, so she couldn't read the rapidly moving lips as they flashed their message. But it didn't matter, and she wasn't afraid.

Look, there's Apollonia.

She understood. She had died. And that was all right.

III.

Nia hid at the edge of the orchard and watched as two men carried her grandmother away.

She nursed grandiose yet halfhearted ideas of running up the porch steps and crying with the rest of them, but every time she'd gone to climb the stairs, she failed. She couldn't do it.

But she didn't want to leave, either, so she stayed and watched her relatives come and go.

Despite the return to manual labor and a lesser lifestyle, her aunt Marjorie looked younger. Her hair had grown out from the fashionable style in which she'd once kept it, and she left it loose down around her shoulders or braided back.

Nia's mother looked older. Her hair was catching up to Grandmother's, sneaking streaks of white through the ash blond it once had been. She'd lost some weight.

"You're easy to find," Mossfeaster said.

Nia had heard it forming behind her, gathering its shape from the ground. She hadn't turned around to watch, and she didn't turn around to greet the creature when it announced itself.

"Took you long enough," she said. "It's been weeks."

"Time is different for me. Eventually, you'll find it's different for you, too."

"If you say so."

It came to stand beside her, and it stared straight ahead, following her gaze and seeing the old orchard with its sturdy old farmhouse. It asked, "Why are you still here, if you aren't going to stay?"

She shrugged. She'd been working on an answer, and as he asked, she found it. She said, "I don't have anywhere to go, and I don't have anywhere to be." Nia squeezed a small leather satchel she kept slung across her chest, and she clicked it open to show Mossfeaster that it was full of money. "I sold the jewelry you gave me from Gaspar's chest. Money's always been tight, and now it's worse than ever. I thought I'd leave this for them, and it would help."

The jewelry had been worth twice what she was offered. Half as much would have been plenty.

"But I can't go home, can I? Not any more than Sam could, if he'd made it out with us." She looked up at Mossfeaster. "I buried him out there, at night. I put him beside the tower. Edward said he didn't mind."

"Edward rarely objected to anything. I always liked that about him," Mossfeaster said. Then it added, "But if you did go home, would it be for them—or for you?"

In a few minutes, the front door closed and everyone was inside or gone.

Nia shut the bag and removed it from around her shoulders. She sprinted up to the porch, left the bag hanging on the front door's knob, knocked loudly, and ran back into the grove—where Mossfeaster hadn't budged.

The creature didn't shift or shuffle as it looked down at her; and Nia didn't flinch or frown when she gazed up at the thing that had made her. She didn't look up with love, or with confusion. She didn't look up in search of answers to any question but one: "So it's just me and you, then, huh?"